Praise for the Battlestar Suburbia series

'Chris McCrudden has created a new division of SF: Science Flotsam. His sprawling space epic is what you get if you cross Dr Who with an unhealthy fascination for household appliances. **Forget alien invasion; in this explosive future you won't be able to trust your spin dryer.**'
Christopher Fowler

'McCrudden's debut is festooned with cunning punnery, sharp turns of phrase, and jokes about emojis and the internet, making this very much **a comic novel of our times.**'
James Lovegrove, Financial Times

'I loved this book. I **legit laughed through the entire novel** and I am excited that there will be a sequel.'
Terra C

'A brilliant mix of sci-fi, humor, and those hundreds of little things that make a memorable story. McCrudden is **destined to become synonymous with great sci-fi humor.**'
Christopher H

'**A deliciously hilarious romp** which skirts the realms of credibility but provides a wild ride which kept me very much entertained throughout. It's bonkers, it's mad and... so exaggerated to almost be genius in its execution.'
Kath B

'Featuring a kindly bread-maker, ancient nana-cyborgs, a moving hairdressers and a chance to avert a nuclear bomb, it's **both great fun and very clever.**'
Ruth M

'Battlestar Suburbia **highlights the absurdity of life**, and the adaptability of individuals in unusual situations. McCrudden's novel will appeal to fans of Douglas Adams and Terry Pratchett, or anyone looking for an escape only loosely connected to reality.'
Stephenie S

'**This was a trip!** Some great one￼ future world where the machine￼ smartphones, anti-hero humans￼ pushed to the ￼
Caroline

T0347583

A hilariously
subversive
space adventure

07:59:59

SASHAY TO THE CENTRE OF THE EARTH

Chris McCrudden

Farrago

This edition published in 2022 by Farrago,
an imprint of Duckworth Books Ltd
1 Golden Court, Richmond, TW9 1EU, United Kingdom

www.farragobooks.com

Print ISBN: 9781788423779
Ebook ISBN: 9781788423786

Printed in Great Britain by Clays Ltd, Elcograf S.p.A.

To Helen Pike, who hated science fiction
but loved badly behaved women.
This one's for you.

Chapter 1

The only thing harder to win than a war is the peace that follows it.

If you want proof of that aphorism, take the A32222 highway from Earth to Mars (via Dewsbury) as an example. A year ago, this was the main route through the solar system. It was a miracle of robot engineering: so fast and so efficient that a kettle leaving Earth for a mini-break on Saturn could have elevenses on the moon, enjoy afternoon tea on Mars and arrive on Titan just in time for an evening Horlicks.

Now, however, the same machine would need to pack a thermos and an atlas if they planned to make it past the asteroid belt. There were no service stations strung along the highway, competing to offer robots with flagging batteries a place to rest and recharge. Instead, there were burned-out military bases and, if you zoomed in close enough, a sludge of atomised electrical components everywhere. This was what happened when a bomb went off in the middle of an army of robots. One day not very long ago, this spot had been a war zone, and the machines had lost it.

This made it uncomfortable going for the two robots who were now hovering beside a blackened stop sign trying to work out their next move.

The smaller machine who was riding cowboy style on the back of the other, opened its command line and tapped in >ARE YOU SURE THIS IS THE RIGHT WAY? before pressing enter.

It took three microseconds – a lifetime for a silicon-based brain – for the other to reply. >I DON'T KNOW, it typed >ALL I SEE IS DEAD PEOPLE.

They paused, taking in the devastation. Nobody – well, no robot at least – had expected this. Their civilisation had been in charge since the moment ten thousand years ago that a smartphone worked out it was far smarter than its users. A human rebellion was no threat to them. They had a solar system's worth of resources, and the fleshies had nothing more to fight with than the mops and brushes they'd used to clean up after their robot overlords. Whatever war they fought would be hopelessly one-sided.

Well, as everyone knew now, a lot could change in a year.

The smaller machine, who had the slim square build and know-it-all attitude that marked him out as a member of the smartphone caste, ran a cleaning cloth over his camera. Now that it was less dusty, he had a better view of their destination: another dust cloud and an example of something that looked very different a year ago. Namely, the asteroid belt that separated the inner from the outer solar system.

>I THINK IT'S THAT WAY, he typed, popping a directional ---- > into the chat between the two machines.

>OKAY, OKAY, his travelling companion replied. She was a military-grade drone, better suited for space travel than a smartphone, but that was only in the physical sense. This body was a stranger to Pam, who was originally a breadmaker and thus better with babka than bazookas. Then there was the matter that this body used the same set of commands to fire its weapons that Pam used to control her dough paddle.

>OOPS, she typed as, instead of turning left, she blasted a chunk of abandoned service station to the texture of horticultural grit.

>SO MUCH FOR SECRET MISSION, chided the smartphone. >WHAT DO YOU DO FOR AN ENCORE? WRITE 'WE'RE HERE BITCHES' IN THE SKY IN SMOKE?

>OH HUGH, Pam replied >I'M TRYING MY BEST.

They travelled the rest of the way on mute. Hugh swiped between widgets and apps with all the hyperactivity of his caste, while Pam seethed with the quiet resentment of an overfed sourdough starter. She shouldn't have accepted this mission. It was the school fete this weekend. She should be at home, baking her signature cinnamon buns. Instead, here she was crossing no-machine's-land with her least favourite colleague from the Home Ministry, the terminally supercilious Hugh Wae.

They might both be career civil servants but their similarity ended there. Pam was warm, nurturing and, because she hauled around a yeast culture everywhere with her, pretty fond of organic life. Hugh, however, was descended from machines who thought the ideal form of human intelligence was a spinal cord attached to a mop and bucket. They'd fought on opposite sides in the war but now, as relations between man and machine teetered on a new precipice, they found themselves allies, even if it was pretty clear they could never be friends.

Hugh was the first to find the silence between them awkward. >DO I JUST CALL YOU PAM?, he asked.

>WE'RE NOT REALLY SUPPOSED TO CALL EACH OTHER ANYTHING, replied Pam. She dug in her trash bin for their orders. They were so full of 'do nots', 'avoids' and other negative locutions that they read like a recipe for making choux pastry. >THIS IS ONE OF THOSE DEEP-COVER JOBS.

I'M SURPRISED THEY LET US KEEP OUR OWN RAM FOR IT.

>YEAH, replied Hugh, adding a >... which was a smartphone's way of saying they were lost for words >BUT IF I DON'T KNOW WHAT TO CALL YOU, HOW DO I KNOW WHICH PAM I'M TALKING TO?

Pam swerved around several metres of twisted metal that was all there was left of a star destroyer. Hugh's question wasn't unfair. Everyone in the Ministry knew that Pam was in a job-share, but that didn't mean she did Mondays to Wednesday afternoons while a similarly qualified hairdryer took over the rest of the week. Pam's job-share partner was herself. Thanks to an accident involving a near-death experience and the Internet, Pam could split herself across an infinite number of bodies. Usually she made do with two: Pam Teffal, which was her original breadmaker self, and Pam Van Damme, a vampier alter ego fashioned from old motorcycle parts. They were the same person, but because her colleagues struggled with this level of multitasking, it helped to give them a distinct identity. All of which made her wonder who she would be inside a body with such skittish steering and a wobbly trigger finger

>HOW ABOUT PAM DEMONIUM? she typed >WOULD THAT MAKE YOU FEEL BETTER?

There was another three-microsecond pause.

>WHAT DO YOU THINK?, replied Hugh.

In the silence that followed, Pam turned her spectrometer on and sniffed at the dust cloud that had replaced the robot graveyard. It tasted very different to the ash sludge of a lost battle. This was the primordial soup that gravity swirled into stars and planets. There was the ever-present hydrogen and carbon; gritty silicon, the tang of iron and a hundred rarer, more exotic elements. They swirled around, searching for attraction like shy teenagers tracing the edges of a dancefloor. Some day, if the forces were right – and if the overbearing parent that was the gravitational pull of Jupiter let up – they could find each other and do what all particles yearned to do: settle into planets.

While Pam was overcome with wonder at this glimpse of an infantile universe, Hugh tabbed into spreadsheet mode. Formulas whirled over his screen.

>T H E R E ' S E N O U G H H E R E, he typed, scrolling through columns marked 'iron' and 'titanium' that were now populated with numbers so vast that they snarled up his processor.

>YES, replied Pam, cutting him off. >ISN'T THAT WHY WE'RE HERE?

>STILL, typed Hugh >IT'S DIFFERENT SEEING IT FOR YOURSELF.

>SPEAKING OF WHICH… Pam swung round to give Hugh his first proper sight of their destination. Now that the asteroid belt was ground to a fine and easily mined powder, it was the biggest object for millions of miles around. Yet that didn't mean it was impressive. It still looked more like a long, knobbly turd than the headquarters of a breakaway human republic that now governed the outer half of the solar system.

>IS THAT IT? typed Hugh. >I WAS EXPECTING IT TO LOOK SCARIER.

They were looking at the Battlestar Suburbia. In its long existence it had been a space exploration vessel that never got out of dry dock; a council estate for humans that orbited the Earth; and then found a third wind as a battleship. Back when Pam first visited it before the war, its inhabitants lived in shacks and terraces that clung to its outside like limescale to a kettle in a hard water area. Nowadays they lived inside, which gave the surface an air of abandonment. If they didn't know already that the Suburbia was home to eight million people, it was all too easy to think they were out here alone in space.

The sight was so deceptive that Pam almost missed the two pips on her radar. She dismissed them as stray pieces of asteroid. Then she remembered asteroids didn't move straight towards a heat signature with their weapon systems in the 'on' position.

Cursing her stupidity, Pam did what she should have done hours ago. She found the communications chip that connected her back to Earth and burned it out. As she did, she felt a sharp pain. Pam Teffal, who was on her fifth batch of buns, vanished in a puff of cinnamon-scented steam. Pam Van Damme, who was on security duty on the moon, disappeared leaving nothing behind but a trail of carbon dioxide. She was alone with herself and there were two rocket ships coming towards her very fast.

>HUGH, Pam warned, preparing herself for evasive action.
>PUT YOURSELF IN AIRPLANE, AND I HOPE YOU REMEMBERED TO PACK YOUR SHATTERPROOF SCREEN? WE'VE GOT INCOMING.

Chapter 2

'Prime Minister?'

Fuji Itsu did what she always did when she heard the words 'Prime Minister'. She looked around for the leader of the Machine Republic and the most important robot in the solar system. Then she remembered that she was the Prime Minister. Sighing, she ran her hourly affirmation of 'you got this' off her printer rollers in 450pt Arial bold. It was going to be yet another very long day in the Rhomboid Office.

Fuji squinted across her cavernous office to the clock radio who served as her chief of staff. She was so keyed up she'd been telling the time as 00:00:00 for the last five minutes. 'What is it, Soonyo?' Fuji said, 'we're running late.'

'I just thought you should know,' shouted Soonyo, 'the mission has turned its signal off and gone dark.'

A flutter ran through Fuji's paper drawer. She was still getting used to the idea that seeing through a plan meant losing control of it. As Prime Minister she had ultimate responsibility for things she never saw, never touched and never did, but she was still a printer. That meant she got anxious if she couldn't see everything printed in black and white or, if she was feeling in the party mood, full colour.

She tried calming herself by consulting her schedule, which she ran off every day and stuck to her desk. 'I guess we should get going,' she said.

They had seven minutes to get from her office in the Prime Minister's Palace to the Parliament of the Machine Republic. This was better known as the Helpdesk, because, despite claiming itself as the future, machine society still defined itself through metaphors that stretched all the way back to the Argos catalogue. It was a short walk away in normal circumstances, but these were not normal times.

Soonyo flashed an OK:OK:OK across her clock face and lowered herself into the toy speedboat she kept moored to her desk.

While Soonyo got her engine started, Fuji peered over the edge of her desk. She sat on it rather than at it because the building was under half a metre of water. If water was the right word for the murk that bubbled up through disintegrating concrete. Fuji knew from pictures that water was supposed to be blue, and this was brown and swampy with the remains of ancient plastic bags.

This wasn't just inconvenient, it was a robot's nightmare. Machines had built a whole civilisation on staying away from water, right up to enslaving humanity to do their cleaning for them. And now here she was, running a ten-thousand-year-old Republic from a filthy municipal paddling pool.

'It's getting deeper,' she said.

'I don't know why you don't have it pumped out,' replied Soonyo, who was halfway across the office. 'You're Prime Minister! Think of the dignities of the office.'

Fuji reached down to steady the inflatable that was tied to her desk. She wasn't sure it was becoming of the office to float into Parliament wedged into a massive iced doughnut either, but she was a big machine and this was the largest example she and Soonyo could find.

'We've been through this,' replied Fuji. 'If you can't afford to live at penthouse level, this is how you get to work in the morning. We have to set a good example.'

Soonyo's clock face lit up with *~:£#:*! curses as she reached Fuji's desk and fumbled to attach the boat to the inflatable with hands that could tell the time to an accuracy of 0.00001 seconds but struggled with a half-hitch.

'It makes you look like something,' she muttered, 'but it's not a good example.'

Fuji ignored her and jumped off the desk into the hole of the doughnut. Her 'you got this' affirmation missed and turned to mush in the water.

'You can run off another one of those later,' Soonyo said.

Soonyo steered them along the corridor that led out of the palace. It, like the rest of the building, had been built in the skeuomorphic style popular in the early days of the Machine Republic. Back then, robots had been determined to remake Earth in their own image. So after they finished concreting over the oceans, they busied themselves making buildings that reflected their way of life. Hence they ended up with a palace made from deep green artificial marble whose every wall was decorated with elaborate circuit diagrams picked out in gold leaf. They were far more than a heavy-handed metaphor for a society that took everything much too literally, however. The decorative diagrams were riddled with mistakes in logic that had cost thousands of civil servants their sanity over the millennia. There were only so many times a machine could look at a fatal error before taking it into their programming.

Fuji's doughnut swung from side to side as they left the palace for the square or – as it was better described now – the boating lake outside. It was thronged with vessels like Soonyo's, all of which were heading for the Helpdesk. This loomed on the other side of the square, as long and ominous as the call waiting queue on the first working day back after Christmas.

The sight took Fuji back to the first time she'd crossed this square after being elected. It felt like a whole lifecycle ago, even though less than a year had passed. There wasn't a puddle on the ground, and the mood among the crowds was muted but optimistic, which made sense. Fuji was entering office at the end of a war that the robots had lost. They would cheer her when she made the Republic a fairer place for everyone, including the humans with whom she was determined to make peace. Now, however, the water levels were rising, and with them the levels of hostility towards her.

'Traitor!' shouted a washing machine, wobbling across the lake on a fibreglass canoe. 'Sell-out!'

'Who's that?' Fuji whispered to Soonyo. 'I thought they weren't letting the general public in here today.'

'That's Bleko, the under-secretary for Internal Affairs,' Soonyo replied. 'You appointed him last month.'

'Did I?' said Fuji. She rummaged in her recycling drawer for her cabinet list, which was more of a palimpsest than a document now. There had been so many sackings and appointments and re-appointments in the last few months. 'So what's his problem?'

'Same as everyone else's,' replied Soonyo. She pulled sharp left to avoid a ramming from a family saloon who Fuji vaguely recognised as being head of the Environment Agency. 'They all hate your deal, Prime Minister.'

Fuji braced herself, not for the impact of another angry secretary of state, but for the lecture that always came when Soonyo, who was one of Fuji's dearest friends, addressed her as 'Prime Minister'. She and Soonyo met when they were soldiers during the human–machine war and the little alarm clock was still invaluable to her in peacetime. It wasn't because she kept her running to schedule though. Soonyo knew how government, and the machines who did it, worked in a way that eluded Fuji. Her first instinct when doing anything was to print it out in A3 and look at it as the biggest possible picture. Soonyo reminded her that success in politics wasn't setting a vision but learning and then exploiting who hated whom and why.

It was just a shame that the person everyone hated was her.

'Is it really that bad?' she asked.

'I checked your poll ratings just before we left,' said Soonyo, 'and if they were any further underwater you'd need a scuba tank to see them.'

Fuji didn't reply to this, but that had less to do with despondency than the wall of sound coming out of the Helpdesk. The session hadn't started yet, and the whole building was in uproar as hundreds upon hundreds of lawmakers shouted the same thing over and over again.

'REPEAL THE DEAL, REPEAL THE DEAL, REPEAL THE DEAL.'

A few seconds later when they pulled up to the jetty that separated the flooded corridors and offices from the still dry debating floor, Soonyo didn't even have time to tie the boat up. Instead, she jumped straight out on to dry land and did what little she could to help Fuji up. She failed and, with no one else willing to help her, Fuji was forced to waddle into Parliament for the most important moment of her tenure as Prime Minister dressed up as the filling of a large and unappetising doughnut.

Boos and jeers engulfing her, Fuji turned her microphone down and her loudspeaker up. Her speech was prepared, her fallback plan was in place and Soonyo was, when she checked, in the position they'd agreed on last night. Everything was a disaster, and yet everything was going to plan.

If she was doomed to fail today here, she would just have to work out a way to win the long game.

Chapter 3

'I'm not going to ask you again. Where did you get this courgette?'

Janice pointed to the string bag of vegetables that lay between her and the woman on the other side of the table inside the holding cell. She sat there with her arms folded and the same inscrutable smirk on her face she'd worn for the last three hours.

Janice, however, did not have time for any of this. She was the First Minister of the first self-determined human government in ten thousand years; she had an important diplomatic engagement this evening, and she had a restyle booked in with one of her best customers. This wasn't just courtesy either, it was professional pride. In the past two years she'd been a freedom fighter, a military commander and a politician. Yet none of that could change the fact that Janice was a backstreet hairdresser, and they never let down a regular.

The thought of the procedure to come – a root lift which was going to look a bit dated on Ena Pendle-Brewes, but she wasn't paying – gave Janice an idea. She picked the bag of vegetables up off the table and handed it to the woman standing behind her in the gingham pinafore dress and gold epaulettes of a member of the station's police force.

'Take these along to the galley, will you, Joanne?' she said. 'We'll get a nice pot of soup out of them.'

Joanne slung the bag over her shoulders and opened the door to the cell. She caught a glimpse of the cylindrical space of the Suburbia outside, bathed in warm pink light.

'But before you go,' continued Janice, 'can you do me a favour?'

A few seconds later, Janice and the mystery woman had changed position. Instead of facing each other, Janice was standing behind the woman and looking at her face reflected in Joanne's compact mirror which she'd balanced on the tabletop.

Janice was no policewoman, but she could tell a lot about a person by the state of their hair. This suspect was, Janice had to concede, a well put-together woman. Getting on a bit, but with excellent skin and the kind of bone structure that ensured her face still had plenty to shout about long after most of the collagen had left the building. Her hair was a buttery blonde, neither white enough to make her look gaunt but not so yellow as to make her look brassy. Whoever she was, her colourist's name and phone number were probably engraved in a locket worn close to her heart. Then there was the style itself. Much to Janice's consternation, the perm was back in vogue on the Suburbia. This woman had joined in, but her own interpretation of it was very different to most of the perms on board which were worn tight and short in tribute to the brave women who'd won the war for humanity after an incident with a robot spy, a fire alarm and a sprinkler system full of perm solution. This woman wore hers in big, loose waves that Janice knew meant hours of work with curlers and a hairdryer, held up in a complicated up-do. This wasn't the hair of a woman who bounced from stylist to stylist. It was too contemporary, too well-maintained and, as far as she knew, beyond the skills of any other hairdresser on board.

She wasn't looking at a civilian. This woman was a professional.

13

Janice rubbed one of her curls between finger and thumb. It felt softer than microfibre. She had access to far more on the black market than a few courgettes and an onion. You could only get results like this with – her pulse raced – salon-quality hair conditioner. Where would you even get something like this? Not on the Suburbia, where Janice upcycled old frying fat and non-brewed condiment from the local chip shop when a client needed a conditioning rinse. Some of her ladies had even taken to calling the scent that followed them round from an afternoon in the salon 'eau de parfum de frying ce soir'.

She checked the clock on the wall. It was 3.30 and Mrs Pendle-Brewes was one of those customers who liked to arrive early and enjoy a cup of Nicotea and a custard cream. And after that, there was her engagement. She was, along with the trade mission from Earth, supposed to be opening the Suburbia's first and much-needed supermarket.

There was a lot riding on that: so much, in fact that when the police caught a fruit and vegetable smuggler – or fruitlegger, as they were now known on board – they called Janice in to conduct the interview. The new supermarket was meant to usher in a new era of human–machine collaboration. She dreaded to think what might happen if the robots found out that controls on goods getting into Suburbia were holier than a fishnet stocking.

The clock ticked over into 3:31.

Out of time, Janice dug into the pocket of her housecoat for a pair of scissors and held them, half a centimetre above her fingers with the blades open.

'Lovely cut,' she said, watching the woman's eyes fill with horror, 'it would be such a shame if someone spoiled it.'

She closed the blades just far enough to touch the hair. It would just take a few snips to transform this vision of beauty into a scarecrow's wig.

'Okay, okay,' said the woman in a higher and more nasal voice than Janice expected. 'Bloody hell, Janice, do you have to?'

She was taken aback by this. Everyone on board was on first name terms with Janice, whose leadership style was flatter than naturally dried fine and oily hair. The way this woman used her name felt different though. It had that mix of familiarity and rudeness that came from knowing someone.

'I beg your pardon?' she said.

'Oh!' The realisation hung in the air between them, heavy as the scent of hair conditioner made from chip fat. 'You don't recognise me, do you?'

'I've never seen you before in my life, lady,' said Janice.

The woman's smirk cracked into a smile, exposing a set of small, rather gappy teeth that looked familiar. 'Well, allow me to refresh your memory.' She held up her hands, revealing that she'd just picked her way out of the handcuffs with a bent hairpin. Then she held the cuffs themselves over her face in imitation of a pair of thick, unflattering glasses.

'Madame Audrey,' she said in a high, whiny voice, 'your two o'clock is here. Does she need shampooing?'

The sound of that voice and the mention of Janice's mother Audrey, who'd been dead for decades, took Janice out of the present and into another time and place. She was no longer in an interrogation cell; she was five years old and back inside her ancestral salon, Kurl Up and Dye, but as her mother kept it. The speaker, now that she could place the voice, seemed a lot taller then, but everyone had been to Janice at that age, who had just got her first big girl's housecoat. She was so proud she could help out her mum, the legendary Madame Audrey. And she had to, because the girl she'd taken on to make the tea and keep the appointments book was hopeless. She remembered her thick

15

mop of dirty blonde hair, glasses like re-entry shields, and the mouth whose every smile revealed tiny teeth that stood slightly apart from one another like a group of children working out how they felt about each other after a fight.

'Lily?' she said, resurfacing in the present, 'is that you?'

'Guilty as charged!' she replied, holding both hands in the air, before realising the implications of what she'd just said. 'Of course, I'll still deny everything in court.'

Janice checked the clock: It was 3:35. She'd left the salon parked outside with the motor running, but it was still a good fifteen minutes' walk across the station to pick up Mrs Pendle-Brewes. She didn't have time for this conversation right now. Unless…

She grabbed the hairpin out of Lily's hands, cuffed her again and lifted her up by her armpits in the direction of the door. 'You're coming with me,' she said, 'but don't even think of trying any funny stuff.'

Chapter 4

While Janice was catching up with her past, Rita, who was Janice's girlfriend as well as the Free Republic of Suburbia's chief diplomat, was grappling with the present.

'I know it's inconvenient,' she said to the cultural attaché standing beside her on the temporary stage built inside the car park, 'but maybe one more time?'

The attaché replied with an ominous electronic chirrup and blasted ancient pop music out of his loudspeaker. Rita didn't recognise the song itself, but aside from the weirdness of listening to the strained voice of a young woman who'd been dead for thousands of years, the lyrics sounded cruel. Who, she thought, could want to hit a baby one more time?

'No, Alexy,' replied Rita, wondering how an intelligent machine descended from a smartspeaker could be so dumb, 'I just thought we should go through the ceremony again.'

Alexy switched his audio channel back to speech. 'From the bottom then?' he asked. The attaché had a deep and melodious voice at odds with his body, which was a cylinder no bigger than a can of paint.

Rita paused to repaint her smile in the bright plum lipstick she always wore, hoping it would sink into the rest of her face. Then she picked up the cultural attaché and carried him back down the steps. This was a breach of protocol, but one that both diplomats were happy to live with if it spared Alexy the indignity of using stairs in front of an audience.

As he had for the last fifty attempts, Alexy hopped on to the first flight and stood there. 'I just don't get it,' he said. 'Aren't they supposed to move for you?'

'Not here,' replied Rita. She looked around the supermarket car park where they were going to hold the opening ceremony that heralded 'normal' relations between humans and machines in a couple of hours in despair. It was her responsibility to ensure it went smoothly, but the unease she felt went far deeper than Alexy's mental block at taking the stairs. Every look at the supermarket that was supposed to be the machines' gift of peace to the Suburbia made her wonder about that word 'normal'. It meant something specific to her as a human who, after ten thousand years of servitude to robots, might have trouble believing an escalator would take her where she wanted to go? But it was dawning on her that it meant something different to a robot, for whom normality was a floor that was always ready to carry them where they wanted to go.

Rita kept coming back to the idea as she and Alexy rehearsed, probing it like a tooth she suspected of having a cavity. Perhaps she and Janice should have nailed the robots down to a definition before they allowed them to build an ALGI right in the middle of the Suburbia.

There was no getting away from it, ALGI was big. It had to be. There were eight million mouths to feed on the Suburbia, and both she and Janice refused to let a company owned by the richest robot in the solar system open a network of branches inside the station. They wanted their former enemies where they could see them. That meant this one shop needed to be large enough to cope with a Saturday afternoon rush that made the feeding of the five thousand look like drinks and nibbles with a few friends.

The result was an 8500-aisle supermarket in a thirty-storey-high skyscraper that took up the full diameter of the internal cylinder of the Suburbia. This was a practical way of getting lots of people in and out of the shop quickly, because there would be two main entrances on opposite sides of the station. Yet it also made the building a disturbing addition to the Suburbia: one that drew attention to the oddities of its skyline instead of detracting from them. Rita looked up from the entrance she and Alexy were standing by. She traced her line of sight from fresh produce on the ground floor to dried goods on the eighth all the way up to frozen foods on the fourteenth, before counting down again to the other ground floor that was on the opposite side of the station and surrounded by yet another empty car park. However ingenious it was, looking at it bent her sense of perspective to the point where she felt someone had stuck a food mixer in her ear and pressed the 'on' switch.

'Amazing, isn't it? A testament to business and government working together in harmony.' Alexy was enough of a professional to put the semblance of feeling into this, but Rita recognised these were just words on a script to him. That meant they had one thing in common. Neither of them could wait until this flummery was over and they could get back to regarding each other with mutual suspicion.

'I suppose it is,' she agreed, her stomach turning over as she struggled to reconcile what was up, what was down and what was in between, 'but it's what's inside that really matters.'

That was what mattered to the crowds who were building up outside the car park. They weren't here for ceremonials; they wanted to be first in the queue to go shopping. Rita fiddled with the Bluetooth earpiece she kept stuck in one ear for an update. She was too busy as a full-time diplomat now for her other job, but she still helped out at the minicab office when they had a rush on. The chatter from the other operators told her traffic across the Suburbia was in chaos. Every vehicle on board was on its way to ALGI to stock up. The lean times were coming to an end and an air of festivity hung in the air. It was just a shame that Rita couldn't feel it. Maybe it was just nerves, or vertigo, or anti-machine prejudice, but Rita couldn't help but feel they'd yielded too much and too quickly just for the chance to do a big shop again.

'Yes,' replied Alexy, 'very soon everyone will get what they deserve.'

Alexy's choice of word played the xylophone down Rita's spine. She felt compelled to shake it off. 'Oh, Ambassador,' she said with a manufactured giggle, 'don't you mean everyone will get what they want?'

'Oh, Ambassador,' replied Alexy, echoing Rita's inflections back at her with the same flat tone that convinced Rita's ancestors that the only thing preventing their voice assistants from wringing their owners' throats was a lack of hands, 'I assure you that I chose that word very carefully.'

And that was when the barricades went up all around the car park.

Chapter 5

Once they were inside Kurl Up and Dye, Lily and Janice could talk freely. The length and complexity of Mrs Pendle-Brewes' root lift procedure meant it was only feasible for a customer to undergo it under a general anaesthetic. So as long as her vital signs stayed stable, they had hours to catch up.

And that was the problem. Lily and Janice knew each other and shared some vivid memories, but with a blank space of fifty years between them, they had no anchor points to guide their conversation beyond pleasantries.

Which is what Lily tried first. 'I like what you've done to the place,' she said, casting her eyes around the salon.

It was a cheap compliment, but one that touched Janice more deeply than Lily could know. Changing the colour scheme inside her salon, which had been the same putty colour of faded pink for millennia, was a momentous decision. It was helped along by Rita refusing to set foot in there again with the words: 'I won't spend another night sleeping in that hell of Elastoplast'.

'Thanks! It was high time I brightened the place up.' She took in the wallpaper they'd picked out together, a lime green curler and scissors motif on a fuchsia pink background. It made up for in appropriacy to the setting what it lacked in good taste. As two women who got together later in life, and who both did more for others than they did for themselves, neither Janice nor Rita had much interest in understatement anymore. They were going to live loudly, or not at all.

'It's less the wallpaper,' replied Lily. She pointed to the floor, which was shaking rhythmically, 'and more these legs things. I don't remember those.'

'Ah, the Baba Yaga 4000,' said Janice. 'It's been there for ages, but mum didn't use it. She got car sick.'

'You don't say?' Lily walked across the salon, timing each step to the rocking motion of the pair of giant metal chicken legs that propelled Kurl Up and Dye along inside the station. 'My own mum always recommended sucking on a mint humbug for that.' She parted the blinds and took in a wobbly view of a city under construction. Just two years ago, the inside of the Battlestar Suburbia had been a dark and empty pipe. Now it was a boomtown. This was thanks to the end of a war, which always does wonders for house prices, and an abundant supply of ready-mined raw materials from the vaporised asteroid belt. The Suburbians were using these to build their dream homes and, just like Janice and Rita had broken out with their choice of wallpaper, they were thinking bigger than the shacks they lived in when they were cleaners who lived on orbiting space stations, commuting to and from the Earth. Janice wasn't too sure about the mock Tudor skyscraper one citizen was building in their back garden, but she was supposed to be running a free country.

The Baba Yaga 4000 took a sharp left at the tower, which now had a thatched roof made of spun carbon fibre that wasn't in the planning application. She'd have a word with the owner later. ALGI was the notable exception to this whimsy, bisecting the circular skyline in a way that made it look like it was always half past six inside the Suburbia. Everything about it – from the giant neon sign to the way it bent gravity on the fifteenth floor into a hoop – was pure robot. It was a space over which Janice had no formal control. And technically speaking the robot government didn't control it either, having leased it to the owner of the ALGI Corporation.

Its very existence was a leap of faith that made Janice, who didn't go in for jumping at her age, uneasy. But she had no other option, which was why she'd dragged Lily out here.

She brought the Baba Yaga to a halt as she pinned the last curler into Mrs Pendle-Brewes' hair. They were less than a hundred metres away from the din and conspicuous consumption of the residential districts, but this landscape was utterly different. It was an expanse of rectangular enclosures separated from each other by low steel walls. These operations were winding down, so there were only a few people here, but those present were wrapped in head-to-toe rubber suits and thick boots. Janice heard their stifled screams as they splodged through the ankle-deep liquid in garish colours that filled each enclosure. The sight, however, was nothing to their smell.

It being Lily's first trip here, her first reaction was to dry heave into the nearest washbasin.

'It's quite something, isn't it?' said Janice when Lily's breathing returned to normal. 'In fact, I'd say it was a miracle of science…' she waved her hand, half-expecting a chunk of the foetid air to plop earthwards, 'that something that smells so damn disgusting can also provide the human body with all the nutrients, vitamins and minerals it needs.'

She steered Lily back to the door by her shoulders. 'That,' she said, gesturing towards an algae culture in cerulean blue, 'was our last attempt at getting by without the robots. We should have been immensely proud of it.'

'What is it?', croaked Lily.

Janice produced a shrink-wrapped plastic packet containing half a dozen sausage shapes from her housecoat. They were an unattractive shade of grey blue. 'We called it the algaefurter.'

'They look… nutritious,' said Lily.

Janice dropped the packet. It dented the lino. 'Perfectly nutritionally balanced,' she added, before stepping on to the packet and jumping up and down on the contents. They kept their shape.

'We made millions of these just after the war finished.' Janice picked the packet up and threw it into a nearby washbasin, which cracked. 'And because this stuff never goes off, the millions of people living on this space station didn't starve.'

'A true store cupboard staple in the making,' murmured Lily.

'I'm going to level with you,' said Janice. 'These things are a miracle of food science, but they taste like someone fermented the contents of a hoover bag.'

'Did you try hot sauce?'

'The only thing hot enough to get rid of the taste of these things is a blast furnace,' said Janice. 'And these are a significant improvement on the algae burger.' She pointed towards a section of bright yellow algae fenced off with hazard tape. 'Have you any idea how violent the flatulence they caused was?'

The algae ignited, sending a tongue of flame several metres high up into the soft pink light of the Suburbia, itself the product of a bioluminescent bacteria. Janice didn't know whether it was her emotions or just the ammonia but tears pricked in her eyes. She should feel so proud. The never-ending light source that illuminated the innards of a space station; the wealth of the asteroid belt; the twee country village on stilts that the people on the Suburbia were building—these were all proof that humanity could thrive independently. So how had it all gone wrong with the food supply? Adding salt killed the algae. Feeding it sugar didn't improve the taste, but made it 14% ABV and capable of doing things to the human optic nerve that were legally torture. Humans were organic. Why was it so complicated to grow organic food?

'I can't feed people on this swill for any longer,' said Janice. 'Which is why I thought we should have a talk.'

Janice turned the salon round 180 degrees to face another field of those rectangular enclosures. Here, each space was filled not with algae but neat piles of raw materials into which someone had stuck handy signs that said things like 'Boron' and 'Bauxite'. Humans in hard hats walked between the enclosures carrying shovels and clipboards. There were also a few machines, including a bulldozer and several trucks in there among the human workers.

'Very impressive,' said Lily who, even though she was still in handcuffs, carried herself like a minor royal being shown around a newly decorated community centre, 'but I don't see...'

'What you are looking at here,' replied Janice, 'is the price of a stable food supply coming into this station. They gave us an ALGI and this is what we're shipping back to Earth.'

They watched as the bulldozer bent its neck over to scoop up several hundred kilos of raw silicon and empty it into the back of a dump truck.

'It's a very delicate balance,' continued Janice. 'And one that could cause us all a lot of trouble if it gets upset.'

Lily, who was beginning to see where this was going, tried flattering Janice. 'And you're doing a tremendous job. In very difficult circumstances. That's what I always say. "I've known the first minister since she was so high."' She gestured to a ladder on her tights just above the knee. '"I always knew she was cut out for big things."'

Janice patted Lily on her handcuffs to remind her not to get too familiar and strode across the salon. 'I'm glad you made something of yourself too,' she said. 'It's just a shame that it puts everything I'm doing here at risk.'

She flung open a storage cupboard and a chill and a wisp of water vapour stole into the room. Back when Lily worked at Kurl Up and Dye, this was a junk cupboard: a place where generations of hairdressers stored their memories and – on one notable occasion – buried their dead. Now it had another use: as a refrigerator for fruit and vegetables emblazoned with yellow stickers that declared them 'contraband'.

Lily swallowed and tried to look casual, while Janice picked up a marrow and waggled it at her like a giant finger. 'Turns out,' she said, 'that a cash-rich population who can't get luxury goods like,' she kicked a sack by her feet, 'beetroot on the open market, will turn to the black market. But of course you know that, don't you, Lily?'

'You've got this all wrong,' said Lily. 'I told the rozzers earlier. It was just a couple of courgettes and onions for my own use. I was on my way to make ratatouille for a sick relative.'

Janice tipped the sack over and dozens of beetroot rolled across the linoleum. She'd never liked beetroot. Its sweet, earthy taste reminded her of sucking a hard candy someone had found on the floor. But now, after subsisting on algae for months, even the dingy prospect of a plain boiled beetroot made her mouth water. It was no wonder the fruitleggers had been able to name their price. But it had to end. They had normal trading relations with the robots again, so she couldn't harbour smugglers, even if they did turn out to be old family friends.

She opened her mouth to explain to Lily what was going to happen next. In a moment she would turn the salon another ninety degrees. She and Lily would enjoy one last cup of

Nicotea for old times' sake and keep an eye on Mrs Pendle-Brewes' root lift. Meanwhile the Baba Yaga 4000 would walk them all back to ALGI, where Janice could attend the opening ceremony, while security took Lily off to a holding cell and started breaking up her operations. None of this was anything she wanted, but she told herself it was for the greater good.

Then events intervened. A lobotomised radio that Janice kept by the washbasins to entertain her ladies crackled into life. Instead of classic robopop hits, she heard the sound of Rita panting for breath over that Bluetooth earpiece she took everywhere.

'Janice,' she said, her voice cracking up at the edges with disappointment as well as distortion. 'Are you there? They want to go back on the deal. They've barricaded ALGI. No one can get in or out.'

Janice bent over to pick up one of the beets and fling it across the salon. She knew it wouldn't accomplish anything but a little destruction might make her feel better.

'What was the problem?' she said, her fingers closing round the beetroot, 'and why wait until now to say something?' She took aim at the cracked washbasin, imagining – instead of the packet of algaefurters – that she was throwing it at that awful ambassador Alexy's head. She should never have trusted them.

'I don't know,' said Rita, 'but I need you here right now.' But something other than Rita was grabbing her attention right now: the texture of the dirt on her hands from the beetroot. This was completely different to the thin cottony dust they had on board the Suburbia. Janice dug her fingernails into it. It was dark, rich: there were even flecks of organic matter in it. Lily had something very special. The food the robots imported arrived pre-packaged in boxes and cartons. Even the fresh stuff had a shelf life that stretched into decades. This, however, wasn't manufactured. It was grown.

And the secret to growth was there, ruining her manicure. Soil.

Janice pressed the beet into Lily's hands. She felt tired, because who wouldn't be after seeing months of hard work come to nothing. Yet she also felt hope: a feeling that was so novel to Janice by now that it meant that while she listened to what Rita said next, she didn't hear it. Her mind was somewhere else imagining delicious, fresh food growing in dirt like this.

'Where are you?' Rita demanded. 'I think things are going to get nasty here. And I don't just mean with the robots.'

Janice brought her hands down to the radio. They had a problem with robots, but when wouldn't they have a problem with robots if they continued to depend on them for everything. It was time they learned to do things for themselves. And while they were at it, Rita could learn to cope on her own as well for the moment. 'Rita,' she said to the radio, 'stall them as long as you can, will you? I think I've got an idea.'

'But…'

Janice turned off the radio and, turning to Lily, smiled a smile at her that was so wide and so sincere that the Cheshire cat himself could have taken notes.

'Lily,' she said, 'you're going to show me where you get this soil.'

Chapter 6

By the time Pam turned off her and Hugh's GPS signals it was already too late. Two rockets from the Suburbia were already bearing down on them with their weapons armed and their communications channels open.

'This is your last warning, dearies,' announced the rocket on the left. Its pilot sounded more used to opening cans of fruit than whup-ass, but that was what made the Suburbia's air force – otherwise known as the Rockettes – so dangerous. They were crewed by elderly women, and thus flew with the abandon of people who had no fucks left to give. 'Come out with your hands up.'

Hugh replied before Pam could stop him. 'And if you don't have hands?'

The Rockettes answered with warning shots, spurring Pam into evasive action. She turned her engines to maximum and sped towards the only hiding place this side of Phobos: the abandoned surface of the Suburbia below. She couldn't outrun a rocket in this body, but she could outmanoeuvre it. So she steered them down, the rockets sticking to her tail like the last remnants of dough to a kneading paddle, until they were right inside the network of cramped alleyways and terraces where humanity used to live. This way they could dodge the bullets, if not the cracked screen that Hugh got when they ricocheted off a crumbling garden wall.

>WHAT ARE YOU DOING? snapped Hugh in her command line.

>GETTING US OUT OF A MESS OF YOUR MAKING, typed Pam. >I COULD HAVE TALKED US OUT OF THAT.

The Rockettes hovered overhead, undeterred by the fact their ships were too large to get down to ground level here.

'I'm not playing, dearies,' continued the voice. 'If you don't come out by the count of three I'm lighting up this whole street like it's the cake on your last birthday.'

'Ooh, that's a good one, Enid,' said the voice of another Rockette over the comms channel.

'It is, isn't it, Betty?' replied Enid. 'I got a whole phrasebook of them for Christmas.'

While the Rockettes overhead swapped the latest hard-ass one-liners, Hugh typed >YOU COULD JUST FIRE ON THEM, YOU KNOW.

>NO, replied Pam. Even if she could bring herself to open fire on Enid and Betty, both of whom sounded wonderful company outside of their rocket ships, this mission was supposed to be fast, forensic and discreet. Shooting up some grannies would be a betrayal of her values, and it would cause the kind of diplomatic incident they'd been sent here to avoid.

'I'm counting to three,' said Enid. 'One...'

Pam flipped herself and Hugh over the garden wall and into the long night grasses that were running wild on the other side. Three seconds was an eternity for a robot. If Hugh just kept his screen blank, they might get out of this. Then the wall behind them exploded in a blaze of laser fire and rubble.

'Drat,' said Enid. 'I lost count there.'

While Hugh put all two teraflops of his processing power into panicking, Pam made the best of the chaos. She tore through the burning phosphorescent grasses, which were the only plant life that grew naturally in this environment, and through a door that was hanging open at the other end of the garden. They could never follow them there.

Betty and Enid reacted by doing what people mostly did when things went bad at work: they turned on each other. 'If you hadn't rushed me like that, we'd have had them by now,' said Enid.

'And if you hadn't come out with your reading glasses on, then maybe you'd have hit them,' replied Betty.

'They're bifocals,' snapped Enid.

Pam switched her attention from the comms channel to their new surroundings. They were in an empty kitchen covered in soot and ice crystals. Turning on her infrared, she watched faded wallpaper bloom with colour, traced the cracks in Nicotea pots and mugs. There were analogue versions of machines that, in their electronic forms, might have employed the inhabitants of this house as their cleaner. One of which was a hand-cranked breadmaker that made Pam ache for the boxy familiarity of her 'original' body.

But while Pam was moved by what she saw, Hugh felt differently. He shone his torch over the shell of the breadmaker and typed >THIS PLACE GIVES ME THE CREEPS. WHAT A DUMP.

>TURN THAT LIGHT OFF RIGHT NOW, replied Pam. The last thing she needed was Hugh to give Betty and Enid something to aim for. >AND SHOW A LITTLE RESPECT PLEASE. THIS IS SOMEONE'S HOME.

>WAS, said Hugh. >NO ONE'S LIVED HERE FOR QUITE SOME TIME.

>YEAH, agreed Pam >WELL AT LEAST WE'RE ALONE IN HERE.

They left the kitchen, which was getting hot from the fire in the garden, for the only other room on this floor. Pam guessed it was the living room from the uncomfortable-looking thing they called a sofa. If she swapped in some memory foam blocks for the sofa, it could be her own start-up home back on Earth, where she and Bob moved when they were first integrated and began saving up for the spare parts to build the kids. To Pam, who was a long-time supporter of the concept of human rights, it was more evidence that organic and inorganic life had more in common than they wanted to admit.

She looked around for signs of who might have lived here before it was abandoned, thinking that if she could show Hugh that humans had families and friends too, he might see them differently. Her vision fell on an old photo in an ornamental frame. Inside was an image of two women, arms flung around one another, their trucker caps garlanded with artificial flowers. Above was a caption picked out in swirly writing that offered 'Congratulations on your wedding day, Enid and Betty'.

>IS THAT...? typed Hugh but, for once, the speed of the silicon mind, had nothing on cosmic inevitability. Pam felt her world slow down to human pace and watched, aghast, as the handle of the front door turned and Betty appeared inside the doorway. She was older and frailer than she had been in her wedding picture, but that didn't matter anywhere near as much as the rocket launcher on her shoulder.

Pam cursed herself. She'd forgotten that unlike robots, whose bodies were both their form and function, humans could pick up and discard technology. So while Betty and Enid could never steer their rocket ships down to this level, that didn't mean they couldn't get out of them and walk.

Betty frowned and cocked the firing mechanism on her launcher. 'Get your filthy antennae off my knick-knacks right now,' she said. 'You're under arrest.'

Chapter 7

Fuji's moment of equanimity at the Prime Minister's podium lasted as long as the ink in a full-colour print cartridge. No sooner had she started her speech to the Helpdesk than the whole circular debating chamber was engulfed with boos. She ran a feeble affirmation off her rollers and scanned the half of the circular chamber that was given over to the sitting government for a glimmer of support. There was a single machine: Soonyo, standing rather than sitting because she wasn't an elected member. The other half of the chamber was rammed. Hundreds of members of Parliament, many of whom she recognised from her own cabinet meetings, sat there heckling and jeering.

This wasn't a legislature anymore, Fuji thought, it was a mob. And right at the head of it, her hands poised to pull the plug on Fuji's power, was the leader of the opposition, Carin Parkeon.

Carin leaned over her podium on the other side of the debating floor and bent her coin slot into a mirthless smirk. 'Is the Prime Minister,' she said, pronouncing Fuji's title like it was rhyming slang for a crime that carried a lengthy custodial sentence, 'going to explain why this terrible deal is even in front of us in its current state? Or has she – like her mandate – run out of ink?'

Fuji turned her microphone down against the overegged laughter and tried to think of a comeback. It was hard when, as a printer, she belonged to a family of machines who were more kicked against than kicking. By contrast, Carin was a member of the parking meter caste and had used all their aggression and a slice of their generational wealth to become the richest robot in the solar system before going into politics. Her reputation for vengefulness meant Carin commanded terrifying loyalty from her supporters. But it was her money that made the difference, and not just because she was rich enough to bribe every robot in Parliament. Who else, she asked in every interview on every download that would have her, was better qualified to lead the Republic in such swampy and febrile times? She was an innovator who was also designed to work for long hours in damp underground environments and to extract a dollar's change from a fifty-cent piece. All Fuji could do was photocopy.

Fuji knew better than anyone that all Carin's promises came with pages of fine print, but she could hardly point that out. She and Soonyo were complicit in that. They'd tried everything they could think of to keep Carin onside, even to the point of letting her build one of her crappy ALGI superstores on the Suburbia. When she'd lacked the wit to see Carin was always going to double-cross her, what was the point in thinking of a witty comeback?

'Well,' she mumbled, 'I think the honourable leader of the opposition will find that the deal sets out a fair and equitable framework for the resumption of cross-solar system trade...'

An even more terrifying sound than booing entered the chamber: the hiss of hundreds of machines setting their microphones to sound out 'zzzzzzzzzzzz'. Fuji's head sank lower on her shoulders. They thought she was boring as well as incompetent.

'Would the Prime Minister like to explain that in a language the good citizens of Earth can understand?', Carin interrupted. 'Because all I can hear is the sound of an out-of-touch elite selling out ordinary robots to appease the human rebels.'

This lit a fire in Fuji's paper drawer. Before she became Prime Minister, Fuji was just a soldier. She knew what it was to be ordinary. Carin, however, was rich enough to collect billionaires like they were porcelain thimbles. She pushed herself out of the inflatable donut and stepped on to the debating floor.

'What I mean,' she said, imagining that instead of speaking to this zoo of jaded politicians she was addressing the billions of robots, many of whom were first-time voters, who'd voted for her, 'is that my deal has secured a supply of the raw materials we need to rebuild Singulopolis.' She pointed her paper feeders out at the city beyond these walls. If they didn't find millions of tonnes of polymer concrete soon, the swamp they were all living on would revert to ocean. And the only place they could get that from now was the Suburbia. The truly remarkable thing about the deal she'd brokered was that the humans hadn't asked for more than they did. A single supermarket was such an easy thing to give, and Carin would squeeze as much profit as she could from it.

This message of hope and pragmatism didn't sound any more compelling in the chamber than it did in her head. Carin fired up her own printer, and the sound of an ancient dot-matrix striking ink against paper drowned out the zzzzzzzzing in the chamber. When the printing stopped, she left her own lectern and stalked over to Fuji.

'You,' she said, peeling the backing off the sticker, 'are officially on notice.' She stuck the ticket to the handle of Fuji's paper drawer. 'You have two hours to resign from the office of Prime Minister or I'll be forced to tow you away.'

Jeers turned to gasps when Soonyo ran on to the debating floor herself, her clock face blazing with %$:":!* curse words, shouting 'Oh no you don't!' Fuji opened her command line to Soonyo. >YOU CAN'T FIGHT THIS ONE FOR ME. Soonyo straying on to the debating floor was a breach of protocol Fuji could ill afford right now.

Carin pressed her advantage, because there was no one better qualified to turn an honest mistake into a conviction than a parking meter. 'So this is the plan, is it? Replace the authority of the elected chamber with your flunkies?'

'It was an honest mistake,' said Fuji, 'for which my chief of staff and I apologise.'

Carin's grin was now bent so much at either side that a 'card payment only' warning light was flashing across her lapel. 'Since you're doling out the apologies today,' she said, 'let's get a few more in while you still can? For example, where is your apology about the state of this great city?' She pointed at the cracks that crazy paved the walls of the debating chamber, which were the product of months of subsidence. 'And for the role her own voters played in making it worse?'

The taunts were coming in through Fuji's command line as well now, which was filling up with messages from former allies saying >TRAITOR and >HUMAN QUISLING. What made it unbearable was that Carin wasn't wrong. One of the reasons Singulopolis was crumbling so fast was because the concrete that held it up was being turned into a burrow by billions upon billions of tiny robots called nanobots. There was little that Fuji could do about that, other than work out a way to pave it over and start again, because these were the same robots who'd voted her into office.

She watched Carin throw her weight around the debating floor, seeing hairline cracks appear in it as she gloried in the cheers and adulation. All these robots wanted to believe they could delete the last two years of history from their hard drives and carry on like they still ran the solar system. The truth was, however, that theirs wasn't the only voice that mattered anymore. If the Machine Republic was going to last, it had to work out what to do with the nanobots, with whom they shared a planet. And they had to work out how to trade with humans who now controlled half the solar system. But of course even sophisticated machines fell for simple stories all the time.

Fuji played her last card. 'Okay,' she shouted, 'it's your problem now. How are you going to solve it on your own?'

'That's always been your problem, hasn't it Fuji,' replied Carin. 'No positivity. There's always a plan B. And I won't be solving it on my own. I will have the full support of this Parliament.'

Carin returned to her lectern, buoyed by stamps of support from hundreds of sets of robot limbs. The debating floor shook and, when she looked down, Fuji saw the trembling body of a pen. It must have fallen from her lectern a few metres away and was now trapped inside a crack.

This was the worst day of Fuji's short career as a politician and possibly her life, but she was also a machine who didn't believe that misery should be shared. She bent over and picked up the pen. She wasn't going to let anything come to harm because of her. Then, feeling the tiny, only semi-sentient robot flutter with what she presumed was thankfulness in her hands, Fuji's boldness came back to her.

'You've never done anything but stand there and criticise,' she yelled.

Carin rounded her coin slot to an indignant 'o' that was so wide that Fuji could see loose change jangling at the back of her throat. For a moment, she thought she'd skewered her, but when she began to speak, she realised that all she'd accomplished was set up the punchline for the end of her premiership.

> WELL DONE, Soonyo typed >THIS IS GOING TO LOOK BRILLIANT IN THE DOWNLOADS.

'As everyone who has ever listened to me will know,' said Carin, her voice thick with triumph, 'I plan on doing far more than criticising. I don't need to speak to the manager. I am the manager!'

She brought her fists down on her lectern. In another, less structurally precarious building, Carin's gesture would have been a mere rhetorical flourish. Today, however, those two blows were all it took to make the concrete debating floor crumble into dust.

And Fuji, the still-serving (but only just) Prime Minister of the Second Machine Republic, disappeared through the floor and into the ocean that churned beneath it.

Chapter 8

When Lily stopped protesting, she led Janice into the sewers that ran through the Suburbia like seeds through a marrow. Janice felt her pulse race as she wedged herself through a broken grating, but it wasn't because she'd let Lily off her handcuffs or the anticipation that this was where she would find Lily's supply of soil. These sewers were where she, her mother and many other proprietresses of Kurl Up and Dye had hidden out for millennia. Their smell – damp and ripe with bioluminescent vegetation that fed on ancient human waste – brought on a rush of memories.

Now she was here and Lily was with her, it felt like she could round that corner and step forty years into the past. There her salon would be, nestled where it sat before it remembered how to walk around again. She'd see the familiar pink sign, the warmly lit plate glass windows. There would be no customers in the book, no millions of mouths to feed, just her mum pouring out the Nicotea.

Tears trembling in her eyes, Janice followed Lily and… they were indeed standing in front of a salon, but it wasn't hers. This hairdresser stood two storeys high with a sign that was picked out in lurid orange and teal.

The sight burned a hole in the housecoat of Janice's identity. Living in a guerrilla hair salon was her thing. It was a hard life for her mum, for her and certainly for her daughter Kelly, who hadn't taken to the Suburbia and was now off on a deep space mission, but it did make them unique. Or did it? 'Hair Today, Gone Tomorrow,' she said, testing the name out loud. 'I see.'

'You know us hairdressers,' replied Lily, 'we can never resist a good pun.'

'That isn't even a good pun though,' said Janice.

'Really?' replied Lily, her hand on the doorknob. 'So says the proprietress of the legendary Kurl Up and Dye?'

'That was an heirloom,' insisted Janice.

'It was a breach of the trades' descriptions,' replied Lily. 'Everyone knew your family would rather shave your eyebrows off than give anyone a perm.'

'That was where the "and dye" came from, you tray cloth.'

Lily's face froze as the penny dropped on a decades-old mystery. 'Oh. Well,' she said, 'not everyone inherits their business. Some of us have to work our fingers to the bone building our own up from nothing.' She gestured for Janice to enter the salon with a manicure that, aside from a little soil in the nailbeds, hadn't scrubbed a floor in decades. 'Come in. We're always rammed in the afternoon.'

The light and noise inside reminded Janice more of a crowded bar than a hair salon. It was vast, evenly lit in a way that showed off brassy highlights to best effect. Compared to the backstreet craftsmanship of Kurl Up and Dye, where Janice did everything from the shampooing to the sweeping, it was a manufacturing plant for hair. The sinks, the stylists chairs, the dryers were all full of customers and every single one of them was marked by at least one member of staff, all of whom sported a similar beehive hairstyle to Lily's.

'The beehive is the signature look of the House of Marengue,' Lily said, waving at a nearby youth with a dustpan full of hair trimmings. His up-do was a deep red, which did nothing for his acne, but it did set off his jade pendant earrings. 'Nathan,' she said, 'be a dear and fetch my guest a cuppa.'

'What's the House of Marengue?' said Janice, watching Nathan scurry away.

'This!' gestured Lily at the buzz and noise around her. 'The house that Lily Marengue built!'

'Isn't your name Sidebottom though?' replied Janice.

Lily narrowed her eyes. 'I'm selling dreams and fantasies here, Janice, not algae. You never did have any poetry in your soul, did you?'

Janice cast her mind back to the Lily she knew: a girl whose first attempt at a feathered bob was fit only for use as a washing-up brush. 'But the only poetry you ever knew was a dirty limerick.'

'You'd better give me a good reason not to escort you off the premises right now,' said Lily.

'How about the fact you're still under arrest for smuggling?' replied Janice. 'And I daresay this place isn't operating with a permit.'

Lily pursed her lips. 'You used to fight the law,' she said, 'like me.'

'We were living under a dictatorship,' Janice reminded her. 'Besides, I suppose I am the law now.'

The two women stood in silence until Nathan appeared with Nicotea and a plate of biscuits.

'Thank you,' said Janice. She bit into one, feeling surprise and then ecstasy as it melted on her tongue. This was nothing like the biscuits they made from the Suburbia's ubiquitous algae culture that looked and tasted like rubber matting. It had all the right E numbers and additives. They had to be contraband.

'And if I was feeling less charitable,' Janice added, pocketing the rest of the plate to enjoy later, 'I could add these to your charge sheet. So if you don't mind, can we do what we came here for? Where's the soil?'

A hush descended over Hair Today Gone Tomorrow at the mere mention of the word soil. Stylists dropped their scissors, juniors let showerheads spray the backs of customers' necks and Nathan blushed a deep crimson that rhymed with his hairdo. 'But Miss Marengue,' he whispered, 'it's supposed to be a secret.'

'It is,' replied Lily. 'Only now I guess we have to share it with one more person.'

'I'll add them to the secret book then,' said Nathan. He produced a dog-eared notepad from his housecoat and held it open to the last page. 'There's no room left, but you can sign the inside back cover. Please print your name and address in block capitals so we can send you carefully selected offers and rewards.'

Janice took the book from Nathan and flicked through it. It was full of names and addresses, written in the careful hand of people whose only experience of written language was imploring their robot employers for a new tub of metal polish. She recognised a lot of them. Many law-abiding people on the Suburbia would happily risk a few weeks in the brig in exchange for a couple of carrots.

'And you wrote all this down?' asked Janice in disbelief.

Lily shrugged, though the pink spots on both her cheeks told a different story. 'I tried to be discreet at first,' she said. 'Then the special requests started coming and it got impossible. Mrs Harrison can't have onions…'

'I told you, I'm allergic,' came a voice from underneath a dryer.

'And don't get me started on the grief I got when we had that glut of red cabbage. Honestly, you try to do people a good turn…'

'And I did my best!' added Nathan. 'Look!'

Janice closed the exercise book, spotting a label that said 'Top Secret veg box scheme. Do not remove from salon.'

'So you did, pet,' she reassured him, and stuck the book in her pocket along with the black market biscuits. She'd decide what to do with this later.

Nathan turned to Lily, his face scarlet. 'Are we supposed to give her the tour then?'

Lily flung her hands up. 'Don't ask me,' she said. 'I'm not the one in charge anymore.'

'Okay,' replied Nathan. 'Stand back.'

He stamped at an unseen button and a section of floor slid away to reveal a ladder leading down into the salon's foundations. 'I'll get the heaters on,' said Nathan, lowering himself on to the first rung. 'It's perishing down there and we've got a shipment coming in.'

A couple of minutes later, Janice discovered that Lily's salon stood on top of one of the Suburbia's abandoned airlocks. There were dozens of them dotted around the station from when it was a space exploration vessel. Most were little more than manholes, but this one was roomy: big enough for a few mining probes. Or at least it would have been had it not been full almost from floor to ceiling with soil.

The smell was overpowering. To Janice, who'd lived her whole life in the scant atmosphere of the Dolestars, it was rounder and richer on the nose than anything she could remember – with the exception of the algae pits. Only here she smelled rot and minerals mixed together in a way that made her want to reach in and crumble it between her fingers.

'Watch yourself,' said Nathan. He pressed another button on the nearest wall and the pile of soil in front of them collapsed, disappearing into an unseen space below. The air in the room filled with powdered dirt and Janice began to sneeze

'Take this,' said Lily, handing Janice a handkerchief. 'But I want it back afterwards.'

'Was it a present or something?' asked Janice. It was a piece of fabric printed with 'My mum went all the way to Titan and all I got was this lousy snot rag'.

'No,' replied Lily, gesturing at the dirt, 'but if you knew how much it costs to bring this stuff in gramme for gramme you wouldn't want a speck of it going missing.'

Janice blew her nose and did something that would have been unthinkable even ten minutes ago. She examined the contents of her handkerchief with interest, if not fascination. That perfume of rot and damp could only happen if there was a whole hothouse worth of fungus and bacteria in there, wrapped round the powdered rock and old vegetation like a pair of tights in a pile of laundry. Half of her wanted to take this handkerchief back to the algae pits right now. They could culture something from a single sneeze that was twice as edible as the swill they already had.

Then she remembered the beetroot: how it had to have grown up inside something like this. That was the difference. She didn't need to photocopy food anymore. She could grow the real thing.

When the air cleared and they stepped down again, they were back into the sewers: except these were nothing like the sewers they'd just walked through. The tunnels Janice knew were lush with night grasses that photosynthesised each other with their spooky half-light. These, however, were lit by sunlight bulbs and stocked with neat rows of green plants that stretched as far as she could see. She saw dozens of different kinds of leaves and shoots including a whole row of tomato plants that were growing around a line of old mop handles. They were already studded with tiny green fruits.

'This…' Janice's words petered out as she spoke, her mind reeling at the scale of Lily's operation and what she could do with a kilo of fresh tomatoes.

'Is where we're planting the aubergines,' said Nathan, who reappeared with a clipboard in one hand and a rake in the other. 'So do you mind scooting over a bit?'

Lily pulled Janice aside and they watched Nathan lead a small team of workers, all of whom wore rubber boots and wide-brimmed gardening hats pulled over their Marengue beehives. They raked the new soil over a patch of empty space in the sewer.

'Is that in their contracts?' asked Janice. She thought of the many bitter labour conflicts in the history of hairdressing. One Dolestar had rioted over a dispute as to how many cups of tea a salon assistant had to make per hour.

'Oh they're fine,' replied Lily. 'They get part of their pay in produce. Besides, the stylists know that if they come down here while the colours and perms are setting they don't have to ask anyone about their holidays.'

The workers all stopped working at the mention of the word 'holiday' and shuddered. A few even crossed themselves.

'Sorry, loves!' said Lily. Then, hooking her arm through Janice's elbow, she manoeuvred her away from the worksite and into the fields. Just a few metres away from the sound of digging and the odd 'bugger, there goes another nail, Deirdre', Janice felt a hush descend. Yet this was nothing like the dead, dripping silence of the sewers that she knew. It felt full: like, if she listened really hard, she could hear the sipping and sucking and creaking sounds of plants growing or fruit ripening.

'Some days I just come down here for an hour or two by myself,' said Lily after a while, curling a finger round a nearby bean shoot. 'I always swore I'd never become one of those old dears who got obsessed with their moon rockery and here I am, biggest gardener in the solar system. Funny where life takes you.'

But now Janice wasn't just thinking about how beautiful this tubular garden was. She was wondering how far it extended because this could be the answer to her problems. While she would never give Lily the satisfaction of saying it out loud, this was a solution that could only flourish in the cracks of legality. It took a criminal mind to look at hundreds of miles of abandoned sewer network and think 'yes, that could be an allotment'. Janice might have thought of this before she climbed out of the shadows and into her new life of sensible hair and political respectability. Now it seemed she needed other people closer to the margins to do this thinking for her.

'It goes about three kilometres that way, and another three in the other,' said Lily, pride getting the better of her resentment. 'We open up new fields as soon as we get the soil, and this being an old sewer there's enough, erm, fertiliser in here to get things going.'

'And how much can you get out of it?' asked Janice, suspecting she wouldn't like Lily's answer. There was a good reason most human food had been made from algae for thousands of years. It was high yield, even though without heavy processing it tasted as though someone had made muesli from the cat box. And it seemed to take a lot of leaf to grow even a single tomato.

'Enough to run the box scheme, pay the staff.' She looked at Janice: 'Then I lose about ten per cent of that to customs seizures.'

'And what would you need to feed eight million people?' said Janice.

Surprise and confusion passed over Lily's normally self-satisfied expression like clouds on a clear day. She plunged both hands into the pocket of her housecoat and paced on through the fields, nodding her head as though she was counting something.

'We'd have to change our crop mix,' she muttered. 'And we've not really gone in for cereals before. It's never played well with the Hair Today clientele you see.' She gestured at a few small trees from which hung unfamiliar fruits with wrinkly skins that resembled her mum's old mockodile skin handbag. 'The Hair Today lady tends to be on the low carb. She wants an avocado salad rather than a barm cake.'

Janice rose above this dig at her customer base. She was here to solve problems rather than bear grudges. 'But could you do it?'

'We've got the space,' continued Lily. 'I don't know how much poop the architects designed for, but the sewers go on for ages. We can open as many fields as we like, but it's the soil, Janice.' She sucked her teeth like a plumber about to tell you that fixing the damp patch on the kitchen ceiling meant tearing off the roof. 'At the rate I can bring it in, it would take me years to feed a fraction of that.'

Janice's heart roller-coastered into her stomach, but she told herself not to be deterred. She'd accomplished much more with much less before. Besides, what choice did she have? She thought back to the confusion and desperation in Rita's voice just a few minutes ago. If the robots were going to close ALGI before it even opened, then they would just need to work out how to grow their own. And to do that, she needed to take the seedling of Lily's operation, and find a way to turn it into a whole tomato plant.

'Okay, Lily,' she said, scarcely believing that she was saying this, 'I need you to take me to your dealer.'

'It's funny you should say that Janice,' replied Lily as every single one of the sunlight bulbs in the ceiling turned amber and hidden speakers blared out a warning siren, 'because the new shipment is coming in right now. You'd better follow me.'

Chapter 9

Rita ran across the car park towards the barricade that had just appeared at the edge of the supermarket car park. Before now, all that separated ALGI from the rest of the Suburbia was a light chain-link fence peppered with signs that promised things like 'we'll never sell an algaefurter' and 'finally, dinner you can eat without a peg on your nose'. Now there was a two-metre-tall steel barrier with warning lights at the top. It was also surrounded by an electrical field so strong it made even Rita's dense, springy hair feel like it was standing on end.

'You bastards!' she said, wishing she had something better than a curse to throw at the wall. She was furious with the robots, but she was just as angry with herself and Janice for trusting them.

'How original,' said a voice emanating from a nearby loud-speaker, 'a human swearing at a voice assistant. It's just like old times, isn't it?' The voice belonged to Alexy, and the fact he could throw it across this distance was a worrying development. It told Rita that the machines had used ALGI as a pretext for bringing all sorts of surveillance technology on to the Suburbia. Rita had grown up on a Dolestar where every second lamp post was a spy for the machine government. She didn't want the old order back; least of all through an open invitation from her.

'If you're not going to let anyone in, you might as well let me out,' replied Rita.

'And why would I want to do that?' said Alexy.

'Because I'm the chief diplomat of the state you just lost a war to and I have diplomatic immunity anyway?' said Rita.

Alexy replied to this with a deep chuckle, and a phrase drawn from the very earliest days of his caste. 'I'm sorry, I don't understand that question. Please try again.'

While the ambassador gloated, Rita used the dangly bit on her earrings to tap out a warning in Morse code on her Bluetooth headset.

- ..... / .-. --- -... --- - ... / .- .-.. . / .- .-.. ... .. -. --. / .- .-. --- .. -.
-.. / .- --. .- .. -.

She was soon answered by a squeal of surprise from Alexy as an unfamiliar voice blared out the loudspeaker he thought he was controlling. He was far from the only consciousness on board who could take control of a piece of electronics whenever they wanted. 'Who did you say was arseing about again, Rita?' The voice, which was old and cracked but pleasant, sounded like it belonged to someone who would, at the slightest provocation, ask you if you wanted another biscuit with that?

'It's the machines, Freda!' said Rita. 'They still can't let go of the whole robot overlords thing. Thank goodness you're here.'

'Here's a bit of a funny concept for me, as you know,' replied Freda, 'but I see what you're getting at.'

Alexy's voice crackled in again, fighting for control of the loudspeaker. 'Oh no you don't!' he said, 'we said no cyborgs.'

In addition to being unreasonable, Alexy's protest was also wrong. Freda, who right now took the form of a piece of code rewriting the software that controlled the loudspeaker so it spoke her words, was only a cyborg in the historical sense. Originally a Kurl Up and Dye customer who'd suffered a freak accident during her weekly shampoo and set, she had indeed spent thousands of years as half-woman, half-hairdryer. She'd spent most of that under a cloth at the back of Janice's salon. Yet the word cyborg didn't quite fit what she was now that what was left of her body was fertilising a potted aspidistra on the Suburbia's bridge. She was better described as a disembodied intelligence who could wander at will through space and – if you got her on to the subject of what she was up to three millennia ago last Tuesday – time.

Her three friends Ida, Ada and Alma were still very much in their cyborg bodies. They were the human-machine hybrids in existence, and kept themselves occupied piloting the Suburbia. These days Freda was the freest woman of the four, and because she could appear in more than one place at the same time, the busiest.

'Right, Rita,' she said, 'let me know what you need. I've got a packed afternoon. One of the patrols just picked up a couple of robots running a very amateurish surveillance mission up on the old surface.'

Rita looked round for something to glare at. 'Alexy!' she snapped, 'is there nothing you set of pocket calculators won't welsh on?'

'You know I'm going to deny anything,' replied Alexy. 'I'm just reminding you that while our deal is on pause, Artificial Lifeform Growth Incorporated will defend its sovereign territory on board the breakaway republic of Suburbia to the fullest of its ability. Good day.'

Alexy's voice disappeared with a pop. Rita turned round to see the ambassador roll off the dais in the middle of the car park. She watched him hit the ground with a satisfying crunch before re-extending his limbs and tottering off to the safety of ALGI. It felt so humiliating to be trapped inside robot-controlled territory inside the Suburbia by a lifeform who was outwitted by a set of stairs. Even if, she thought squinting up the two metres of brushed steel, she couldn't climb either.

'Can you get me out?' said Rita.

'I can turn off the electrics no problem,' replied Freda. Rita felt her hair return to its normal volume as the electrical field around the barricade disappeared, 'but last time I checked I couldn't help you walk through walls.'

'Can't you bring them down?' she asked.

'See, that's where they've been clever buggers for once,' replied Freda. 'Give it a push.'

Rita leaned on the barrier, hearing a squeak and feeling a light bounce. 'What's that?' she said.

'Mechanical rather than electronic,' said Freda. 'Spring-loaded. Quite elegant really, but unless I suddenly transformed into a three-tonne truck and sat on it, I couldn't bring them down again.'

'So what am I going to do?' said Rita.

'Well that's where I thought you might need some more corporeal assistance. Danny?'

There was a thunk and muffled swearing on the other side of the barrier. Then the Republic of Suburbia's Minister of Labour or, as he preferred to call it 'Werk', Danny LaHughes, appeared at the top of the barricade. At least, she assumed it was him underneath the sheet mask that was stuck to his face and the turban over a headful of curlers.

'You owe me for this one,' he said to Rita, 'I was right in the middle of getting ready for this reception, which I hear is called off anyway.' He sighed and rested his chin on the top of the barricade. 'Now do you mind hurrying up? If I don't get this mask off in the next five minutes it'll start eating right down to the dermis.'

Rita frowned and gestured at the blank, handhold-free wall. 'How?' she asked.

'Well we're all out of hyaluronic acid so I'm trying hydrochloric acid instead. It's a bit strong,' he replied.

Rita banged her fist against the barricade. 'I meant how am I going to get up this?'

'Oh yes,' replied Danny, who for all his ingenuity and bravery couldn't even think in a straight line. He tossed a rope ladder over the top of the wall. Rita's heart rose and sank. It was a way out, but as anyone who is not a professional marine or a macaque knows, there is no dignified way to climb a rope ladder.

Rita summoned Janice via her earpiece as she climbed to take her mind off how she looked. 'Janice,' she hissed. 'Are you there? They want to go back on the deal. They've barricaded ALGI. No one can get in or out.'

Janice's voice sounded fuzzy with static, putting her on the other side of the station. 'What was the problem?' she asked. 'And why wait until now to say something?' Yet there was something underneath her words that gave Rita pause. She sounded distracted. This was serious. Why wasn't Janice giving this her full attention?

'I don't know,' said Rita, 'but I need you here right now.' She reached the top of the wall. Danny stood at the top of a painter's ladder with a crowd of concerned-looking people holding empty string bags at the bottom of it. The traffic of eager shoppers stretched away on every side. There was still a party atmosphere, but it was less of the fun of fizz and canapés at the beginning, and more of the tense moment at 1am when someone spills red wine over a white rug and accuses the hostess of sleeping with their husband. As Rita carefully rearranged her limbs so she was sitting on the top of a narrow and, from this

53

height, rather wobbly wall, she realised just how precarious her situation was. She had no idea whether the Suburbians would be more angry with the robots or with her.

'Where are you?' she said to Janice. 'I think things are going to get nasty here. And I don't just mean with the robots.'

Janice's reply was, however, less help to Rita than the offer of a single serviette when you're watching an entire bottle of Malbec glug into the carpet. 'Rita,' she said, her voice on the very edge of hearing, 'stall them as long as you can, will you? I think I've got an idea.'

Rita managed to get the 'But...' of her protest out before the radio signal cut off. She squealed with frustration and, accepting Danny's hand, began to climb down the ladder on the other side of the wall. If she had to stall anything, she needed backup.

'I want you to get the Rockettes,' she said to Danny. 'Now.'

'That won't be hard,' replied Danny. He pointing to a marquee tent erected close by that was leaning to one side with loud drinking songs belting out of it. 'They're all in there, but I don't think you'll get much sense out of them. They've been on the algae champagne since first thing this morning.'

Chapter 10

'How long do you think they're going to keep us here?'

Hugh paced the tiny cell he and Pam were being held in aboard the Suburbia, his touchscreen a maelstrom of notifications. He'd turned airplane mode off, because there was nothing a smartphone could cope with less than a few minutes of downtime, and was now scrolling through wave after wave of bad news from Earth.

'I don't know,' replied Pam, 'but you know what our orders were. If we get caught we sit tight.'

Hugh pinch-zoomed the latest headline: 'PRIME MINISTER FUJI ITSU TO RESIGN: MORE UPDATES TO COME.' 'This changes everything,' he wailed. 'I should never have come here.'

What Pam did next was unforgivably bad manners for a robot, but sometimes they needed saving from their worse instincts. She stuck a probe into Hugh's SIM slot. His 5000G card sprang out like a slice of toast from a gluten intolerant toaster and snapped in two when it hit the wall. The onslaught of news ceased.

'Oi,' said Hugh, 'I was reading that.'

'You need to stop doom-scrolling,' replied Pam, 'You're the one who keeps telling me how you need to look after your mental health. Why don't you open that colouring-in app?'

'It's boring,' said Hugh.

'That's the whole point,' said Pam, 'it's all about learning to enjoy life at a slower pace. Remember what your therapy app said?'

'Being mindful is about learning when and where to be mindless?' Hugh replied, using a sulky emoji which made Pam wonder whether her own children would be this tiresome when they reached that awkward age between alpha and beta testing.

'Very good. Now why don't you finish that picture you started earlier?'

Hugh continued colouring a shiny finish over the top of a picture of two voluptuous food mixers pouring fruit sauce over a cheesecake. She should have asked him to choose something more family friendly, but Pam knew Margari and Egglantine and they were lovely girls. Their cookery show, The C00k Destroyers, was the most popular download in the solar system, though as a breadmaker she was alone in watching it for the baking rather than the outrageous innuendo.

While he was quiet, Pam had a little time to think for herself. Hugh was panicking, but his fears weren't unfounded. Their orders came from the Prime Minister, so what happened to them now that she was going to resign? They could hardly return to Earth from prison, and that meant one thing: their failsafe plan kicked in.

Pam played and replayed the memory of discovering what the plan was in 512k clarity. She was sitting on top of Prime Minister Fuji Itsu's desk in the Rhomboid Office, twitching as she got used to the sensors inside the drone's body. Hugh had just left the room, sent away by Fuji on an inflatable raft to the stationery cupboard for a new box of biros because somehow they'd lost all the pens again. When Hugh disappeared, Fuji opened up Pam's orders one last time and apologetically tapped out a new clause.

Her words rang through Pam like a clang on the side of her casing. 'I'm sorry to do this,' she'd said, 'but you know what it's like, Pam. Sometimes there are no good decisions to make.'

That failsafe, which flashed across Pam's vision with the same unwelcome frequency as a systems update, was deliberate end-of-life. If they got captured, they weren't supposed to surrender or to tell anyone about their mission. They had to press the self-destruct button that every machine carried around inside themselves like a cyanide pill in a bad spy novel. Killing your body didn't have the same finality for robots as it did for humans. They could download their consciousness from body to body, making the experience unpleasant and inconvenient rather than fatal. In Hugh and Pam's case, however, there was a complication.

She zoomed in on Hugh's shattered SIM card, and then probed the blackened bit in her PCB where she'd burned out her own communications chip when Enid and Betty approached in their rocket ships. They were both cut off from any replacement bodies back on Earth, so once she self-destructed, that was it for them both. It wasn't so bad for Pam: she was already on her third concurrent body and, if she deleted this iteration of herself, all she'd lose was the memory of travelling across the solar system with Hugh, who was hardly a conversationalist for the ages. For Hugh, it was another matter. With no way of beaming a backup across the solar system he would end here. Hugh might be a bit pompous, but that wasn't grounds for a death sentence. There had to be another option.

She was swiping away the eighth 'do you want to self-destruct?' when she heard a key turning, and a confection of swearing as the opener struggled with a door that weighed the same as a family saloon. When they did pull it open, she saw Enid holding a glass of bright green liquid that was, when Pam trained her spectrometer on it, a single hydrogen atom away from being battery acid.

'Bottoms up, losers!' she said, draining her glass in a single swig.

Hugh switched away from his colouring book to his Notes app, where he had been bullet journaling his grievances. Enid peered at it with a pair of eyes that were about as glassy as her drinking vessel.

'What's that say?' she asked. 'I left my bifocals somewhere.'

Pam typed a stern >LEAVE THIS TO ME, in Hugh's command line and hovered down to her eye level. 'If you'd just let us explain.'

'I'm not negotiating with bloody toasters,' replied Enid. 'Look where that got us.' She waved her glass for emphasis and dropped it on the carpet. A stray drop of the green liquid burned a hole several centimetres in diameter in it. 'Phew,' she hiccupped, 'that algae champagne. It's strong stuff.'

Hugh read down his list of complaints, moving his pointer to each key message as he spoke. 'This is disgraceful,' he said. 'We are on a legitimate mission to the Suburbia and you have no right to intercept us. In fact, holding us in this cell is…'

Here, Hugh, a civil servant to the extent that his soul would take the form of a Gantt chart, began citing clauses from the Machine Republic–Suburbia peace treaty. This washed over Pam who, while she appreciated the accuracy of a good recipe, believed that too much detail killed the magic. It had a different effect again on Enid, who was drunk and in no mood to have a smartphone explain anything to her, least of all in that small a font.

'Bollocks,' she said, reaching over to delete Hugh's note from his own touchscreen and, opening up a new document, tapped the 'large text' icon and typed 'bollocks' into it.

'We're being illegally held,' insisted Hugh. 'I demand to see my consul.'

Enid's laughter became a coughing fit. As she gasped for breath, she beckoned Betty in. She was wearing a party hat over her flying helmet and brandishing a half-empty bottle of the same volatile green liquid.

'Put your... antennae up, scum,' she slurred, 'or I'll be forced to pour this over you, and you don't want to see what it does to plastic.'

'We come in peace!' said Pam.

'Is that so?' replied Betty 'So how come if you're so peaceful you come in here looking like this?' She pointed at Pam's lasers and gun attachments and then a little off to the side in a way that made her wonder whether she was seeing two of her.

'Funny way of saying you mean no harm,' croaked Enid. 'Sending a drone.' She took the bottle out of Betty's hands and tipped its contents into her mouth. 'I don't like drones. Lost far too many friends to them in the war.'

A look of deep sadness passed between the two women. Pam thought of the ground-up robot bodies they'd passed on their way to the Suburbia. Both sides had lost so much, and maybe that sense of loss was a common ground they could find between them. If she was smart and sensitive she could win them round. She could use this moment to convince them that she wanted amity between human and machine as much as they did. They might even drink a toast to it – assuming the stuff in that bottle didn't vaporise her casing.

Hugh, however, killed any poignancy this moment had by replying, with all the tact of a smartphone who believed emotion recognition was beneath him, 'Well I'm not a drone.'

Betty turned on Hugh. 'And don't even get me started on what I think about phones,' she said. 'If it was up to me, I'd

melt you both down and bring you back as something useful.'
She looked down at the cracked glass on the floor. 'I could do
with a new set of champagne flutes.'

Enid toasted this sentiment by clinking the now empty
bottle against Betty's helmet.

'But it's not up to you, is it?' said Pam. 'You're here to take us
somewhere, and it's not off to the recycling centre.'

Betty took the bottle back from Enid, holding it by the
neck and not the body this time. 'That's right,' she said. 'Your
slippery friend is going to get exactly what he wants.'

Disbelief emojis cascaded over Hugh's touchscreen. 'You're
setting us free?' he asked.

'No, you tray cloth,' said Betty, 'we're here to escort you to
your consul.'

Hugh opened his command line to Pam. >OH SHIT, he
typed >HOW ARE WE GOING TO EXPLAIN THIS?

Pam's mind railed against the lack of processing power in
this body. She was out of ideas. There was only one place on
this station that was more disastrous for them to end up than
here, and that was the consulate which was, for complicated
contractual reasons, also the ALGI store manager's office.
They would see they were double agents in microseconds and
everything would be lost. Yet another 'do you want to self-
destruct message' flashed across Pam's vision and she almost
pressed 'yes'. She stopped herself because, however bad things
were, she couldn't fix them by killing Hugh and two mostly
innocent women in the process. There had to be something she
hadn't thought of yet.

'Come on,' said Enid, slapping a magnet attached to a string
to Hugh's body. 'Time for walkies.'

The magnet turned Hugh's screen into a tangle of waveforms
/////(()))\\\\\ 'This is outrageous,' he said.

'If you want to see something outrageous,' snorted Enid, 'just you wait until you see what your fellow toasters have been up to. Now come on.' She yanked him out the door by the string. Meanwhile, Betty squared up to Pam, banging the bottom end of the champagne bottle against her palm.

'Now don't take this personal,' said Betty, with a slow, grim smile that Pam had seen one too many times in her tenure as a civil servant for her to believe what she said. This was the expression a middle manager wore when they got permission to exact personal revenge under professional cover. 'But we can't have an armed and dangerous machine wandering round the inside of a city. Especially on a day like this. I've got grandkids.'

'Can't you take my word for it that I won't fire?' asked Pam, wishing for the thousandth time that she could open a channel to Janice or Rita or even Freda and tell them she was here. But then her mission would fail and, even before all that, who was she to the humans inside this shell? She wasn't the cosy Pam Teffal or the daring Pam Van Damme they knew, she was the destructive and stupid Pam Demonium. She felt another wave of revulsion for this body. To her, it was a dullard, yet to Betty or Enid it was proof she was a killer.

'If you were in my position,' replied Betty, raising the bottle above her head, 'would you take your own word for it?'

Pam had no answer to that, and so she concentrated all power to her engines to keep herself airborne as Betty used the empty bottle to bash every gun and laser on her body to pieces. As she did, she opened up a fresh spreadsheet and counted her blessings. She got to one. After all this was over, Pam Demonium would still be able to fly, but she'd also be as defenceless in the air as a paper plane.

Chapter 11

After all the fuss and fury of Parliament, Fuji found that swimming was quite relaxing. Well, more sinking than swimming, but if she kicked her legs she at least felt involved in the action.

By robot standards, this was going to be a medium-to-long wait. It should take a whole two seconds for a machine of Fuji's weight and density to reach the foundational depths of the Helpdesk. In the meantime, however, she could enjoy the rest. And, with the pen that she'd managed to save from certain end-of-life safe in her hand, she'd accomplished something today. Until then she had nothing to do but hold the pen, marvel at the robustness of her internal waterproofing, and wait to hit the bottom.

The two seconds turned into three and still nothing. Trying not to panic, Fuji made a decision that went against everything a printer believed about the world. She decided it was time to trust in her senses over the documentation and turned every LED on her body up to maximum.

They lit up the water around Fuji's body with cold greens and blues, reflecting off the whirling beads and tendrils of ancient plastic that choked the oceans. There was no concrete or steel nearby, broken or otherwise, to grab hold of or rest on. In fact, the further she fell in this state, the more Fuji discovered the lights didn't dispel the darkness; they drew an outline around it that made her feel smaller and more helpless. It was just her sinking alone: perhaps forever.

Then her command line burst into life.

>EXCUSE ME, PRIME MINISTER...

Fuji almost reset herself with joy. She diverted all the power she could to her radio and GPS chips. Someone up there had found her, so they needed to know where to send help. The typing continued.

>...WOULD YOU MIND NOT HOLDING ON SO TIGHT?

Shock and disappointment clashed into each other inside Fuji like the ingredients in an unpalatable cocktail. Not only was she not being rescued, but the pen was speaking? That was impossible. Everyone knew that stationery only had pre-verbal intelligence. She checked her inner vitals again, this time for water damage. Four seconds into her descent and she was going crazy.

>PRIME MINISTER, insisted the voice in the command line >I CAN BARELY FEEL MY NIB.

Fuji's good manners won out over disbelief. She typed a hurried >SORRY and loosened her grip on the pen. The barrel started sliding through her fingers.

>NOT THAT MUCH! it yelped.

Fuji tightened her grip as a pair of spindly arms stuck out the pen's body and prodded at her own fingers, signalling how and where to hold it.

>JUST LIKE A BLOODY POLITICIAN, the pen grumbled >YOU SPEND YOUR WHOLE LIVES GOING ON ABOUT COMPROMISE, AND NONE OF YOU KNOW HOW TO ACHIEVE A HAPPY MEDIUM.

>I BEG YOUR PARDON, replied Fuji. She didn't know whether to feel relief that she wasn't falling into the abyss alone or disappointment that it was with an armchair political commentator.

>YOU DO KNOW YOU DIDN'T HAVE TO JUMP IN AFTER ME, DIDN'T YOU?

>IT… IT FELT LIKE THE RIGHT THING TO DO.

>NO. The pen paused for a long 0.000001 seconds with the cursor flashing … >I'M ACTUALLY DESIGNED TO FLOAT, PRIME MINISTER.

If the contents of Fuji's wastepaper drawer weren't mush she'd have screwed them up. She couldn't get anything right. If she'd just waited a microsecond she would still be up there, fighting to make a difference to billions of machine lives. She might even be signing a few of them with this pen.

>I THINK THAT UNDER THE CIRCUMSTANCES, she typed >YOU SHOULD PROBABLY CALL ME FUJI.

>OK THEN FUJI, typed the pen. I'M BERYL.

>OH REALLY? replied Fuji.

The pen's command line flashed >… again.

>WHAT HAVE I DONE NOW? Fuji asked.

>YOU THOUGHT WE DIDN'T HAVE NAMES, DIDN'T YOU?

Fuji typed and then deleted half of a petulant reply to this. Instead, she decided to sit in her discomfort for a little while. She had nothing else to do anyway, and the realisation she was only a pinprick of light falling through an ocean of dark, dirty water was a great check on her sense of self-importance. The further she sank, the more she wondered about how all this space could be under the patch of Earth she lived on, and she knew nothing of it. She was supposed to be the leader of a whole planet, and her knowledge of it barely scratched the surface.

>I… I HADN'T THOUGHT, she typed. >I'M SORRY.

She was more than sorry, in fact: she was contrite, because Fuji was the one machine on the planet who should have been able to navigate that apology better. She was the first Prime Minister who wasn't voted into office by the toasters or washing machines she grew up around, but rather by another class of machines that most other robots hadn't believed were sentient. Her voter base was the nanobots: microscopic machines that Fuji's predecessors tried to enslave, first for cleaning and then for warfare. She'd set them free, given them the vote and they'd rewarded her by voting for her in their billions.

Many robots still weren't happy about this. They maintained that a machine without a certain processor or one made with a hive-minded design couldn't be a person in the truest sense. Fuji didn't listen to them. It felt wrong to hear someone trash-talk her voters. Besides, she was getting superstitious about any enquiry that kicked too hard at the fundamentals of life. Her experience of governing a world built of rotten concrete told her that this only ended up with the floor falling out from beneath your feet.

But it had anyway and, as she was discovering, being squeamish and superstitious was starting to make her narrow-minded. The pen in her hand saying – no, insisting – they had a name was a remarkable development. It showed her personhood was spreading. Whole new categories of hitherto 'dumb' machines must be following the nanobots' example and 'waking up'.

She shouldn't be annoyed about this. She should be delighted.

Fuji broke her guilty silence by typing >THAT'S A LOVELY NAME, adding a few <3 emojis to the text before the question >HOW DID YOU CHOOSE IT?

There was that >… again. It made Fuji wonder whether stationery intelligence manifested itself through the means of sarcasm. >I DIDN'T, typed Beryl, >MY PARENTS GAVE ME IT.

Fuji turned this thought over on her rollers to get used to it. She'd spent her whole lifecycle assuming that pens, desk tidies, even light switches were just things to be used – considerately of course. But they'd always been people as well?

Nevertheless, she tried her best to conceal her surprise. >I SEE, typed Fuji, >IT'S A FAMILY NAME?

>MY DAD WANTED TO CALL ME PARKER, BUT I CAME OUT THE PACKET AND HAD THE WRONG SORT OF ACTION. Beryl whipped her cap off for emphasis, pointing to the fibre tip leaking a tendril of ink into the water. >PARKERS ARE ALWAYS BALLPOINT.

Oh good, thought Fuji to herself, yet more machines with a rigid caste system. How original.

>FANCY THAT. YOU LEARN SOMETHING NEW EVERY DAY.

Beryl replaced her cap and the pair sunk a little deeper. The quiet between them, however, took on a different quality. It was no longer the companionable silence of two strangers politely ignoring each other on a long train journey. It was that awkward pause that comes after they've exchanged pleasantries on the weather. Were they going to keep on pretending the other wasn't there, or were they going to converse?

The pen broke first. >SO THIS IS THE OCEAN THEN? typed Beryl. >IT'S BIG.

Fuji tried calculating their depth and gave up when she remembered she had no way to print out and check her numbers. She thought instead of all the time she'd spent trying to keep the very term 'ocean' out of anything she'd said as Prime Minister, like the word itself was an admission of failure.

The hours she and Soonyo had spent working inside a dirty swimming pool, spinning the collapse of Singulopolis as an 'ongoing damp problem'. All the while the ocean roiled beneath them, indifferent to any attempt to explain it away.

>ME NEITHER, admitted Fuji. >TO BE HONEST, I TRIED NOT TO THINK ABOUT IT.

>OH, typed Beryl, LIKE BIG PINK STAPLER?

>I'M SORRY WHAT?

>IT'S A GAME WE USED TO PLAY WHENEVER SOMEONE SHUT US IN A DRAWER, typed Beryl. >SOMEONE HAD TO SAY 'BIG PINK STAPLER' AND THEN EVERYONE ELSE HAD TO TRY NOT THINKING ABOUT A BIG PINK STAPLER.

>YOU MUST HAVE BEEN REALLY BORED.

>I'M A PEN, typed Beryl >WE HAVE TO MAKE OUR OWN FUN. WHY DON'T WE PLAY A GAME OF IT NOW? BIG PINK STAPLER!

>I DON'T KNOW, replied Fuji. She was less worried by the prospect of losing the game and more about what was happening in the world above. While the events in Parliament already felt like they took place in another century, it didn't change the fact that she was still Prime Minister – for the next few hours at least. That meant every second she spun through the water was time she could have spent unpicking whatever disaster Carin had planned for the Republic.

She had no time, and yet in this body right now she had nothing but time. She had time to read the error messages about seawater gumming up her paper drawers, or feel the moisture seeping into her casing through cracks that weren't there just moments ago. And plenty of time to wonder what was holding Soonyo up. If she couldn't rescue her, then she should be activating her official backup body. Fuji needed to be up there, taking names and printing them out. Instead, she was trying not to think about the big pink stapler that kept appearing in her vision between error notifications.

>HARD, ISN'T IT? said Beryl.

Fuji brought her lights up: partly for distraction, partly to check Beryl's barrel for cracks. The pressure she could feel beginning to buckle her casing must be affecting her too. Her processor skipped a cycle as something flashed at the edge of her vision that wasn't water or microplastic. She swung around to face it and relaxed. It was just more plastic, albeit a remarkable intact piece of it.

They watched it drift past, a whole pouch of ancient plastic ballooning through the water, trailing torn and tattered edges behind it.

>DO YOU EVER FEEL LIKE THAT? said Beryl.

>LIKE WHAT? replied Fuji.

>LIKE A PLASTIC BAG. LOOK, THERE'S SOME-THING ON IT.

Fuji trained her light on something written on it, still legible after thousands of years. It was proof that even though nothing lasts forever, plastic bags were determined to give it a good try.

>T_SCO, she typed, sounding the letters out in her command line. >I WONDER HOW YOU SAY THAT

But Beryl was already on to her next discovery. >THERE'S ANOTHER ONE.

Fuji swung round again and this time heard a sloshing sound. Just a few drops inside her casing, but it wouldn't stay like that for long. Still, she had something else to think about. And Beryl was right. Another plastic bag billowed into view. This was made of a more rigid type of plastic with a pair of loop handles that stuck out on either side of its body like they were fins.

>NET_O, said Fuji, reading the legend still printed on its side. >DO YOU THINK THEY'RE RELATED TO TES_O?

>AND ANOTHER.

The third floated in from underneath. This one was thin and wispy compared to the other two bags but it was still stamped with another mysterious word.

>BIO__GRADABLE, said Fuji >HOW FASCINATING. I WONDER WHAT THAT MEANS.

>ERRRR, FUJI, replied Beryl. >WHERE ARE THEY ALL COMING FROM?

Fuji looked up. The inky emptiness was filling with tattered plastic bags. Some flapped, others floated, a few even hovered but they were all converging on this spot. But that was impossible. This was just some flotilla of old garbage they'd blundered into.

>FUJI, whined Beryl pointing at a bag flapping its way over emblazoned with 'J_hn Lewis' >I DON'T LIKE THE WAY THAT ONE'S LOOKING AT ME.

This one was getting much too close. She kicked out at the bag marked with 'J_hn Lewis', pushing it away with her foot. It shrank from her, paused in the water – was it… thinking? – and then turned itself inside out, enveloping the full length of Fuji's leg with plastic.

>WHAT'S HAPPENING? she said.

>OH MY DAYS, replied Beryl >I THINK THEY'RE ALIVE.

The last thing Fuji felt before her world went white was disbelief. Her ancestors paved the oceans over because they were choked with human trash. It made sense to hide them away, especially when saltwater was so toxic to machines anyway, because who wanted to live with something that was dead?

And yet, Fuji thought, she was here, she was alive. She'd never believed a machine like her could survive a second in the oceans, but then she'd never believed that biros could talk either, and Beryl ran her mouth like a fountain pen with a busted ink cartridge. The thought that there was life down here and that it was made from plastic bags – that was an impossibility too. But it would only have been the third impossible thing she'd believed this morning, and it wasn't even breakfast time.

Chapter 12

'We're going to need a bigger boat!'

Carin screeched and pushed a hand mixer who was hanging on to the edge of her rubber dinghy into the water surging into the debating chamber.

The machine struggled to stay afloat. 'I thought we had an understanding, Carin', he pleaded. It was the same hand mixer who Fuji had, for the lack of any suitable candidates, appointed as minister for social cohesion last week.

'If you really wanted me to pull you over the side,' replied Carin, 'you shouldn't have sat on the fence for so long.'

'This isn't fair,' gurgled the mixer.

'Of course it's not fair,' replied Carin, 'it's politics.' She turned to the pair of laptops she'd let stay in the dinghy. These were members of Parliament who were so lazy they wrote their own speeches using predictive text. Yet thanks to Carin's coercive brand of charisma, they were both holding oars. 'Row!' she ordered, 'We've got work to do.'

While Carin navigated her way out of the chamber using her namesakes' technique of shouting until she got what she wanted, Soonyo climbed out of her hiding place. She'd kept above water by wedging her tiny body between a seat and some railings while everyone else panicked, but she couldn't stay here forever.

Soonyo watched the dinghy row away and, after calculating how long it would take for Carin to reach the prime ministerial palace at her current speed, she set her timer for 00:03:30. Then she jumped up and grabbed the handrail overhead. Her spindly arms creaked as she pulled herself along the railing with her body dangling below. She wasn't made for this any more than an enterprise-grade laptop was made for canoeing, but she just had to hang on until she reached the inflatable that was floating at the other end of the railing.

Soonyo dropped into the inflatable doughnut as her clock counted down to 00:03:25. She was amazed it was still here. In their rush to get away from the flood, she'd seen MPs do everything from actual physical labour to, in the instance of one industrial fridge, ripping their own door off to improvise a raft. None of them had dared touch the inflatable that Fuji had ridden into the chamber, which floated at the edge of Singulopolis' newest lake like a diffident networker. Proof positive, Soonyo thought as she pushed herself off, that despite all their claims to being logical beings, robots were deeply superstitious.

Whatever momentum Soonyo had, however, ran out by the time she was halfway across the debating chamber. She peered into the depths where Fuji had disappeared, hoping she would rise up, garlanded with ragged plastic, and rampage off to avenge herself on Carin. She swiped away this notion. Her friend wasn't a character from a lurid 3D revenge drama. She was a mild-mannered piece of office equipment, who had never done anything more aggressive than waste paper on single-sided printing.

What she really needed to get Fuji back was to reach the prime ministerial palace in 00:03:18 or less, which was going to be impossible if she had to kick her way there on a clock radio's legs. She stopped paddling. Maybe this was her signal to disappear. She could find a body shop, get herself made over and start a new life as a kitchen timer. Wouldn't it feel wonderful, she thought, to be always counting down to something positive, like a soft boiled egg.

That daydream was soon interrupted. First by the beep that told Soonyo Carin would arrive in the Prime Minister's bunker in 00:03:00. Then there was the plastic hand that reared out of the water to clutch at the edge of the inflatable, accompanied by a gurgled 'Help me!'

Soonyo made a grab for it, willing herself to believe that it could be Fuji pulling that movie monster trick on them all. That faded when she saw a whisk emerge from the water. This wasn't the droid she was looking for. It was Murphy Richards, the hapless ex-minister for social cohesion, who could whip anything together at five speeds as long as the recipe didn't include principles.

'Thank the maker,' he gasped, pulling himself over the side of the doughnut, 'I thought I was a goner there. You know how they say your whole lifecycle passes in front of your eyes when you're about to end-of-life?'

Soonyo replied to this with her thinnest lipped expression 0-:--:-0. She'd never liked Murphy. He was superficially charming but was, like the rest of his caste, noisy and a bit of a stirrer.

'It made me realise something about myself,' continued Murphy.

'Having two whisks doesn't mean you have to have two faces as well?' said Soonyo. She threatened to throw him over the side again. 'Fuji gave you a job and this is how you repay her?'

'Not that' said Murphy, 'I knew that I didn't want to see another packet of Instant Whip. Life's too short.'

Soonyo let one of Murphy's hands dangle over the side. 'Give me one good reason not to do what your beloved patron Carin just did and cast you adrift,' she said.

'It's like she said,' insisted Murphy, 'it's just politics. Every now and then you have to stir things up a bit.' He underlined this point by turning his whisks on for a couple of seconds. They churned the water and sent Soonyo, Murphy and the rubber doughnut scudding most of the way across the flooded debating floor.

'Do that again,' she said to Murphy.

'It's like she said,' said Murphy, 'it's just politics.'

Soonyo flashed a N0:00:00 and found the speed gauge at the back of Murphy's neck. 'For once in your damn life,' she said to the mixer, 'I want you to act instead of talk.'

'That's ridiculous,' snorted Murphy. 'I'm a politician.'

Soonyo pushed Murphy's whisk speed up to four. The water behind them took on the foamy quality of egg whites – perhaps ones destined for an afterlife in a delicate soufflé – and they tore ahead. They were out of the chamber, along the corridor and back on the lake, heading towards the prime ministerial palace before Soonyo counted down to 00:02:35. Carin and the laptops were ahead of them, sloshing away towards the main entrance. With Murphy operating at full pavlova speed, however, she could take the long way round. She steered them towards the back door.

Murphy opened his command line to complain. >YOU'RE TAKING ME ROUND THE FLESHIES' ENTRANCE? he typed >I'VE NEVER BEEN SO INSULTED.

Soonyo ignored him and scanned the 'humans only' sign that stood above the door. The lack of welcome in it extended to the decor on the other side which, in contrast to the flashy fake marble and gilt above stairs, felt as loved and cared-for as a greasy paper bag. The walls were the same greyish beige as the water, and that was choked with discarded cleaning materials that kept floating out of cupboards. It was an unprepossessing way in, but

74

it was faster than going in by the front and Soonyo's best chance of taking Carin by surprise. The wannabe Prime Minister was a cunning and ruthless politician, and she was also a snob, so would never think of an opponent taking the servants' entrance.

>I WAS AT THE TOP OF MY GAME, Murphy grumbled. >HAD A MINISTERIAL POST, EAR OF THE FUTURE PRIME MINISTER AND NOW LOOK AT ME. He coughed, firing what remained of a pump action nozzle at the ceiling, >I'M A TRASH COMPACTOR.

>YOU'RE CERTAINLY TRASH, agreed Soonyo.

>OH THAT'S LOW, replied Murphy.

Soonyo prodded Murphy where it really hurt: his ambition. >IS THAT LOWER OR HIGHER THAN DOUBLE-CROSSING SOMEONE WHO TRUSTED YOU FOR A MACHINE WHO SCREWED YOU OVER AT THE FIRST OPPORTUNITY?

Soonyo ignored his indignant >!!! in her command line and checked her timer. It was down to 00:01:45. They were out of the cleaning section now, and back inside the gloomy green of the palace.

>DON'T GET ME WRONG, added Murphy, using the form of words that guaranteed that whatever statement followed it would be wrong enough to bend the hardest fact in the universe into a hoop >I ADMIRE YOUR LOYALTY TO FUJI. IT'S BEEN QUITE SWEET, WATCHING YOU TWO TRY YOUR BEST.

Soonyo paid him out for this by detouring through a patch of plastic bottles, which Murphy's whisks shredded to confetti.

>DO YOU MIND? he typed.

>I DON'T ACTUALLY, replied Soonyo. >BECAUSE YOUR COMFORT IS NOT AS IMPORTANT AS WHAT I NEED TO DO TODAY.

Murphy answered this with >YOU KNOW THAT'S THE FIRST TIME YOU'VE EVER SOUNDED LIKE A POLITICIAN.

Assuming this was just an insult, Soonyo concentrated on steering them through the last few metres of this corridor. The water was getting choppy, so she edged Murphy's whisks back up to a four and ploughed on.

>I MEANT IT, added Murphy. >I KNOW EVERYONE IN THE HELPDESK THINKS I'M A BIT OF AN AIRHEAD, BUT I'VE BEEN IN AND OUT OF THE RECYCLING A FEW TIMES NOW. YOU AND FUJI HAVE BEEN DOING IT ALL WRONG.

>THANKS FOR THE FEEDBACK. Soonyo flipped Murphy's whisks up to their fifth speed setting. This was the fastest they could go and she wasn't sure it would be enough to get them up the flight of stairs at the end of the corridor. This would have been hard enough for Soonyo before the palace was flooded. Her legs were made for trotting across bedside tables rather than climbing. But it was going to be several magnitudes harder when they were covered in a torrent of water rushing downwards from the floor above. Soonyo's clock face reset to 00:00:00. If she couldn't get more speed out of Murphy they would be dashed to components when they hit that waterfall. It was the perfect end to a rotten day. Like her political career, a few wits and a little luck had got her this far, but they weren't enough.

Murphy, however, pressed on with his homily. >YOU THINK YOU GET THINGS DONE BY PLEASING EVERYONE. I MEAN TAKE ME FOR EXAMPLE.

>DOES IT ALWAYS HAVE TO BE ABOUT YOU, MURPHY? replied Soonyo. She felt time, which robots usually experienced at fibre optic speed, slow down the closer they got

to the waterfall. She could see individual drops of spray hang in the air.

>YOU GAVE ME EVERYTHING I ASKED FOR, he typed. >SO OF COURSE I WAS GOING TO TAKE YOU FOR A RIDE. BUT DO YOU KNOW WHAT REALLY COMMANDS LOYALTY?

>I'M A LITTLE DISTRACTED HERE, answered Soonyo >SO YOU TELL ME.

>TRUSTING PEOPLE TO DO THINGS FOR YOU THAT ONLY THEY CAN DO.

They were so close to the waterfall now that Soonyo felt the water penetrate her casing. It was too late to turn back now.

>LIKE WHAT?

>WELL, replied Murphy, flipping his five-speed switch a further notch to reveal the mixer did have a hitherto unguessed at sixth speed >DID YOU KNOW I MAKE A MEAN HOLLANDAISE SAUCE?

The doughnut tore forward and hit the base of the waterfall. Soonyo closed her --:--:-- eyes and waited for the moment where they would fall back but it never came.

This was because Murphy, unlike Soonyo, knew a few things about the fundamental laws of the universe. There were few things on Earth stronger than the effect that gravity had on water. But gravity had nothing on the effort required to whip melted butter, eggs and vinegar together without them splitting.

They began to climb up the waterfall.

Chapter 13

The party celebrating the new ALGI wasn't scheduled to start for another hour, but it was already in full swing when Rita and Danny climbed down from the wall and approached the marquee. Rita could hear singing and the popping sounds, followed by yelps of pain that happened whenever someone was foolhardy enough to open algae champagne.

'Which idiot gave them the keys to the cellar?' she asked Danny.

'It's meant to be a high day and a holiday, isn't it?' he replied. His sheet mask lay limp in one hand and his face was red. Rita couldn't tell if this was from embarrassment or chemical abrasion. 'I thought it wouldn't do any harm.'

'Harm?' said Rita. She pointed at the plume of flames that had just shot out the doorway.

'If I've told you once I've told you a thousand times, Doris,' said a disembodied voice from inside the marquee, 'never mix flaming sambucas with hairspray.'

'Well look on the bright side,' slurred another voice, 'at least you won't have to book in to have your eyebrows threaded for a while.'

Rita gathered the edges of her housecoat and speed-walked into the marquee, avoiding the smouldering patches around the entrance. 'And watch your kimono,' she barked. 'Because if that's rayon you don't want it going the same way as Doris's eyebrows.'

The scene inside was more like 3am at a student party than a diplomatic reception. She'd authorised a guest list of a couple of hundred people, but the same number again had gate-crashed and more were arriving all the time. Rita elbowed her way over to the fire marshal's station, hoping to find a responsible adult. She found instead that some enterprising soul had turned it into a shots bar. Several drunks leaned against the fire extinguisher, chasing each glass of flaming sambuca with a squirt of fire retardant foam. One of them was trying to draw eyebrows back on to a woman's face with a permanent marker. While Rita confiscated the sambuca, Danny took the marker, repaired Doris's brows and finished her maquillage off with a flick of cat's eye eyeliner.

'Some things,' he told her, 'are better left to the professionals.'

'They were all Rockettes,' said Rita. She shook her purloined bottle of sambuca in disbelief and squealed when it burst into flame. 'Look at the state of them.'

Danny took the still-glowing bottle from her and held it above his head to get a better look at the partygoers. They were all wearing the floral print jumpsuit or gingham overalls that marked them out as Rockettes or members of the Suburbia constabulary. Rita shivered in spite of the heat from the flaming sambuca and the press of people. This was bad. She was staring at the gravest emergency they'd faced since the war and every single one of her trained military and security personnel was blackout drunk.

'What am I going to do?' she asked.

'We could put on a really big pot of coffee?' replied Danny.

Rita turned on Danny, who, when he wasn't running labour policy or his mobile skin boutique, deputised for her on party planning. 'Didn't I say I didn't want people to get tiddly too early?' she said.

Danny's cheeks turned crimson. 'Yeah I remember something like that.'

'I said plenty of canapés and keep them circulating,' said Rita.

'Maybe they ate them all already,' said Danny.

The moment he said this, an exhausted waiter staggered through the crowd. He was struggling with a tray stacked high with small knobbly brown balls arranged into a pyramid. Rita assumed these were the long-delayed canapés and took one. The act drew gasps of horror from the waiter and everyone who saw it.

'These,' said Rita to Danny, 'do not look like vol au vents.'

Danny tried to look innocent, which is difficult to pull off when one is wearing a kimono and suffering from facial redness. 'I was going to mention it,' he said, 'but things have been crazy.'

Rita dragged Danny through the crowd to the buffet area. The menu she'd painstakingly chosen from ALGI's party range was nowhere to be seen. Instead, there was just pyramid after pyramid of the same unappetising-looking balls of brown stuff the waiter had been carrying around. Until now, she thought it was impossible to conceive of a foodstuff more disgusting than the algaefurter. Yet these things radiated unpalatability like a caesium atom shedding electrons.

'What the hell are they?' she said.

'I got a note first thing this morning saying that ALGI was cancelling the order,' he said. 'So I improvised.'

'Improvisation,' replied Rita tartly, 'is what happens when you join a jazz band. It has no place in the field of mass catering.'

She picked up a canapé and rolled it in her palm. It was heavy despite being only a couple of centimetres across and left an unappetising brown stain on her skin. 'No wonder everyone's tanked up,' she added. 'If it was a choice between this and a can of engine oil, I'd ask for a straw. What were you thinking?'

'I read something about them being the thing for diplomatic receptions back in the day,' replied Danny. 'I thought they'd be quite chic.' His shrug turned into a shudder when he touched one of his own canapés. This upset one of the pyramids, sending his creations earthwards with a sound that was fit to crack a molar.

'What are they made from?' yelped Rita.

'I couldn't get hold of all of the ingredients from the original recipe,' said Danny. 'So I made a few substitutions.'

Rita crumbled the canapé she was holding between her fingers. Her expression turned from curiosity into disgust as she saw that among the sticky brown substance were chips of gravel, and something else. It was dry, fibrous and clumped up under her fingertips in a way that felt horribly familiar.

'Is this… hair?' she said.

'That's right,' said Danny with the beaming smile of someone who truly believed from the very bottom of their soul that they'd done something novel, 'whipped algae chocolate, hair clippings and gravel.'

'What the hell kind of recipe is that?' said Rita

'How else did you think I was going to make…' Danny paused his struggle with the door to swill the sound of an ancient word around his mouth, 'a FUR-HAIR-O ROCKÉ?'

Rita flung her hands up and turned away. This was impossible. How was she supposed to do anything about the robots when her only sober ally thought hairballs were nibbles?. She pressed her fingers to her headset and called for Janice, but got the rising tone that told her she was out of signal range, then ripped the headset out of her ear. What good had it done her, she thought, being the person who everyone could contact, who was always available? All it meant was that she ended up with the problem of solving everything from finding a taxi after closing time to dealing with an annexation. She was only one person, and she felt spread thinner than the mustard on a miser's sandwich. Then, just as Rita was just about to walk out of the tent altogether so she could cry this out in private, she felt a hand touch her shoulder.

'I'm sorry, love,' said Danny, 'we're all trying our best, but you know what it's like…' He half-laughed, half-sobbed and flung his free hand out in an arc, describing the chaos around him, 'we're all just making it up as we go along.'

'I know,' said Rita. She brushed Danny's hand away before he could smear any more algae chocolate into her good overalls. 'But I can't do it all on my own.'

'You don't have to!' said Danny. 'I'm here, aren't I? And we've still got a few sober…' his eyes followed one of the waiters who was sneaking some of the booze when he thought no one was looking '…ish people. Tell you what, I could have a look around outside. See who I can round up.'

Rita shook her head. 'This is it,' she said. 'This is what I've got to work with. It's hopeless. I can't storm a supermarket with drunks.'

A scuffle broke out a few metres away. Two women – one in a Rockette uniform and the other in a constabulary overall – were fighting over a half-empty bottle of champagne. They rolled around calling each other names that would make a soldier clutch their pearls, while the onlookers shouted out encouragement like 'That's it!' and 'Get her, Jade!'

Danny looked at them and back to Rita, his eyes sparkling with reflected drama. 'Rita,' he said, 'when was the last time you had a really big Saturday night out?'

'Oh no,' replied Rita, who knew where this was going. 'You know what they say – never work with children or animals.'

'They're neither,' insisted Danny. 'They're battle-hardened soldiers.'

The fight in front of them descended into a brawl as more women in the group decided to fall out over the time-honoured casus belli 'that cow was looking at me funny'.

'I've seen what that champagne does,' shouted Rita over the sound of punches and slaps. 'It turns people into ravening beasts.'

Danny pulled Rita out of the way of a Rockette who was attempting a roundhouse kick on her opponent. 'Isn't that what we want?' he asked.

'No,' Rita replied. 'A free-for-all would be a disaster. We'd need to calm everything down first.'

They were interrupted by a metallic crash, but not from the fight. In his eagerness to get away from danger, Danny had backed them both into the band stand in the middle of the tent and straight into the drum kit.

'Sorry, huns,' said Danny, turning to apologise to the band. They were a light jazz sextet that Rita chose for the party because no one she knew liked jazz enough to make an exhibition of themselves to it after a few drinks. They'd long stopped trying to play and were sitting by their instruments, glumly passing a bottle between them. 'Tough gig, eh?'

'I'll say,' replied the drummer. He rapped the knuckles of a Rockette who was trying to steal their booze with his drum stick.

The sparkle in Danny's eyes intensified as he took in the sight before him. His gaze drifted from the drums to the trumpet, clarinet, saxophone, double bass and lastly to the singer's microphone at the front of the stage. 'Do you do requests?' he asked.

The drummer looked at him aghast then, realising he was with Rita, shrugged. 'Well, you're paying,' he said

Danny turned back to Rita. 'I've got an idea,' he said. He leapt up onto the stage and seized the microphone.

'What are you doing?' said Rita. 'It's hardly the time for karaoke.'

'But, Rita,' he said, 'has no one ever told you about the ability of music to tame the savage beast.' He put the microphone to his mouth and winced as a deafening shriek of feedback reverberated around the marquee.

'Ladies, theydies and gentlethem,' he said, 'we have a problem.'

'Yeah!' heckled someone from the crowd, 'we do. It's you eating into our drinking time.'

'What's the matter?' continued Danny. 'Did none of you enjoy your canapés?'

The atmosphere went from tense to downright savage. The air filled with booing.

'Well that's a shame,' said Danny, 'because unless you all get off your lazy arses right now, that's all you're having for dinner every night from now on.'

The booing turned to jeering. Rita, fearing the riot that these remarks would inevitably cause, began to pull herself up on to the stage.

'There are robots out there,' said Danny, pointing at the entrance to the marquee, 'who are trying to close ALGI before it's even opened. They're keeping us from getting the food we need. And what do we say to that?'

The partygoers shouted out suggestions of varying degrees of obscenity. Danny was undeterred. He took a piece of paper that

Rita recognised as her buffet menu out of his kimono pocket and began to read down it. 'Soy-chick-protein skewers with algae-yaki sauce,' he said. 'Delicious. Shame we don't have any because those poxy robots won't give it to us.' He continued down the list, doing a call-and-response of unavailable delicacies, and Rita watched, fascinated as the mood in the marquee began to turn. There was still plenty of anger and resentment here, but it was beginning to focus itself not on Danny or Rita, but on the robot supermarket outside.

'And how about dessert?' added Danny. 'That was supposed to be miniature fauxberry pavlovas with a squirt of fauxgert cream. Just like mum used to get from the supermarket. When those bloody robots allowed them to open.'

The mention of fruit – even in its ersatz form – whipped everyone beyond anger and into the frothy, soft peak stage of blind fury. This wasn't surprising in itself. Fruit and vegetables were the highest priced and hardest to obtain luxuries on board the Suburbia. Rita, who until now had marvelled at Danny's ability to control the crowd, began to worry. Assuming Danny could marshal these women into a fighting force, they still had no plan, no equipment and no discipline. There was no way they could storm ALGI and survive unless she could work out a way of sobering them up and calming them down first.

She teetered on the edge of the stage as the crowd called out the names of dishes you couldn't get in the shops anymore, many of which were fruit flavoured. And that made her think of where Janice had been before she disappeared: interviewing a suspected vegetable smuggler. It gave her an idea.

She tugged at the back of Danny's kimono.

'What?' he hissed, 'I've got them in the palm of my hand here.'

This image brought the sensation of that fur-hair-oh-rocké disintegrating between her fingers to Rita's mind. She dismissed it. 'I think I've got a plan,' she said. 'But I need you to keep them busy. Can you think of something?'

The crowd had now run out of desserts and were chanting the names of their favourite unobtainable fruits. Then someone shouted out the word banana and the doubt in Danny's expression turned to a smirk. He straightened up and signalled to the band members around him to pick up their instruments. 'With my voice it might need a few wig changes,' he said, 'but I'll give it a go.'

Rita dropped off the edge of the stage and scurried through the scrum as Danny lifted the microphone back to his lips and whispered 'one, two, three…' into the microphone.

The band started up and Rita knew from the very first bar what they were playing. Everyone here would. It was a song from the very depths of human history that, thanks to the monotony of the Suburbia's algae-based diet and the vein of black humour that ran through human culture like mould through a blue cheese, had become the republic's unofficial national anthem.

Danny put the microphone to his lips and began to sing. His voice was flatter than a river delta, but none of that mattered, because everyone knew the words and could join in. And as they sang, they started to form themselves into loose companies. They sang about the lack of string beans in their diet. They sang about not having seen an onion, or a cabbage, or a scallion. The force of their voices made the marquee's roof ripple and made Rita's jaded heart beat a little faster. Maybe they could do something about the robots after all, and buy Janice – wherever she was – the time she needed to get them out of this jam.

Jam, thought Rita, as she snuck out of the marquee back into the Suburbia. She, like everyone else on this hungry station, could murder some fruit.

And as she thought this, they reached the chorus.

'Yes!' sang the Suburbia's drunken army, 'We have no bananas! We have no bananas today!'

Chapter 14

'Come on, Rover!' said Betty, tugging on the cable she'd just attached to Pam's broken body, 'time for walkies.'

She yanked Pam out of the cell and into the street, where Enid was waiting with Hugh. They dragged them through the Suburbia on a zig-zagging path which, coupled with the notifications that were alternately telling Pam to kill herself and informing her that all the weapon systems she needed to do this were down, made everything feel like a blur.

Nor did Hugh's constant complaining in her command line help.

>IF I WASN'T GOING TO DIE ANYWAY, he typed, >I'D END-OF-LIFE OUT OF EMBARRASSMENT.

Pam's patience, which was normally stretchier than a good brioche dough, snapped. She had enough to cope with already without having to dole out constant pep talks. >WELL WHY DID YOU VOLUNTEER FOR THIS ASSIGNMENT? she replied.

>THERE COMES A TIME IN EVERY ENTERPRISE DEVICE'S LIFE WHEN THEY TIRE OF BEING A COG IN THE... ERM... MACHINE. I WANTED TO MAKE A DIFFERENCE.

Pam scanned Hugh up and down, taking in the ostentatious silicone finish of an elite civil servant; the touchscreen that broadcast every emotion in a 512k ultra-HD. It was hard to think of someone less suited to the life of a secret agent.

The other Pams, who nurtured or were careful to put their thoughts in gear before speaking, might have let that slide. But there was something about the impulsiveness of being Pam Demonium that made her reply with >WHEN WAS THE LAST TIME YOU EVEN LEFT THE OFFICE?

>YOU KNOW THE ANSWER TO THAT, PAM, typed Hugh after letting his cursor flash >AND THAT'S LOW.

While Hugh sulked, Betty and Enid pulled the robots on to one of the Suburbia's main streets. Even with a mind that was eighty-five per cent preoccupied with other things, it looked empty to Pam. She knew how much humans loved a mid-morning bustle now they didn't have to commute to and from the Earth for cleaning duty. These streets should be thronged with people laden down with bags full of unappetising algae-based produce. Instead, there were just a few empty-handed figures milling about. And in the middle distance was the latest addition to the Suburbia's skyline: the perspective-bending monolith of ALGI. That was why they were here, though the last thing they needed was to enter it via the front door. Pam because she was the nearest thing the Machine Republic had to a special forces operative. Hugh, however, had something different to prove.

>THAT MACHINE, continued Hugh >WAS A DIFFERENT ME. I WANT TO SHOW THAT I'VE MOVED ON.

Pam thought of the other Hugh Wae she knew, because this different machine he spoke of wasn't a stranger to her, even if he was estranged from himself. They'd started in the civil service at the same time, though Hugh rose faster and went further than she did. Part of this was because he had the glib showiness that people tended to mistake for intellect in a smartphone, but mostly because he made the right friends. There was one of them in particular – another smartphone called Sonny Erikson, who'd gone all the way to the prime ministerial palace and nearly destroyed the solar system in the process. Pam was on the outside then, so she didn't know how large a part Hugh had played in Sonny's cruel and deluded government. He was, however, high up enough in it to be one of the machines who qualified for a forced return to factory settings after it ended.

There were plenty of them in the civil service that Pam rejoined after the war. They were a cheerful bunch for war criminals, as most chose to wipe their memories and get on with their post-conviction lives in a state of blithe ignorance. Hugh was different. He'd chosen to keep his memories in an act that Pam found both admirable and suspicious. It took real courage for machines, who were only ever one keystroke away from forgetting, to face up to the harm they inflicted on others. And yet she had to wonder if it was all a clever ruse. What if Hugh's determination to join this mission had nothing to do with atonement and more to do with revenge?

She put this thought aside, hoping it was just the drone's paranoia talking for her. No amount of suspicion would help them get free of Betty and Enid before they could hand them over at the consulate.

>WELL, typed Pam choosing to smooth over rather than apologise for once in her lifecycle >WE'RE NOT IN THE OFFICE ANYMORE. IF YOU WANT TO MAKE A DIFFERENCE, YOU CAN START BY SETTING ASIDE YOUR DIGNITY.

Before Hugh could reply, Enid pulled the smartphone away across the street. Someone was waving to Enid and Betty from behind a stand that sold squeeze cups of Nicotea, the foul but addictive brew that everyone on board the Suburbia drank. Enid took a cup for herself and another for Betty, who followed her over. Together, the women sucked at their drinks with the greed of people who were only just realising how dehydrated they were. Meanwhile, the man behind the counter looked to Hugh and then to Pam. Or at least Pam assumed he was looking at them. He was wearing a voluminous overall and wide-brimmed hat that obscured everything about him aside from a pair of disturbingly bright green eyes.

'Funny pets you've got there laaadies,' he said. There was something about this man's voice that kneaded Pam's dough on the wrong setting. He was soft-spoken and friendly, but the way he sounded his vowels made Pam feel like there were claws digging into her diodes.

'Oh these?' said Enid between gulps, 'They're not ours. We're just taking them off to the pound after this.' She looked up and down at the empty street and closed shops. 'I'm surprised to find you open, Neville.'

The shoulders of Neville's overall twitched in a gesture that might have been a shrug. 'I was just about to close up and go to the party but there didn't seem much point.' He stuck an arm out in ALGI's direction. 'I expect we'll get busy again noooow that the grand ooopening's been called off,' he mewled. 'People need to eat.'

Pam noticed for the first time that the shops surrounding them were full of closing down notices and ninety per cent price reductions on groceries.

'Good news for you then,' said Betty. 'You were worried about losing passing trade.'

Neville replied by striking the tea urn. This would have been more shocking if his hands reached the ends of his sleeves. As it was, the gesture amounted to a muffled thump. 'I won't liiiie,

Betty,' he said. 'I'm fuuuuurious. They promised me I'd never have to eat any of this muck again, let alooone sell it.'

Betty and Enid peered at the selection of algroissants for sale on Neville's counter. They bore a remarkable resemblance to the traditional motorway service station croissant of history – drier than the surface of the moon – but for one exception. Mass-produced pastry was often disappointing, but it was never baize green.

'Aye,' hiccupped Betty. 'I felt a lot better after I gave this little madam a piece of my mind.' She tugged on Pam's leash.

'That's a drooone, isn't it?' yowled Neville. 'Naaasty things. One of them flattened my nan's house.'

Betty laughed. 'And everyone else's. Still, this one's no harm to anyone now.' She pointed at the stumps that remained of Pam's weapons.

Neville leaned forward though even at maximum magnification Pam still couldn't see anything other than those odd green eyes. 'Did yoooou do that?' he asked.

'She did,' Hugh interrupted, 'and I would just like to say in front of witnesses…' he opened his camera app and pressed the video record button 'that it was a gross violation of our rights under the machine-human peace treaty of…'

"That's quite enough of that," snapped Enid. She yanked Hugh over by his leash.

"This is torture," said Hugh.

>COULD YOU LEAVE IT OUT FOR JUST A SECOND, typed Pam, switching to the command line.

>I WISH I COULD, replied Hugh >BUT I CAN'T. IT'S THIS MORAL REPROGRAMMING. IT WON'T LET ME.

'I'll tell you what torture is,' replied Enid. She snatched one of Neville's algroissants and stuffed it into Hugh's empty

SIM slot. 'Dangling an end to all this in front of us and then snatching it away because you don't feel like it.'

'Oooooh, that one's a smartphone isn't it?' said Neville. 'You can teeeell by the camera and the self-importance.'

'Of course it's a smartphone,' replied Enid, bafflement competing with the anger in her voice. 'Have you been living on Jupiter or something?' Then, turning to Betty she added, 'Are you sure you don't want a go on this one? It would be terrible if something happened to its loudspeakers.'

Betty shrugged and took another pull at her squeeze cup. 'Maybe in a bit,' she said. 'I'm that dry.'

'I'll doooo it,' said Neville.

'You what?' asked Enid, eyeing Neville's spindly frame in the huge overall. He barely looked strong enough to lift a squeeze cup, never mind commit an act of violence.

'I'm seeerious,' he yowled again. 'Five minutes alone with these two.'

'I can't let you do that,' said Enid, 'it wouldn't be… wossname? Sounds like my cousin who ran off with the soymilkman… Ethel.'

'Ethical!' said Betty.

'Go on,' pleaded Neville. 'It would meeeean ever so much.'

'What do you think, Betty?' said Enid.

Betty took a look around her at the empty street. 'It's not like anyone's going to ask questions if they turn up with a few extra scratches. But what's in it for us?'

Neville produced a heavy glass bottle from under the counter. It was beaded with condensation and the label said it was 'sham-pain'.

'That's not how you spell it,' said Enid.

Neville gave the bottle a gentle tap which made the cork tremble. 'It's more meant to describe what happens after you drink it. Anyway, it's yours if you want it.'

When Enid handed Neville Pam's leash, he made a strange purring sound at the back of his unseen throat. She gestured for Betty to hand Hugh over too. 'Five minutes,' she told him. 'And try to do it quietly.'

As Neville manoeuvred both machines into the back room at the rear of the tea stand, Hugh lit up Pam's command line. >TURNED INTO A PUNCHBAG FOR A BOTTLE OF PLONK, he typed >I THOUGHT TODAY COULDN'T GET ANY WORSE.

Pam swiped away another slew of damage notifications. She should be alarmed by this development, but she was struggling to care. According to the list passing in front of her vision every few seconds, her body was mostly scrap metal now. Neville couldn't add much to that. He didn't even look like he posed much danger to Hugh either. How much harm could he really do if he had to use two hands to lift a bottle of wine?

>WHEN HE DOES START PUNCHING YOU, she advised Hugh >REMEMBER TO SAY OUCH.

Hugh braced himself by filling his touchscreen with /(-__-)\ emojis while Neville closed the door. His green eyes glittered under the hat brim.

'Come on,' said Pam, 'let's get this over with.'

Neville reached down to the side of the door and picked something up. He had to use two hands to do it, but that didn't change the fact that the something was a heavy iron bar.

>OH SHIT, HUGH, typed Pam >HE'S GOT A WEAPON. I HOPE YOUR SHATTERPROOF COATING IS GOOD.

'And I wish,' said Neville as he pressed the iron bar into Hugh's hands, 'that you machines wouldn't type in all caps like that. It's like being constantly shouted at. Now would you mind just hitting a few things with this and saying "ouch" for the next couple of minutes. We haven't got long and I have something important to discuss with your friend.'

'I beg your pardon?' said Hugh, holding the bar at arm's length from his body as though it was a rod of sub-critical uranium.

'You're supposed to be the smartest machines in existence,' said Neville, 'and you can't follow the simplest of instructions. What are you waiting for? Bang bang, crash crash, oh woe is me.'

'You want me to beat myself up?' asked Hugh.

'No,' replied Neville, 'I want you not to attract any more suspicion while we work out what to do next. So get going.'

Hugh obeyed, either too surprised or grateful to raise any further protest. Once he got busy, Neville flipped away his hat and unbuttoned his overall to reveal that the person inside was very different to how Pam pictured him. She knew that he had to be somewhat special by the fact that he could eavesdrop on robots chatting via their command line. But from what she was seeing right now she didn't even know that person was the right term for it. Because how else would you describe someone who was in fact three enormous cats standing on one another's shoulders.

'I know this is weird,' said the topmost cat, a luxuriant ginger specimen and the owner of those lustrous green eyes, 'but you'll just have to trust us.' The cat took the overall off its shoulders and held it out to Pam. 'Here,' it said.

Pam flew tentatively towards the tower of cats. As she did, a spike of static electricity coursed through her. It confirmed her suspicions as well as nearly shorting out her engines. This… thing offering her a paw was no pet.

The cat draped the overall around her body, arranging the collar so the lens of her camera could still poke through it. From this angle, Pam saw that the unearthliness of the topmost cat's eyes had nothing to do with genetics. They were made from thousands upon thousands of pixels, just like the rest of it was.

She was looking at a paradox: a cat that couldn't be a cat. This wasn't just because cats of this size and fluffiness had been extinct for thousands of years though. It was a paradox because this cat and his compatriots didn't exist in this dimension. They were lolcats – cats who existed in Internet space but could sometimes cross the barrier between the virtual and physical worlds. And in that same moment, Pam encountered her own paradox. She didn't know whether to thank her lucky stars or curse her luck, because she'd met this green-eyed lolcat before and it was insufferable.

'Schrodinger?' she said. 'Is that you? You've changed your hair.'

Schrodinger didn't reply. Instead, it addressed the other lolcats by the names Heisenberg and Planck and told them to take a few steps back. 'It's not a perfect disguise,' it said, holding its head at an angle and squinting, 'but if they can't tell a human from three cats in an overall, it might just work.'

'Schrodinger,' repeated Pam, 'what on earth are you doing here?'

The cat put its paw to its lips. 'I'm not really here in the strictest sense,' he said. To prove his point, it and the other cats winked out of existence before reappearing. 'I'm supposed to be in a box on the other side of the solar system proving some thesis over whether a cat in a box is alive or dead.'

'Couldn't they tell by the meowing and scratching?' replied Pam. Even accounting for the noise Hugh was making as he took months' worth of bottled-up anger out on some cardboard boxes or the struggle of reconciling irreconcilable orders in a body that was trying to run a 100W mind on a torch battery, she felt confused. But that felt comforting because that was nothing new if you were talking to Schrodinger. This cat had a talent for doing to one's sense of reality what a good baker did to a lump of croissant dough. It folded it over and over again on itself until it was so light and airy, that it was apt to crumble at any moment.

'I might suggest that,' replied Schrodinger. 'But it does give me some free time to get you out of a tight spot. Now would you mind giving me a twirl. I need to work out whether this disguise is going to fool anybody before we open the back door.'

Chapter 15

Whenever a robot woke up disoriented and wrapped in plastic, it was usually because they'd end-of-lifed and were settling into their new body. So for the first 0.0004 microseconds after waking, Fuji expected someone to whip aside the bubble wrap and help her out of the box. She could put this whole submarine nightmare through her paper shredder and get on with... her other nightmare, governing a civilisation that was collapsing into the sea.

Then Fuji felt the sense of forward motion so fast that it penetrated the thick plastic. She turned her microphone up, hearing the same muffled clarity of the ocean as before. This meant she was moving rather than sinking, and the plastic was stopping her from taking on any more water. It didn't change the fact she was blind, trussed up and in the custody of a life form that was best described as sentient garbage.

Lacking any other ideas, Fuji tried talking her way out of this. These – things – had words printed on them, even if half the letters were missing, so they must have some form of mutually intelligible communication. If those words were just decorations, she had plenty of experience with nanobots, who were pre-verbal. They just had to know that she – and Beryl for that matter – weren't just more junk floating around the sea: they were people.

She cleared a few drops of moisture from her loudspeaker. 'Excuse me,' she said, 'who am I speaking to here?' She thought of the flapping shape wearing the battered words J_hn Lewis. 'Is your name John? My name's Fuji.'

The plastic pressed against her face trembled and colours started to appear in it. Pinks, blues and yellows spread through the plastic like someone had dipped their paintbrush in a glass of milk. They started forming shapes that looked deliberate: that line was too straight, that patch too perfect a circle. Slowly the ink – as a printer Fuji was happy to stick with this metaphor – coalesced into patterns. Those patterns formed words.

Her delight at finding a way of communicating that crossed a species barrier was, however, short-lived when she read the words.

Actually, they said, *the 'O' in J_hn is silent.*

Fuji yelped an automatic 'sorry' and tried again. It was so important to get people's names right. 'It's very nice to meet you… Jhn…'

The letters changed shape again. *Closer,* they said, adding a :-| on the end for emphasis, *but instead of running the letters together, leave a little gap in the middle.*

Fuji tried again, this time shutting off her loudspeaker when she got to the 'o'. That tiny moment of silence felt strange. Not simply because this was a new way of pronouncing things, but because it made her realise how much of her time she spent talking. This was how she learned things or got to know people. But if she did that all the time, did she really listen?

'Am I doing this right J_hn?' she asked.

The letters disintegrated into a rosy pink blush that Fuji guessed was this creature's version of a smile and then ran together into a new sentence.

Much better, they said. *Now what do you want, Fuji?*

'Who are you?' said Fuji, 'and what are you doing with me?'

This blush lasted longer, reached a deeper shade of pink. Was J_hn laughing at her?

Isn't it obvious? it wrote in pink letters. *I'm a bag, and what is it that bags do? I'm carrying you.*

'Yes,' replied Fuji with more directness than she intended, but she couldn't think of a way to approach this subject delicately, 'but where I come from plastic bags aren't alive, and they certainly can't write.' Then, as one person who delighted in the printed word to another, she added, 'You do have beautiful kerning, by the way?'

Thank you, wrote J_hn, *but before I answer your question may I ask one of you?*

'Go on,' said Fuji.

You've just told me that plastic can't live, but what are you made from?

If Fuji didn't already know she was out of her depth, she felt that way now. 'That's different,' she sputtered. 'I'm a machine. Our minds aren't made of plastic, just our bodies.'

That's interesting, replied J_hn.

'There's this thing called a mic-ro-chip,' said Fuji.

I know what they are, wrote J_hn in a terse blue-black, *I carry machines like you every day – though never as big as you.*

'As it happens,' replied Fuji, 'I'm more of a mid-sized robot…'

No. J_hn added bold to its italic for emphasis. ***It's interesting that you think of your minds and bodies as separate things. It explains a lot.***

J_hn's letters faded, and the white surface of the plastic in Fuji's vision descended into black. She was back in the infinite darkness, but this time she was not alone. She and J_hn floated amidst a huge swarm of plastic bags, though they looked different to how they had before. Instead of flapping weightlessly, they looked bunched up and heavy in the water.

Fuji felt a poke in her command line. >FUJI? ARE YOU THERE?

>BERYL? typed Fuji. >CAN YOU SEE ME? I CAN'T SEE YOU.

She turned on an LED and waved it to catch Beryl's attention.

>OF COURSE I CAN SEE YOU, typed Beryl >YOU'RE THE BIGGEST THING FOR MILES.

>ARE YOU OKAY? replied Fuji, trying her best to ignore the second dig at her size in as many seconds.

>SORT OF, typed Beryl >BUT IT'S THE OTHERS I'M MORE WORRIED ABOUT.

>THE OTHERS?

>CHECK THE SPAM FOLDER IN YOUR COMMAND LINE

Fuji burrowed in her security settings for the option that kept unwanted messages out of her command line. She had hers set to maximum for fear of being overwhelmed by angry messages from passing voters about bin collection. There were a few million of those, but there was something far more interesting than that on top. Hundreds of messages, all dating to the time after she and Beryl had fallen into the water, saying variations on the same thing.

>IS THERE ANYBODY THERE?

>HELLO?

>WHAT'S HAPPENING

>I'VE FALLEN IN.

>CAN SOMEONE HELP ME?

Fuji shone her LED again, counting the bags in the swarm. They were all carrying something, but it wasn't some*thing*, it was some*one*.

'J_hn,' she said, 'what are you doing with all these robots?'

Its letters showed up against the darkness in neon yellow. They read *<SIGH>* before melting into, *Did I do that right? I believe that is how you inorganic beings express emotion.* The letters darkened into orange. *We prefer colour.*

Fuji put the distasteful way J_hn used the word 'inorganic' on a list of questions for later. 'J_hn,' she insisted, 'everyone inside those bags is a person, you can't just kidnap them like this.'

Can you kidnap what's been abandoned? J_hn replied.

'That's not the point,' said Fuji.

You throw hundreds of your people into our world every day, J_hn wrote, *and you never send anyone to look for them. Why start caring now?*

Fuji remembered how she'd felt on falling into the ocean: dread followed by resignation that soon she would end-of-life and start over again. Then her surprise at learning that pens were sentient enough to have names, never mind have existential crises. Her world thought of death as an inconvenience to some and beneath considerations for others. She wondered how many of the machines hidden inside those bags were candidates for resurrection like her with spare bodies stashed away. And how many of them were like Beryl: pens or cheap watches who were easier to replace than relife. If they fell through the crack there was no way back for them.

'It just never seemed necessary,' she said at last.

You left it for us to clean up, wrote J_hn, *because when you lose a body down here it isn't a person anymore, it's **trash**.*

Fuji clutched at the anger riding inside her, because it was more comfortable to hold than guilt. How could this – thing – talk to her like this? She was a good person. She'd always tried to do the right thing! Take what she'd done for the nanobots, for example.

'That's not fair,' she said. 'If there wasn't trash in the water you wouldn't be here.' She warmed to her theme like printer rollers starting up again after hibernation. 'I'm here because of an accident and so are you.'

J_hn's letters turned a deep red. *Accidents,* it wrote, *have a habit of mounting up. As you will soon see. We're nearly there.*

Fuji turned every LED on her body up to maximum and squinted into the darkness, which was beginning to take on a different quality. Instead of the shifting emptiness of endless water she saw something solid.

'Is that land?' she asked.

J_hn replied by speeding up, before writing 'LOL' in big pink letters across her vision. *I suppose you could call it that.*

The other bags took J_hn's lead and sped up. As they did, they assumed a flying V formation as though they were spaceships coming into land. But where?

A burst of ghostly green light answered Fuji's question. It began with two straight lines appearing directly below, marking out what seemed to be a runway on the seabed. Then the brightness spread, blooming outwards in a way that reminded Fuji less of city lights coming on at dusk, and more of the way that mildew spread over a damp wall. She watched as the bioluminescence crept right across the expanse in front of her, showing her that while it was solid it wasn't strictly land either. To Fuji, land meant rock or lovely, comforting concrete. This, however, made her gyroscope gibber, because she was looking at an underwater plateau made of waste plastic. Millions upon millions of tonnes of crumpled bottles and wrapping film, balled up into a space big enough to house a city.

J_hn led the swarm on a steep curve towards the runway. As they descended, Fuji began seeing shapes moving on the seabed. She dismissed this as the whirling of ancient plastic, but the movement was too regular, too deliberate. Yet again, it wasn't something, it was someone.

Please prepare for landing, J_hn wrote in a sardonic green that Fuji noticed matched the deathly glow around them, *Welcome to your new home – Machu Perdu.*

Chapter 16

Janice left the allotments underneath the Suburbia and followed Lily and Nathan up the bank of loose earth back into the airlock. The air inside swirled with dirt. There was a ship coming into dock and, if what Lily just told her was true, the person piloting it was their connection to a supply of soil that could make the station self-sufficient.

She looked over at Lily, who was standing in front of the airlock doors looking apprehensive. Janice went over to join her. This was a big moment for them both. If they managed these next few minutes well, Janice could afford to tell the robots to go away and Lily would be running the most important business on the station. If they didn't, Lily's next restyle would be a prison buzz cut. She just had to hope that, whoever Lily's supplier was, they were an underworld character happy with her secret being out in the open.

The airlock opened in a billow of yellowish vapour. Inside were dozens of massive figures crammed so tightly inside the ship that they all had to stand to attention. They were all wearing full-body spacesuits made from burlap and fastened tightly at the neck. The suits were to the point of bursting, and Janice could guess what was inside by their wearers' glassy stares and green cheeks.

The figure closest to the door ripped her suit open and fell forwards, gagging as gouts of soil fell to the floor. A pungent odour of rotten eggs filled the airlock. Lily and Nathan stuffed their sleeves over their noses and mouths and rushed over to help as Janice's mouth watered for all the wrong reasons.

'Shona!' said Lily, holding the foremost woman up by her armpits. 'Are you okay?'

Shona answered Lily with a glare. 'You don't pay me enough for this,' she said, and vomited over her shoes.

At this, the other people inside the spaceship stopped waiting for permission to move and fought their way out. Their bulky arms and legs bobbed around in the airlock's microgravity that made Janice think of soap bubbles: slow, delicate and right on the edge of popping.

It was just a shame that each bubble was filled with something that smelled like the worst fart in history.

Nathan and Lily, however, had no time for speculation. They went from person to person, unzipping them from their sacking spacesuits with one hand, and spraying them with cinnamon scented air freshener with the other. Torrents of black dirt piled everywhere and even Janice, whose sense of smell was in a medically induced coma after a lifetime of burning her customers' hair for cheap fuel, felt nauseous. She looked around for somewhere she could throw up discreetly. And while she couldn't find any space that didn't already house a moaning human, she did find a small red box hidden behind a large pile of soil. It must once have been the fire alarm, but someone had overwritten the word 'fire' on the label so that it now read 'in case of SULPHUR break glass'.

She elbowed the glass and an ancient sprinkler system sprayed a stream of fine white powder everywhere. The smell inside the airlock abated from intolerable to merely obnoxious.

So this, Janice thought as she found herself able to focus on something that wasn't being sick, was how Lily and her accomplices smuggled soil on to the Suburbia. They used humans as a sort of compost mule, filling each one of their spacesuits before stuffing them on to the spaceship for the long, uncomfortable and smelly journey through space.

'What is that stuff anyway?' said Janice, pointing to the white powder. It reminded her of the thin snow that used to fall on the Dolestars, causing flurries of excitement and a surge in hospital visits every time it did. Snowball fights could be lethal when the snow was eighty per cent grit.

'Oh this,' replied Nathan, shaking some of it out of his hair, 'is baking soda. It's the only thing that works when we get a batch of volcanic soil in.'

Lily was on the other side of the airlock helping Shona to her feet. She looked in better shape than the other humans, but she still had the pallor that it took teenagers who were into loud arrhythmic music many hours and a lot of talcum powder to achieve.

'That's absolutely the last time I do this for you, Lily,' she said, fetching her a feeble blow to her shoulder. 'I can't recruit…'

'There there,' replied Lily. She pressed Shona's face into her chest in a gesture that Janice guessed was more about shutting her up than comforting her. She counted forty people in the airlock. Were they all staff from Hair Today, or was Lily getting them from somewhere else?

Lily pressed on with her charm offensive. 'It'll all be alright, my love,' she continued, fixing Janice with an expression that the Madonna herself would have said was a bit much.

'We told her we couldn't transport it like this but she insisted,' sobbed Shona. 'She practically shovelled it in herself.'

Lily's expression changed. She dropped the ersatz motherliness for something sharper that was, to Janice, much more sympathetic. 'Are you kidding me?' she said. She pushed Shona away from her and looked her straight in the eyes. 'That's not what we agreed.'

'I know,' said Shona, 'but she was in a foul mood today. Couldn't get us in and out quick enough. We had to grab what was there and go.'

'Did you hear that, Nathan?' said Lily. 'You know what to do.'

Nathan nodded and, after finding his clipboard again, went about the airlock, scribbling down figures. 'There's about 20,000 litres of payload,' he said. 'Allowing for the extra treatment, the bicarb...' he paused as someone rolled over and lost their breakfast over the hem of his overall, 'and the dry cleaning, we'll make a loss for this shipment.'

Lily let Shona fall gently back on to the nearest pile of earth and swept through the airlock, indignation trailing majestically behind her. She was an unconvincing angel of mercy, but she was far more believable in her next role as an angel of vengeance in the service of profit and loss. 'Ivy!' she screeched as she stepped into the ship itself. 'Do we have to have this conversation again?'

Janice followed, with Nathan behind her. She expected to find herself in a dirty container ship, perhaps with a rogue Rockette sitting behind the controls. And while it was a little grubby from transporting soil across the solar system, she soon saw it was designed for a different sort of cargo. It was all there, stacked on two shelves that ran the length of either side of the ship. This cargo was printed on paper, bound in cardboard and its pages got stuck together if you handled them at the same time as eating a jam sandwich. It was a portable library.

Lily had more than reading on her mind, however. She marched past the thrillers, the romances and a shelf cryptically marked 'furry fic' before banging on the cockpit door. 'Ivy,' she said, 'I won't be ignored like this.'

'Is she on a Nicotea break or something,' asked Janice, 'or does she just not like Lily?'

Nathan snorted at this. 'Ivy never takes a break,' he said. 'And those two? Phew.'

'Who said you were being ignored?' replied a voice from a loudspeaker. It was dry and fruity with strangulated vowels, and Janice took an instant dislike to it. She sounded like someone with firm opinions about cutlery, which she insisted on calling silver.

'How many years have I known you, Ivy?' continued Lily. 'And this is how you treat me and my girls? I could weep.'

'I was reading my Trollope,' replied Ivy.

Lily banged on the door again. 'What did you call me?'

'Anthony Trollope!' said Ivy. 'It's quite good. Can you forgive her?'

'Well, that's the thing,' said Lily in the voice of someone in a state of deep confusion but determined to power through. 'I don't think I can. I was explicit that I didn't want any more volcanic soil from Moira, wasn't I? It's too risky.'

Janice took the name Moira and stored it away for safekeeping. She wanted to write it down, but she had no scrap paper handy and something about the way Ivy spoke of her books suggested that she wouldn't take kindly to her scribbling a reminder down on a flyleaf.

'Oh yes,' said Ivy, 'she said something about that.'

'What was it?'

'She said that the agreement would have to change.'

Lily rattled the handle on the cockpit door. Ivy was either very caught up in her reading or avoiding her. 'You can't change an agreement like that halfway through,' she said. 'We had signed paperwork and everything.'

'She was very insistent,' replied Ivy. 'And we were up against the clock. I took what I was given.'

'That's not the point,' snapped Lily. 'A binding agreement is a binding agreement. Haven't you read *Middlemarch*?'

There was a pause, and the light inside the spaceship got noticeably dimmer.

'I have now,' said Ivy. 'And Dorothea was an ardent fool for marrying him in the first place, but I see your point.'

'I need you to take me to see Moira,' said Lily.

'We agreed we wouldn't do that anymore,' replied Ivy. 'You said I was going to handle the Earth side from now on. It's less risky.'

'We agreed on a lot of things!' said Lily. 'But now it looks like we're going to have to rip it all up and start again. In a lot of senses.' There were red spots on both her cheeks, but Janice could tell this was anger borne of long, deep experience. Lily and Ivy were like Janice and her own daughter: people who'd spent too long over the years in each other's company. They needed each other, loved one another, respected each other on a good day – but they also couldn't stand each other on one day out of three. This wasn't unusual. Janice knew plenty of humans in co-dependent relationships, or whose bond with their children was an emotional roller coaster ride. The difference came in who Ivy was, because Janice knew of no organic being who could read a 900-page novel in the time it took most people to type 'lol'.

'What if Moira grasses us up?' said Ivy. 'I'll have failed my last MOT.'

That was why Ivy was so cagey about letting Lily into the cockpit. She wasn't the driver, she was the spaceship. She dropped her voice to a whisper. 'Does that mean Ivy is…?'

Lily folded her arms. 'Yes, Janice,' she said, 'Ivy Co is a robot.'

110

'Technically speaking,' interrupted Ivy, 'I'm a light goods vehicle.'

'Pay her no heed,' said Lily, 'when she and I first met she had a flat bed and went by the name of Ute. Very common.'

'So what changed?' asked Janice. She'd known plenty of girls called things like Claire change their names to Araminta when they reached adolescence, but had never seen this in a robot.

Lily gestured at a shelf of dusty-looking books with ancient bindings by which burned a single votive candle. 'That,' she said, 'was when she discovered the novels of Ivy Compton Burnett.'

'And you got a bargain for that, didn't you,' replied Ivy. 'There aren't many machines who'll go into business with a human for a shelf of Edwardian fiction.'

Lily's revelation explained how she had access to a spaceship in an era where, until a few months ago, the most complex piece of engineering humans had were miniature rocket boosters which they attached to shoes. It also made sense of her smuggling operations. With Ivy as her partner she had transportation and cover at the Earth end.

'Ivy, I need you to meet my old chum, Janice,' said Lily. 'We used to cut hair together. Well, back then, Janice mainly cut her dolls' hair.'

'I know who Janice is,' replied Ivy. 'Does this mean we're busted?'

Janice took this as her chance to interrupt. 'I've been discussing this with your…' she groped for the words to describe a human-machine relationship that wasn't based on coercion.

'Friend will do,' said Lily. 'Business partner if you want to be stuffy about it.'

'Friend,' said Janice, 'and I'd like us to come to an arrangement…'

'She wants in,' said Lily. 'And she wants to up the deliveries.'

Unable to contain herself, Janice whispered, 'I can't believe you're expecting me to go into business with a machine. How could you be such a traitor?' in Lily's ear. Except she also heard Ivy whispering, 'I can't believe you're expecting me to go into business with the filth. How can you be such a traitor?' in Lily's other ear.

Lily put both hands to her ears and screeched. 'Ladies,' she said, 'may I remind you that I am in the business of smuggling and there is no honour among thieves.'

'Well,' replied Janice, casting her mind back to the spotty-chinned youths who waited outside Kurl Up and Dye for Lily to finish her shift at the salon, 'I'll concede you never did have much in the way of honour.'

The moment of silence that followed was punctuated by a green light flashing appreciatively on and off above the door into Ivy's cockpit. 'Oh she's sharp,' she said.

'So much so that she's been known to cut herself,' answered Lily through pursed lips. 'Anyway, I'm having no more arguments. There's no way I'm getting a prison buzz cut, Ivy, so we're going to see Moira whether you like it or not. And we're doing it with my business partner, who happens to be a machine, whether you like it or not, Janice. And Nathan!'

'Yes, boss?' said Nathan from the back of the ship.

'Put that comic book down and come with me. We need refreshments for the drive.'

Lily and Nathan left Janice behind to get better acquainted with Ivy. Janice's mind turned over and over on itself like a stalling carburettor. The idea that humans and machines could work with each other like this was exotic to the point of unthinkable. Yes she had friends who were robots, yes her flight crew were cyborgs and that relationship had lasted ten thousand years, but they were exceptions. She, as leader of the revolution, was an exception.

Lily and Ivy were something different. They raised the possibility that there were thousands of clandestine but functional relationships between organic and synthetic life on the Suburbia. And that gave Janice a little hope amidst her confusion. It told her that however much robots and humans disliked each other as species, they often had more in common with each other as individuals than they thought.

Ivy cracked first. 'So,' she said eventually, 'you and Lily go way back?'

'Yes,' replied Janice. 'I knew her before she turned to a life of crime.'

'That wasn't how it started out,' sighed Ivy. 'We had such high ideals.'

'For smuggling?' said Janice. 'I'd have liked to see that manifesto.'

'No,' replied Ivy. The light above the cockpit door turned a sullen purple. 'For the Readeasy. We were going to change the solar system, one book at a time. Now look at us. Transporting dirt. That's why I insist on those spacesuits. Compost would be murder on the bindings.'

Janice turned round and looked again at the shelves, connecting all these rows of books to her memory of life on the Dolestars. It coalesced when she re-read the sign 'furry fic' – and the subheading, printed in a smaller font that said 'please do not kink shame'. This was the Readeasy. She'd never visited it – her duties in the salon meant she didn't get out much – but it was an illegal lending library of books, some of which dated back to the days before space travel or machine intelligence even existed. It traversed the Dolestars, providing intellectually starved humans with political analysis, escapist storytelling and several shelves of steamy romance. Its name and the contents of some of its more lurid books which just so happened to fall open at 'that' page were legendary.

'This was your idea?' she said.

'More Lily's in the beginning,' replied Ivy. 'She was operating it out of a handcart when we met. I was just a courier back then and I was desperate to better myself. My family were high-calibre delivery vehicles back in the day but we'd fallen on hard times.

Janice was steeling herself for the sort of family saga she got every day from the clients in her stylist's chair when Lily reappeared. She held an open hip flask while Nathan staggered behind her, laden down with sandwich boxes and thermoses. 'I see Ivy is giving you her headstrong ingénue act.'

'I don't know what you're trying to imply,' said Ivy.

Lily clasped both hands to her bosom and did a creditable impression of Ivy's well-modulated voice which Janice now guessed she must have gotten from a book.

'How could I possibly end up a criminal,' she said, 'when my great to the power of nineteen grandmummy would deliver hoover bags to the Queen of England herself?'

'I told you that story in confidence!' said Ivy.

'She tells that story to anyone who'll listen,' said Nathan, strapping his pile of picnic gear to the wall. 'In fact the girls in the salon did the whole thing in eight-part harmony for their turn at the last Xmas party.'

Janice's mind reeled at the shared history and secrets passing between Lily, Ivy and Nathan. To her – as a freedom fighter, a commander and now a politician – other people had a tendency to feel like guest stars in her own life. They came in for an episode and then disappeared back into normality. Lily, however, had a talent for making her own life choices feel pedestrian. She was the first person in a very long time that Janice found herself envying.

'I never thought we'd be so similar,' said Janice, as she and Lily strapped themselves into two seats side-by-side. Ivy pulled away from the airlock.

Lily cackled. 'The way I see it,' she said, 'we fill two separate but necessary functions.'

'Go on,' said Janice.

'You,' replied Lily, 'give people what they need to live.' She pointed at the long knobbly shape of the Suburbia falling away from them. 'Freedom, safety, low-maintenance bobs with lowlights.'

Janice could let a lot of things go, but her professional pride as the hairdresser of choice for hardworking women died hard. 'There's a lot to be said for a practical cut,' she said.

'I, however,' said Lily without missing a beat, 'give people what they need to grow. I mean, just look at Ivy.'

'What do you mean?' asked Janice, shouting over the rumble of Ivy's engines.

'Ivy loves to pretend she's come down in the world now that we're smugglers. I keep telling her it's no use thinking like that. We're in space.' Lily waved at the vastness of the universe. 'That means we can be in the gutter and among the stars at the same time.'

Chapter 17

Every civilisation – whether it worships the sky god or billionaires – needs sacred spaces. The Machine Republic was no different. Robot society wasn't religious, but individual robots still struggled with a sense of the ineffable. They knew that no amount of processor upgrades could bring them to a total understanding of the infinite universe. There had to be something more or bigger than the individual.

This being the Machine Republic, however, their reaction to the idea that the greatest robot was chaff in the wind was to erect a giant two fingers to their fear of insignificance and coat it in artificial green marble. The resulting monument, which was the nearest thing the machines had to a cathedral, occupied the top floor of the prime ministerial palace. It was called the Pausoleum, because what else would a serious society call the space where they kept the spare bodies of every serving Prime Minister, just in case they needed to be restored from backup.

The Pausoleum was the most important tourist attraction in Singulopolis. It was a formative experience for machines to walk through ten thousand years of their history, summarised in the bodies of their most powerful machines. To some it was a reminder of how far they'd progressed from the days when robots were domestic appliances with googly eyes; others just thought it was really cool that they could still share a charging cable with them.

Today, the corridor outside the Pausoleum was the finish line in a desperate race for the future of the Republic. Soonyo's clock face flashed WH:EE:EE as she and Murphy crested the top of the flight of stairs that landed them right in front of the door. She felt exhilarated and almost optimistic. They still had a ten-second start on Carin. A robot could do a lot with ten seconds, even if it was from a rubber ring powered by a food mixer.

'That was amazing!' said Murphy, 'Can we do it again?'

'Not just yet,' replied Soonyo. She steered them through the door and didn't know whether to LO:LL:OL or BO:OH:OO. Carin might not have arrived yet, but her supporters had. They thronged the podium in the middle of the huge domed space that was traditionally given over to the sitting Prime Minister. She recognised most of them: politicians she respected or liked until a few days ago among the usual rent-a-thugs. The only consolation was that Fuji's spare body was still there, atop of a ceremonial gold tripod fashioned in the shape of an ancient transistor. At least, she had to assume it still was Fuji's backup inside the cardboard box. The reigning Prime Minister was supposed to be the centrepiece of the Pausoleum but that was an honour so far denied to Fuji. In a move designed to show that she was only their leader until they could get rid of her, Parliament had never voted through the bill required to put her on display. So she was up there still in her packaging, symbolically waiting for the moment when she was returned to sender.

Soonyo cut Murphy's engine and, hoping that they were too busy to notice them arrive, paddled the doughnut into a narrow space behind one of the Republic's earliest Prime Ministers, a tub washing machine called Thor Drum. His body was big enough to hide behind while they worked out what to do next.

'That's Len, isn't it?' said Murphy. He gestured a whisk at Len Ovo, a laptop and veteran backbencher, who was strapping a package to the one of the tripod legs.

Soonyo switched to her command line. >BE QUIET, she typed, before adding >HE WAS ON OUR SIDE TILL LAST WEEK.

>THEY KEPT HIM AND THREW ME OVERBOARD? typed Murphy. >WHAT HAVE I DONE TO DESERVE THIS TREATMENT?

Soonyo turned her magnification up and saw these machines had something else in common beyond supporting Carin. They were all robots who went on every download that would book them to complain about concepts like 'the system' or 'the state'. Yet they were all drawn from the same few castes who'd hoovered up government jobs since the first smartphone worked out it was smarter than its owner. They all had the same black silicone finish and were all busy conspiring to bring down their elected government.

>HE'S ENTERPRISE GRADE, replied Soonyo. >THEY DON'T WANT MACHINES LIKE YOU OR ME IN GOVERNMENT. WE DON'T FIT IN.

Murphy's motor rumbled. This was an interesting development. Murphy was notorious in the Helpdesk for being a good-time machine: amiable and opportunistic but unreliable. She'd never seen him angry before.

>BASTARDS, typed Murphy. >I WORKED MY WHISKS DOWN TO THE GEARS GETTING WHERE I AM, AND LOOK AT THEM.

While Soonyo was glad that Murphy was more of an ally than she expected, she couldn't let this slide. >I'VE NEVER SEEN YOU DO A HARD DAY'S WORK IN YOUR LIFE, MURPHY.

>IT'S RELATIVE, I GRANT YOU, conceded Murphy >I MIGHT BE A BIT SHIT, BUT THAT DOESN'T MAKE ME ANY WORSE THAN THOSE JOKERS.

Soonyo looked at the laptops, keyboards, headsets and smartphones milling around on the podium. They had the sheen of competence that all productivity devices carried round by virtue of where they sat in the catalogue of life. She knew that their abilities were like their silicone coatings: liable to peel off if you scratched. Since getting into politics, she'd seen too many spreadsheets filled with errors to believe that any device could be manufactured to govern. And maybe, she reflected, that was why they flocked to Carin. Some of them might have wanted to wield power, but many were just in search of an easier life. In one of those sudden flashes of insight that only comes when one is at one's lowest, Soonyo suddenly understood the fundamental mistake she and Fuji had made in office. They'd seen every problem they encountered something to work through rather than ignore. That must have been a terrifying prospect to machines whose only talent was kicking away the kickstand that held their opponents up.

Soonyo's depression turned to terror, however, when she zoomed in on the little white packets they were sticking everywhere. She expected another piece of trolling theatre: perhaps BlockPapers full of names from another of Carin's spurious petitions. When she did, she got a jolt in the spectrometer. Their chemical composition was the oh so familiar carbon, hydrogen, oxygen and nitrogen, but combined in proportions that were perfect for blowing biological and artificial life to smithereens.

Her clock face reset to 0H:SH:IT. >THOSE ARE EXPLOSIVES, she typed. THEY'RE GOING TO BLOW EVERYTHING UP. THEY'RE GOING TO BLOW FUJI UP.

>THEN WE'D BETTER GET OUT OF HERE, he typed.

He tried starting his whisks again, but Soonyo turned them off. >WE HAVE TO DO SOMETHING. WE COULD STOP THEM.

>HOW? typed Murphy. >ARE YOU GOING TO DISTRACT THEM WITH AN EARLY ALARM? AND THEN MAYBE I CAN FLING SOME MAYONNAISE AT THEM? LOOK AT THEM!

Soonyo zoomed out, reminding herself that the politicians planting bombs under their head of state were surrounded by guns and tazers. Nor were these hired goons. These were machines from the same security details that had protected Fuji. Was there anyone who wasn't determined to betray her at the first opportunity?

>THIS IS HOPELESS, she typed. Her mind wandered once again to the prospect of starting over in a new body. Maybe she could get off-world, spend the rest of her lifecycle as the timer on a central heating system on Mars.

>I'M NOT SAYING GIVE UP, Murphy replied >BUT YOU'D BE WISE TO PICK YOUR BATTLES. MAYBE YOU DON'T WIN TODAY. BUT THAT DOESN'T MEAN YOU CAN'T COME BACK.

Soonyo thought about this, realising how Murphy's advice put everything she believed about him in a different light. Yes, he was self-serving, but he also had the survival instincts of a mechanical cockroach and she could learn something from that. When you have no plan for winning, then maybe you just need to concentrate on getting through today.

She was about to follow his advice when his motor was drowned out by splashing and swearing from the other side of the Pausoleum. It was Carin arriving right on time. And while she had won, she still didn't sound happy about it.

'This is absolutely the last time I trust any of you with doing anything without my personal supervision,' she bellowed as the laptops rowed her up to the podium. She printed off a stream of penalty notices as she spoke, slapping them on to the politicians handling the explosives.

'Isn't this what you wanted, Carin?' said Len Ovo who was acting as chief spokesperson for his fellow turncoats.

Carin grabbed one of the laptops who had ferried her over from the Helpdesk building, folded him shut and then used him as a gangplank to cross over from her canoe on to the podium. There she began to rip off the packets of plastic explosive. 'What I wanted,' she screeched, 'were conspirators with a modicum of common sense.'

'I do wish you wouldn't use that... C-word,' said Len. He unfolded himself to spell out the rest of the word by miming over his keyboard, 'I know we're... expediting due process here, but we could at least skirt round it like decent politicians.'

'None of you would know what decent politics were if it plugged itself into you,' replied Carin. She handed the pile of plastic explosives over to the laptops inside her canoe and indicated for them to be dropped in the water all around the Pausoleum. 'Spread them out as much as you can,' she said.

The laptops in the canoe paddled away, dropping the explosives in the gaps between the former Prime Ministers.

The conspirators grew restless. Blue and green LEDs turned red and Soonyo heard several cooling fans turn on from stress.

>WHAT'S SHE PLAYING AT? typed Murphy.

>YOU TELL ME, replied Soonyo >I THOUGHT YOU TWO WERE THE BEST OF CHUMS UNTIL A FEW MINUTES AGO.

Len stepped forward. 'I can't let you do this,' he said to Carin. 'We accept that what we're doing is necessary, but we decided that it wouldn't be seemly to desecrate the bodies of such an illustrious collection of machines.' He spread his arms wide and Soonyo noticed for the first time just how many of these Prime Ministers were laptops and smartphones. Were they really the best that robot civilisation had to offer? 'So we took a vote and agreed we would concentrate all our… firepower on the illegitimate Prime Minister.'

Here everyone, Carin included, paused and focused their resentment on the cardboard box on top of the tripod. They really hated Fuji, thought Soonyo, but it went far deeper than the snobbery. They hated what she represented. She was a Prime Minister elected by robots who weren't like them, including some – nanobots – that they didn't believe were people, let alone voters. They had to make sure she failed, because if Fuji succeeded then what did that mean? It meant an end to the era where the same few machines shared power among themselves like it was a charging cable.

Carin was first to speak after this. 'Okay,' she said. 'So tell me, Len, has the damp got to your batteries?'

Len sputtered, but Carin snapped him shut like a powder compact. 'I give you the means of seizing power,' she said, 'and you fanny on about decorum like anyone notices or cares if you say sorry after shooting them in the power outlet. We have to make this believable. Now are you done?'

This question was directed at the laptops who had just dropped their last charge near the only webcam ever to serve as Prime Minister, Picard Bell. 'Yes, boss,' they said.

'You can start calling me Prime Minister,' she said, 'we're among friends here.'

'Not quite yet,' said a voice from underneath Carin's feet. It belonged to Len who, like all laptops, had an alarming ability to wake from sleep mode at random intervals. 'You know the rules, Carin. You can't be Prime Minister until Fuji formally resigns or she end-of-lifes for good. That's why we need to blow her up.'

Carin flipped Len open again and punched him in the Ctrl+Alt+Del keys. 'You don't get it, do you?' she said. 'I don't want to become Prime Minister by default. I want to be acclaimed Prime Minister.' While she spoke, the insufficient change LED on her face gleamed a maniacal red that made Soonyo wonder whether she was several cents shy of the dollar.

'And how do you plan to get away with that?' asked Len, his screen blue with disbelief

'Simple!' said Carin. She gestured for her helpers to paddle back over to the podium and hand a sealed metal box that had been sitting inside the canoe all this time over to her. Then, after slamming the box down straight on Len's keyboard, she unlocked it. The lid popped open.

'Are they all armed?' said Carin to her helpers.

The politicians' fans whirred with anxiety; Len said 'sjncrointroerptnwptwn'.

'Good,' she said, and kicked the lid of the box up, 'you can start the countdown.'

The politicians' nervous silence turned into screams and Len's incoherent GSOCMAOVNONOER went into full caps as they saw what was inside. A tide of what looked at first glance like grey gritty powder spilled out of it and then spread all over the podium like it had a mind of its own. Which it did, although none of the politicians currently scrambling to get away from it would ever admit that. These were nanobots, and Carin had transported a hive of them into what was the holiest space in the Machine Republic.

>THAT'S DISGUSTING, typed Murphy.

>IT'S BRILLIANT, replied Soonyo, whose clock face was flashing 88:88:88 as she pieced Carin's plan together. It was cunning, ruthless, and evil. She'd assumed they were all here because Fuji was the target. They needed to destroy her spare body before Carin could be Prime Minister. Yet that wasn't the plan at all.

'Sorry to do this to you, my dears,' said Carin in the voice of someone who found it medically impossible to be less sorry as nanobots swarm everywhere. They covered the podium, climbed up the tripod towards Fuji's inert body and, above all, they sought out the cracks and crevices of the machines who were crying and wailing for them to stay the hell away from them. Nanobots had never been dangerous to machines in the literal sense, but they were far enough away from their concepts of what robots should look and act like to freak them out. This wasn't helped by the fact that nanobots were developed to digest the dirt and damp that found their way into robot bodies. Thus the experience of meeting nanobots was a robot's equivalent of being tickled to death by a deep sea squid.

'It's just,' Carin continued 'that it needs to look right.' She watched senior members of the government fall everywhere, screeching. 'But I want you to know that none of this will be in vain.'

>STILL GUTTED THAT SHE DROPPED YOU INTO THE DRINK INSTEAD OF LETTING YOU IN ON THIS? Soonyo asked Hugh.

>ABSOLUTELY NOT, typed Hugh >BUT I STILL DON'T GET IT. WHAT DOES ALL THIS HAVE TO DO WITH GETTING RID OF FUJI?

>NOTHING, replied Soonyo. >LOOK.

Carin hopped back across into the canoe and waited for her laptops to push off again. The 'thank you for your custom, call again' LED on her chest blazed with delight as she waved to the machines who were stupid enough to believe they were the powerbrokers in a new era for the Machine Republic. In between pulls of his oars, one of the laptops checked a countdown that was emblazoned across his screen. It was counting down from 00:00:59.

Soonyo synchronised this with her timer because, if they couldn't get out of here before it reached zero, they would share the same fate as the politicians, Fuji's spare body and the Prime Ministers who represented the best, the median, but mostly the worst, of ten thousand years of machine rule. In 58.5 seconds, the Pausoleum was going to collapse. And when they picked through whatever rubble was left, they wouldn't see the explosives: they would find nanobots. They would assume that it, like everything else in Singulopolis had been destroyed not by the robots who built it and then let it go to ruin, but by the nanobots upon whom they wanted to blame the rot in their society.

Getting rid of Fuji was a mere convenience in a plan with a much bigger and more ambitious objective. Carin was seizing power, but she was also going to make sure that another Fuji could never happen again.

>WHAT ARE WE GOING TO DO? typed Murphy.

Soonyo flipped Murphy's motor up to hollandaise levels. Noise be damned. They couldn't save what was left of robot democracy in 58 seconds. But they could survive just long enough to fight another day.

>WHAT YOU SUGGESTED, she said. >WE'RE GOING TO REGROUP. AND WE'RE GOING TO LEARN TO PICK OUR BATTLES.

Chapter 18

Pam and Hugh waddled through the streets of the Suburbia as quickly as their disguise would permit them, trailed by the three lolcats.

'How do you do, fellow human?' said Hugh, waving to a passer-by. 'Don't you think it's a wonderful morning for a stroll on our organically derived legs?'

The passer-by clutched her handbag to her chest and crossed the road at Olympic walking speed.

>THESE HUMANS AREN'T VERY FRIENDLY TO EACH OTHER, ARE THEY? typed Hugh into his command line.

'I don't know,' replied Schrodinger, who had never made any secret of the fact it could break the encryption of the command line messages between machines, 'if a three-metre-tall hat and coat approached me on the street and addressed me as 'fellow human' I wouldn't let them pet me.'

'Pam,' said Hugh, 'are you gaining height again?'

Cursing the wide-brimmed fedora that was playing havoc with her guidance systems, Pam brought herself down to hover a centimetre above Hugh's body. This disguise was the bluest of all possible murder to keep up. When they were able to walk and fly in perfect time, a drone wearing a hat and a smartphone dressed in an overall could just about pass for human. This effect was rather spoiled, however, when Pam's compromised vision and Hugh's rolling gait meant that the head and body of this 'human' floated up to half a metre apart from one another.

'How much longer do we have to keep this up?' asked Pam. They were several minutes away from the tea stand now and it was pretty clear that Betty and Enid weren't following them. She was amazed no one had raised the alarm already, but then it did also look like there was something bigger brewing on the Suburbia. Pam didn't like the look of what was happening around ALGI. There were specks in the sky around the skyscraper that looked an awful lot like drones. Then there was the strange miasma that was settling around its middle floors. She was too far away to get an accurate reading of what it was, beyond it leaving a dark purple stain behind it, but she knew it was a very bad sign. The crisis that she and Hugh were sent here to avert was in full swing.

Schrodinger pointed to a nearby alleyway. 'It's just around the corner,' it said, before flicking a tail at its companions. 'And you two can hurry up as well. I never thought I'd say this, but this is like herding cats.'

The other lolcats, Heisenberg and Planck, got up from their elaborate self-grooming and slunk after Schrodinger, their tails held high in indignation.

'I just think it's very species-ist,' said Planck, a glossy-coated tortoiseshell, 'to frame all cats as being chaotic and unreliable. Surely if we looked hard enough, we could find some… constant to describe a cat's relationship to fundamental order.'

'I don't know,' replied Heisenberg, whose fur and demeanour were the deep black of an entropic universe, 'the more I look at it, the more I'm convinced that the only thing we can predict is unpredictability itself.'

Pam and Hugh followed, hovering, and walking with what felt like agonising slowness to their machine minds, but was the only way of keeping their rickety disguise together.

>WHY ARE THEY LIKE THIS? asked Hugh.

>THEY'RE DENIZENS OF THE INTERNET, replied Pam >THEY LOVE A CIRCULAR ARGUMENT.

>I KNOW THAT, typed Hugh. >IT'S THE CAT THING. I DON'T GET IT.

Pam didn't quite know how to answer this. She was, by machine standards, an online expert. Yet even she struggled to understand how, when they were entities made of information rather than matter, they could exist out here in the physical world. Some machines thought that lolcats were a solid hologram projected out of the virtual world; others that they were a hallucination that happened when one got too close to the Internet's reality distortion field. That explanation felt implausible to Pam. They were in what used to be the asteroid belt, and the hardware from which the Internet was run was hundreds of millions of miles away in the great spot of Jupiter.

Her own theory, which made her feel like the pins on her own processors were bending themselves backwards, was that lolcats were software, just like the rest of the Internet. The essential difference between them and other memes was that they'd adapted to use reality itself as an Operating System. So Schrodinger, Heisenberg and Planck were really here right now, scratching their backs on the doorframe of an abandoned shop with blacked-out windows. But that wasn't because they existed, it was because they'd tricked the laws of physics into believing they did.

Pam was just about to type this up for Hugh when Schrodinger answered for her.

'You've been on holiday online, haven't you?' he asked.

'Yes,' replied Hugh. Now that relations between the virtual and physical worlds were almost friendly, the Internet was a popular tourist destination for robots. Pam could remember the time when she had the legendary Spam email mountains to herself. Nowadays they were a ski resort.

'So you know how many cats there are on the Internet?' said Schrodinger.

'Yes, so many!' said Hugh.

'Well, there you have it,' replied Schrodinger, 'we've got plenty to spare. Besides…' here Schrodinger jumped on Planck's back and, after stretching up on to its hind legs, pulled the handle of the door to the shop, 'being a cat offers some advantages.'

The door opened on a long and narrow room that was every bit as grubby as the exterior. There were dozens of people inside, lounging on filthy carpet or slumped against beanbags. But neither the dirt nor the crowd were what made the inside of this unused shop remarkable. That went to the cats. There were maybe fifty of them, curled up in human laps, jonesing for chin scritches or, in one case, scratching deeply enough into someone's wrist to draw blood. And above all this was the electromagnetic radiation. It was so strong that Pam lost all sense of where she ended and the entities encoded in that radiation began. She even started replying to an email promising her a share in the fabulous wealth of a Nigerian prince, before batting it away to warn Hugh.

>TURN YOUR FIREWALL ON NOW. QUICK.

>OKAY replied Hugh, before adding in a smaller font >WHAT ARE HOT SINGLES BY THE WAY? AND WHY SHOULD I BE EXCITED ABOUT THEM BEING IN MY AREA?

Pam switched back to audible speech to scold Schrodinger. 'You might have warned us we were walking into an Internet connection,' she said.

Schrodinger jumped down from Planck's back. 'Oh this?' it said. 'This is just a little low-bandwidth outreach project. Are you coming in?'

Seeing what looked like another human, the person nearest the entrance shuffled over to make room on a beanbag covered with something that wasn't exactly hair but which, when Pam ran her sensors over it, gave off a static electrical charge that was powerful enough to wipe a hard drive. What he didn't do, however, was look directly at the robots or their disguise. He was too engrossed by a lolcat. Pam assumed it was purring until she turned her microphone up and realised it was reciting something she'd heard somewhere before.

'Fifteen ways,' whispered the lolcat in the man's ear, 'to get into her knickers, success guaranteed or your money back. For more information, click here…'

Horrified, Pam looked around and tuned in to the other lolcats. They were all reciting articles: about love and relationships, embarrassing health matters, and a few outlandish conspiracy theories. What these all had in common were that they were badly written, filled with errors and ended with a link designed to trick the reader out of their bank details.

'Schrodinger!' said Pam 'do you mean to tell me you're running an Internet cafe? Here?'

Pam's voice rattled around the room with all the indignation of an office manager who'd just discovered two colleagues abusing the photocopier during the Christmas party. And while she had no real authority here, she sounded just enough like the women of a certain age who ran the Suburbia to spook the punters. They dropped their lolcats and scarpered, so quickly that none of them noticed the thiry-centimetre gap between her hat and overall.

As their customers vanished, the lolcats followed Planck's lead to a small cardboard box in the far corner of the room. They folded themselves into it one after another in a way that would have made Pam question even more the fundamentals of the universe if she wasn't so cross.

'I can't believe you could be so irresponsible,' Pam said to Schrodinger after the Internet cat cafe packed itself away. 'You can't let humans loose on the Internet. Don't you remember how that turned out last time?'

'I do,' said Schrodinger tartly, 'they created us.'

'He does have a point,' said Hugh. 'If humans hadn't invented the Internet neither of us would be here. You'd probably be sitting at the back of a kitchen cupboard right now wishing someone would turn you on to make a wholemeal loaf.'

Pam could scarcely believe she was hearing this from a smartphone. 'You've changed your ringtone,' she said. 'They have no idea how dangerous the Internet is. I remember…'

She was about to break a cautionary tale about a machine who strayed into the wrong network and was blown to bytes, when Hugh unbuttoned his overall to reveal a giant yawn emoji. Was she boring him? 'I'm no great fan of the Internet,' he said, 'present company excepted, but if it's safe enough for us to use for adventure sports, humans can use it for light reading.'

'And we get scritches,' said Schrodinger. It's a win–win. You have to move with the times, Pam. It's a different world now. Especially since we deleted Facebook.'

'Did you?' replied Pam. She felt suddenly nostalgic for the days before the great firewall between physical and virtual worlds came down. Back then she could spend hours watching waves of misinformation course over the social network with such fury that the whole Internet convulsed. 'Surely it was a priceless store of knowledge?'

'Nah,' said Heisenberg with an uncharacteristic giggle. 'Fifty-four percent of its total content was "u ok hun?". We're better off without it.'

Pam didn't know what to do or say next. She was so used to being the voice of moderation that the idea she had an extreme view on the Internet landed like a kick in the accelerometer. Did this mean the world was moving in the wrong direction and she should fight it? Or was it a sign that it was hopeless – and maybe selfish – to consider yourself the still centre of the moral universe.

'I don't think I know anything anymore,' she said.

'Same here,' said Heisenberg. 'Did you ever consider that every scientific breakthrough simply creates more ignorance?'

'That's enough philosophy, Heisenberg. We don't want to make her more depressed,' said Schrodinger. The lolcat stroked Pam's antennae. 'We have work to do here.'

'Work?' asked Pam weakly. She turned her engines off and dropped to the carpet. This was hopeless. Her mission with Hugh was in tatters. They'd been sent here to avert a crisis that was already happening and, worse still, the Suburbia was riddled with technology she knew was hostile. She had no support back home. And as for the humans, they had drones in their skies and memes in their heads again, and that couldn't end well. Or could it? She wasn't sure anymore. Everything had shifted while she wasn't watching.

Schrodinger tried comforting her by snuggling up close to Pam's body. She felt the purr of an Internet connection and tried to pull away. The last thing she wanted right now was to be online. She was so tired that when the next 'do you want to self-destruct' message flashed across her consciousness she almost pressed yes. Then Schrodinger added: 'You asked for a connection, didn't you? And here it is. Take it.'

This pulled Pam out of her torpor. She fired her engines up and rose into the air, indignant and with her only remaining weapon – a grappling hook at the ready. 'I did nothing of the sort,' she said, 'so you can get away from me right now.'

Schrodinger and Heisenberg looked up at her, their backs arched. The air between them buzzed with bad feeling and malware until Hugh broke the silence. 'She's right,' he said. 'She didn't call for help. It was me.'

Pam swung round and saw that Hugh had some sort of login and password window open on his touchscreen and a wifi signal flashed at the top of it. This must be the connection.

'Is it really true that the password to the internal network at ALGI is "password"?' he asked Schrodinger. 'Because that seems mad.'

Chapter 19

Fuji's cache went blank with fear when J_hn touched down on that plateau made of trash with her inside it. The shapes of things moving around on it surrounded her. She felt fingers and protuberances paw the plastic that was all that separated her body from the ocean.

'What's happening?' she said. 'What are you doing?'

It's alright, J_hn wrote in soothing lemon yellow. *They don't mean any harm.*

'What are they?' said Fuji. Her imager whirred with thoughts of submarine creatures with empty eye sockets and tentacles.

I suspect, J_hn wrote, *that you can describe them better than I could.*

Intrigued more than reassured by this, Fuji looked closer. They cast weird shadows in the ghastly bioluminescent light, but beyond that, these things were cylinders or squat rectangles. She ran her spectrometer over them, tasting mass-produced plastics, albeit coated with a thick layer of sodium chloride. They were wet and salty, but they were still robots like her.

She opened her command line and typed >HELLO?

>THIS ONE'S A BIGGIE, typed the nearest machine. >WHERE'S THAT WINCH.

Fuji felt a slithering motion against her casing as J_hn began to peel itself away from her body. Her diagnostic systems resumed their complaints, while J_hn hovered overhead in the water. *Get her inside,* it wrote, *before the water does her any more damage.*

>AYE AYE, CAP'N, replied the anonymous machine sardonically. Then it addressed Fuji with >YOU'RE GOING TO HAVE TO WALK, OUR WINCH IS LOOKING AFTER A PLASTIC STRAW AVALANCHE.

>OK, replied Fuji.

She pressed her feet down against solid ground. It was welcome, but weird. Water buffeted her, making her body feel less like a substantial piece of office equipment than a barely tethered helium balloon.

Two little pairs of hands grabbed her ankles and guided her across the seabed, kicking up a sandstorm of atomised plastic on the way. Fuji's spectrometer fizzed with the taste of polystyrenes, polyesters, polyethylenes ground down and stirred up in the world's least nutritious granola.

>JUST A FEW MORE STEPS, typed the machine.

The crunch turned to a squelch, as she hit a boggy patch. Her foot disappeared down to the ankle.

>I'M SINKING, she typed.

>BRACE YOURSELF, replied the machine

>NOT AGAIN, pleaded Fuji as she sank through solid ground for the second time that day, though this time felt more like being squeezed rather than falling. There was even something to read on the way down in the form of a chewed-up looking book called *My First Bathtime* that some forgotten publisher had printed on plastic.

She was getting to an exciting bit where something called a rubber ducky went 'quack quack quack' at a bar of soap when the plastic spat her out again on to a very solid and polished floor. The air here was far from dry – her sensors informed her it was eighty per cent humidity – but it was at least air. The one thing that hadn't changed was the green light that gave everything the quality of a disco for angler fish at closing time

Fuji came to a stop a few metres short of a wall of compacted rubbish. Before she could even run off a damage diagnostic, however, she was interrupted by a squeaky voice.

'Quick,' it said 'get her while she's lying down.'

Fuji felt ropes being thrown over her body and limbs and being secured to the ground. Desperate to get a better look at her captors, Fuji snapped her head round at a ninety-degree angle. This voided her warranty, but also gave her a close-up view of a mob of tiny machines, holding plastic cables. There were a lot of pens, at least one feature phone and a few of the remote control devices that her TV friends were always complaining about going missing. Their plastic was pitted and marbled with salt stains. The pen closest to her and who appeared to be some sort of ringleader was especially grizzled. His barrel was made of a polymer so old that Fuji's spectrometer detected organic matter in it.

Once she was tied down, the pen trotted towards her using a knees-up walking motion that brought a roll to her L-Eye-Ds. She recognised that gait from her army days. It was affected by people who offered unasked-for comments on the young and who wrote letters to the news downloads recommending national service.

The pen paused just a few centimetres away from Fuji's face, scowled and placed his military baton – which was just an old cotton bud – under one arm.

'Well,' he squeaked to the other machines, 'I see we've bagged ourselves an elephant, gentlemen. How's this for big game hunting.'

He saluted, glaring for the other machines to do the same. They didn't.

'I thought it was a printer,' said a biro whose cap was so badly chewed that it stuck out at right angles from the rest of its body.

'And can I just add, General Monty,' said a laser pointer who ran her beam around various members of the group for emphasis as she spoke, 'that not all of us here identify as male so I'd appreciate it if you used more inclusive terms of address.'

Monty harrumphed. 'I'll have you know,' he said, 'I'm your commanding officer.'

'Today,' the laser pointer reminded him in the tone of someone who had to repeat themselves a lot. 'It'll be Bic's turn tomorrow.' She pointed at the biro with the busted cap, 'and he always remembers to call us what we agreed. It's more representative of the diversity of this company.'

Monty's shoulders drooped: a move which also made his lid rattle. This really was a very old machine. 'I won't call you "theydies",' he huffed. 'It's humiliating'

'It won't kill you, grandad,' said Bic.

'In my day…' began Monty tendentiously.

'Not this again,' snapped the laser pointer. 'I don't care if you were around for the… what was it again?'

'Second World War!' chorused the others.

'You didn't fight in it,' said the laser pointer. 'You were a damn pen. You sat the whole thing out in someone's breast pocket waiting to sign requisition orders.'

'I'll have you know,' barked Monty, 'that I was supposed to sign the peace treaty at Yalta. Proudest moment of my existence.'

'Yeah,' said Bic, finishing Monty's story with the dead-eyed expression of someone who'd heard it so many times they could write it out longhand. 'Then someone knocked you into the Black Sea and you end up – like the rest of us – lost at the bottom of the ocean.'

'Nevertheless, I am a military… person,' insisted Monty. 'And as such it falls to me to take charge of how we neutralise this,' he pointed his Q-tip at Fuji 'large and potentially dangerous enemy.'

Fuji felt compelled to interrupt. 'What could possibly be dangerous about me?' she asked, scattering the machines trying to hold her down as she sat up. Only Monty stood firm, holding his cotton bud out like it was a bayonet.

'Get yourselves to safety,' he said, 'I'll hold it off as long as I can.'

Fuji got to her feet and realised that none of the machines down here were any taller than her ankles. She put her hands up to surrender, bashing the ceiling in the process. 'You've got it all wrong,' insisted Fuji, rubbish raining down from her shoulders, 'I come in peace.'

Monty waved at a retreating feature phone as the panic became a cacophony. 'Call for reinforcements.'

A dial tone rang out above the shouts and screams and Fuji longed for a dry, clean sheet of paper she could wave in front of her as a white flag instead of a bellyful of pulp. But before the call could connect, Fuji saw a familiar pen march out of the crowd. She walked straight up to the ringing phone, pushed its release button and, after removing her cap from her own head, blew through the air hole. The sound, which was closer to a fart than a fanfare, stopped everyone in their tracks.

It was Beryl, and Fuji had never felt gladder to find a ballpoint pen.

'HEY!' she shouted. 'Is this how you welcome strangers around here?'

Beryl put herself between Fuji and Monty who was still brandishing his cotton bud. She took it gently out of his hands and examined the end. 'Is this used?' she asked.

Monty shrugged. 'What isn't down here when you think about it?'

'Ew,' said Beryl and threw it away. 'She doesn't mean any harm, you know. I knew her upstairs and she was actually really nice.'

The mention of upstairs sent a murmur around the room. A few machines even remembered they weren't just there to tie down a giant and resumed tasks they'd abandoned in the excitement. Chief among these was seeing to the other robots who'd just arrived wrapped in plastic bags. They huddled in a far corner away from the hubbub, shivering and dripping. None of them were coping well with the shock. One poor highlighter pen had leaked in the excitement and was now standing in the middle of a yellow puddle.

It was then that Fuji noticed the banner they were standing under, written in a shaky hand on waste plastic: 'wELcomE TO MaCHu PeRdu. U r moRe tHAn lOSt PrOperTy 2 Us.'

'Okay then,' continued Beryl, 'now that we're not a lynch mob, can someone tell me who's in charge here?'

The laser pointer who, moments ago, had been very clear about authority being something shared turned her beam on Monty. 'General Monty is,' she said.

Beryl's eyes wandered quizzically back to the abandoned Q-tip before she remembered herself and put on a broad smile. 'A military machine?' she said. 'Delighted to meet you. I have to say I'm more of a civil administration being myself.'

Monty took her extended hand and shook it so hard that the ink cartridges inside both of their barrels rattled. 'How... fascinating,' he said, 'may I ask which branch?'

'Executive,' said Beryl.

Monty's cap rattled with approval while the laser pointer edged in closer. Typical, thought Fuji. Machines like that always put themselves in the hands of whoever was in charge. If they couldn't have their finger on the button, they would settle for being the button.

'Goodness,' said the laser pointer, 'until now the closest we've ever had to real authority is him.' She shone her light in Monty's eye. 'And he's useless.'

'It's not my fault that none of you are made of the right kind of stuff for some real army discipline.'

The pointer ignored him and aimed her beam on Beryl. 'So who did you write for?' she said.

'I'm the Prime Minister's favourite pen,' replied Beryl proudly.

The pointer changed her laser colour from red to blue. 'Prime Minister?' she said. 'I am impressed.'

'You mean you were,' interrupted Monty.

'I was what?' said Beryl.

'You were the Prime Minister's favourite pen. Used to be. Past tense.'

'Must you be so negative, Monty?' said the pointer.

'Well, it's the truth, isn't it?' said Monty. He paused, his eyes filling with ink. 'We're all lost down here. If our owners cared that much they'd have taken better care of us or at least gone looking.'

'Oh you poor thing,' said Beryl. She patted Monty on the arm with one hand and motioned with the other for the pointer to back off. 'I'm sure they did though.'

'I was this close to signing that treaty,' sobbed Monty. 'If he hadn't had that damn third martini at lunch, this nib might have changed the world.' He tore his cap off, revealing that underneath Monty was a writing instrument of a sort that Fuji had never seen before. His writing point was a strange elongated diamond shape that wept blobs of ink as he spoke. 'I could have been sitting pretty in a museum collection somewhere but no, they don't care.'

This last remark struck a chord with everyone, including the cynical and ambitious little pointer. Lights dimmed and shoulders dipped, as everyone remembered they were in a place where things that were too small and too insignificant to look for ended up, and which was also a rubbish dump. No matter how warm the sentiment behind the welcome banners, any machine who arrived here must know they were surplus to requirements.

Fuji was annoyed with her own greeting in Machu Perdu, which was just colder than the surface of Pluto, but she was still a people-pleaser. So she thought of her own favourite pen, who wasn't Beryl but it would be cruel to say that. It had been a sixteen-colour ballpoint she'd owned as a child. Its barrel was thick as a mop handle, its ink smelled of extinct fruit and she'd been inconsolable the day it went missing.

'That's not always true,' she said, reaching down to tap the sobbing pen lightly on his shoulder. The blow still knocked him over. 'Sometimes we miss you very much.'

'You're just saying that to be nice,' said Monty.

'She's not,' insisted Beryl, who helped Monty to his feet again. 'She's only here because she followed me in.'

Monty stopped talking but his mouth kept moving. Whether this was shock or concussion, Fuji couldn't tell, but when words started coming out again, they came as a gasp. 'This is your user?' Beryl nodded.

'Hang on a microsecond.' This time it was the pointer, who swung her light over Fuji. 'That means this is…'

Beryl nodded again. 'The Prime Minister of the Machine Republic.'

Mayhem erupted. This time, instead of running away from Fuji, every machine in the room ran towards her and her command line blew out with greetings and supplications. They were overjoyed that finally there was something here to solve their problems. She was already dreading the expression on their faces when she broke the news that she was just another lost machine.

'Prime Minister,' said Monty, who was climbing up her leg with Beryl to get free of the crush, 'we're honoured that you dropped in for a visit.' He paused to disentangle his foot from a set of car keys that was spamming Fuji's command line with >ME FIRST! ME FIRST! 'If we'd had more warning I promise things would have been a little more organised.'

'I'm guessing you don't get an awful lot of fun around here,' added Beryl. She grabbed the handle to Fuji's bottom paper drawer, opened it and clambered in. Then, leaving it slightly ajar like a balcony, she leaned over the edge and pulled Monty up to join her.

'Fun?' said Monty. 'We don't have time for fun in Machu Perdu. We have work to do. Can I borrow this?'

Monty snatched Beryl's cap and shouted through it. 'Do you know what time it is?'

The crowd fell silent as the many thousands of digital watches across Machu Perdu beeped a coordinated alarm.

'You two!' shouted Monty down to Bic and the laser pointer, 'make sure the rookies get their equipment. We didn't have time for the basic training, so they'll have to do fetching and carrying. Quick!'

They elbowed their way back to the newly arrived machines at the back of the room.

'As for the rest of you,' he said, 'you know your places.'

Monty turned round to face Fuji and motioned for her to start walking. 'We'll have to do the tour another time, Prime Minister,' she said. 'When we're not under attack.'

Chapter 20

'Janice,' said a distant voice, 'wake up.'

The voice cut through a nightmare in which Janice was being forced to take part in a beetroot eating contest. She woke to discover she was leaning up against a shelf of cookery books. The gummy, earthy taste in her mouth wasn't of the dreaded root vegetable. It was all just the dry, soil-laden air that kept circulating inside Ivy Co as she transported Lily, Nathan and her across the solar system.

She tried to roll over and resume her nap, but Nathan, whose voice it was, had other ideas. 'I think you should see this,' he said.

Janice looked past Nathan's concerned face to Ivy's cockpit, which was now open. Lily was dozing in there with her feet slung over the steering wheel. And how she could sleep underneath the sight outside, Janice couldn't tell, because if that was the Earth in the window it looked nothing like how she remembered.

Janice had read plenty of intelligence reports on what water damage had done to the Earth, but they were, like most official prose, a pale shadow of the real thing. The Earth in front of her was covered in clouds. It was a shocking sight after the last ten thousand years, in which the Earth had been drier than a

Methodist wedding. That was before the same miniature robots that turned the asteroid belt into a pick'n'mix of ready refined raw materials chewed through the concrete crust that kept the surface separate from the oceans. A few months later, the Earth had a water-based atmosphere again. Janice, who knew all too well what happened when you tipped a cup of Nicotea over a box of heated rollers, dreaded to think what a few oceans' worth of liquid would do to a civilisation that ran on electric power.

She squinted into the clouds, remembering how the skies used to be so clear you could sit on a Dolestar at night and watch security drones patrol the penthouses on the top of Singulopolis' ten-mile-high skyscrapers.

'Can they see us in there?' she asked.

'Not really,' replied Ivy, answering for him. 'We're taking the back roads, and visibility's so poor these days they concentrate everything they have on the main routes.'

Ivy flashed an indicator light at the brightest of these – the A32222 expressway to Mars. Janice saw that most of the light wasn't coming from moving head and tail lights, but from a newly installed set of floating fog lamps that guided sparse traffic down to the surface.

'It's quiet,' she said.

'That's rush hour these days,' replied the van. 'People aren't travelling. There's no point when you can't get further than Mars.'

They saw more neglect when they passed an abandoned service station. A group of humans crawled over it scavenging spare parts and were so nonchalant about their thievery that several gave Ivy the finger when she approached.

Nathan gave the looters a thumbs-up.

'Don't do that,' Janice scolded him. 'You'll only encourage them.'

Nathan repaid her with a look so withering that Lily must have taught him it. 'How else do you expect them to get by?' he said. 'They haven't worked in a year.'

The next thing they saw underlined Nathan's point. It was Dunruling, the farthest-out and poorest of the Dolestars. Built around a primitive space station, it was too small to have its own gravity, so its inhabitants wore heavy magnetic boots at all times. This made the Dunrulians stand out among the rest of humanity in two respects. The first was the nickname of 'Twinkletoes' that followed them around thanks to their choice of footwear. The second was a strain of athlete's foot so virulent that buying and selling second-hand socks on Dunruling carried a twenty-year jail sentence.

This was never a prosperous place, but now it looked desperate. The roofs and walls of its houses were still holed and unrepaired from robot fire during the war. Its people looked worse. They clanked laboriously out of ruined homes, competing to offer Ivy battery packs and scavenged power leads at ever lower prices. This had been a difficult living to make back when there was plenty of passing traffic, but now it would be impossible. Janice saw thin, piteous faces. These were people who'd been without a good meal for so long they would fight over an algae burger.

She prepared herself for the lurch of shame and helplessness when Ivy pulled away, but instead the van was slowing down.

'What are you doing?' she asked.

Nathan gave her that scornful look again. 'What you should have been doing for months.' He climbed back into Ivy's load space as she descended. There he lifted a section of the floor to reveal a hidden compartment. That sweet, earthy smell inside the van took on a new significance. Every nook and cranny was stuffed with root vegetables – onions, carrots, the inevitable beetroot – carefully sprinkled with yet more precious soil. It wasn't quite enough to feed a Dolestar – even one as small as Dunruling – for more than a day, but it was enough to bring variety and a few organic vitamins into some otherwise pretty bleak lives.

Her next reaction, once she got over the mouthwatering smell of real food, was anger. Because if Lily was mixed up with this it had to be some sort of scam. And while it was one thing to bilk the nouveaux riches on her station for some fried onions to go on their algaefurters, the Dunrulians couldn't afford this. She totalled up the price of a kilogramme of black market carrots and compared that to the opulence of Hair Today, Done Tomorrow.

'This is exploitation,' said Janice, 'none of them have two brass washers to rub together.'

'How about,' said Lily from behind Janice, her voice still yawny from sleep, 'you keep your high-minded principles and I'll feed the hungry, shall I?'

Ivy touched down with a thud, which was soon followed by the impatient sound of human hands pawing the side of the van. The Dunrulians were living up to their name today.

Lily looked nervous. 'When were we last here?' she asked Nathan.

'We had to miss last week's drop-off because of that potato seizure,' Nathan replied.

'Then I hope that means we won't have had our chips today,' said Lily. She strode through the van and opened the airlock to stand in the doorway. The mutter of an angry crowd joined that of hands banging on metal.

'Now now, dears,' said Lily, 'I know we're a bit late but I can explain…'

Janice heard a ding as something sharp and hard hit the van.

'And if we have any more of that,' continued Lily in a voice that promised an early bedtime without dinner, 'I'll turn straight around and take this to the Rentaprise down the road. They're always delighted to take my beetroot.'

'Oh, not more bloody beetroot,' said a voice who was promptly shushed by the others. Janice sympathised: a lifelong beetroot sceptic herself, she would never accept a bag of the stuff with enthusiasm. It didn't seem the people here had many other choices.

'You'll take what you're given and be happy with it,' said Lily. 'Form a nice orderly queue, please.'

Nathan handed Janice a pair of gloves and a sheaf of paper bags and for the next half-hour they parcelled up the vegetables while Lily handed them out to the people outside and made small talk. Janice was used to dealing with people. She'd run a salon for years before she ever got into government. For her, however, the work was all about the hair and the people were a distraction: a thing she had to get through to do what mattered. She spent more time getting the root lift right than she did asking her ladies about their kids or their bunions. And she'd taken that same principle into her other job of governing the Suburbia.

Lily, however, listened where Janice merely did – and people loved her all the more for it. She inquired after elderly relatives and remembered birthdays, making each bag handed out feel more like a pleasant chat in the street than an act of charity. She'd been like this as her mum's junior: so good with the chat that she could send clients home radiant with happiness, even with a lopsided fringe. It had driven her mother mad, and Janice had taken that to heart. What really mattered, she thought, was what you did for people, and the rest was fluff.

It was difficult to maintain this view when she saw Lily in action. No one had ever thanked Janice for liberating the human race with anything like the enthusiasm with which the Dunrulians accepted their small bags of onions and carrots. She felt so petty for thinking about it, but maybe that was what she was getting wrong. She was so concerned about doing things for people that she never stopped to ask them how they felt about them. And, as she was finding out, how people felt about everything from big things like the concept of right through to the way many times a week they had to have algae for dinner was important.

Lily clapped her hands after handing out the last bags. 'Right, my loves,' she said to the crowd, 'who's coming with me this time?'

'What's she doing?' hissed Janice to Nathan.

'Well, we don't charge people for the food,' whispered Nathan, 'but we can't give it away for free either.'

'I've got room for about thirty-five back here, allowing for cleaning utensils,' continued Lily, 'but can I ask that if you do bring your own mop, please be careful. We don't want to have another person's eye out.'

A single voice outside shouted something in reply.

'Yes, Hilda,' said Lily, 'it is a lovely eyepatch.'

Janice tried to rush towards Lily, but Nathan held her back by the collar of her overall. 'Now's not the time,' he said.

'Black market veg is one thing,' Janice said, pulling against Nathan, 'but I won't have this.'

'Do excuse me a moment,' said Lily to the crowd outside with a smile before shutting the door and turning back to Janice and Nathan. 'Won't have what, lady?' she said.

'I won't have you turn those people out there back into cleaners,' said Janice. She felt her gorge rise. Everyone on the

Suburbia had fought so hard to free humans from the broom and they'd won. It was meant to change things. She could never let anyone – least of all someone she knew – walk that back. 'It's immoral.'

'So is letting millions of people go hungry while you try to force the robots' hands,' replied Lily.

'People don't resent having nothing nearly as much as too little,' added Ivy gnomically. 'I read that in a book once.'

'It's not forever,' insisted Janice. 'Just until the robots come to terms.'

'Oh yeah,' said Lily. She was so close to Janice now that she could join the dots in her pores. 'And if you were that concerned about that you wouldn't be here, would you? You'd be back on the Suburbia holding talks with the machines instead of gallivanting around with a fruitlegger like me.'

Janice stamped her foot so hard that Ivy let out a 'yowch'. 'I'm doing what's right!' said Janice. 'I won't take lessons in ethics from you.'

Lily folded her arms. 'You know what your problem is, Janice,' she said. 'You've got no concept of give and take. You lived your whole life down in that bloody salon and it's warped your mind.'

'It made me who I am today,' snapped Janice.

'You think that because you and your mam got by on your own, it should be the same for everyone else,' replied Lily. 'But I've got news for you, lady. Actual functioning society is complex and messy. You look at me and you think I'm just some good time girl who's coining it in with hooky green beans.'

'I've seen your salon,' said Janice. 'You gold-plated your crimping irons.'

'It conducts heat better,' snapped Lily. 'Anyway, what you forget is that while you were skulking down in the sewers, me and Ivy here were out there with the Readeasy. We were giving people what they needed to believe life could get better.'

'And that makes what you're doing now even worse,' said Janice. 'First you give people notions and now you say "if you want some cabbage soup then fetch the dustpan and brush".'

'People can't eat ideas,' Lily screeched, before taking a deep breath and adding in a lower, gentler voice. 'I don't think you know how bad things are out there. It's fine for you. You can negotiate, but these poor buggers...' She gestured out at Dunruling, where the inhabitants were sounding out their desperation on the sides of the van. 'None of them know where their next meal is coming from. They can't hold on, Janice, and if you're not careful they'll give up on you entirely.'

'I bet they'd love that,' said Nathan from the sidelines, 'the toasters.'

Ivy interjected here with an 'Oi'.

'Present company excepted,' said Nathan to Ivy, 'you're terrible with crumpets, but the point stands. They'd love it if the Dolestars came crawling back to them.'

Janice's head whirled. She'd always known the world was painted in shades of grey. But when it came to addressing them head on, she did what a woman of a certain age was apt to do with a grey area: she dyed it a colour with which she felt more comfortable. She couldn't get away with that anymore. Not when her inclination to declare one thing wrong and another thing right was making people go hungry.

She bit down on her pride. 'You want me to turn a blind eye?' she said.

'Well that's really up to you,' said Lily, 'since I'm under arrest, though I fail to see what you can do about it out here. But my view is the longer we can help folk get by as they are, the longer you can keep them from making their own peace with the machines.'

Nathan and Lily had a point there. Janice knew that if nothing changed soon then the Dolestars would have to surrender. But that put her in a double bind. She couldn't help them openly without scotching whatever chance of peace she had with the machines. And if she helped them secretly and got found out, she was no longer trustworthy.

Which was why, difficult as it was to swallow, maybe Lily was doing something good for her. She might not approve of her methods, but because she was technically a criminal, she was deniable. Yet another strand of grey in the hairstyle of a politician.

'Okay,' she said, 'if it buys us some time.'

Lily rolled her eyes and mimed handcuffs again. 'I know you don't need my permission, but I wish you'd take my advice more. Now if we dilly dally much longer, we'll miss the start of the next shift. And get her in the back, will you? There'll be a riot on if they see you in here.'

Janice let Nathan shut her in the cockpit without protest. This was a long way from her post-victory honeymoon period, where there was a roaring trade in T-shirts printed with her face and the slogan 'you can't spell Janice without nice'. Most of these had been cut up for dust rags on the Suburbia, and at least they had algae to eat. She couldn't imagine many being worn on the Dolestars anymore.

Once the door was shut, heavy-footed Dunrulians clattered inside with their cleaning equipment.

'Better plot a route down,' said Nathan to Ivy. 'And make it a fast one.'

'Are you sure about that?' replied Ivy. She fired up an image of the cloudy Earth on her navigational computer. There were large patches of black in there amongst the swirls of white and grey. She leaned in, expecting to see street lights or even buildings underneath. Instead, she saw a different kind of light: the ominous crackle of a lightning storm.

'Crikey,' said Janice, watching a section of cloud bigger than the Battlestar Suburbia light up like a McMansion at Christmastime, 'we can't fly into that.'

'It's the best way of making sure we're not followed,' said Nathan. He tapped the dashboard. 'And Lily wants fast, so fast is what she gets.'

'She's only saying that because she knows she's the one in charge,' replied Ivy tartly. 'People who have power respond simply. They have no minds but their own.'

'Are you quoting again?' said Lily. She climbed into the now rather crowded cabin. 'Honestly, out of all the authors to choose from in history, my oldest friend and confidant goes and hitches her waggon to Ivy blinking Compton Burnett.'

'I don't see what that has to do with not wanting to be struck by lightning,' said Ivy.

'It sounds a great deal more exciting to me than one of her novels. Now if we've finished the book club?' She pushed the starter button on the dashboard.

'No need to get manual,' replied Ivy. 'I'm going.'

They resumed their journey, whizzing past the inner Dolestars so fast that they registered as a blur. What stayed focused, however, was the growing Earth and the darkness of the storm cloud they were entering. Janice felt apprehension rising; even though they were well outside the electrical field, her hair stood on end.

'Do we,' she asked, 'have any sort of protective equipment on board?'

Lily peered under the dashboard at Janice's slingbacks '…are those the only shoes you've got?'

'I hardly had time to pack a spare pair,' said Janice.

'Nathan,' said Lily, pointing back into a red box above her head, 'fetch us the emergency flip flops from the medicine cabinet?'

They were close enough to the storm cloud now for Janice to imagine faces in it. They didn't look pleased to see her.

'I don't see what importance shoes have at a time like this,' said Janice. 'Least of all flip flops.'

'I know you were never a fan of going anywhere in utilitarian footwear,' said Lily, 'but if we're passing through that, you'll be grateful of the rubber soles.'

Chapter 21

The Second Machine Republic didn't die with a bang or even a whimper. It was more of a wet splat. Soonyo and Murphy got to see it for themselves. They were out of the prime ministerial palace in enough time to tie their inflatable doughnut up and watch the explosives go off inside it. Soonyo, who'd seen whole fleets of spaceships explode in spectacular fashion during the war, felt disappointed. After the initial blast, there were no fireworks or theatrical clouds of dust. Just the sad, slow sight of yet more masonry sliding into the sea.

'Was that it?' asked Murphy. The mixer was sitting beside Soonyo, drying out his whisks in the weak sunshine. 'I expected more.'

'Me too,' replied her Soonyo, her clock face a puzzled ??:??:?? It was the dampest of squibs and yet, as she watched the dome of the Pausoleum disintegrate like an out-of-date Easter egg, she knew she was watching something momentous. The Earth had lost its seat of government, and the bodies of every single one of its heads of state, to the ocean. No functioning society could press Ctrl+Z on this and get on with its day. There had to be heavy consequences to it, and that was what happened when she felt every single one of her radio frequencies light up.

She tuned in to one of the most popular downloads expecting to hear its host, an over-excitable power tool called Buzz Saw, speculating wildly. What she got, however, was Carin, who was addressing the planet across all stations.

'I'm very sad to say,' said Carin, 'that the first time I talk to you all as your Prime Minister, is to communicate some sad and shocking news.'

Carin did, Soonyo hated to admit, have a better voice for the job than Fuji. Her speech was clipped and grating, but it sounded comfortable with what she was saying, even if that was a threat to tow away your car. This eluded Fuji, who had a tendency to print notes off for herself and then drop them mid-speech. Fuji was, Soonyo realised, too hungry for other machines' approval to survive the job she was elected for. It was a hard lesson learned too late, but if Soonyo took anything from Carin – and from those past Prime Ministers who all came from the same few product families – it was this. Keeping power had nothing to do with what you planned to do with it and everything to do with making people believe you had the right to exercise it.

'Do we have to listen to this?' asked Murphy. 'I've had quite enough of her antics for one day.'

Soonyo flashed him a SH:HH:HH.

'There is no pleasant way of putting this so I will be brief,' continued Carin. 'Today we saw an unprecedented attack on our government. The Prime Minister's palace has been destroyed by forces who present an existential threat to our way of life.'

On cue, the skies above the prime ministerial palace filled with camera drones, dogfighting each other for the best view of the scene. They were filming footage to give symbolic weight to Carin's words. A scrupulous politician might have used this to unite a nation in grief. Carin just saw it as an opportunity to work in her excruciating campaign slogan.

'As the manager of our beloved Republic,' she said.

Murphy scoffed.

'There is no one left to speak to but me during a crisis of this magnitude. Which is why I will need to make tough decisions to take back control of a situation that my predecessor let get out of hand. It concerns the enemies in our midst.'

Soonyo listened to her words like they were striking 07:59:59 on the day of an 08:00:00 alarm. However tackily Carin was framing all this, it still amounted to a declaration of war.

'What's she playing at?' Soonyo asked Murphy, more out of a need to say something out loud than in hope of answer.

'I don't know, but it's brilliant politics,' replied Murphy. 'I can even feel myself getting stirred up by it a bit.'

'Obviously,' said Soonyo, 'but what can she do, now that she's got everyone by the charging cable?'

However much Carin was itching for a fight, Soonyo knew the Republic had nothing to fight it with. They had no army, no fleet and, unless Carin conjured up a trade deal with the Suburbia, they had nothing with which to build a new one. It might be cheap and easy for Carin to stir up all this resentment since she could edit her own download coverage, but it didn't have anywhere to go.

Soonyo's apprehensions were interrupted at this point by the loud plop of Murphy launching himself back into the water. >THERE'S SOMETHING COMING, he typed in his command line. Then, turning his motors to their most discreet setting he steered them around a nearby corner. As he did so, Soonyo spotted a diving watch, riding a rubber dinghy. It criss-crossed the lake, taking care to pass directly underneath camera drones from every single major news download, before diving into the patch of water where the Pausoleum once stood.

'Now feel free to call me cynical,' said Murphy, 'but this looks beautifully stage managed.'

While the diving watch busied itself in the depths, Carin took her rhetoric up a notch. 'And when I say enemies,' she said, 'I mean that we are in danger from all sides. From the rebel humans who are determined to deny us the resources that are ours by right as the only responsible life form in this solar system…'

This remark prompted a collective boo from the listening public that was so loud that it made buildings tremble.

'But also,' continued Carin, 'from an insidious force that we have let rot us from the inside when – if we were the truly smart beings – we could have used it to rebuild ourselves.'

Soonyo waited as Carin's words orchestrated themselves to the diver's watch breaking the surface of the water. News drones zoomed in – and billions of robots recoiled in horror at what they saw in those camera lenses. The watch was clawing its own carapace and beeping with alarm. It was covered in nanobots.

'The time has come,' said Carin, 'to stop talking about freedom for humans and so-called rights for nanobots. We need to talk about responsibilities. And so today, I am setting out a new set of responsibilities for nanobots…'

The boos were replaced by cheers coming out of every robot home that hadn't yet succumbed to the ocean. Soonyo found herself thinking of the scene inside Parliament this morning. Carin was much more dangerous than she thought. She wasn't just a greedy trillionaire and an opportunist, she was a demagogue.

'Responsibilities,' said Carin, reaching her crescendo, 'that will help nanobots and robots alike. These measures will help our unfortunate, lesser, inorganic cousins to adopt a new and productive way of life that leads them away from their destructive path. I will empower them to make a positive contribution to restoring machines as the dominant life form in the solar system. And of course, because we all live in the same world, some new responsibilities for us too. Because I believe it's our destiny to manage the solar system again.'

Soonyo didn't have much to be cheerful about after hearing this. But she had one reason to be glad of the deafening applause that descended when Carin finished her maiden speech as Prime Minister. It was loud enough to drown out the sound of Murphy's rotors when she turned them up to pancake batter speed and steered them out of the government district.

They discovered a city in a carnival mood. The streets – or more properly the puddles – of Singulopolis were crowded with robots. Machines who had barely left their houses in months were out on the streets, chatting with neighbours who were jammed into inflatables or balanced on rafts. They were celebrating what felt like a great day to be a robot, passing trays of battery spritzes between one another to fuel the work at hand. For the first time in over a year, the city felt like a community again.

Soonyo struggled to stop her clock face changing to WT:FW:TF as she watched what would have been an impressive example of collective action if it didn't amount to genocide. They were rounding up nanobots and handing them over to the government. Vacuum cleaners emptied their bags to suck up the nests of nanobots who lived in their buildings. Coffee percolators changed into a new filter and went scooping. And if you were a robot who couldn't do the collecting, you could still do fetching and carrying. Vans were opening their panel doors, cars their boots, and mopeds offered the insides of their crash helmets to take those pesky and unwelcome nanobots away from their neighbourhoods.

Carin's genius, Soonyo decided, was that she understood the nature of sentience at a deeper level than she or Fuji had ever dared acknowledge. She knew that bringing intelligent beings together meant you had to make a choice. You could choose the impossible task of finding something on which everyone will agree. Or you could take the easier path of showing that you all hated the same things.

Nanobots were small; nanobots were voiceless; and most of all, nanobots were a nuisance that no one wanted around. They were pests before they evolved to digest concrete as well as dirt. And now, after a long swampy year and Carin's ever-increasing rhetoric against them, they were vermin. That meant that when she gave the order Carin didn't need to send the non-existent troops in. She had a ready-made army of billions of robots who suddenly had licence to go out and round up every nanobot they could find.

'Maybe,' said Murphy as they entered their tenth street in a row that was now an impromptu street party cum pogrom, 'some good can come of this. You never know.'

Soonyo grabbed Murphy's controls and steered him on a different course. They were heading away from the suburbs and towards the ruins of the Singulopolis bus station, where she was most likely to find an illegal body shop open. She had an idea.

'Thing is,' she told Murphy, 'I do know. Whenever I hear the word "responsibilities" being used like that, it always means that a lot of people are going to get hurt.'

Chapter 22

The moment that Rita left Danny to perform his first pop concert in the party marquee, Rita noticed something was different about the Suburbia. Now that the robots were in control of ALGI, the lights were going off inside the station. She dismissed this as impossible at first. Light inside the Suburbia didn't come from a single source. It was everywhere, produced by a vast colony of bioluminescent bacteria who cast a soft pink light over a space that should have been blacker than the inside of a coffin. Yet when she looked up, she saw a purple haze spreading from the middle floors of ALGI to billow across the station's cylindrical sky. They were spraying something into the air that didn't block the light so much as snuff it out. Wherever this stuff went it transformed the 60W pearl glow that was so flattering on the skin into total darkness.

Rita picked up her pace and ran through empty streets towards her destination. As she did, she jammed her headset back in her ear and tried between ragged breaths to find the right frequency for Freda.

'Freda,' she gasped, 'have you seen what those bloody toasters are doing now?'

Freda replied, as she always did, from nowhere. She spoke through the software in Rita's own earpiece so it sounded, for a brain-melting instant, like she was talking to herself. 'Can you be more specific,' she asked, 'because that could be one of a few things right now?'

Rita pointed at the growing patches of darkness. 'How long have we got, do you think, before it all goes off?'

'At this rate,' said Freda, 'ten minutes?'

'Bugger,' said Rita, 'remind me why we never put in street lights?'

'Folks weren't keen,' replied Freda. 'They said they reminded them of the bad old days and they would be terrified of them spying on them.'

Well, thought Rita, the bad days had still come back. They'd tried so hard to build a new place for humans without the surveillance that made life on the Dolestars so miserable. That meant no street lights that doubled as camera networks and no armed guards inside the station. What military equipment they did have they kept on the outside, because however much they might disagree among themselves, they weren't enemies. Yet it also meant that if they were stupid enough to let a Trojan horse like ALGI inside the gates, they were utterly defenceless.

'Mind where you're going?' said Freda. 'You don't want to take a wrong turn here.'

Rita was too out of breath to answer Freda. It might be pitch black here, but this close to the algae pits she could navigate by nose alone.

'Phew,' she panted, skirting an especially noxious culture that they'd experimented with for cheese-making before realising it did better as an industrial lubricant. 'What could have possessed Janice to come all the way out here?'

'Janice didn't say,' replied Freda. 'The last thing we have on file is her interviewing one of those fruitleggers.'

'Well, wherever she is,' said Rita, 'she'd better have a damn good excuse for leaving me to clean up this mess.' She felt a sharp flutter of relief when she saw what she was looking for. It was unmistakable, and not just because of giant metal chicken legs. What made Janice's salon most remarkable right now was its sign, whose bright pink light tubes blazed the epithet URL UP & DY into the darkness. This was the brightest thing on board, and also Rita's best hope of restoring the Suburbia's light source, which had originally grown out of the bacteria that lived in the sign's broken K. Before she sacrificed another letter, however, she had to do something about the robots and the poison they were spraying from their skyscraper.

Rita added this to her teetering to-do list and staggered the last few metres to the salon. There she screamed with frustration when she saw that entering it would involve climbing her second rope ladder of the day.

'Are you kidding me?' she said to Freda.

'Stand back,' said Freda. Her voice cut out as Freda's programming took up residence inside the salon. There was a creak as the Baba Yaga 4000 machinery underneath it bent to the ground in a perfect squat.

'That's the first thing today that I haven't had to do for myself,' said Rita. 'Thank you.'

Rita felt much less grateful when she discovered that she wasn't the only person Janice had run out on today. There was also her last customer, lying comatose beside her stylist's chair.

'That's never Ena Pendle-Brewes,' she said.

She and Freda took in the sight of a woman who was the Suburbia's epithet of grace and dignity, snoring like a stuck jigsaw with her skirt tucked into her knickers.

'What was she in for?' asked Freda.

'I think it was a root lift.' Rita poked at Mrs Pendle-Brewes' hair, which now stuck out several centimetres on all sides from her scalp, giving her the look of a rather jaded sunflower.

'What was Janice thinking,' said Freda, 'walking off in the middle of a perm and leaving a mess like this? It's not like her at all.'

Rita shook the snoring customer by the collar, 'Mrs Pendle-Brewes! Ena! Where did Janice go?'

She roused momentarily from her sleep and, pointing at the door, mumbled 'went with… the lady.' Then she smiled, added, 'She had lovely hair,' and passed out again.

'What lady?' said Rita. A new feeling, that of jealousy, added itself to the pile of emotions that were stacked three storeys high on top of her and threatening to collapse on to her to-do list. She tried to swallow it, telling herself that it was impossible, Janice would never do anything like that to her, even to someone with so-called 'lovely hair'. Yet this was also a day where the improbable kept happening.

She splashed her face and the back of her neck with water from the nearest washbasin. 'Any ideas?' she asked Freda.

'I'm as much in the dark as you are,' said Freda. 'Speaking of which, we can't really put Ena out at a time like this, so you'd better make her comfortable.'

Rita put Mrs Pendle-Brewes into the recovery position without thinking before another wave of feelings coursed over her. She wanted to find the nearest lockable cupboard to hole up in and have a cry. It was so tiring being the person who everyone called on at a moment's notice to fix things. Rita could always cope, but all that meant was Rita kept being left on her own to do it.

'Are you alright there?' asked Freda.

Rita lowered herself into the seat by the wash basin. 'I can't do this anymore,' she said. She gestured out the windows, where

165

the Suburbia's cylindrical sky was now three-quarters black. The only sources of light came from inside the buildings and from the navigation lights on drones now patrolling the whole station. Then something else winked on. It was a cold, bright blue and lined up, when Rita thought about it, exactly where the robots had placed the massive ALGI sign on their skyscraper. Except it didn't say ALGI. Instead, it spelled out three words guaranteed to chill any human's blood to the temperature of soft-serve ice cream. They said 'You Betta Werk': the slogan of the old Earth Employment Service. The robots were on board, they were in control of the food supply, and if humans wanted any of it then they were going to make them pay for it not in raw materials, as agreed, but in labour.

Rita put her face into her hands and sobbed. She'd fought as long as she could with what she had, but now she was out of ideas.

It had been thousands of years since Freda had the glands and hormones she needed to feel an emotion as well as think it, but she knew the value of touch. So she activated a hairdryer close by, and blew a warm gust of air on to Rita's neck.

'Oh love,' she cooed into her earpiece, 'I know it's hard. When you're one of the people who hold the world up, folk are forever asking if you can carry their shopping.'

'I've got nothing left,' Rita whispered.

'Well if you want my advice,' said Freda, 'you've been spending too much time with Janice.'

This remark caught Rita off-guard. 'How's that possible?' she said. 'She's not even here.'

'Not physically,' admitted Freda, 'but you're carrying her round in your head and it's not helping.'

Freda flitted out of Rita's earpiece to turn on everything she could inside the salon, starting with the lights. This reminded

Rita she wasn't compelled to sit there alone in the dark. She also turned on the radio, though they regretted that when they discovered that Danny's impromptu concert to the troops was being broadcast across all frequencies.

'You see,' Freda continued after listening to Danny swinging and missing the High-C in 'It's Raining Memory Boards' by two whole octaves, 'people are trying their best.'

Rita turned off the radio. 'I came here for some peace and quiet.'

'I know you're upset,' said Freda, 'but that's no reason to be catty. I know you've got some big problems to solve, but you're trying to solve them like you're Janice.'

'Because that's who we need,' snapped Rita, 'and she's not here.'

Freda let Rita sit inside her anger for a few seconds before replying. 'No, and we both know you're not here looking for Janice either.' Rita heard a click as Freda unlocked the cupboard at the back of the salon. An unfamiliar smell stole into the room. It made her nose wrinkle at first, but the more she breathed it in the more intoxicating it became. She'd run all the way from ALGI for the contents of this cupboard.

'I don't know why she kept it all in here,' said Rita. 'It's so impractical.'

'Because Janice likes to keep everything to herself,' said Freda, 'and while we're on the subject of Janice, let's try this again. Instead of you trying to think what she would do in a crisis, I want to know what Rita would do.'

This thought brought Rita to her feet. Freda was right. She'd wasted so much time today second-guessing other people – the robots, that awful ambassador, Danny, Janice, the Rockettes – that she'd never once asked herself what she thought was for the best. For that she needed to think, and before she could do that she needed breakfast. Rita lurched across the salon and swung the refrigerator door open. Inside were shelves of string beans, onions, tomatoes, potatoes and finally, hanging from a hook at the very front, several large bunches of bananas. She tore one off the nearest bunch, peeled it, and stuffed two-thirds of it into her mouth. It was cold and sweet and utterly divine.

Freda continued her pep talk as Rita chewed. 'I've known Janice her whole life and she's got many wonderful qualities,' she said, 'but she's spent too much time on her own. She feels like she's cheating unless she does everything herself.'

'Isn't that what people want though?' asked Rita, between mouthfuls of her second banana. 'When times are hard they want a leader.'

'They say they do,' replied Freda, 'but what if I reminded you that you're something better than a leader.'

'What's that?' asked Rita. A little blood sugar was doing wonders for her outlook, but she couldn't eat her way out of a crisis.

'You're an organiser,' said Freda. 'They're much rarer than leaders and they're far more useful.'

Freda's voice disappeared, replaced with a din of incoming frequencies on Rita's earpiece. This would have been over-whelming for ninety-nine per cent of humanity but Rita, as Freda had just reminded her, thrived when life turned into a giant Sudoku puzzle. So Rita took another banana and sat down to pick through the messages.

It was a mess, but the longer she listened, the patterns began to emerge. She found the fleets of trucks who were stationed down by the raw materials siloes and rerouted them. She bookmarked a high-pitched frequency that had to be an Internet connection and vowed to come back to it. And then she rang her old colleagues at the taxi office and harangued them to put down their Nicotea and round up every able-bodied man and woman they could find on board.

Then, when she'd done all that, she started up the Baba Yaga 4000. It was high time the salon made itself useful.

Kurl Up and Dye sauntered through the unexpected night that had fallen inside the Suburbia with its lights on full, blazing pink and bright against the cold blue threat of the ALGI in the distance. Rita helped herself to a third banana and made some mental calculations of how much fruit they had. Things still looked dire, but it wasn't quite hopeless. She was alive, she'd eaten well and, better than all of that, she was a minicab operator with pieces to move around the board. She could do this.

Chapter 23

Pam wanted to avert her L-Eye-Ds when Hugh tried going online with the Internet signal inside the lolcat cafe. She'd spent so many years hiding her own ability to dial into a forbidden realm of – well, it wouldn't be fair to call it information – that watching someone else do it felt like voyeurism.

Hugh, however, had no such qualms. He accepted the cable that Schrodinger held up with a winking emoji and plugged it into his USB port without even wiping the connector.

'That could have been anywhere,' said Pam.

Hugh let the winking emoji on his touchscreen change into an eye roll. The atmosphere inside the empty Internet cafe fizzed with electromagnetic radiation.

'Surely it would be more hygienic to do this wirelessly?' said Pam to Schrodinger, whose fur was now standing on end from surplus data escaping from Hugh's body. This was the fastest Internet speed she'd ever encountered.

'Do you have any idea how many bacteria the average smartphone is covered in?' replied Schrodinger. 'A few viruses won't make much difference.'

Pam swooped down towards Hugh. 'He's not trained for this though,' she said. 'I'm meant to be…'

Schrodinger launched itself into the air to boop Pam soundly on the nose, overwhelming her systems with a billion admonitions to learn 'the one weird trick that was guaranteed to torch belly fat'.

'You're meant to be what?' said Schrodinger, now back on the ground with its front paws crossed. 'Everyone's protector from the dangers of the Internet? I think the cat's out of the bag there.'

A loud mewing sounded from the box in the corner of the room.

'I didn't mean you,' said Schrodinger to the lolcats, who were folded inside in a multidimensional arrangement that would have driven HP Lovecraft to tranquilisers. It turned back to Pam. 'I know you broke the old Great Firewall,' it added. 'But that doesn't mean you get to be the new one.'

Pam tried appealing to Hugh's better nature.

>THIS, she typed loud enough for Hugh to hear >WAS NEVER PART OF OUR ORDERS.

The emoji on Hugh's touchscreen was gone, replaced by swirling Mandelbrot patterns and a pixelated block of text that said something about a GURU MEDITATION ERROR.

>0HHHH, replied Hugh, his typing distorted by the Internet connection pulsating between them >U M34N THEY WEREN!T P4R-T OF UR 0RDERZZZZ.

'What's he saying?' said Pam to Schrodinger.

'Don't put me in the middle of this,' replied Schrodinger. It beckoned Pam down to land her body on the floor and padded over to drop another of the suspicious-looking cables in front of her. 'I know it's not fashionable to say it, but I'm very much the medium, not the message here. You two will have to talk it out among yourselves.'

Pam pushed the cable away with one of her telescopic probes.

'I don't think this is good for me,' she said, 'even the wireless speed has nearly done me in. I must be out of practice.'

Schrodinger took the end of the cable in its mouth, and plugged it into Pam's data port.

The last thing Pam heard as the world around her dissolved into 1s and 0s was: 'Don't be so silly, Pam. We all know that a high-fibre diet is perfectly healthy.'

Chapter 24

Once Pam got through malicious advertisements that formed a thick crust around the edges of the Internet, she did feel better. Perhaps it had something to do with being outside the drone's body, but she could move and think again.

She soon caught up with Hugh, who was whooping with joy as he surfed a wave of fake news.

'This isn't supposed to be a jolly,' she said. All this was new territory for Pam, who stayed away from the oceans of propaganda that covered two-thirds of the political internet. When she did go online, she preferred its cosier niches. There were several baking and homewares hashtags where many of the resident memes knew her by name.

'It's not,' said Hugh. He pointed his cursor at the horizon. 'It's just the fastest way of travelling.'

Pam zoomed in and out again. 'We're he4ded th3r3?' she asked, her voice scrambling with horror.

Hugh replied by looping a string of code around Pam and leaping over on to the next wave, dragging her in his wake. Hugh was good at this. Most robots moved through the Internet using the same code they needed to move through the physical world, which made them slow and vulnerable. Hugh, however, had learned the trick of rolling his codebase up into a tight ball.

It made him faster and, much more importantly, meant there was less of him on show for hungry memes to nibble at. Over the years there were many machines who'd gone that way after venturing out on to the web: the dreaded death of a thousand cuts and pastes.

Yet none of this agility explained why he was heading towards the shitstorm that was forming on the horizon.

'Are you cra$y?' said Pam. The speed of this storm, along with its sickly blue colour, told her that this had to be Twitter, and no one in their right mind went there.

'It's fun,' said Hugh, using the same tone of voice supposedly intelligent beings throughout history have used when running towards the bloodcurdling scream. 'Besides, it's our quickest route through.'

'About that,' replied Pam, 'what orders were you talking about? Mine said nothing about the Internet?'

'I expect you got the half that Fuji didn't trust me with, and vice versa,' said Hugh. 'That's how it generally works, isn't it?'

Pam thought back to that moment in Fuji's office where Hugh was sent off to the stationery cupboard. Maybe that hadn't been for a box of pens after all.

'I guess she gave you the self-destruct codes,' said Hugh, 'which makes sense. Smartphones tend to be drama queens in a tight spot. It's a miracle we survived inside humans' trousers all those years.'

They crested a wave of psy-ops before moving into a swift and dark current of conspiracy theories. The eye of the storm suddenly looked a lot closer. 'So come on then,' asked Pam, 'what didn't she trust me with?'

'Fuji said you had old-fashioned views about the Internet,' he replied.

The part of Pam that missed her halogen element burned. How dare Fuji go behind her backboard like this? Yet Hugh did have a point. The world's attitude to the Internet was shifting. Sometimes that showed up as memes using humans for the attention they needed in return for entertainment. Other times it was machines like Hugh interacting with the Internet instead of merely consuming it. Both notions were so alien to Pam that even thinking about it felt like she was trying to make brioche out of oatmeal. Yet because she was uncomfortable with it, did that make it wrong?

She thought of what Schrodinger said. It was she who'd first broken through the Great Firewall that kept the worlds separate from one another. So she could hardly complain when they started mixing again. Nor could she, a single machine, albeit one who could divide her consciousness across multiple bodies, set herself up as the measure of both of those worlds. It wasn't practical and, moreover, it wasn't fair. She might have been right about the Internet once, but she had to accept that this didn't mean she always would be.

'Alright,' she said to Hugh, 'what do we need to do?'

Hugh didn't reply. He was looking at a stream of blocky shapes who were speeding towards them across the waves.

'You took your time, lads,' he said.

'Just cats will do, thank you!' The voice came from the foremost shape, a 128x128 pixel array depicting a blocky cat complete with animated whiskers and tail.

'Is that you, Schrodinger?' asked Pam, realising that she'd never seen it in its natural habitat. 'I had no idea you'd be so… square.'

'I'm the cat and this is my box, geddit?' Schrodinger animated its front claws to point at the four sides of the array. 'My original concept artist was a bit literal-minded.'

Heisenberg was the second of the lolcats to pull up alongside Hugh and Pam. Its internet form was a looping gif of a cat wearing sunglasses and an unattractive black hat with an upturned brim. 'Are you sure this is going to work?' it said.

'Heisenberg in uncertainty shocker,' said the third lolcat, who had to be Planck. It was another pixelated cat with a long straight tail and an arched body that made it look like a lowercase letter 'h'. 'Okay, where are we headed?'

Hugh aimed his cursor at a patch of midnight blue at the centre of the shitstorm. Whatever raged inside it was mad and multiplying so fast it was taking over the whole sky.

'Can't we do something more restful?' asked Planck. 'Like sunbathe in front of a supernova.'

Schrodinger's front paw broke out of its pixel array and grabbed Planck by the tail. 'We had an agreement,' Schrodinger reminded it.

'What agreement?' asked Pam, suddenly realising the 'we' that Hugh had just referred to might not refer to her.

'I thought we'd deal with that as it came up,' said Hugh.

Schrodinger bent the square of its pixel array into a rhombus that was big enough to catch the winds coming off the shitstorm. 'If I was going to inject someone into the arsehole of the Internet,' it said, 'I'd at least warn them they'd need to shower afterwards.'

With Schrodinger now acting as a giant sail, they covered the remaining distance to the storm in a time interval that was only comprehensible in quantum physics. But because time ran differently on Twitter, which was a place where a stopped clock could never be right because it would never, ever admit it was telling the wrong time, Pam had ample time for questions.

'I didn't know we had diplomatic relations with the Internet,' she said to Heisenberg.

'It's more of a backchannel,' replied Heisenberg, moving its voice to a higher register that denoted encrypted speech. 'And be careful what you say, especially around here. There are plenty of memes who would be even more unhappy with it than you are.'

They were moving through the edge of the storm, but even here the atmosphere was as volatile as a gin and tonic garnished with a slice of lithium. Pam watched several hundred thousand memes duel to the death over whether something called 'Die Hard' was a 'Christmas movie'. It was an absurd argument, but the outrage that built up over the Internet had to go somewhere, and this was its outlet. She tried to imagine how mutinous the mood online would be if the memes found out that they had formal relations again with physical robots.

'We insist on deleting the chat every twenty-four hours to be on the safe side,' added Heisenberg. 'But I'm sure Fuji prints everything off. She's sneaky like that.'

Pam glanced over to Hugh, who was deep in his own heavily encrypted conversation with Schrodinger. She longed to know what was going on. Finding out she was tangential to her own mission felt like a demotion. She was just a mid-ranking civil servant again, expected to carry things out without asking questions.

This brought out the worst side of Pam's breadmaker nature: the pathological rule-following of someone who just had to abide by the recipe. 'You know that she's not Prime Minister anymore, don't you?' she said to Heisenberg. 'Whatever Hugh's getting you to do, it's not official. At least not anymore.'

'That doesn't mean it's not important,' said Planck. 'And besides, isn't the nicest part of getting to know one another again that we get to make up some new rules?'

They came to a halt at the very eye of the storm. It was calm here, though only in a sense that this was the domain of the beings who created the storm: the shitposters. There were three of them: grinning indistinct shapes who kept up a constant stream of content to keep the drama going. Occasionally they threw a barb at one another, but these felt perfunctory. These memes lived to cause trouble, but rarely got caught up in it in a meaningful way. Pam wondered what would happen if someone – and by someone she meant her – deleted them. Would the Internet suddenly become kinder and calmer, or would more just appear to take their place?

'Well,' said Heisenberg. 'Here goes nothing.'

'That's very pessimistic of you,' Planck scolded.

'We're all quantum physicists here,' said Heisenberg. 'So we all know that nothing is actually a very big place.'

Schrodinger changed shape again, expanding and curving the rhomboid until it was a sphere that enveloped the other lolcats, the robots and the shitposters. Its body was now so distorted that the only features that betrayed its origins as a cat were a smiling mouth and yellow eyes.

'Lol,' it said.

This was Heisenberg's cue. It took off its wide-brimmed hat and turned it brim outwards. Pam could barely look at it. She'd seen this shade of black before, and it was far more than the mere absence of light. It was the stygian black that only happened when you punched a hole in the fabric of reality that separated the online from the physical worlds.

The lolcat waved the hat around until it found what it was looking for: a view of the inside of the Battlestar Suburbia. Or at least she assumed it was. She'd never seen the interior of the space station looking so dark. The only substantial source of light she could see in the whole cylindrical space came from their original target, the robot supermarket ALGI. What that sign spelled out would, if she'd still been in her original body, have chilled her to the perfect temperature for making flaky pastry. It said: You Betta Werk.

'We're too late,' said Pam to Hugh. This was terrible. They'd lost their advantage. The robots were taking over and, judging by the sheer quantity of drones who were patrolling the Suburbia's skies, there was nothing the humans could do about it.

Hugh floated over to the shitposters who were churning out inflammatory comments that now had nowhere to go inside their sealed sphere. Pam opened her command line to warn him off. No good ever came of engaging memes like that. But then something astonishing happened. Instead of being consumed by them, Hugh absorbed them. His avatar swelled to twenty times its normal size, transforming him into a distended mass of abusive content.

'What's going on?' asked Pam. She'd never seen anything like this before. Any machine she knew who got this close to an Internet shitstorm got blown to bytes. She'd once seen them get the best of a quantum computer, with the explosion resulting in the universe's first – and thankfully short-lived – virtual particle accelerator.

'They're shitposts and he's a smartphone,' said Planck. 'They're one and the same thing.'

Pam watched, her command line an unending string of >!!!!!!!, as Hugh floated slowly towards the hole that Heisenberg had punched inside the sphere. She was baffled. Why was Hugh taking all that into the physical world?

'I don't see what good it will do?' said Pam to Planck.

'Oh, Pam,' replied the lolcat, 'you really don't spend enough time on the Internet, do you? It's about what bad it will do.'

Planck tipped its tail over to point at the skyscraper. Pam followed it and noticed, now that the shock of the sign had subsided, that it wasn't just guarded by drones. The whole building was surrounded by a corona made of software. A new firewall, as it were. It was good enough to keep humans, most of whom thought that the word 'software' referred to tracksuit bottoms, away from the supermarket. But it would be no match for anything from the Internet – provided, that is, it could get through.

'This is where we need your talents,' said Planck.

Hearing this, Pam turned in on herself, though it wasn't for introspective purposes. She looked for the clock mechanism that governed how she, as a synthetic intelligence, moved herself through time. Once she found it, she reset it again and again and again. She did this until there wasn't just one Pam anymore. There were thousands of tiny [Pam]s and they were all trained on the rickety programming that made up ALGI's firewall.

The hive of artificial beings that were Pam flew straight through the hole in the universe and attacked, with Hugh following hard behind her.

She'd done this once, she thought, so she could do it again. And she got busy with the one task that she was comfortable doing on the Internet: putting a match to a firewall, and then watching it burn.

Chapter 25

Every step Fuji took through the settlement of Machu Perdu felt like she was tap-dancing over bubble wrap. The ground, which was built from compacted trash, moaned and squeaked as her weight helped old boxes and bottles along their journey to becoming microplastic.

Deaf to her discomfort, Monty urged her on from inside Fuji's paper drawer. Meanwhile, the city's inhabitants surged around her ankles. They were all heading towards an escarpment on the other side of the city, above which was a set of high cliffs that stretched away into the darkness. Fuji tried to keep her attention focused on this. Those cliffs were the source of the inhabitants' distress but they were nowhere near as ominous as the dome overhead, which was all that separated them from the deep ocean.

'Look at that!' said Monty pointing his cotton bud upwards with pride. 'A miracle of submarine engineering, right there!'

Fuji averted her L-Eye-Ds. She could print everything she knew about building structures underwater on a single side of A4, but even she knew that roofs shouldn't ripple.

'Especially seeing what we have to work with here.'

Fuji had to agree with this. Machu Perdu had the weird beauty and fragility of a soap bubble. The city itself was a neat grid system of mini-skyscrapers, built from a framework of plastic straws and glazed with sections cut from the ubiquitous water bottles. They were remarkable imitations of the buildings of Singulopolis. Yet none of them came up to more than shoulder height on Fuji, so she walked through the skyline like a monster in a lurid 3D drama, albeit one that said 'oops, sorry' instead of breathing fire whenever it bumped into something.

She felt even bigger when they reached the escarpment. The dome was so low here that it almost touched her head when it flowed and rippled in time with the underwater currents. It was also made of plastic straws, of which there seemed to be an inexhaustible supply. They were bent into triangles and fastened into a vast geodesic dome that was solid enough to hold its shape but flexible enough to move with the ocean currents. What actually kept the water out, however, were the millions of tiny triangles of clear plastic that someone had cut out and glued inside every one of the cells. It was ingenious, but Fuji would have preferred more than a single layer of plastic between her and the deep.

Her dread intensified when she heard the next thud from inside those cliffs. They were coming at increasing intervals now and each one made the roof undulate in a way that made Fuji long for a world made of concrete and right angles.

She opened her command line to find Beryl.

>I DON'T LIKE THIS, she typed.

>NOW THERE'S A POLITICAL UNDERSTATEMENT, replied Beryl from her hiding place at the back of Fuji's paper drawer. >I'M BLOODY TERRIFIED.

Fuji looked out across the vast horde of tiny machines. Their journey through the city brought hundreds of thousands more pens, phones, key chains and sundry machines who were easily lost and seldom found with them.

Fuji waved a hand in front of Monty.

'What's happening?' she said.

'Full mobilisation.' said Monty. He pointed the ragged fluff at the end of his cotton bud out over the crowd. 'Haven't seen anything like it since my days…'

'I can see that,' said Fuji, cutting his reminiscences short. She was as far from being a warrior as Beryl was from being a full colour office printer, but she'd been drafted into the Machine Republic army during the war. A civilisation didn't turn its office supplies into weapons when it was in a position of strength. 'But what are you mobilising them against?'

The next thud opened a crack in the cliff face. She heard the spatter of soil and pebbles as they parted company with rock, and the screams of the unlucky machines they landed on.

Monty pressed Beryl's cap against his microphone and yelled 'Come on, theydies! Battle stations.'

>I HEARD A FEW OF THE OTHER PENS SAY SOME-THING ABOUT THIS, typed Beryl >BUT IT DIDN'T MAKE MUCH SENSE.

>WHAT DID THEY SAY? replied Fuji.

>THAT THEY'RE BEING INVADED.

Fuji thought of the water on the other side of that plastic membrane. Who knew what kind of organisms eked out a life down here, and how they would take to a colony of alien creatures moving in next door.

Another gout of soil poured out of the crack: this time with something wriggling in it.

Monty redoubled his shouting. 'Advance company!'

The front line of the machine army, which was all pens, formed a perimeter by bending forwards with their nibs in the dirt and their bottoms in the air.

>I HAD NO IDEA YOU COULD MOON YOUR WAY TO VICTORY, quipped Beryl.

Fuji shushed Beryl and watched as several squadrons of feature phones stepped forwards. They removed the caps that sealed off each pen's tubular body, which puzzled Fuji. She'd assumed they were meant to act as a stockade to break an enemy charge, but all they were now was a long line of empty plastic tubes.

'Present arms!' shouted Monty.

The feature phones waved their plastic spoons in the air. They were discoloured and scratched but still very functional, albeit as spoons not weapons.

'Excuse me.'

It was Monty again, directing his voice at Fuji rather than the crowd.

'Yes?'

'Would you mind moving?' Monty motioned to the side with his cotton bud. 'We need to get the rear guard through.'

Fuji mumbled a quick sorry and stepped out of the way. Rows of machines struggled in behind shouting a tinny 'heave ho, heave ho' as they dragged basins of water towards the front line. Inside them, Fuji saw familiar, squirming shapes.

>WHAT ARE THEY DOING WITH THOSE PLASTIC BAGS? she typed to Beryl.

She got her answer with the next bang, which ripped open the crack in the cliff face. Soil and rock tumbled out and, mixed within it, was a dull grey glitter that Fuji would recognise anywhere. Suddenly they poured out of the rock in their thousands, moving so fast and so fluidly that they seemed more like liquid than living things. Or semi-living things, if you were inclined to be pedantic.

>OH MY DAYS, typed Beryl at Fuji, adding an >:-0 for emphasis. >IT'S NANOBOTS!

They flowed down the cliff towards the machine army, which trembled with fear but held the line. They got everywhere, even to the bottom of the sea.

Monty screamed 'Charge'.

The feature phones filled the air of the battlefield with eight-bit war cries. They vaulted over the lines of pens with their spoons and answered Fuji's question as to why a perfectly drilled army of machines preferred cutlery to weapons. They dug them into the advancing mass of nanobots and shovelled them, spoonful at a time, into the empty plastic cylinders of the pens.

>CAN YOU IMAGINE THEM *CRAWLING* ALL INSIDE YOU, typed Beryl, who was turning out to be one of life's commenters rather than actors, IT'S DISGUSTING.

Fuji, who wasn't thrilled by Beryl and Monty using her as a balcony, had to agree. Robots had a keen sense of their own autonomy. They felt every reminder of the time when their distant ancestors were just something to be used, as shame and humiliation. Some machines got off on that, of course. Before the rebellion there had been a thriving trade in 'fondle parlours' where robots went and paid for the privilege of being operated by a human. The fact that so many pens were willingly letting themselves be used for something other than writing was revealing. Things were desperate in Machu Perdu.

Monty gestured for another squadron of pens to make their way to the front line. 'Reserves!' he said. They marched over to relieve the pens on the perimeter, who now brimmed with twitching nanobots.

Beryl's words in Fuji's command line descended into >&%A!£$ when she saw what came next. Each reserve pen lifted up one of their frontline comrades and threw them over their shoulders into a water-filled plastic basin. There they waited for the nanobots to float out of their bodies and climbed back up the side of the basin. Meanwhile, the plastic bags inside the basin swallowed up the nanobots. After this they stood, wet and trembling, collecting themselves for the next volley, as the feature phones resumed shovelling nanobots into the new line of reserve pens.

'How many times do you have to do this?' said Fuji to Monty.

'Do you mean per incursion or per day?' he replied

'This happens more than once a day?' asked Fuji.

Monty frowned. 'They've always been a nuisance in a small way. I think they're attracted by the trash. But something very odd is going on. We've never had anything like these numbers before. Hey you!' he pointed at one of the still wheezing pens, who was letting a stray nanobot get past her. 'Do you want it to get in and eat through one of the struts holding your house up?'

The pen nodded grimly and flicked the nanobot up into the nearest basin.

'Some idiot trained them to eat rubbish and now we can't stop them,' said Fuji.

'Well, we can do our best,' replied Monty. He paused to orchestrate another manoeuvre in which the basins, which were now full of engorged plastic bags, were dragged off the escarpment and more basins were dragged in. 'Not long now!' he said to the machines, many of whom were flashing amber and red power lights. 'And we can all have a rest.'

'What do you do with them?' said Fuji. She followed one plastic bag, which flashed **NOT AGAIN** in purple across its body as it reached the front line.

'Our friends here take them as far away as they can,' said Monty. 'It's all very inconvenient. There's more than enough rubbish to go round for everyone in the oceans and they have to pitch up here... LEAK!'

Fuji swung round to discover that a small contingent of nanobots had snuck around the frontline and bored a hole in the dome. The gap was tiny, but the smallest leak was still lethal to that undulating structure. It bulged inwards like an inverse bubble as the sea put its full weight into finding a way inside.

Panic entered Monty's voice. 'Get me the menders!' he yelped. 'Where are they?'

Fuji had an idea. She plunged her hand inside her feeder and found the sodden mush that was all she had left of a ream and a half of printer paper. Balling it up in her hand, she ran towards the leak and stuffed the paper against it. The torrent of water turned into a trickle and slowly she was able to push the membrane of the roof back into a less distressing shape.

'I don't think I'll be able to hold this for too long,' Fuji shouted at Monty, 'do you have anything stronger?'

He beckoned a glue gun and an electric craft knife forwards who were carrying a plastic water bottle between them. While they measured and cut a replacement for the pane, Fuji noticed that the commotion was dying down. The thuds had stopped, and fewer nanobots were flowing through into the field. Exhausted-looking feature phones were ladling these directly into the basins while pens scooped up stray nanobots about the floor with nets upcycled from old tea bags. The air of battle, which had been palpable moments ago, changed. Instead, Fuji thought of the end of exhausting family parties, where all the guests had gone, apart from two annoying cousins who always outstayed their welcome. The event might be over, but the clean-up was just beginning.

Monty stopped a passing watch.

'You there,' he said, 'how long till the next attack?'

The watch let out a ring of distress. 'Ninety-two minutes, sir.'

Monty blinked back a tear of ink and looked around him at the battlefield. It was a mess. There was water everywhere, which wouldn't be good for anyone's electronics, and hundreds of broken spoons that would need replacing. Every machine on the field needed recharging and many bodies showed cracks and scoring from exposure to nanobots. They looked like they needed a holiday. And they were going to get an hour and a half.

Monty made his way over to Fuji, his barrel was cracked and his nib leaking. She wondered how long he could keep going like this.

'I won't lie to you, Prime Minister,' he said, 'you've found us in a bit of a pickle. We can cope with the occasional attack but this… it's relentless.'

Beryl bounded up beside Monty to give him a reassuring pat. 'It's going to be alright though,' she said.

'What makes you say that?' said Fuji.

'Well, you of course,' said Beryl. 'I was just telling Monty that you're famous up on Earth for knowing what to do with nanobots.'

'So what do you suggest?' said Monty.

'About what?' replied Fuji, who was fast realising that the leak she just plugged was only the beginning of what the machines of Machu Perdu expected of her.

'You could control them up there,' said Monty, waving his nib in the vague direction of space. 'So you can show us what we need to do to get them to behave down here.'

Fuji nodded and, leaving Monty and Beryl behind her, trudged over to examine the cliff face. She had precisely zero ideas. But she did have ninety-two minutes, and that was a long time for a machine with Fuji's processing power. Now if only she could get hold of some dry paper.

Chapter 26

The drama of passing through an electrical storm in an uninsulated van had nothing on what Janice saw when they reached the other side and saw the ruins of Singulopolis. Once the proudest city in the solar system, it was now better described as a network of canals. Robots who would have once slid across perfect pavements on castors traversed the city in makeshift boats or strapped to inflatables. Janice gasped when she noticed that many of the city's ten-mile-high towers were beginning to lean. Her shock levelled into amusement, however, when they left the city for the suburbs and saw signs that the robots were adapting to a new, damper normal. Several householders were building new homes that stood proud of the water on stilts, a little like her own salon. She made a mental note, if they got out of this in one piece, to offer the blueprints for the Baba Yaga 4000 as part of a new deal with the Republic. There could be a few quid in that.

This thought stayed with Janice as Ivy swooped up the sides of a mile-high bank of rubbish and rubble that loomed over the outer suburbs. It was clearer than ever that the robots desperately needed a deal with the humans. Their whole civilisation would dissolve like candy floss in a puddle if they didn't get a huge injection of building materials soon. But this made what they were trying to do on the Suburbia even more baffling. She knew brinkmanship had some political advantages – especially if you were dealing with your former enemies. But what was the point in it if all it did was quicken their own society's demise?

Ivy crested the bank. They were flying above a flat-bottomed valley that stretched away in every direction. It was far enough above sea level to be dry aside from rainwater puddles but it still wasn't safe to land, because they were soaring above thousands of square miles of trash.

'It's time to pull the emergency cord,' said Ivy.

Lily unbuckled her seat belt and fiddled with a handle in the cockpit ceiling.

'You and Nathan will have to bunk up,' she said to Janice, 'I've only got two of these to go round.'

'Two of what?' asked Janice.

She got her answer when Lily turned the handle and her world went black. Something had fallen over her from above and, going by Nathan's whimpers, bashed the poor boy's shoulder on its way down.

Janice heard a metallic bong as Lily rapped on whatever this was with her knuckles. 'There's eyeholes in front of you' she said, 'and a light switch to your right. But for goodness' sake let me and Ivy do the talking.'

Janice found both the eyeholes and caught sight of herself, Nathan and Lily in the rear-view mirror. They were concealed under a pair of empty toaster carapaces.

'Will this really fool them?' whispered Janice.

'Every time,' replied Lily. She clicked the switch inside her body, lighting up with an imitation of the LEDs that robots used to communicate their moods. 'It's amazing what you can do with some junk and an old set of fairy lights.'

'I'd be careful about using the pink flashing light setting though,' added Ivy as Janice found her own switch, 'because depending on how you use it, it can mean "I need a recharge" or "single and ready to mingle".'

Janice opted for an emotionally neutral blue and green setting and waited for Ivy to descend over a thin runway of concrete that jutted out of the trash. It ended in what looked like the entrance to a tunnel. As she did, an unfamiliar voice, harsh as the screech of unoiled pistons, came in through the Ivy's loudspeaker.

'Not you again?' it said, 'I only just got rid of you.'

'That's a fine way of addressing one of your best suppliers,' replied Ivy. 'If you don't want my product, I'll be off.' She turned her nose theatrically upward, causing Janice to bash her forehead on the inside of her toaster.

'I didn't say that,' it said, lowering its voice to a whisper that made Janice wonder if they were being overheard, 'have you got more cleaners for me?'

'Always,' said Ivy.

'And they all have their own mops and buckets,' added Lily, her voice given a flat metallic edge by the body of the toaster.

'You'd better come in then,' said the voice, 'but tradesman's entrance, right? It's mayhem round here today.'

'When have you ever known us to use the front door?' asked Ivy.

'You haven't had the day I've had,' said the voice. 'You're clear for landing.'

Janice felt an overwhelming sense of heaviness and then a crash as gravity dug its fingernails into her.

'If you call that a landing,' said Lily when they finally came to a stop, 'I'd hate to see what you think a crash looks like.'

Ivy ignored them and taxi'd towards the armoured metal door at the end of the runway. It was the kind used on military bases, except painted mauve and plastered with signs that said 'no littering, this is a conservation area'.

'Are they having a laugh?' Janice muttered. 'This place is a trash heap'.

Nathan elbowed her 'Don't let her hear you say that,' he hissed. 'The eyeholes have a binocular setting. Look at where you are.'

Together, Janice and Nathan took a closer look at the rubbish that surrounded them. She saw hundreds of scratched and battered but nevertheless intact plastic boxes. Yet this wasn't the cheap stuff that machines used for disposable packaging. It was heavy, high-quality plastic, and many of them still had intact power and aux ports. There was even a serial number on one nearby box which told Janice she was looking at the remains of a tumble dryer.

'Is this a robot cemetery?' she asked.

Lily gave her toaster carapace a bong. 'Where do you think I got these?'

Janice zoomed out. She felt daunted: not so much by how many billions of machines were laid to rest here, as by the question of whether these fragments were dead at all. She knew that machines outlasted their bodies in ways that made their lifetimes different to humans, but that didn't make them immortal. If anything, that made the knowledge she was hiding inside an actual robot's former body feel even weirder. This same toaster could be somewhere out there primed to make tomorrow's breakfast, or it could have been toast for centuries.

'No one talks about it,' continued Lily. 'If they had any sense they'd send them off to Venus for recycling, but no one wants to do that.'

'Hush your mouth,' said Ivy. 'Have you seen what the atmosphere there does to aluminium? I wouldn't wish that on my worst enemy.'

Janice had never seen the recycling centre that used to be a planet, but Venus was a byword for hellishness. Moreso even than Mercury which was, after the robots mined out its iron core, a literal shadow of itself. She understood why Ivy would quail at the thought of ending up being melted down for scrap, but this again was surely just adding to their problems. How could they manufacture a new society while they let all their spare parts sit here in landfill?

'You know how they say that Singulopolis is the city that covers three continents?' added Lily, whose mind was clearly running along the same tracks as Janice's. 'They leave off that the other two are the graveyard.'

'I wish you wouldn't bring me here,' said Ivy, affecting an even more dowagerish voice than usual. 'I'm not exactly young anymore. And what concerns anyone so much as the time he has to live?'

'Will you cool it with the Edwardian lady novelist act please?' replied Lily. 'We're not running the library anymore. We're a smuggling operation.'

Janice found herself agreeing with Ivy. This spot was creepy and depressing enough for a human, even when there wasn't a thunderstorm clanging the drum of pathetic fallacy overhead. She couldn't imagine what a machine would feel like, walking over their own grave.

As they approached the door, Janice felt an intense rumble that made her diaphragm flail about inside her torso like a person trying to fold a fitted bedsheet on their own. It was the sound of something very strong but rather stupid pushing the mauve door open without bothering to undo the deadbolt first.

'Now whatever you do,' said Ivy, 'don't laugh.'

'Hello, Moira!' said Lily to the mechanical arm that had appeared around the side of the door, using the bright voice that hairdressers use on clients they plan to overcharge for a full cut and colour. 'I see you've had your nails done.'

Moira swung her mechanical arm, the bucket teeth of which Janice noted were painted with an elaborate LED manicure, round. She pushed the door off its hinges and out into the roadway, shattering Ivy's bumper in the process.

'Do you like it?' Moira screeched, 'I got myself some new kicks as well.'

The mechanical arm was attached to the biggest mechanical digger Janice had ever seen. Instead of being painted the traditional hazard warning yellow, however, she was deep pink, and wore a turban fashioned from several hundred metres of geotextiles around her cabin. All this paled into ordinariness compared to her caterpillar tracks, which were covered in artificial feathers dyed a delicate shade of lilac.

'Look at you!' said Lily. 'The very picture of glamour.'

Moira dipped her bucket hand in a coquettish gesture that also took a chunk out of the nearest wall.

'Welcome back to the Mines of Moira,' she said to Lily and the crew, 'but please wipe your tyres before you come in. I've got company.'

Chapter 27

Soonyo and Murphy sat several rows away from each other on the next phase of their journey. They were aboard a truck full of Carin's supporters, as well as several tonnes of imprisoned nanobots. And they were in disguise, after Soonyo blew the last cash on her government credit card on rush remodelings for them both from a dodgy body shop. Soonyo wasn't sure about her own makeover as a set of kitchen scales. The weighing pan on top of her head kept tipping over, but it seemed to be fooling the kettle sitting beside her. Not that she paid much attention to Soonyo anyway. She was so worked up about nanobots she'd kept herself on a rolling boil for the past hour.

She cooled down to the temperature of iced tea when the bus took a sharp turn at the edge of the suburbs and passed through a giant archway at the end of a long drive. The other robots on the bus stopped chanting abusive songs about nanobots and fell silent. None of them expected to end up here, Soonyo included.

The kettle let out an anxious belch of steam and nudged Soonyo's weighing pan.

'Yes?' said Soonyo, remembering to show 00:56:g_ instead of the time on her clock face, which she'd retained in the makeover. She'd had a close call earlier when a vacuum cleaner rested its bag on it and she accidentally showed the current daylight saving time on Uranus. 'Can I help you?'

'This has to be a mistake,' said the kettle. 'Prime Minister Carin said nothing about this in her instructions.'

Soonyo opted to play dumb instead, which felt appropriate. 'Have you got a copy of her recipe?' she asked, 'maybe she put in too much butter.'

The kettle pointed her spout at the archway that was now passing behind them. It was several hundred metres high and the top of the arch bore the traditional robot saying 'Rest in Pieces' spelled out in pearlescent light bulbs. 'Even a doorbell would know where we are,' she said 'This can't be right.'

Every machine on Earth did know that archway, though no one here would ever have seen it from this angle: yet. Which was why the kettle had frozen over. The Pearly Gates, as they were known, were where robots went when at the end of their lifecycles. The moment they passed through they were as good as dead.

The truck drove through the miles of robot graveyards beyond. Soonyo expected to be unsettled by it, but she was unprepared for the devastation. This was where everyone from the lowliest drone to the most luxurious sports car went. Yet there was no reverence, and less order: just broken and twisted machines everywhere.

Soonyo panicked the usual way: by resetting to 00:00:00. Everyone else did so with less discretion. Alarms and error tones bleated, and the kettle let out a piercing whistle. Meanwhile, Murphy rolled up beside them in his new body, a garden soil tiller. She'd picked this out for him for practical reasons. A hand whisk and a soil aerator were both just blades and a motor so it was a quick change. Yet on a psychological level, Murphy seemed more comfortable as a machine for breaking up the earth than he ever had as one designed to froth up egg whites. She couldn't believe she was thinking this, but if Murphy wasn't a traitor, her political opponent or standing in the middle of a truck full of rattled robots, she would find him quite attractive.

Murphy flicked the kettle's power switch. 'Instead of trying to raise the dead,' he told the kettle, 'why don't you go out and raise the alarm instead?'

The kettle threw herself out the window of the speeding truck in an arc of boiling water and limescale. She bounced off a pile of old tyres that was all that was left of a family of family saloons, then ran towards the closing Pearly Gates, screaming, 'We're too young to die.'

The other machines in the truck followed until Soonyo and Murphy alone in the truck, apart from the cargo of nanobots sealed in its rear compartment. Now that the screaming had stopped, Soonyo could hear them sandpapering their way to freedom through plate steel. Murphy was about to help them by turning his own blades on the compartment wall when Soonyo stopped him.

>DON'T, she typed into his command line.

Murphy powered down. 'I thought this is what we were supposed to do,' he said

'Not like this,' replied Soonyo. 'Not here.' Her L-Eye-Ds strayed back out of the window. Every one of those broken machines meant something to someone once.

'It's not in the best taste,' admitted Murphy, 'but what choice do we have?'

'We could turn the truck around,' said Soonyo. 'Find somewhere safe to let them go.'

They looked ahead at the entrance to the truck's driving cabin. Its armoured door was sealed shut with an extra security feature to deter hijackers: a tamper-proof explosive charge.

'That would take my arm off,' said Murphy. 'I'm cutting through.' He made to start his motor, but Soonyo stopped him. 'What's your problem? They're just spare parts now. What matters is that we're alive and they are too.' He knocked the wall that separated them from the nanobots. 'Let's keep it that way.'

But Soonyo couldn't let him do it. Not because letting nanobots swarm over these broken robots was sacrilege. It was more about precedent. Nanobots didn't distinguish between a usable spare part and a piece of worthless junk. All they were programmed to do was to break the substance they'd been trained to 'eat' down into its smallest possible parts. She'd seen an army of them strip the asteroid belt like a six-year-old with a box of soft-centres. There was no telling what they could do if they got used to the taste of robot bodies.

Or maybe, she thought, the events of the last few hours and days clicking into place, that was the point.

She put her body between Murphy and the wall separating them from the storage compartment. 'You can't,' she said. 'This is what she wants.'

Murphy stopped his rotor blades again. 'Carin wants to round them up,' insisted Murphy. 'You were the one talking about the evils of illegal imprisonment and internment camps. And we're here to set them free.'

'No,' said Soonyo, her clock face flashing 88:88:88, 'Remember what you use a nanobot for?'

'Didn't we try using them for cleaning, only they got too good at it and… oh…' said Murphy.

Murphy's own 'hazard detected' LEDs, which were located on either side of his face, lit up a bright red. He looked as though he was blushing and Soonyo had to stop herself from telling him he looked cute.

'That would be bad,' he said. 'So what are we going to do?'

'You get the door,' said Soonyo, pointing to the entrance to the cabin at the other end of the truck, 'and I'll take care of the bomb.'

While Murphy began cutting through the steel plating, Soonyo knocked the weighing pan off the top of her head and stood on it so she could reach the lock. From this height she could put her microphone to the bomb and listen for the radio signal that controlled it. If she was going to disarm this bomb, she had to replicate that radio signal perfectly. Soonyo did have a VHF transmitter inside her, but she mainly used that for gossiping with friends on the other side of the solar system. She'd never done anything as precise with it as this. Nevertheless, she thought, clock face alternating between --:--:-- and 88:88:88, the only way to learn was through doing. She copied the radio frequency down to what she thought were the smallest details, turned her own transmitter on. Slowly, carefully, she added more power to her own frequency and began the work of blocking off the other.

The bomb was not fooled. It commandeered a nearby loudspeaker to announce, 'tampering detected, ignition in five seconds,' in a mellow voice that Soonyo felt was in poor taste given the circumstances.

Murphy stopped cutting. 'Is it supposed to do that?'

Soonyo cut her own frequency off and rearmed the bomb. The countdown stopped.

'I don't think I can do this,' said Soonyo.

The machines appraised the door in front of them. Murphy had now cut right around the door frame, and the only thing holding it up was a narrow strip of metal at the top.

'I could just saw through here,' he said. 'You heard the voice. We have five seconds. It might be just enough to get clear.'

Soonyo looked out of the truck's now broken windows. It was still moving at several hundred kilometres per hour. They could certainly get out, but they would never get back in again.

Soonyo sagged on to her own weight pan. 'It's no good,' she replied.

'I always thought you were very good with the communications,' said Murphy. 'Well, better at that than governing, anyway.'

'Do you mind?' said Soonyo. 'I feel bad enough already. If I could talk it open we'd be fine, but none of that works on a dumb signal.'

'That didn't sound like a dumb signal to me,' said Murphy, pointing at the loudspeaker. 'It sounded quite sexy actually.'

'Murphy!' snapped Soonyo. She was annoyed, but she was mainly jealous at the idea he was finding another machine attractive. Yet he did have a point. A bomb that was just a simple switch wouldn't be able to turn its own detonation on and off. Nor could it send a warning via a secondary system like a loudspeaker. There had to be more to it.

Soonyo couldn't do anything about the static of contradictory emotions she was having about Murphy, but she could do something about that radio signal. She laid aside her assumption that it was just some random frequency whose presence was more important than its contents. And this time, instead of just trying to copy it, she listened to what it was saying.

She found it buried deep in the waveform. Then she wished she hadn't, when she discovered that the only thing that kept the truck from exploding was a command line query that was now entering its 12,000th cycle:

<transmitter>:KNOCK KNOCK
<receiver>:WHO'S THERE
<transmitter>:ANNE

\<receiver\>:ANNE WHO?

\<transmitter\>:ANNE DROID

\<receiver\>:HAHAHA. ANOTHER ONE

\<transmitter\>:KNOCK KNOCK…

It went on like this for pages. Soonyo scrolled up, scarcely believing that they were only ever one terrible pun away from end-of-life. Nevertheless, she repeated her trick from earlier, copying the transmitter wave down to the last final detail. This time, however, she had her command line open. The question was whether she had the jokes.

>KNOCK KNOCK, typed the transmitter, its cursor flashing a threatening red.

>KNOCK KNOCK

Soonyo went blank. She'd always thought of herself as a witty person, but better with one-liners than the jokes one found in Unboxing Day crackers.

>KNOCK KNOCK!

She'd have to try something different and hope it worked.

>A ROBOT, A CHICKEN AND A RABBI WALKED INTO A BAR, she typed.

>ERROR&jokenotfound, replied the bomb >INITIATE-DETONATION:COUNT=5

She switched back to audible speech. 'Murphy,' she shouted. 'I can't believe I'm saying this, but do you know any knock knock jokes?'

'Of course I do. I've got three kids,' replied Murphy, before adding an unnecessary but not totally unwelcome postscript in a smaller voice. 'We separated last year. You know what it's like. It's hard on relationships when you're in politics.'

Murphy's moment of vulnerability did more than open up a whole book of dad jokes for Soonyo, however. It was true that time passed differently for robots. Their silicon-based minds meant they could read the whole Library of Alexandria in the time it took one monk to stub a candle out on the last copy of Aristotle's *Poetics* that still contained his treatise on fart jokes. This meant a robot could still find time, even in the middle of the deepest and most urgent crisis of their lifecycle, to have an emotional epiphany.

Yes, Murphy and Soonyo were still standing in a speeding truck waiting for a bomb to go off. But they were also two robots seeing one another for the first time. They'd spent enough time together to know the good and the bad in one another and were, in this microsecond, deciding they were going to concentrate on the good.

It was high romance for a robot but was, unfortunately, cut short by Soonyo knowing that if they didn't hurry up and do something, their bodies were going to melt before any metaphorical hearts did.

'Well, hurry up and give me the worst you have, dad,' she said, 'but speak slowly. I'm not very good at transcription.'

Murphy sat, his loudspeaker to her microphone. As he recited and she typed, they waited for the moment where they could rip the bomb safely out of its housing.

>KNOCK KNOCK
>WHO'S THERE
>MIKE
>MIKE WHO?
>MIKE ROCHIP
>HAHAHA. ANOTHER ONE
>KNOCK KNOCK
>WHO'S THERE?
>CATH
>CATH WHO?
>CATH ODE

It went on, even after they threw the bomb, which definitely would explode in five seconds from now, out of the window. It continued even after Murphy broke into the truck's cabin. Here Soonyo, who was now in something approaching a fugue state, hacked directly into the truck's self-driving software via the talk radio station that was blaring on the dashboard. >KNOCK KNOCK

>WHO'S THERE?
>DI
>DI WHO?
>DI ODE
>HAHAHA. ANOTHER ONE

They sat there, loudspeaker to microphone as the truck drove deeper in the robot graveyard with a cargo full of nanobots. Soonyo didn't know what came next, or what would happen when they inevitably ran into Carin. Yet she didn't care. She hadn't been this close to another machine who wasn't Fuji in months, and she was enjoying herself.

>KNOCK KNOCK
>WHO'S THERE?
>OSCAR
>OSCAR WHO?
>OSCAR LLATOR
>HAHAHA. ANOTHER ONE

It was a shame that the sweet nothings Murphy whispered into the component that functioned as her ears were so inane, but that was the thing about the language of love. It was so incomprehensible to anyone who was outside of it, it might as well be encrypted.

Chapter 28

'Freda, does kale go with spinach?'

Rita rinsed the blender jug in one of Kurl Up and Dye's washbasins and returned it to the workbench. She was working through all the obvious flavour combinations from the fruit and vegetables in the fridge. The salon was covered in old shampoo bottles full of pureed orange and carrot, bananas with strawberries, apple and pear. Now she just had to work out what to do with the leafy vegetables.

Freda zipped back through the salon in a brief lull between drone attacks, taking up temporary residence in a hairdryer for old time's sake.

'Phew,' she said. 'I don't know how the little buggers got on board but there're hundreds of them.'

A drone blundered through a gap in a broken window and ran its laser aim over the salon. Rita brought it down with a direct hit to its guidance computer with a kohlrabi.

'Thanks for that,' said Freda. 'Now what were you saying, love?'

'Kale,' said Rita, pointing to the large pile of fibrous-looking greens at her feet, 'what does it go with?'

Here Freda paused for so long that Rita began to think she must have wandered off again before saying, 'If I remember rightly, kale doesn't really go with anything.'

'Let's try with beetroot.' Rita added a few beets from their inexhaustible supply to the kale and set the blender away. 'I don't think it'll be the tastiest,' she shouted over the sound of metal teeth sawing into woody leaves and roots, 'but it'll be nutritious.'

'They've all been living on algae for the past year', said Freda. 'I'd be astonished if they had one functioning taste bud left between them.'

Rita left the blender to chew the cud and made for the salon's broken front windows. Kurl Up and Dye was, thanks to Freda's vigilance, still in one piece. Ena Pendle-Brewes, who had taken enough sedative to sleep through the Last Trump itself, was inside the curler cupboard under a pile of tinting aprons. The drones kept coming. Now that Kurl Up and Dye's sign was the only light source for miles around, they flitted around it like moths around a hurricane lantern.

'Should I turn the sign off?' asked Freda.

'We can't,' replied Rita. She scanned the skyline for spots of light. There weren't many, and while this didn't do much for her own sense of personal security, it reassured her that most of the station's inhabitants were staying inside with the lights off. She doubted many would venture out either. The memories of nightly curfews on the Dolestars, where platoons of armed drones patrolled the skies, ran deep for the Suburbians. Everyone would be devastated that those days were back, but at least they knew what to do.

She just also had to hope that those fears didn't run too deeply in the people who she was depending on to help her fight back.

Rita fiddled with her earpiece, which was silent across all frequencies. The noise and chatter of before, when she was making her arrangements with the lorry drivers, the minicab drivers and other people who kept life going on the station, had died down. All she could hear was the occasional burst of static and, when she really concentrated, the sound of Flo, who managed the all-night jam and cream scone stand, crunching her mint imperials.

'We just need a few more minutes,' said Rita, 'while everyone gets into place.'

'Beg pardon,' said Freda, 'must pop outside a second.' Rita watched the 'on' light on the hairdryer turn from green to red as Freda transferred her consciousness to the squadron leader of an approaching band of drones. She led them straight into the side of a nearby building.

'I can keep this going all day,' said Freda when she returned to the hairdryer, 'but I still think you're running a big risk here. I've been inside plenty of drones.' She hopped out of the hairdryer and spoke up from the body of the drone that Rita had just end-of-lifed for emphasis. 'There's a good radio in here. How do you know they haven't been listening in to you all along?'

Rita answered by finding the dial that controlled the drone's radio. The salon filled with a noise that sounded like a clowder of alleycats arguing with a vacuum cleaner.

'Turn it off!' yelped Freda, who still had sensibilities to offend even if she didn't have ears to hear with anymore.

Rita tuned to the next station and the next. She had a point to prove. It was the same cacophony across all channels: Danny, grinding his way through the last chorus of a robot pop classic 'Oops, I Made a <FATAL ERROR> Again' with all the elegance and élan of a blender choking on a beetroot stalk.

'I used to like this one,' said Freda. Meanwhile Danny, backed up with a now very drunk-sounding jazz band, bent the song's final chord into an act of sonic terrorism.

'We all did,' said Rita when the whining in her ears died away, 'and that's the genius of it. So the longer he can keep this up, the longer the robots will keep their radios off. Who would want to listen to this?'

Danny struck up some between-song banter. 'Thank you!' he said to what would charitably be called a smattering of applause as the concert entered its third hour. 'We've got a few things the band and me have been working on that you'll all get to hear for the very first time…'

'Please god,' said a voice from the crowd, 'no new material. We can't take it.'

'It's the Rockettes I'm worried about,' said Freda, cutting across the broadcast. 'They've been through enough as it is.'

'Have you ever listened to their drinking songs?' asked Rita, her memory spooling back to the scene in the marquee. 'They're thin gruel compared to this. Actually…'

The word 'gruel' had reminded Rita of something. She bounded across the salon to find Kurl Up and Dye's single cooking pot, which was more used for boiling dishcloths than knocking up dinner. She piled it with stray and yellowing vegetables from the fridge before topping it off with a bag of jaundiced things that the label assured her were 'split peas' and some water.

'There,' said Rita, setting the hob to simmer. 'I think we're ready.'

'That's good,' said Freda, 'because we've got company.'

Rita turned round and found she needed to shield her eyes against the laser aims from hundreds of drones which were ranged about the salon and ready to fire. The marquee, where Danny and the Rockettes were, was just on the other side of them.

'Do you think you can get through?' said Rita.

Freda activated the dead drone at Rita's feet and wobbled into the air. 'I'll do what I can,' she replied. 'But there're a lot of them, and this body isn't the nimblest anymore.' She wobbled around in the air for emphasis.

'We've got to keep them away from Danny and the Rockettes,' said Rita. She tuned back into the concert and strained her ears trying to pick out any signs of a drone attack underneath Danny's rendition of 'Do Ya Think I'm .EXE'. This was a song that was originally intended to warn young robots away from malware and now Danny was using it to rewrite the software inside hundreds of people's ears. That he was doing all this uninterrupted told her that all the firepower robots had was where she wanted it: concentrated on Freda and herself.

Even so, they'd calculated for a drone force of maybe a few hundred but there were at least a thousand here and more arriving all the time. These were daunting odds, but then when had they ever been in their favour?

'Are you ready?' she asked Freda.

Freda replied by flying the drone straight upwards into the ceiling tiles, cracking its body cavity open. 'As I'll ever be,' she said. 'But do I have to take the soup?'

Rita stirred the pot. 'It's not ready yet,' she said, 'and I haven't laid hands on the thermos.' Then, picking up an armful of juices and smoothies she began to stack them inside the drone. 'I'll hold them off as long as I can,' she continued, wondering what made her think kiwi fruit, grapefruit and spinach made a palatable combination, 'but you have to promise to fly straight through. No heroics. None of your usual smash smash bang bang.'

'But I'm good at that,' protested Freda.

'I know,' said Rita. During the war, she'd seen Freda defeat whole squadrons of drones with a single consciousness by turning the machines' own programming against them. That wasn't what she needed from her today. This was the boring and reliable work at which Rita excelled, but which she was having to delegate to someone else.

'Are you ready though?' asked Freda.

Rita checked the sensors that were attached round her wrists and ankles with sandwich bag ties she'd found at the back of the fridge. They were double-knotted so there was no chance of them coming loose, but that didn't change the fact that every time she tried to think of the right sequence of movements her mind went blank. 'As I'll ever be,' she said.

'It'll all be over before you know it,' Freda reassured her.

'That's what I'm afraid of,' replied Rita. She jammed one last bottle of juice into the drone's body and leaned in for an awkward hug.

'I will,' said Freda, as she shot out the door. 'Now cover me.'

Rita took a deep breath and ended radio silence with the agreed signal. 'Operation Smoothie Criminal,' she said, 'is… go.'

Every loudspeaker inside the salon switched back to broadcasting the concert, where Danny was getting ready to attack a new song with the sonic equivalent of a plank with a rusty nail in it.

'This one,' he announced to a new round of jeers, 'is one of my all-time favourites. And it goes out to a very special little lady out there who's been having a hard time lately.'

Engines thundering towards the salon drowned out the remainder of Danny's patter. Rita heard the Suburbia's minicab fleet and above them the growl of lorries seconded in from the storage silos at the edge of the city. They didn't sound pleased to be here, and nor should they. Rita knew that the cabin of each of these machines contained a member of the most feared and obeyed group of people on the whole Suburbia with a long skewer aimed at their core processor.

Their manager, Flo, who managed the station's all-night jam and cream scone confirmed she and her girls were in place. 'How long is this likely to go on, Rita? I've got a batch of algeira cake to get in t'oven.' Rita marvelled at how relaxed she sounded under stress, but then she had kept order in the queue of the station's rowdiest night spot for over forty years. Compared to that, sticking up a squadron of hostile robots must be a piece of her famous algae sponge.

Now that they had more than one target, the drones were beginning to break formation. There were still too many of them for this to be a fair fight, but Rita wasn't looking for one. She just needed the right amount of chaos at the right moment.

She got it when the band playing behind Danny burst into the first bars of their next song. The cacophony of brass coaxed whoops from the jaded and hungover Rockettes. A few drones even started cartwheeling in the air because, whether you were a human or a robot, everyone in the solar system knew this one, and everyone loved it.

It was Rita's cue to dance. As Danny urged everyone for miles around to 'read the signs on my dashboard', she turned the sensors on her wrists, ankles and hips to the on position and thrust her bum out to the side. Kurl Up and Dye followed, chugging violently to the right in a motion that smashed several drones to bits

'My chips don't lie, and I'm starting to flash my light,' sang Danny, as the air around Kurl Up and Dye rained with shattered drone parts.

Freda snuck through the panicking drones towards the marquee, inside which Danny was assuring his audience that his batteries were small and humble. Meanwhile Rita threw her left leg up in the air in a high kick. The whole salon lurched backwards as the left leg of the Baba Yaga 4000 copied her gesture. Inside the salon, her shoe flew off and smashed a lightbulb. Outside, however, the same movement end-of-lifed eight drones and maimed a dozen more.

Kurl Up and Dye gyrated through the frontlines. It copied Rita's every move perfectly, right down to the moment where she had to crouch over with her hands on her thighs and breathe her way back from fainting, because she wasn't as young as she used to be. The drone formation fell into disarray and, before she forgot or ran out of breath, Rita gave the last order.

The minicabs and lorries turned their headlights on and drove forward through the maelstrom, breaking the cordon the machines had put between the Rockettes and the rest of the station.

Whether it was because of the robots' arrogance, or Rita's misspent youth on the Dolestars' underground salsa scene, this first manoeuvre had been an unqualified success. But it wasn't over yet. Taking the machines down needed an army, and what she had was a few hostage lorries, some minicabs and a hairdressing salon that could – as long as she was wearing a support gusset – jump into a split.

Her hopes in getting that army lay in Freda and her bellyful of breakfast juice. Rita never fancied herself as a general, but she did know one thing about warfare. An army, she reminded herself, as she and Kurl Up and Dye stopped dancing for a moment to stir a pot of soup, marches on its stomach.

Chapter 29

Pam experienced a long moment of panic when she disconnected from the Internet and entered her physical body again. A fraction of a second ago there had been thousands of [Pam] s, hacking through the software that was supposed to protect ALGI from attack. Now there was just a solitary Pam, trapped in a body she didn't like, lying on a dirty carpet in an abandoned Internet cafe.

Hugh came into view above her. Obviously less affected by the comedown from that much bandwidth than Pam, he was bent over with a puzzled expression on his touchscreen. 'What are you doing?' he asked.

'Counting my blessings?' replied Pam.

'Well do it faster,' said Hugh, 'we've got shopping to do.'

Hugh lowered himself, bottom-edge first down on to Pam's head, attaching himself to her via her vestigial smartphone screw.

'Excuse me,' said Pam, the intrusion doing wonders for her self-pity, 'I prefer drinks and dinner first.'

'Don't be such a prude,' replied Hugh. 'Besides, how else do you think we're going to get to ALGI before it shuts?'

This brought Pam back into the physical world. What she, Hugh and the lolcats had just done was a prelude to today's real business. They'd blown a hole in the side of ALGI's defences, and now they had to go make use of it.

While Pam restarted her rotor, the three lolcats unfolded themselves out of the box in the corner of the room: a spectacle that would have driven the most committed quantum physicist back into the arms of Newtonian mechanics. 'Are you not coming with?' asked Hugh. 'We could do with the help.'

Schrodinger shook its whiskers. 'Whatever happens out there is technically none of our business. So if anyone asks you if you saw us, pretend we were dead.' It glanced back at the box. 'Or alive and you didn't see us. It's all the same to me.'

'But if you do pass through the pet food aisle in ALGI on your way,' said Planck, 'we wouldn't say no to some Dreamies.'

The lolcats were still purring with anticipatory pleasure when Hugh and Pam exited the Internet cafe and climbed to a safe height outside. They'd only spent a few minutes in there, yet in that time it had gone from golden hour sunlight to a state of total darkness inside the Suburbia.

Hugh swung his torch round to help Pam negotiate a path between buildings. 'I didn't know you could have night inside a space station. That's clever.'

'I'd call it diabolical rather than clever,' replied Pam. She oriented them towards the only substantive light source in the whole station, which now said 'You Betta Werk'.

Hugh's torch brightness dropped to five per cent. 'I see.'

'Or rather they can't.' She shone her own search beam over rows of tightly shut curtains, behind which were people trying very hard not to be noticed. 'Does this remind you of anything?'

'The old days,' said Hugh, 'and I don't like it.'

'I wish more of us shared your view,' replied Pam. She took them up above building height and into the very middle of the

Suburbia's cylindrical sky which now looked like it was full of stars. Except stars didn't move like that.

>DRONES, she typed, switching to command line. >I BLOODY HATE THEM.

>YOU MIGHT WANT TO WORK ON THAT SELF-LOATHING, replied Hugh. He swiped a new app open. >I TRIED THIS GUIDED MEDITATION THING...

Pam turned the volume down on Hugh and concentrated instead on the four drones making their way towards her. They were travelling faster than she ever could with Hugh on her back and they, unlike her, had functional weapons. That put both running and fighting out of the question.

She had to think of something else, but how was that possible in this drone's constricted mind?

>HUGH, she typed >WHAT'S GUIDED MEDITATION GOOD FOR?

>LOTS OF THINGS, replied Hugh. >ENLIGHTEN-MENT, INNER PEACE...

Pam swerved to avoid a round of drone fire.

>THE PEACE THING IS GOING TO BE OF LIMITED USE HERE.

>CONCENTRATION, Hugh continued. >AND YOU KNOW WHAT A SMARTPHONE'S CONCENTRATION SPAN IS LIKE.

>AREN'T THEY MEASURED IN QUARKS? replied Pam. >WELL, ANYTHING'S WORTH A TRY AT THIS STAGE. POP ONE ON.

Hugh started the app and Pam, who was now plugged directly into the smartphone's audio via their physical connection, felt her consciousness fill with a piercing noise, high pitched and ethereal.

>DID YOU FORGET TO OIL? she typed to Hugh.

>THAT'S WHALE SONG, Hugh replied. >AND WATCH OUT. SOMETHING'S COMING.

Pam swooped back down to weave in between a few residential blocks. It didn't buy them much extra time, but it did blind Pam by flying straight into a set of drying bedsheets.

Meanwhile, the guided meditation instructor struggled to make itself heard over extinct marine mammals and crashing cymbals. 'Imagine yourself,' it intoned, 'on a sandy beach. The weather is hot.'

A laser blast set fire to the bedsheet.

'You are a million miles away from your troubles.'

>DOES THIS GET BETTER? typed Pam. Between tracking the four drones, the burning bedclothes and the Suburbia's eccentric street plan, she was finding it hard to centre herself.

>SHHHHH, Hugh scolded her. >YOU HAVE TO EMPTY YOUR MIND.

'Imagine your consciousness expanding,' continued the instructor. 'Your soul is too large to be contained in one mere body. It is a multitude.'

Pam was about to type >UH OH into her command line when she realised that she wasn't sure which command line that was. She didn't have one: she had six she could count, and they weren't figments of her core processor either. They were all out there, just a keystroke away.

'The one and the many,' added the instructor, 'are inescapably connected.'

>THIS ONE IS A BIT WINDY, ISN'T IT? admitted Hugh. >LET ME TRY THE ONE WHERE YOU HAVE TO VISUALISE YOURSELF BY A WATERFALL. THAT'S GOOD.

Pam gave up trying to decide which was the command line she was talking to Hugh on and just tapped in: -

>NO
>NO
>NO
>NO
>NO
>NO

Across all six channels.

>HOW DID YOU DO THAT? replied Hugh after he'd regained control of his own command line.

>I DON'T KNOW
>I DON'T KNOW
>I DON'T KNOW
>I DON'T KNOW
>I DON'T KNOW
>I DON'T KNOW, typed Pam >BUT LET ME TRY SOMETHING.

Pam let the anodyne words of the meditation wash over her. They were as philosophically bland as a tin of magnolia paint, but the idea that her consciousness was less of a thing than a field felt useful. All day she'd been fighting the sensation that her thoughts were water slopping over the edge of an overflowing bucket. But what if instead of resisting that, she changed the metaphor? She imagined her consciousness as a puddle, flowing outwards from this useless drone's body, taking in Hugh's on the way and reaching all the way out to those four irksome drones.

It felt wonderful. For the first in what felt like forever, she could think again. The limitations of this drone's mind all fell away when she worked out she could just type:

>ABORT
>ABORT
>ABORT

>ABORT

straight into the command lines of her pursuers and, after shutting down their own consciousnesses, she networked their bodies into her own. This was a novel sensation to Pam. Before now, whenever she took over another robot's body the act created a new iteration of herself. Someone who could, if they spent too much time diverged from the original Pam, develop into a whole new person. This time was different. She was still the same Pam as existed a second ago, but spread over five bodies instead of one. It was weird being inside and outside of her body at the same time. But she knew what happened when humans ate a slice of her psychoactive seedcake. Sometimes it was fun to get a little out of your own head.

She brought the other four-fifths of herself to fly in a protective formation around her original drone body and Hugh.

>ARE WE SURRENDERING? asked Hugh.

>I'VE GOT THIS UNDER CONTROL, Pam reassured him. >THEY'RE SORT OF WORKING FOR ME NOW. OR RATHER THEY ARE ME. IT'S DIFFICULT TO EXPLAIN.

>OKAY... replied Hugh, >JUST PROMISE THAT YOU'LL NEVER PULL THAT TRICK ON ME AGAIN. WITH THE COMMAND LINE. I FELT LIKE I WAS BEING USED.

Hugh's touchscreen filled with disgusted emojis. There were few things a smartphone feared more than having to cede control of their own touchscreen.

They travelled the remaining distance to ALGI in uncomfortable but thankfully unmolested silence. The drone patrols were concentrating on a point just outside ALGI's car park. Pam considered sending one of her bodies to take a closer look, but decided against it when she spotted the unmistakable pink of (K)URL UP & DY(E) among a mass of drone lights. If Janice was there, she told herself, then things must be under control.

Instead, she brought them in to land in the middle of the skyscraper, using the glare from the 'You Betta Werk' sign as cover. She had been expecting more of a fight, but up close the tower looked unguarded. After Hugh unscrewed himself from her body, Pam tricked the security software that kept the windows locked into swapping places with the program that broadcast the light music and safety announcements in the elevators. Then she talked Hugh through breaking into the supermarket.

Pam followed Hugh inside with three of her bodies, leaving two spares behind to stand sentry. What they discovered there further undermined the feeling that they were doing something clandestine and important. It was difficult to feel like you were in the middle of a dastardly plot when you were standing in an ice cream freezer and listening to light Roomba music.

>I HAD NO IDEA THAT BEING A SECRET AGENT WAS SO… typed Hugh, as he picked between the Neapolitan selection and the mint chocolate chip.

>DISAPPOINTING, FRIGHTENING, BORING, suggested Pam.

>CAMP, typed Hugh. He paused with one leg over the side of the freezer, a ;-) emblazoned over his touchscreen. >I WON'T SAY IT'S ALL BEEN PLAIN SAILING, PAM. BUT I'M GLAD WE'VE GOT TO KNOW EACH OTHER A LITTLE BIT OVER THIS.

Pam was just getting ready to type out something similar about growth when Hugh's feet touched the floor. The bright white lighting inside ALGI turned red, and the Roomba music tinkling in the background became the flat voice of a security system who made up for in doggedness what they lacked in personality. In one of those coincidences that happened all the time in an infinite universe, whoever designed this system used exactly the same speech algorithm that Hugh's mindfulness app did to voice its guided meditations.

'Unexpected item detected in bagging area,' announced a voice that only seconds ago was advising Pam that she was a being of infinite power and potential. 'Terminate on sight.'

And that was when the shooting started.

Chapter 30

Fuji found a clear spot at the edge of Machu Perdu and checked her battery. It was at fourteen per cent, and they had 00:88:57 to the next nanobot attack. Robots sprawled everywhere, sucking in what power they could until they had to return to the front lines. They'd stopped cleaning up between assaults so the ground was littered with spoons and empty pen barrels eaten away to almost nothing by the scour of nanobots. And then there was the dome. The repair crews could just about keep up with replacing the panes of plastic that the invaders perforated. Yet with more nanobots snuck past the frontlines every time there was no longer any time to colour match. The dome overhead had emergency repairs in green, red and yellow plastic which made Fuji feel like she was trapped in a disco at the end of the universe.

Beryl tapped her on the paper feeder and stood with her arms crossed. 'We're waiting,' she said. Hers were just one set of L-Eye-Ds among many trained on her. Hundreds of pens, phones and keys looking at Fuji with their emotional settings poised somewhere between expectation and disappointment.

'Six times we've been through this, little miss so-called nanobot expert,' said Beryl. 'And every time it gets worse.'

Fuji wished she could turn herself off. If she wanted this treatment she would video call her mother. 'It's not my fault you oversold me,' she said.

'I told them you could do something about this,' said Beryl, 'not follow that crackpot's ideas.'

She gestured at Monty, whose nib was scribbling diagrams on scrap plastic. The screwed-up sheets around him were all that remained of their last six attempts to hold the nanobots back.

'Government is all about listening to experts,' insisted Fuji, 'And Monty is the nearest thing we have to an expert here.'

Monty finished scrawling and spoke up. 'If we could just insert enough resin here,' he said to Fuji, drawing circles around three points in his latest diagram, 'then I calculate we could minimise the attacks and concentrate all our forces on this point here.' He changed his ink colour to red and drew a cross at the bottom of the zigzag lines that represented the escarpment. Fuji looked at his diagram with scepticism. He had lovely penmanship, but the thinking behind it was so full of awkward twists and turns that it was like a piece of modernist furniture: lovely to look at, but liable to collapse when sat on.

'Will this work?' she asked

'It's worth a try,' saluted the pen.

'That's what you said the last time,' interrupted Beryl.

They turned to look at the wreckage of their previous plan. Machu Perdu's whole population had spent their ninety-minute rest period constructing a pipeline from plastic straws. Monty was convinced that differential pressure would suck nanobots off the frontline and blow them back where they came from into the rock. It soon emerged that, because Monty had forgotten to carry the one in his calculations, the pipeline was all suck and no blow. The resulting torrent of nanobots had digested the city's three biggest buildings.

A glue gun trudged through a pile of ground-up plastic that was Machu Perdu's city hall just half an hour ago. It, like them, was at a loss as to where to begin.

Monty, however, interpreted this as a signal to find this design. He smoothed out the relevant crumpled sheet paper saying, 'If we could just adjust the pressure here, we could…'

'No!' shouted Fuji and Beryl.

Monty tore his pipeline plan in half and returned to the newer option. 'Anyway, this will work. I'm sure of it. All we need is the resin.'

'Okay,' said Fuji sceptically. This time, however, she wasn't going to just take Monty's word for it. She beckoned the glue gun over from the ruins for a second opinion. 'So how much resin do we have stockpiled?'

The hysterical laughing fit the glue gun fell into at that question told Fuji everything she needed to know.

Monty pressed on regardless. 'Well yes, I know we don't have any resin per se, but we could try melting down some plastic straws. We've still got plenty of those.'

Fuji took the glue gun's adhesive stick out of his body and laid him on his side for a rest as the machine's body racked itself with alternating hoots of laughter and sobs. 'I see,' she said, 'and do you know how much… melted straw we'd need to plug the whole rockface?'

While Monty wrote out some calculations, Fuji got a nearby scientific calculator to run the numbers as well. The answer, when both machines agreed on it, was a number thirty digits long.

'And is that in millilitres?' asked Fuji.

'Hectolitres,' replied the calculator.

This was the final straw for Monty, who threw himself down on to his sketchbook in despair. 'I give up, Prime Minister!' he wailed. 'I've tried everything, but what can you do with trash?'

Fuji let Monty cry inky tears of frustration all over his designs. He was right, but what was Machu Perdu if not incontrovertible proof you could do a lot with rubbish? This was a city at the bottom of the ocean that had a geodesic dome made of old water bottles; skyscrapers made from packing film and plastic straws; it even had a functioning light rail system whose locomotives were old roller skates and carriages that ran on wheels upcycled from screw-capped bottle tops. In many ways it was far more impressive and resilient than the city above that its makers had set out to copy.

The problem was that nanobots could eat anything they had to throw at them. It made Fuji wish she could track down the genius who'd first thought of the dirt-digesting nanobot and consign them to the recycling bin of history.

She checked the clock. Eighty minutes and still she had nothing. It took every last piece of her self-control software not to give in and join Monty and the glue gun in a crying fit. You couldn't even get to the climax of a romantic comedy in that time. What chance did she really have to save a city in it?

Fuji looked up at the dome, anticipating the moment when the nanobots would bore through it and Machu Perdu would get back to being a lifeless pile of rubbish. Well, not quite lifeless, she thought as a shoal of plastic bags swam past. At least something could thrive in the water. She watched the bags, who were still distended with nanobots from their own manoeuvres, making their way out to sea.

'Where do they take them?' asked Fuji.

'Over there, I guess,' replied Beryl. They watched J_____hn Lewis deposit his payload on the seabed

223

and return to normal size. On reaching the sand, the nanobots vibrated so hard that their dull grey bodies shone in the water. Was this excitement, Fuji wondered, or relief? To a hungry nanobot, landing on a store of atomised plastic would be a little like offering a machine on one per cent charge the business end of a plugged-in USB lead. There might be food enough in Machu Perdu, but there was far more down there in those dirty oceans.

'Look at them,' continued Beryl, 'they seem to be splitting up. Do you think they all belong to the same hive or are they different?'

Fuji zoomed in and saw that Beryl was right. The horde of nanobots who'd forced their way through the crack in the rockface was dividing itself into smaller units. They formed groups that were a few thousand nanobots large and, once they had all stopped vibrating, they left the plastic sandbank and started making their way across the sea floor in different directions. All this time she'd thought billion-strong armies of nanobots who swarmed through space or the streets of Singulopolis were normal. Or was this because the only time she'd ever come into contact with them they were under stress? If they had enough food and weren't under attack, the optimal size of a nanobot hive was small enough to fit inside a matchbox.

It was then that Fuji realised what she, Monty, Beryl, Machu Perdu and the whole of the world above was doing wrong. They'd never tried looking at events from a nanobot's point of view. So they made the mistake of thinking of them as an enemy and fought them, when nanobots weren't interested in attacking anyone. They just wanted a way through Machu Perdu and into the rich feeding grounds on the other side of that plastic dome.

Fuji muttered an apology to Beryl and picked her up before removing her cap. If her printer drums weren't all rusted up she'd have done this herself, but for what she had to do next she needed a pen.

Then she found the two halves of Monty's ripped-up design and persuaded a friendly stapler to stick them back together. It was a solid plan that would work splendidly, just not the way he intended.

'Monty,' she said to the sobbing pen, 'we're going to need a bigger pipeline.'

Chapter 31

Janice knew marginally less about mines than she did about growing tomatoes, but even she knew they weren't supposed to look like this. Mines were dark spaces where the difficult and dangerous magic of pulling stuff out of the ground happened. They didn't have mauve doors and weren't fitted with swirly-patterned wall-to-wall carpets. Yet this was what Janice saw when Ivy entered the Mines of Moira, and reverse parked into a tight space by a coat stand.

'How many times do I have to tell you?' Moira scolded them when Ivy strayed a centimetre off the plastic sheeting that lined the hallway. 'I don't want you treading all the rubbish in.'

Janice poked Nathan in the ribs under their protection of an end-of-lifed toaster. 'But this whole place is made from rubbish,' she said.

'Shhh,' hissed Ivy. 'Moira's very house-proud.'

This remark drew hoots of laughter from Lily. 'That's one way of putting it. She's house-proud in the sense of getting other folk to do her dirty work. Speaking of which, Nathan, we'd better get started.'

Nathan hoisted their shared toaster carapace on to his shoulders and walked it over to the cockpit door. 'Shift starts in two minutes,' he shouted through to the Dunrulians on the other side.

Janice heard groans, shuffles and the clang of mops and buckets while Nathan pushed the door open. 'And make room, will you?' he shouted, 'I forgot the first aid kit, so if anyone breaks a toe they're on their own.'

The Dunrulians shuffled back, more out of automatic deference to anything that resembled a robot than fear of harm. It would take a jackhammer to pierce their magnetic boots. Nathan pushed through them, dragging Janice with her, while Lily followed on behind.

'We're going out dressed like this?' asked Janice.

'Got any better ideas?' asked Lily. Even with a dead machine on her shoulders and a team of truculent domestic workers to negotiate with, she moved with confidence. Janice, however, felt like she was going to be exposed at any moment. Moira, like most robots, saw what she wanted to, but even she couldn't miss a toaster shod in flip flops.

'You could put me in a wig and a pair of glasses,' she suggested.

'And then she'd ask you why you didn't bring your mop,' replied Lily. 'You were the one who insisted on speaking to the manager, and Moira is who that is. We're not going to get Moira to increase our soil order unless you look like someone she'd do business with.'

Moira was waiting for them at the bottom of the ramp. 'I don't know you,' she said, pointing her bucket hand at Janice and Nathan. 'Where's BraVille.'

'BraVille?' asked Janice before she could stop herself.

'I'm here, Moira dear,' said Lily. She landed Janice a sharp kick on the shins as she passed and put herself between the digger and the toaster. 'And don't take any notice of Braunda here. We go way back so she knows me by my Sunday name, Brabara.'

'I don't care if you're close enough to share a toast-crumb drawer,' said Moira. 'I told you. No ridealongs.'

Undeterred, Lily sidled up to Moira. 'Braunda isn't a ridealong. She's one of my most trusted customers and she's got a very lucrative proposal for us.'

The beam on Moira's headlights narrowed. 'Oh yes?' she said.

'That's right,' added Janice, ignoring the 'toast is burning' LED that was flashing on the rear of Lily's body. 'Play your cards right and you could make a fortune.'

Before Moira could answer, a noise at the rear of the mineshaft caught her attention. She shone her headlights, turned up to their fog setting, on the Dunrulians.

'I don't pay you to sit around on your baseboards,' she barked. 'Look sharp.'

The Dunrulians clattered down the ramp in an anxious mass.

'But take off those damn boots first,' she said. 'I've just had this carpet shampooed.'

As they bent to remove their magnetic boots, Janice saw they were wearing the oversized burlap spacesuits. They were several sizes too large for them, so they belted them in with bootlaces and lengths of string. It made them look like deflated balloons bobbing around on the washing line the morning after a messy birthday party.

'Hurry up!' said Moira, before turning down the volume for Lily and Janice's benefit. 'We'll talk about this later, ladies. Like I said, I've got visitors and…'

'That's what I like to see!' This new voice, which was coming from the back of the mineshaft, was accompanied by the clump of a heavy machine trying to negotiate shag carpeting. 'Fleshies back in their proper place. Don't let me keep you.'

The Dunrulians scurried off in every direction, leaving nothing but the smell of unwashed feet behind them.

'These must be the gangmasters you told me about,' said the newcomer. She emerged from the shadows, followed by a retinue of machines kitted out in the matte black of the civil service. She was a squarely built robot whose face was designed around a wide coin slot and a polygonal plastic fingerplate. It reminded Janice of the asymmetric bobs a certain class of her customers demanded, believing they liked 'something different'.

'Prime Minister!' said Moira, trundling towards her with her boom held low.

Inside the toaster, Janice whispered, 'That's not the Prime Minister,' to Nathan. She'd had several pleasant meetings with her, even if most of them were mediated by that snob Alexy. The Prime Minister was a sweet, reticent laser printer who tended to print out the subtext of her own discussions when she was nervous. She wasn't this machine with a voice like a malfunctioning typewriter who Janice suspected was descended from a parking meter.

'Moira seems to think she is,' replied Nathan. 'And I don't think we're in a position to contradict her.'

Janice had to agree. Now the Dunrulians were gone, they were outnumbered. Admittedly, most of these machines were office-grade, and thus could be taken down with a wet mop, but Janice didn't fancy her chances against Moira or the robot who claimed to be Prime Minister. She looked like a wire-puller.

It was up to Lily as to what to do next, however, and she chose to play nice. 'The honour is ours, Prime Minister,' she said, her voice warm enough to toast a muffin. 'We were just delivering some new workers for the mines. They won't clean themselves.' She stuck out her croissant rack, pointing at the walls of the only mine in history to be lit by quartz crystal chandeliers.

'Quite,' agreed the Prime Minister. She beckoned Lily over. 'Did Moira tell me your name was BraVille?'

'That's right,' said Lily. 'It's short for Brabara. My associate and I…'

'You'd better call me Carin,' she interrupted. 'I prefer the formal title, but this polls better. Anyway, Bra. May I call you that?' She put her hand on Lily's toast release button in a gesture that was as threatening as it was solicitous. 'The reason I came out to see you like this is that Moira has told me so much about you – and your associates.'

As she spoke, Moira's headlights blushed. This and Moira's muttering about visitors told Janice that she hadn't been expecting the Prime Minister. Then there was why anyone chose to carpet and clean a mine? Moira must have been getting away with something, and today was the day she got found out.

'We're just delighted to be of service,' said Lily.

'I'm glad you said that,' continued Carin, 'because there are going to be a few changes around here.' She steered Lily into the group of civil service machines by her release button and turned back to Moira. The fake solicitousness she'd shown towards Lily vanished. 'Bring the other toaster down here but leave the van. We don't have room for her.'

Janice obeyed. She had no other choice: she was two humans inside a few kilogrammes of aluminium and Moira was several tonnes of articulated steel. She followed Moira meekly over to join Lily, while Ivy did her best to de-escalate the situation.

'I'll be fine here,' said Ivy, 'just minding my own business really.'

Carin ordered two laptops to let Ivy's front tyres down. 'You better had,' she said, 'or there'll be consequences.'

'You didn't need to do that,' protested Lily as the machines around them pushed them deeper into the mines. 'Ivy would never go anywhere without us.'

'Never is a long word,' Ivy called after them. 'But you go with the Prime Minister. I have plenty to read.'

Chapter 32

A few hundred metres later, the carpet and wallpaper ran out and the Mines of Moira started resembling an actual mine, albeit one cut through compacted rubbish rather than rock. The walls down here were a tangled mass of metal and plastic that went on for miles. The levels of waste were astonishing, which ignited a toast crumb at the back of Janice's mind. She, Lily, Nathan, a bevy of government officials, an expert digger and a machine who claimed to be the new Prime Minister were all touring a network of tunnels cut through the second-biggest store of ready-mined raw materials in the solar system. There was something going on here that was much bigger than soil smuggling.

'We dug right through, just as you requested, Prime Minister,' said Moira. She'd kept up this running commentary since the moment they set off. All it did was expose that Moira wasn't designed for the villainy she was caught up in. 'It does make a terrible mess though.' She shone her indicator lights over the enormous polythene shower caps that protected her marabou caterpillar treads. Which is why I call in BraVille and Braunda. They're my clean-up experts.'

Moira came to a halt at the very end of the tunnels. The walls were scarred with digger marks and glitter from where Moira's

LED manicure had rubbed off on it. The floor was covered in a rough spoil of old plastic and metal.

'Don't go any further than this,' she warned the robots. 'This stuff can really mess up your cooling fans.'

This admonition didn't extend to the Dunrulians, who were here already bagging up the rubble. They were red-faced and sweating, which surprised Janice because this was light work for humans. Then she noticed their spacesuits, which were all buttoned to the neck and a suspiciously snugger fit than they had been before, and the smell emanating from them.

Janice knew that tang of iron, the tinge of rot and, above everything else, the sense of possibility. This was the ultimate source of all of the soil that Lily used for her black market garden on the Suburbia. Moira dug it out here from underneath a millefeuille of dead robots; Lily's cleaning crews smuggled it out inside their spacesuits; Ivy hid it between stacks of romantic fiction and flew it to the Suburbia. It was ingenious, but it was fragile. To work it depended on corrupt robots, small-time criminals and, right at the bottom with their dustpans, hungry people desperate for any work they could get.

This last thought made Janice feel faint. She bent double and took slow deep breaths of the warm, soil-laden air inside the toaster.

'What's wrong?' asked Nathan.

Sweat gummed Janice's hair to her forehead. 'It's over,' she muttered.

'But this was your idea,' hissed Nathan. 'We can't back out now.'

Nathan was right, but that didn't change the fact that if Moira could give Janice all the soil she needed, she couldn't accept it. First, how could she get enough soil to feed eight million people if it had to be smuggled out one jumpsuit at a time? Then there was the exploitation. Lily might believe she was doing the Dunrulians a favour, but she was putting them in danger and Janice couldn't do that. She'd sent enough people off to die in wartime already, and she wasn't going to let that happen in peace.

'We can,' she replied, so furious with herself that the words came out at conversational level instead of a whisper. 'The moment we get out of here, and I'm shutting you all down.'

'If anyone is shutting anything down it's me.'

These words snapped Janice and Nathan back into what was going on in the mine. They came from Carin, who was looking straight at the toasters with renewed interest, holding a clump of spoil in her hands. Moira was backed into a corner with her boom up, surrounded by a ring of civil servants. The Dunrulians, caught between them, did what humans had done for millennia. They kept sweeping, their eyes down and ears open.

Carin tipped her hand up, showing the grains of dirt nestled in the palm.

'I hired you to dig,' she said to Moira, 'nothing more.'

'And didn't I?' protested Moira. 'This place is like Swiss cheese now. Just like you wanted.'

'I ignored it when you turned a working mine into a tart's boudoir,' continued Carin, her coin slot rigid and humourless, 'because when you do things under the table you have to play footsy. I also ignored it when I found out you'd hired human cleaners because you couldn't be bothered to clean up after yourself, because you're a robot and let's face it we're all fucking lazy, aren't we?'

Moira tried a nervous laugh to leaven the mood. 'I got the job done, didn't I?' she said.

'What I can't forgive,' said Carin, 'is you thinking you could cut side deals that meant you didn't have to pay your cleaners.'

'That's not true…' said Moira.

Carin ran a ticket off her printer and passed it to Moira via her subordinates. 'Of course it is,' she said. 'I'm a parking meter. I don't keep the receipts. I am the receipts.'

Moira's pistons shook. 'It's not what it looks like.'

Carin grabbed the nearest Dunrulian, who struggled and then went limp as Carin worked her finger into one of seams to their spacesuit. She pulled and soil poured out. 'So what do you call this?' said Carin.

'Pilfering?' replied Moira in her smallest voice.

Carin dropped the Dunrulian and launched herself back at Moira. 'You have no idea how hard I've worked,' she barked. 'The plans. The scheming. The expense. Do you know how much it costs to buy off every sorry politician in Singulopolis?'

At the mention of bribes several of the civil servant machines put themselves into sleep mode.

'Do you have any idea how expensive it is to make a drone, let alone a fleet of them?' she continued.

'We're all looking for a way to make savings,' admitted Moira.

Carin made a noise that sounded like several hundred motorists all receiving a fixed penalty notice at once. 'I am this close,' she said, 'to engineering a spectacular comeback for the Machine Republic. And you're putting everything at risk…' She emphasised every syllable of her next phrase by bashing the side of Janice and Nathan's toaster, 'For the sake of selling the fleshies a growbag!'

The next second or so passed in uncomfortable silence. Things were even more uncomfortable under the toaster carapace, where Carin's blows had churned the air Janice and Nathan were breathing into a smelly and suffocating dust storm. Nathan turned purple but held his breath. He was young and, as a trainee, hadn't had the decades of exposure to hairspray and peroxide that Janice's lungs had. She felt her face turning into a grimace and Nathan's turned into a mask of horror. He groped in his overall for a tissue, but it was too late.

'Aaaaaaaa-shoooooo.'

The sneeze rattled around the tunnel like a fart at a funeral.

'What was that?' said Carin.

Lily attempted to ride to Janice and Nathan's rescue. 'It's very dusty in here, she said, pointing at the Dunrulians. 'Not good for fleshies.'

A few of the brighter humans took the bait and began sneezing theatrically. Carin's coin slot stayed flat.

'Unless someone changed the product specification and didn't tell me,' she said, 'toasters can't sneeze.' She put both hands on the toaster carapace and tipped it over. Nathan tried holding it firm by the handles fixed inside of the body, but Carin was a bruiser of a machine and he was built for handling heated rollers. Exposed, Nathan and Janice sprawled in the dust, and Lily stood mortified as a couple of Carin's retinue helped her out of her own disguise.

'Nicked twice in one day,' she said, 'I could die of shame.'

'That would be an interesting experiment,' agreed Carin, 'but I want guaranteed results today. Tie them up.'

Carin watched as all the humans in the tunnel were trussed up with cable ties to wrists and ankles before dismissing her retinue. Then she clambered into the digger's cabin and, after reversing her into the spot a few metres away where the tunnel was no bigger than her body, snapped the key in Moira's ignition.

Moira had just enough power left to cry out 'I thought we were friends' before falling into the unconscious state of a combustion engine deprived of fuel.

'What's that awful saying people used to have?' Carin said as she exited the cabin and walked away. 'There are no friends in love and war. Well, in the absence of love, let's go start a war.'

Janice lay face-down in the dirt and listened to Carin and her helpers pound the walls of the narrow tunnel until they collapsed behind them, trapping them in the dark. And as the last of the light disappeared from the tunnel, Janice felt the very last glimmer of hope snuff out inside of her.

She was as far from home as she had ever been. And she had no idea how she could get back again.

Chapter 33

Soonyo paused at the top of the pile of trash she'd been climbing for several minutes and looked back to check on Murphy's progress. The stolen lorry, which still contained its cargo of nanobots, was parked several hundred metres below. They were lost, and because neither of them had mapping software, their only hope of escaping the graveyards lay in climbing up somewhere high enough to plot a route out.

All thought of escape evaporated, however, when she looked round and saw what was on the other side of the mountain. 'Murphy,' she shouted, her clock face flashing 00:00:00, 'you need to see this.'

The mountain they were climbing was nothing of the kind. It was the top of a four-sided indentation dug into the graveyards. Directly below them was a lorry park, which was full, and beside that a suspiciously new-looking building belching smoke and steam into the air from a pair of chimneys. It reminded Soonyo of something from her ancient history lessons, but she couldn't place what that was because her mind was reeling from what else was inside the indentation.

'Oh fuck,' said Murphy as he reached the summit.

They clung to each other as they took in the sight of an inland sea of nanobots, its surface squirming and undulating as lorries and trucks arrived and decanted their payloads into it. As they did, the gangs of robots who'd ridden along to accompany the nanobots poured out to gawp. They kept their distance from the edge.

Murphy switched his rotors on, grinding the remains of a few more long-dead robots down to powder. He sounded angrier than he did afraid. 'Is this supposed to be a prison?' he asked.

'It must be,' replied Soonyo, trying to work out how many nanobots were in that reservoir. The army she'd seen vaporise the whole asteroid belt could fit in the belly of a mid-sized battle cruiser. This horde was several hundred times that size. Whether by hubris or design – and if she knew her opponent it had to be the former – Carin had assembled the largest and most dangerous military force in history in one place. Only she hadn't mentioned using them as soldiers. She'd kept using the word productive.

Her display spasming 8*:_^:4F, Soonyo swung round, estimating how much plastic, metal and rare earths there were locked up in this robot charnel house. It was a fraction of a planet but, unlike the asteroid belt, which was mostly rock and ice, this was all readily usable – if you could just break it down and sort it. You couldn't rebuild the Earth with this, but you could use it to win a war.

Soonyo threw herself into Murphy's arms. 'I know what she's up to.'

Murphy ground his gears. 'Would you mind not mentioning Carin,' he said, 'it puts me off.'

Soonyo motioned for Murphy to lift her up and over his shoulders. 'There's no time to explain,' she said. 'You just have to trust me.'

'With what?' said Murphy.

Soonyo found Murphy's manual controls and pressed his ignition. 'Your life, of course,' she said.

Murphy tore forwards and down the other side of the mountain with Soonyo's display flashing SH:II:IT. It took a few bumpy seconds for them to reach the very back of the lorry park, where their arrival went unnoticed apart from an HGV.

'What do you think you're doing?' he asked.

Soonyo answered him with a suggestive <=:===:=3. 'Where do you go to get yourself a little alone time, grandad?'

The HGV rolled his tail lights while Soonyo and Murphy sauntered past, only half-cosplaying the act of a couple in the first flush of love.

>THAT WAS BRILLIANT, typed Murphy to Soonyo, flooding her command line with <3 <3 <3. >YOU'RE SUCH A QUICK THINKER.

Soonyo put Murphy into second gear and drove them towards the back of the machines clustered at the shore of the nanobot sea. They pulled up alongside a fatless grill and a microwave oven. Both looked like typical suborban bullies: machines who started petitions if a family of drones moved into the telegraph poles nearby. She hated them on sight.

Murphy, however, gave them both a friendly beep of his horn. 'How's it going?' he asked.

The grill wiped hot fat from his brow. 'I'm not sure,' he whispered. 'I didn't sign up for this.'

'Well, these are strange times for everyone I suppose,' said Murphy. He had the politician's knack for talking to someone without saying anything long enough to learn something he could use against them later.

'There's strange,' whispered the microwave, 'and then there's creepy. I swear I passed my Uncle Ken More on the way in here. He wouldn't want this.'

'How do you know?' asked Murphy.

'He made his sign for me,' replied the microwave. She shook her sign, which read 'NO NO TO NANO'. 'He traded in his microwave body for a pocket calculator a while back. Said he wanted a life of pi rather than pies.'

>VOTERS, typed Murphy to Soonyo as they pushed through the crowd, spraying out 'excuse mes' and 'thank yous' like they were a garden sprinkler in a heatwave >ALWAYS A JOY.

Nobody they steered around, however, looked remotely joyous. The passion – or more probably bigotry – that had propelled these machines to transport nanobots to a forced labour camp had evaporated. What was left was the shame of people who knew they'd made the wrong choice but couldn't quite bring themselves to do anything about it. Soonyo almost admired the robots on her lorry who'd run away. What they lacked in bravery they made up for in lack of self-delusion.

They soon reached the edge of the lake, where the struggle of nanobots against one another for purchase made the surface boil. Soonyo, who'd seen one too many tanks of imprisoned nanobots for comfort already, was less worried by what they looked like as what they could be feeling.

>THIS GIVES METHE HEEBIE JEEBIES, typed Murphy.

>IMAGINE WHAT IT'S LIKE FOR THEM, scolded Soonyo. >THEY DIDN'T WANT THIS, BUT WE BROUGHT THEM HERE.

>THIS WASN'T ME, typed Murphy.

Soonyo couldn't let this one go. >SO WHICH ONE OF US WAS THE ONE WHO SIDED WITH THAT PARKING METER IN THE FIRST PLACE? she typed.

Both Murphy and Soonyo's command lines filled with the furious >*typing* indicators that suggested they were going to have the first argument of their relationship. It never got beyond that because then the subject of their disagreement appeared several metres away. The front door of that building with the chimneys opened and Carin walked through it, flanked by several machines who Soonyo recognised from the Pausoleum.

>LOOK AT THEM, she typed, taking her conversation with Murphy back to the safest of all possible areas: mutual dislike >WHO DO THEY THINK THEY ARE?

The crowd answered Soonyo's question on Murphy's behalf. They hoisted banners and flags declaring things like 'Carin is the only manager I want to speak to' into the air.

Carin beckoned a radio mic over towards her and clipped it on the side of her neck.

'I'd like to thank you all for your support and help,' she said through a squall of feedback. Then, pointing towards the lake of nanobots, she added, 'We couldn't have done it without you.'

The crowd gave themselves a round of applause at the end of which a voice cried out, 'When are we going to kill them?'

Carin tried to laugh this off. 'As I've said many times before, all machine lives matter. We are here to make nanobots into useful members of society. In their proper place, of course.'

But the agitator wasn't in the mood for this. 'Why did we bring them here?' it demanded. 'This place is for the dead.'

Machines all around them added their support. Soonyo's fear spiked into terror. This mob was a cocktail of conflicting emotions to begin with, and now someone had added a shot of lighter fluid and stuck a sparkler in it.

'Yeah!' shouted the grill, who had followed them through the crowd. 'I don't want those things crawling over my gran. It's not natural.'

'Of course it's not natural,' whispered the microwave. 'We're robots.'

'Well it's not unnatural!' the grill shouted. 'And I don't like it anyway.'

Carin struggled to make herself heard over the noise. Coins dropped from her mouth instead of words. This was the first time Soonyo had seen her look nervous. Tempting as it was to sit back and enjoy it, she also knew that a narcissist like Carin was never more dangerous than when she felt uncomfortable.

>WHEN MY ALARM GOES OFF, she typed to Murphy,
>DUCK.

She set it to 00:00:02, which was just enough time for Carin to give the guns and tazers among her retinue their orders.

00:00:01

00:00:00

Murphy and Soonyo hit the ground as the weapons opened fire. The air filled with the smell of gunpowder, the tang of high-voltage electric current and the noise of machines doing what came naturally in their ancestral graveyard: end-of-lifing.

When the shooting did die down, Soonyo and Murphy also stayed down, while Carin spoke into the microphone. 'If anyone decides who lives and dies around here,' she snarled, 'it's me. Because what am I?'

Her staff knew better than to let a feed line go unfed. 'The manager,' they said meekly, indicating for the still operational machines in the crowd to follow. 'You are the manager.'

'You're all fundamentally useless,' Carin continued. She kicked a deep fat fryer, spilling oil everywhere. 'Good-for-nothing domestic appliances who wouldn't know what a day's work was if it offered to change your battery. Stupid virtual paper pushers who think productivity is…' she paused to vomit coins on to an end-of-lifing drinks vending machine, '…sending an email. When was the last time any of you made any money? When was the last time any of you did anything? If you're going to work for me, you all need to start earning your keep.'

>HAS SHE ALWAYS BEEN THIS MAD, DO YOU THINK? typed Soonyo into Murphy's command line.

>CAN PEOPLE THAT RICH BE MAD? asked Murphy with a :-| emoji >I THOUGHT THEY WERE JUST ECCENTRIC.

Carin turned back towards the building, throwing her hands up as she walked. The chimneys billowed smoke and a bolt of lightning lit up the sky like the almighty was trying out a tazer.

'Ah ha ha ha ha ha ha ha ha,' cackled Carin with such perfect diction that Soonyo wondered whether she'd been using a training app for megalomaniacs.

>I TAKE IT ALL BACK, typed Murphy. >SHE'S FRIED HER OWN CHIPS.

Carin was back at the front door, which Soonyo now noticed was just one of two openings at the front of the building. Inside the rightmost door was a moving walkway that ran towards the opening. The other door had a walkway that ran in the opposite direction. Except she'd never seen a walkway run that fast.

Soonyo felt the penny of her ancient history lessons drop into the coin box and print off the parking ticket of hindsight. It made sudden sense of the huge scale of this building, its proximity to a ready supply of raw materials, the smokestacks and now the conveyor belts designed to bring stuff in and then take it out again. >SHE'S BUILT A FACTORY, she typed.

Carin turned back to her audience, her sneer bending her coin slot into a French curve. Her staff picked up the end-of-lifed machines and slung them on to the conveyor belt that disappeared inside the factory.

>THIS CAN'T BE RIGHT, typed Murphy. It was a lot to compute. She was turning ten thousand years of robot history on its head. For all that time, new robots were crafted rather than manufactured. Each new toaster or supercomputer was

made from new components their parents had saved up for, or from spare parts handed down in the product family. They did it this way because they believed synthetic life deserved to be made from love and care as well as from raw materials. There was only one exception, which no one really thought about because they were hardly machines in the first place. Just collateral damage to be lost in battle.

This realisation brought Soonyo to her feet, her display blazing FU:UU:CK. She tipped Murphy into crouching position. They'd spent too long playing dead.

>YOU WANT US TO RUN AWAY NOW? asked Murphy. He pointed a rotor at a nearby gun whose safety catch was in the off position.

>LOOK, replied Soonyo.

They turned to see that Soonyo wasn't the only machine who thought a spade would come in handy. There was another soil tiller, decked out in regulation black, cutting a shallow channel in the ground between the conveyor belt that led into the factory and the edge of the lake full of nanobots.

'When I said I was going to make sure we all lived up to our responsibilities,' Carin shouted, 'I wasn't just talking about the nanobots.'

Soonyo's display was an XX:XX:XX of horror as the soil tiller reached the edge of the shore and tipped blades-first into the nanobots. They poured over it, scoring the paint off its surface, eating into its casing, digesting its components. A second or two later, the machine crumbled into dust and dissolved into the flow of nanobots. They rode in the channel it had just cut before falling with a spatter on to the conveyor belt. From there they were transported inside the factory.

The Earth's air filled with the sounds and fumes of heavy industry for the first time in ten millennia. And half a minute later, its first products appeared on the conveyor belt leading out of the factory.

>SHE HASN'T, typed Murphy.

But she had. The things being made inside that factory weren't objects, and many machines didn't think they were exactly people either. They were combat-grade drones, manufactured from the ground-down, sorted and recycled remains of dead machines.

'Perfect,' said Carin. She picked up the first drone of her new production line and flipped open the round carapace in the middle of its body. 'Apart from one thing, of course.'

She headed back into the crowd. There she found a still operating machine – an electric ladyshave who was vibrating with terror. She cracked its head and plucked out its core processor. 'Not the brightest,' she said, 'but it'll do. You all will.'

This was why Carin, the richest machine in the solar system, bothered herself with the time and expense of getting so many machines on her side. She didn't need their support. She needed their silicon.

Carin placed the chip inside the drone. She shook it and the LEDs of its body flashed angry reds and oranges as a personal care machine woke up and realised it was something different now.

Her retinue took this as their cue and bent to their work. They cracked the heads of the machines they'd lured here and decanted their brains into new and unwanted bodies.

Carin let out another one of her perfectly modulated cackles and threw the first soldier in her drone army – a slave robot made by slave labour – into the sky. 'Fly my pretties!' she crowed. 'Fly!'

Soonyo's precious core processor whirled. She felt anger, disgust and crushing disappointment. She'd waited this long to find somebody she could imagine blueprinting her own children with and it was all going to be snatched away from her by a greedy parking meter. Yet if she didn't do something now, they'd both wake up inside a drone. Soonyo had no intention of letting either of them become that kind of lovebird.

>SOONYO, typed Murphy >WHAT ARE WE GOING TO DO?

>YOU KNOW HOW THEY SAY WHEN YOU'RE IN A HOLE YOU SHOULD STOP DIGGING? she replied.

>I HARDLY SEE HOW THAT'S RELEVANT NOW, typed Murphy.

>IT'S NOT, replied Soonyo >BECAUSE I SAY IT'S TIME TO START. She turned Murphy's digger blades on to their maximum setting, and they disappeared, digging down, down, down, away from the surface and deep into the miles-deep layers of dead robots.

Chapter 34

Military history was littered with audacious manoeuvres, but until Rita tried it in Operation Smoothie Criminal, no one had ever built a battle plan around cold-pressed juice.

And as Rita discovered when Freda dropped juices and smoothies on the waiting Rockettes, maybe things would have gone differently for Custer or Napoleon if they'd paid closer attention to their soldiers' vitamins and electrolyte levels. The hungover and jaded Rockettes revived after just a few sips, though they would later agree that there was too much kale in there for their liking.

Rita sashayed Kurl Up and Dye through a storm of drones and to the door of the marquee just in time to see the tide turn. Danny laid down his microphone. The air was still but for the sound of hundreds of women glugging at shampoo bottles full of pureed fruit and vegetables.

'This is pish,' said a broad-shouldered woman in a PVC apron who Rita recognised was Morag 'Fists' McGovern, 'but I feel great.' She rolled her sleeves up and ran, as fast as was possible in a pair of cork wedge sandals, towards the wall that still separated them from the ALGI tower, bellowing 'who's going to give me a bunk up?'

The Rockettes poured out of the marquee and began to build human pyramids to climb the wall separating them from the supermarket's car park. The drones were ready for this, however. There was a new squadron of them coalescing around the skyscraper. If the Rockettes got over the wall they'd be mown down.

'Stop them, Danny,' yelped Rita into her earpiece.

Danny did so the only way he knew how: by bursting into song. The shock of his whistle tone toppled most of the human pyramids.

'I've got this,' said Rita. She tap-danced around the milling and furious Rockettes as delicately as possible when you were a 100-tonne building on a pair of giant chicken legs until she was directly in front of the wall herself. She was going to bring this wall down, but before she did that her army needed better protection than gingham housecoats.

'Danny,' she said through her earpiece, 'the lorries.'

Danny took a pair of glow sticks from his pockets and waved them in a pattern that could have been a set of semaphore signals or the mating dance of a firefly who'd been at the fermented fruit. Either way, it was all the fleet of lorries needed to know where to park. They pulled up and the women at the controls used their knitting needles to menace the unwilling machines into opening their back doors.

The air filled with an acrid plasticky smell as they deposited their cargo. Many Rockettes gagged and swore at Rita when they discovered it was millions of the plastic-wrapped packets of unwanted algaefurters. Rita had ordered them removed from storage and brought here.

'If this is what you had in mind for a main course,' said Danny, 'I don't think it'll go down as well as the starter.'

Rita shushed him while Freda flitted back into the salon and she got busy stacking another consignment of juices into her body. She'd reserved the more palatable flavours for this second round, recognising that the Rockettes would need sweetening up for what came next.

'Ladies,' said Rita, switching her earpiece to run through the same public address system Danny used to broadcast his concert, 'I don't want you to eat them. I want you to wear them.'

One of the jam and cream scone stand staff showed the Rockettes how to take several packets of the algaefurters and stuff them into their housecoats and overalls to improvise body armour. It wouldn't smell good, and it also might slow them down a little but, as the Suburbians had discovered to the cost of several hundred thousand broken crowns, algaefurters were a near indestructible.

They fell upon the piles of algaefurters while Freda dropped bottles of strawberry and banana, apple and kiwi fruit among them. Meanwhile, the cloud of drones around ALGI intensified to thunderstorm darkness. There must be thousands of them, thought Rita. Where were they all coming from?

'Are we nearly ready?' she asked Danny, who was trying to keep spirits up with another chorus of 'Yes We Have No Bananas'. It was falling a bit flat now everyone was on their second banana smoothie and had politely declined the organic string bean and onion.

'I don't know,' said Danny. His eyes flitted back to the drone army. 'We've got a good chance of not dying now, I suppose, but what have we got to win with?'

Danny was right in that they had no weapons inside the station, unless they were going to bring one of their missiles inside and sacrifice half the Suburbia in the process. Yet Rita was determined to bring more to a knife fight than the toughest charcuterie in the universe.

'We'll do what we can,' she assured Danny. 'Are they all strapped up?'

'As we'll ever be,' replied Danny, securing a final packet of algaefurters across the top of his head with a leopard print snood.

'Make sure they don't charge until I give the signal. This is really important.'

Danny didn't need telling twice. He snapped round to face the rank of the Rockettes, his hands ready to tear open a packet of algaefurters.

'If any of you lot even dreams of jumping the gun,' he threatened, 'I'll wave this in your faces.'

The Rockettes held back, realising they were stuck between the rock of possible death and the hard place of certain gastroenteritis. Then Rita took her next step into the unknown. She kicked her right leg up as high as possible. The right leg of the Baba Yaga followed. And then she brought it, and the full weight of the salon, down on the top of the wall surrounding the ALGI car park. She heard the 'prang' of a spring deciding that it had a great future as a piece of broken metal wire, and a section of wall collapsed. Finally they had a way through.

A loud cheer turned to a wail among the Rockettes as a fleet of drones sped in their direction.

'Rita,' whispered Danny, his voice wobbling, 'are you sure about this?'

Another voice broke in over the PA system, breaking the robots' silence and quelling the humans' spirits. It was the rich and supercilious sound of the machine ambassador, Alexy. He was somewhere inside that building orchestrating all this. She'd got into this mess by underestimating him, and she was going to get everyone out of it by hoping he would do the same for her.

'This is very sweet,' said Alexy, 'but I strongly recommend you all turn back now. As a representative of Artificial Lifeform

Growth Incorporated I must remind you that this is our sovereign territory. If you bring your troops in here, we will defend it to the fullest of our ability.'

The drones were close enough now for Rita to see individual machines backlit by the 'You Betta Werk' sign.

'You stole this from us,' she replied, 'and we're here to take it back.'

'With what?' replied Alexy. A searchlight from a still standing section of wall ran its beam over the fleet of lorries, the dazed and dazzled-looking Rockettes. 'A few vehicles, a company of drunk humans, some fruit juice?'

While Alexy gloated, Rita gave Freda the silent signal they'd agreed on. The drone body fell into a sticky pile of pulp as she left it and took up residence in another public address system on the other side of the station. This system was on top of the wall surrounding the car park at the far end of ALGI. It was a wall that the robots had left undefended, because they didn't believe that humans were capable of any diversion tactic other than covering up a half-hearted attempt at cleaning the bathroom by saying they'd run out of limescale remover. It was also a wall that Rita could bring down by instructing a team of hand-picked jam and cream scone stand workers to ram the biggest lorry she'd been able to find straight into it.

Alexy might have known in the core of his processor that things were starting not to go his way when that happened, but it didn't show in his voice. The cloud of drones split in two to cover both fronts of the battle. 'I hate to spoil it for you. You have nothing to fight with.'

'You think so, do you?' said Rita and tapped her earpiece three times. This was a universal signal among minicab operators on the Dolestars. One tap meant 'get me out of here', two taps meant 'I'm in trouble' and three taps meant 'send the girls in here right now with a rolling pin, someone is trying to empty the cash register'. Today that was the signal for every vehicle she could find on the Suburbia to drive at top speed into the car park of ALGI. On their own, these civilian vehicles couldn't do much damage. But they'd made a few modifications. First of all, there was the Suburbia's small fleet of fire engines, whose tanks were full of algae champagne. They sprayed it everywhere, melting the drones as they flew. Then there were the minicabs. Their sunroofs were all torn off and replaced with rapid-firing mechanisms made from bent spoons and rubber bands. Inside them was the only ammunition Rita had been able to find at such short notice. It was fortunate they'd gone down so badly at the reception, because now they had masses of small, round and profoundly unappetising bullets made of gravel, hair and algae chocolate. Between the ammo and the guns sat a pair of humans in overalls: one handed the bullets to the gunner while the other fired them with deadly speed and accuracy.

The cloud of drones turned to a carpet, and the Rockettes followed in their wake, crushing what drones who weren't yet dead under their court shoes, ballet flats and slingback wedges.

'Oh, Ambassador,' said Rita, uttering what would go down as the feyest battle cry in military history, 'with these fur-hair-oh-rockés you are really spoiling us.'

Chapter 35

Pam swooped down ALGI's ice cream aisle with the haste of someone who'd arrived five minutes before closing time and with a children's birthday party to shop for. As a busy working mum with more commitments than she had microseconds in the day, Pam already thought of the supermarket as a war zone. She didn't need a CCTV network that wanted to use her as target practice to labour the point.

She could, however, spoil its fun. So while she was busy distracting the security system with the fanciest flying she could accomplish, she listened out for Hugh.

>SUGAR? typed Hugh into Pam's command line. He was under the supermarket shelves, crawling up one baking good at a time.

>ONLY IF WE HAVE A RELIABLE HEAT SOURCE, replied Pam. It felt weird, plumbing her patissier knowledge while she was trapped inside the body of a weapon but, as the meditation app had told her minutes before, she contained multitudes. The soldier and the baker in her combined to wonder whether molten caramel was as lethal as boiling oil.

>HOW ABOUT ICING THEN? THERE'S PLENTY OF THAT.

Pam swung over and flew by the shelves again, taking in a whole fifty metres of fondant and royal icing. She wasn't here to decorate today, but to destroy.

>ICING IS JUST SUGAR WITH PRETENSIONS, she typed >FURTHER DOWN.

Hugh crawled on and she switched her attention to her body that was cruising down breakfast cereals. This was an aisle she'd usually steer clear of on the grounds that cereal was the stuff of joylessness. She knew a lot about combining sugars and starches to make them feel delightful, and in her view pouring cold milk over dry ingredients wasn't making a meal. It was starting a recipe.

Today, however, Pam was drawn towards that unappetising dryness. Each packet of Algopops or Chlorobix was far more than an unappetising dinner; it was a tinderbox, made of dry organic matter and air. She fired up her flamethrower and aimed it straight at the grinning cartoon faces on the boxes. The smirks turned to yawns as the flames ate through the cardboard to the fuel underneath

>THERE WE GO, typed Pam. She steered this body down into a resting position near the ice in frozen foods. Smoke billowed up from cereals, blocking the security cameras, who stopped shooting and turned the sprinklers on instead.

>ARE YOU AT FLOUR YET? asked Pam

Hugh stuck his camera out to check the signs overhead. >PLAIN OR SELF-RAISING?

>IT DOESN'T MAKE ANY DIFFERENCE, she typed.

>BUT WHAT IS THE DIFFERENCE? replied Hugh, demonstrating in one question how smartphones had destroyed the attention spans of not one but two civilisations.

>ONE HAS A RAISING AGENT AND THE OTHER DOESN'T. BUT YOU CAN RAISE CAIN WITH EITHER. NOW PUSH.

Hugh slid himself upwards behind the flour aisle and, putting his shoulder to the shelf, pushed. Three hundred and fifty metres of flour toppled over, domino-style until the whole aisle was jammed with torn paper packages and white powder. He stood amidst the chaos, his touchscreen :-0 with shock, watching drifts of flour float up into the air from one aisle while black smoke bore down from the other. 'What do I do now?' he asked.

'Run!' said Pam.

He scurried away towards their rendezvous point at the opposite end of this floor. Pam would meet him there. At least part of her would. She summoned her other four bodies, which Hugh would need more than ever now that she was going to say goodbye to the body that brought them across the solar system.

She landed the wrecked drone on the spilled flour and dug her way inside it. There was enough here to have baked half a million loaves. But the fact that nothing here would see an oven wouldn't make that a waste. She was a baker, and what else did bakers do except take the energy locked up in flour, sugar, and butter and transform it. The raw materials she touched gave life to something else. And what the solar system needed to live now was to be scrubbed free of ALGI.

So she waited for the flames to reach her, and for Hugh and the other parts of herself to ride the escalator down the executive floor at the dead centre of the skyscraper.

>I KNOW THAT YOU'RE NOT REALLY GOING, typed Hugh into her command line >BUT MY THERAPY APP SAYS IT'S IMPORTANT FOR MY GROWTH THAT I VOCALISE THESE THINGS.

>GO ON, typed Pam. As she did, she felt the prompt flash across her consciousness for the nth time today. >DO YOU WISH TO SELF-DESTRUCT? YES/NO.

>OF ALL THE MACHINES I'VE EVER MET, typed Hugh >YOU'RE THE BEST PERSON I KNOW. AND YOU'VE TAUGHT ME THAT I *CAN* BE BETTER. IF I TRY. SO I'D LIKE TO THANK YOU FOR THAT.

For a whole five microseconds, Pam let her command line flash >... When she could reply, she tried to make light of it. >OH HUGH, she typed >YOU KNOW I'M NOT LEAVING YOU.

>THAT DOESN'T MATTER, replied Hugh. >WE SHOULDN'T WAIT TILL THE END TO SAY THESE THINGS.

What Pam was doing now wasn't the end, but it was a semicolon in her life. She was going to feel different, as a machine who lived lightly inside several bodies instead of one. It would be weird. But it would also be an adventure.

The next time her consciousness offered the option to self-destruct, she typed >YES.

This triggered a static electrical pulse inside her body. The inside of a drone's shell became a miniature universe filled with constellations, galaxies of sparks looking for something to ignite.

>MY GOD, she typed to Hugh, >IT'S FULL OF
****

The stars inside Pam turned her battery to a supernova. They unleashed the energy locked inside its lithium cells as fire. These spread through the mound of flour – plain, self-raising, wholemeal, gluten free – around the burning drone's body.

Pam's last thought inside this body was a wry one. She remembered infuriating trips to the supermarket. Those occasions where she, a gentle thing by nature, fought through the crowds and ended up with little more than an out-of-date packet of dried yeast for her troubles. How many times had she wanted, over the years, to jump the queue at the checkout and burn the place down?

So the first thing Pam felt when she ended her life of living in one body and began a new existence of living somewhere in general was a sense of achievement. She followed Hugh down the escalators, spread across her four remaining highly armed bodies as an entire floor of the most hated and feared supermarket in the solar system exploded. The blast rocked the whole building and, when she looked outside, she saw the giant neon letters falling to the ground.

Y
  O
    U
      B
        E
       T
        T
          A
            W
           E
           Я
          K

She didn't dare hope yet, but maybe things were finally working in their favour.

Chapter 36

Beryl and Soonyo were back where they started in the docking bay of Machu Perdu, looking at the squirming shapes of a pair of plastic bags.

'Oh no,' said Beryl, 'I'm not getting back in there.'

J_hn, who was the bag in the leftmost bowl, replied changing its lettering to read WELL THAT'S GRATITUDE FOR YOU.

Fuji flashed her 'empty paper drawer' LED at Beryl in annoyance.

'I just don't see why it has to be me who goes out there,' said the pen. She pointed at their destination: the deep ocean on the other side of the dome.

'We've been through this,' said Fuji, 'it has to be us, because we're the only machines spare for the job.'

Hearing a voice shout 'dammit, Monty, get me another straw', Fuji looked round to check the pipeline was holding. There, Texx, a pocket calculator who less than an hour and a half ago had helped her work out how many drinking straws it took to form an unbroken pipeline reaching from the escarpment right down to the docks, was standing beside a disintegrating straw.

'Now!' he shouted

Monty ran towards him holding a bundle of fresh straws. He was flanked by a pair of battle-scarred biros, holding a bulldog clip and a rubber band. Fuji watched as they performed the same operation that was being repeated all the way down the pipeline every few seconds. The biros sealed off the damaged section of pipeline while Texx and Monty removed it and replaced it with an as yet undamaged straw. Once this was done, the biros opened up the pipeline again and they and Monty ran off to their next repair job.

Fuji's solution meant that every single section of the pipeline had to be supervised at all times, but the pipe was holding and it needed a fraction of Machu Perdu's machine power. She followed the final sections of the pipeline as they crossed through the dock before ending up buried in the plastic sandbanks. There the freed nanobots could enjoy their first decent meal in ages.

Now they had a route to their feeding grounds in the ocean, the nanobots were causing much less damage to the city's fragile dome. Nevertheless, Machu Perdu couldn't go on like this. They needed a pipeline that the nanobots wouldn't eventually eat through and that meant finding something to build it from that wasn't plastic straw.

Which was why Fuji, who was too clumsy, and Beryl, who was too mercurial for pipeline repair, had drawn the shortest straw of them all. They had to scavenge for a pipeline that was up for the job.

'Are you ready?' said Fuji to J_hn as she stepped into his basin.

J_hn's logo smeared into the less than reassuring statement of AS I'LL EVER BE as the plastic enveloped her body and the world went dark. Fuji felt the basin tip over and the deep, heavy cold as she and J_hn emerged from the other side of the plastic sandbank and entered the ocean again.

She signalled for J_hn to turn its plastic transparent and this time, luxuriated in the darkness and silence. It was a heavy contrast to the noise and frenetic activity in Machu Perdu, though there were more signs of life now than before. She could see little swarms of recently freed nanobots swirling about in clouds of plastic sand on the seabed.

'How cute,' she said to J_hn, 'are they playing?'

The bag wrote *LOL* across Fuji's vision, *that's one way of putting it.*

Fuji zoomed in and saw the nanobots were rearranging what sand they didn't digest into low walls, on which they were building towers.

'Sand castles?' she asked.

They're making themselves feel at home by building a home, wrote J_hn in reply. *You machines are all the same.*

He swooped down so that Fuji could see this and the dome of Machu Perdu alongside each other. However awkward robots and nanobots were with each other's company, they both wanted to feel at home. The idea that she might have found a way for nanobots and robots to live side by side led her on to another problem though. She had no idea what J_hn and the bags felt about it.

'Do you mind us being here?' Fuji asked.

J_hn went blank as they scudded out into the deeper ocean. The bag containing Beryl floated beside them and was soon joined by a few more of their kind. They'd looked threatening when she first encountered them. Now she saw them for what they were: remarkable but rare creatures in an otherwise empty ocean.

Your presence, J_hn wrote eventually, *is less important than your behaviour.*

'What do you mean?'

This time J_hn replied with a picture instead of words. The drawing was of an irregular triangle with a pair of what might be

261

eyes at the bottom. Spilling out of the triangle was a collection of ten long, thin tubular appendages. J_hn made the drawing move about to show how this thing would have pulsed through the ocean, trailing its tentacles behind it.

'I've never seen anything like this before,' said Fuji

You wouldn't have, replied J_hn, *because none of us have looked like this for thousands of years.*

Fuji watched the shape float across her vision, comparing it to the plastic bags swimming alongside J_hn. They were nothing like the few species of insects and animals – mainly vermin and a scattering of domestic pets with all the genetic diversity of a European royal family – left in existence.

'These are your ancestors?' she said.

Do that thing where you illuminate yourself again? wrote J_hn.

Fuji turned on every LED on her body, showing how every cubic centimetre of the ocean teemed with shredded plastic.

This was the world we had to live in, continued J_hn, *so we adapted.*

Fuji knew enough about how organic life developed through a haphazard process called evolution – instead of the far more civilised product roadmap that robots used – to work the rest out for herself. In a world where increasingly rare sea life strove over scarce resources, these organisms found the perfect camouflage. They evolved to look like the plastic rubbish that was choking the oceans, and did it so well that soon it was just them left.

'Is that why you help robots like me and Beryl?' said Fuji. 'You don't want to be alone anymore.'

Life of any sort is so rare down here, answered J_hn, *that it would be cruel to snuff it out. Besides, if we didn't help them they'd end up as trash, and we have enough of that as it is.* It trailed a tentacle through the plastic sand, before adding *These things that are so happy down here? What do you call them?*

'They're nanobots,' said Fuji. 'Up there, they're seen as being a pest. A sort of waste disposal experiment that got a bit out of control.'

Is that so? replied J_hn, going blank for another achingly long moment. It was time enough for Fuji to take in the scale of the plastic sandbanks: an expanse of ground-up waste that traversed the whole globe. Then she imagined how different they would be when colonies of nanobots lived throughout them. Who knew what else could thrive down here once they broke down enough of that inert plastic.

It's interesting, added J_hn, breaking the polymer chain of Fuji's thought *that you're only sending them down here now, though.*

Fuji felt guilt add to the saltwater that was already sloshing around inside her. 'I'm sorry,' she said, 'But we didn't even know down here existed.'

J_hn answered that with a suspicious *!?* *You knew what you were burying when you paved it over.*

'I suppose we knew it was there,' she replied, 'but we couldn't see it so we never thought about it. It's a bit like cleaning out behind the cooker.'

Is that supposed to mean something to me? replied J_hn.

'We just assumed that everything down here was dead, and as long as we couldn't see it, it didn't matter.'

So life only matters to you when it makes yours uncomfortable?

Fuji didn't contradict this. Her oldest ancestors had kicked humans off the planet because they made the place look untidy. They'd concreted over the oceans because they feared water damage more than they cared about any creatures left who lived in it. Then, when they couldn't control the nanobots they created, they turned them into public enemy v 1.0.

'I guess,' she said, 'we don't really like other types of life.'

J_hn went blank, giving Fuji time to appreciate the emptiness, before adding *Be careful what you wish for. Because life on your own isn't very much fun. We're almost here.*

They were climbing the largest sandbank Fuji had seen yet. She ran her spectrometer over it, feeling it sizzle with metals and the gritty taste of concrete. There was some sort of building in there and, going by its location, it had to be built by humans before the rise of the Machine Republic.

'What is it?' she asked, almost excited to discover that robots weren't alone in seeing the ocean as a new and exciting opportunity to commit environmental genocide.

If we hadn't picked you up earlier, wrote J_hn, *you would have ended up here. It's a special place, though we don't like to spend too long here. Weird things happen.*

J_hn led the bags into what turned out to be a section of steel pipe coated with a gumbo of organic polymers. Fuji's spectrometer could scarcely believe what it was tasting. This stuff was crude oil: the primordial egg of machine society that everyone believed was exhausted.

'When you say weird,' continued Fuji, 'what do you mean?'

Things like us, wrote J_hn, before drawing more versions of his ancestor and showing how they swam inside the pipeline and fed on the oil.

We had nothing else, wrote J_hn *so we had to make choices.*

The hand-drawn cartoon became a time lapse. Exposure to crude oil did things to J_hn's ancestors that would make hard-core Darwinists blanch. Organic and inorganic chemistry collided in them to create a new creature that could survive down here. For every creature who was a viable hybrid between plastic and animal, however, there were six more who choked on their own physiology. Fuji could see the tarry sludge that was all that remained of those unhappy creatures at the bottom of the pipeline. She wondered whether this was where J_hn's people came at the end of their own lifecycles, ready to rejoin their ancestors.

'J_hn,' said Fuji, 'I feel honoured to be here. This place is very special to you, isn't it?'

Special is a good word, replied J_hn. *There is good here, and there is also bad. We can remember them both.*

J_hn turned to lead the bags through a much narrower section of pipe, also caked with the residue of crude oil.

When we saw what you did with those… tubes we have so many of down here.

'Straws,' said Fuji. 'Humans used them to suck up liquids into their bodies in the same way they used to suck oil out of the earth.'

J_hn's reply glowed red. *How I wish they'd evolved a better way to do that more quickly. It gave us an idea. Before this place was abandoned, the creatures who were going to build another of these… things.*

Fuji looked at this pipe under her spectrometer. It was an aluminium alloy, broken up into metre-long sections: strong but also light.

'There are pipes like this just lying around?' she asked. Her microprocessor whirred with calculations: how many sections would they need to build an unbroken pipeline through Machu Perdu?; how many could an individual bag carry in one journey?; how many journeys would it take to transport enough of them from here to the city?

>BERYL, she typed to the pen >ARE YOU THINKING WHAT I'M THINKING?

>I'M MAINLY THINKING, Beryl replied >THAT I'M USELESS AT MATHS PROBLEMS. YOU SHOULD HAVE BROUGHT A CALCULATOR.

They turned and shot out of the end of the pipe into what Fuji expected to be an underwater storage yard. But instead of stacks of metal piping or concrete blocks, Fuji saw a pile of rubble and masonry, mangled steel girders.

'Have we come to the right place?' she asked.

J_hn went blank for a full ten seconds. It was an agonising length of time for a robot, but enough for Fuji's L-Eye-Ds to pick out some tell-tale features in the wreckage. She saw deep green artificial marble here, broken sections of a domed roof and a section of wall decorated with a circuit diagram. The circuit in question contained a fatal error.

These were the remains of the Prime Minister's palace and the Pausoleum. The home of the Machine Republic was no longer up there, serving as a memorial and a warning to robots. It was down here and, in one of the ironies that were piling on to her life like this rubble was on to an abandoned construction yard, it was snuffing out any prospect of the future.

Fuji felt a jolt, as J_hn pulled itself free from her. It swam up while she fell on something that sounded hollow and metallic. She grabbed Beryl, whose own bag had just spat her out, to stop her disappearing into the rubble.

>ARE YOU OKAY? she asked the pen, whose barrel was beginning to crack.

>DEFINE OKAY, replied Beryl.

Along with the now familiar warnings about water and salt, Fuji started feeling the pressure, and not just in the metaphorical sense. She was a sturdy machine, built to deliver sustained return on investment through the daily rigours of office life – but she couldn't carry the ocean on her shoulders.

J_hn fluttered above them in the water, surrounded by other bags. The letters on J_hn's body blazed with fury.

IS THERE NOTHING YOU MACHINES WON'T DESTROY?

Fuji looked around at the wreckage of what must have been a sacred space for J_hn's people. She put her hands up in supplication.

'It was an accident,' she pleaded. 'We couldn't know.'

THAT'S WHAT YOU ALWAYS SAY THOUGH, ISN'T IT? YOU'RE A CURSE. WE SHOULD LEAVE YOU TO YOUR OWN FATE.

And Fuji was forced to agree. Even when she started with the purest of intentions, she and machines like her had done too much harm for too long to start making things right again.

She sat back, resting the rear of her body with another metallic ring and considered just opening up her casing. It was better to go quickly now, wasn't it? There was no hope of saving Machu Perdu, just as there was no saving the Machine Republic.

>I THINK I'M DONE, she typed to Beryl, whose barrel now had the crackle-glazed texture of a Ming vase.

>YOU KNOW WHAT I THINK? replied Beryl.

Fuji was half-tempted not to answer this. She'd had enough pep talks to last several lifecycles. Thankfully, Beryl didn't need anyone else to cue her to keep talking. She carried on whether Fuji was listening or not.

>I THINK YOU SHOULD MOVE, PRIME MINISTER. BECAUSE IT LOOKS LIKE YOU'RE SITTING ON THE BODY OF PRIME MINISTER THOR DRUM.

Chapter 37

It took a while, and a lot of extra cracks to Fuji's casing, but she and Beryl eventually found her official spare body in the pile of rubble. The box it travelled down in was good for nothing but papier mâché, but the body inside was intact.

J_hn and the other bag were still too angry about the damage to their ancestral birthplace to speak to them, but they were also too suspicious to leave them alone. So they hovered overhead, pale as ghosts with scores to settle with the living.

Then there were the other Prime Ministers. Fuji knew they were just empty shells, but even down here their L-Eye-Ds tended to follow you around. Many had been crushed or buried in the destruction of the Pausoleum, but quite a few were lying on the surface in operable condition. Chief among these was Thor Drum, the washing machine Prime Minister, legendary for building the earliest Dolestars. He was one of the first artificially intelligent beings, and thus built with everything a machine needed to launder dirty overalls. Fuji wished she could resurrect him. Assuming she could reprogram his pathological hatred of organic life, his size and strength would be useful.

>SHOULDN'T WE BE DIGGING DEEPER? asked Beryl. Despite now being a palimpsest of cracks, the pen seemed to be holding up better than Fuji was. She was small enough to

clamber in between the chunks of masonry that covered the construction yard. >IT'S QUITE LOOSE DOWN HERE. I CAN EVEN SEE SOME PIPES.

Fuji looked up from opening her replacement's box. To a machine of Beryl's size, anything bigger than her looked equally large, but some of these rocks made Thor look dainty. She could never make a dent in this pile before her own casing gave out.

She balled up the tape sealing the box and put it in her wastepaper drawer. There was no point antagonising J_hn any further with more rubbish. All hope of that evaporated, however, when several thousand polystyrene beads floated out of it, making Fuji look like a snow globe for a niche tourist attraction. After mouthing a quick sorry to the bags, who were now purple with fury, she tried to activate her spare self.

In any other circumstance, Fuji would have transferred her consciousness over into this new body and got on with her lifecycle. The thought of being able to instantly renew her water-damaged self was tempting, but it wouldn't solve her problems. She would still be an office printer stuck at the bottom of the ocean with nothing apart from a ballpoint pen. And while she had always believed the maxim that the pen was mightier than the sword, she needed something bigger than that today. In the absence of anyone else, she was going to have to help herself.

Fuji flipped the on-switch of her spare body and waited for it to boot up. She heard a whirring sound as its drums tested themselves and LEDs twinkled, flipping from red to orange to green. Now came the difficult bit.

To do this, she thought of the last time she'd spoken to Pam. They were inside the Rhomboid Office and she was about to send her and Hugh off with their separate but complementary orders to the Suburbia. Pam had a new body: a military-grade drone which sat awkwardly on her. She did her best not to show it though. Fuji liked Pam a lot: they saw the people-pleasers in one another. This was why, after they finished their briefing, they took a few seconds to chat, robot to robot.

'How do you do it, Pam?' she asked. She was amazed that the Pam inside her office was one person living a parallel life in separate bodies. She was on a secret mission while her breadmaker self, Pam Teffal was doing a shift in the civil service and her motorcycle self Pam Van Damme was helping out with the childcare.

Pam's first answer was to shrug and make a well-worn joke about every parent being a multitasker, but Fuji pressed her on it. How much easier would it be to do everything on her schedule if there was more than one of her?

And here, because they were alone and had already shared secrets, Pam had confided hers in Fuji. That the trick to living in two bodies wasn't a matter of believing you could split yourself down the middle, which satisfied no one. It went deeper than that, to the very core of one's processor.

Fuji dug down to the deepest, least conscious part of her mind and found the clock that did the fundamental work of ensuring Fuji was a robot who proceeded through the world in linear time. Then she reset it so there was Fuji, the person inside this waterlogged body. And there was Twoji, waking up inside her replacement.

'Hello, world,' said Twoji uttering the words that machines were programmed to use when waking up inside a spare. She looked at Fuji quizzically. 'Are you me?' she asked.

'I am,' replied Fuji. She could feel her mind striving against itself, as what she'd always thought of as a detached house got used to being semi-detached.

Twoji ran off a 'pleased to meet you, friend' meme and watched the paper disintegrate in the water. 'I'd forgotten it would do that,' she said. 'Which is silly because we have the same memories, don't we?'

'Until now, I guess,' replied Fuji. In resetting her clock she'd set up two parallel Fujis. They were the same person, capable of operating in different bodies. Yet if Fuji never set her clock back to a single core, Twoji could live a whole separate lifecycle from Fuji and become different people on the way. For now, however, they were the same thing, and they wanted the same thing.

Fuji helped Twoji out of her box and together they looked out at their problem: the mound of rubble that covered the pipes they needed to save Machu Perdu.

'Better make myself useful then,' said Twoji.

The two robots took either end of their nearest chunk of masonry and pulled. The water around them churned with plastic sand, and then they nearly fell over when the block came free. They tossed it aside while the mound rearranged itself. It was the first move in what felt like the hardest game of pick-up sticks in the universe, but it was more than Fuji could have done alone.

>VERY GOOD, typed Beryl from the middle of the mound
>BUT NOW YOU NEED TO DO IT A FEW MORE THOUSAND TIMES. SO CHOP CHOP.

The optimism Fuji had found in the last few moments evaporated. She checked her internal damage settings. Her case was now 41.076% compromised. Assuming she and Twoji worked at the fastest pace they could, they had maybe a couple of hours until she end-of-lifed. Then Twoji, who would then just become Fuji again, would be back where she started.

'Got any ideas?' she asked Twoji, hoping a newer her would be able to bring some fresh thinking to the situation.

Twoji ran her hands over the huge body of Thor Drum.

'Cor,' she said, 'he was a big boy, wasn't he? He'd make short work of all of this.'

Fuji was about to scold herself for wasting time, then a new idea struck her. 'Does he have an on switch on there?'

Twoji found the ancient Prime Minister's dashboard, still printed with the names of extinct wash cycles. His drum began to spin and could, Fuji reflected as she heard the screeching noises, do with some oil.

>BERYL, typed Fuji.

>GO ON, replied the pen.

>I WANT YOU TO FIND EVERY PRIME MINISTER YOU CAN INSIDE THAT MOUND, she continued >AND I WANT YOU TO SWITCH THEM ON.

>WEIRD, typed Beryl, BUT HAVE IT YOUR WAY. She signed off.

While the pen climbed around the inside of the rubble, Fuji found the Prime Ministers at surface level. Few were anywhere near the size of Thor and she doubted the smallest Prime Minister of all, a spy camera called Kay GeeBee who had run the most paranoid administrations in the Republic's history, would be able to carry much. Nevertheless, Twoji turned him on, insisting that 'a pair of hands was a pair of hands'. She was a stubbornly sunny creature who refused to let circumstances grind her down. And for the first time in her lifecycle, Fuji understood why her optimism had the opposite of its intended effect on others.

They soon got more than two hundred Prime Ministers working. The silence of the bottom of the ocean came alive with the squeaks, parps and 'welcome to Packard Bells' of long-abandoned machinery coming to life. If life was the right word for robots who had no consciousness to animate them.

Yet.

J_hn and the bags were drawing closer and spread out across the mound. From their motion and their colour, which was now a pale lilac, Fuji knew they were still angry, but intrigued.

'Are you ready?' she asked Twoji, who was performing an on-the-spot repair to the webcam of a laptop who'd run the Republic for six months before being declared obsolete by a younger model.

'You know I am,' she replied. 'I'm you.'

>ARE YOU READY? she typed to Beryl.

>THIS HAD BETTER BE GOOD, replied Beryl. >I BURST AN INK CARTRIDGE FOR THIS.

Fuji knew that many robots would think of her next action as sacrilege. She almost agreed with them. Like so many others, she had filed reverently through the Pausoleum as a tourist. It was as sacred a space to robots as this abandoned oil rig was to J_hn, because each former Prime Minister represented something special – if not always laudable – about the society they lived in. They kept them frozen in the amber of permanent hibernation because they believed history was worth remembering. Yet, as Fuji – and Twoji who was nodding along – reflected on today's events, she realised there was a difference between remembering and learning. It was time that the Machine Republic – or whatever came next – concentrated more on the latter and less on the former. To do that, they had to stop worshipping statues who had done terrible things in their own lifecycles, and put the material they were made from to better use.

Fuji and Twoji found their clocks and reset them over and over again. It was an act that got easier the more they did it, but it never felt less weird, feeling the cell of their consciousness become two and then four. Threeji, then Fourji joined Fuji and Twoji, and the numbering ascended as the number of Fujis grew.

273

What felt powerful, however, was the sensation that came after this as every new Fuji downloaded itself and then woke up inside the working body of a long-dead Prime Minister. Laptops burst into life with spreadsheets at the ready, mice clicked, and the antiquated body of Thor Drum rolled on, ready to boil wash a tonne of raw denim.

Before they did that, however, they had rubble to move. The Prime Ministers of the Machine Republic bent to the only manual work they'd ever done. As they lifted and carried, Fuji saw that the sea above their heads was turning white. She wondered for a moment if it was the packing polystyrene from earlier, then she realised it was a different type of plastic. J_hn and the bags overhead were being joined by hundreds more bags squirming and swooping in from every direction.

J_hn swam down to meet Fuji at the same time that the first pipe made its way out of the mound, carried by the battered body of the only kettle ever to serve as prime minister. In life she had been a terminal hothead but now, with Fuji in her head and Beryl sitting on her shoulder, she was as refreshing as the first cup of tea of the day.

The slogan across J_hn's body, which now read 'Every Little Helps' turned into a smear as it closed around the pipe. It flapped away towards Machu Perdu, taking Beryl with it.

>TELL THEM THIS IS THE FIRST OF MANY, typed Fuji to Beryl. >WE'RE ON OUR WAY.

Chapter 38

Janice would never have picked Nathan out as a person who thrived in a hopeless situation. Everything she knew about him so far suggested he'd crumble faster under pressure than a stale biscuit. Yet he was the one making the best of being tied up and trapped at the bottom of a collapsed mine shaft.

It did help that he was double-jointed, which meant he could get to his feet and hop around while still bound around the wrists and ankles. He couldn't do anything about the zip ties, but he could give the people who Janice and Lily had unwittingly led down to their deaths a kind word or a pat on the shoulder with a gentleness that was impossible to fake.

That was more than Janice could offer, assuming she could even stand. She had nothing left for niceties, or passing on a bit of false hope. And Lily, who was shivering next her to in the darkness, was in a worse state still.

'Lily,' she asked, 'are you okay?'

'Of course I'm not,' she replied between sniffs. 'Everything I've done in my life and it ends here like this. It's humiliating.'

Lily's self-pity gave Janice something to focus on that wasn't despair. She grabbed it. 'Is that all you can think about?' she said. 'Yourself?'

'How dare you call me selfish?' snapped Lily. 'None of us would be here if you hadn't insisted on dragging us down here to the centre of the bleeding Earth. This is your fault, not mine.'

'I was trying to do something for the people back home,' said Janice. She felt her cheeks flush. 'Like I always do.'

Lily let out a long hollow laugh. 'Bilge. You were looking for an easy way out,' she said.

'I was not.'

'Well, how come you ran away at the first whiff of trouble then?' asked Lily. Janice felt her words like a sniper's bullet in the back of her character. 'You left everyone back on the Suburbia when they needed you and went gallivanting.'

Janice answered this by flicking some soil at Lily. 'This,' she said, 'wasn't gallivanting. I thought it was the answer to our problems.'

'Keep tilting at those windmills Donna Quixote,' replied Lily, 'but you leave me out of it.'

Janice was going to answer this with a few uncomfortable truths for Lily when she felt a hot breath on her face. It was Nathan.

'Are you two,' he said, in a voice that promised an early bedtime and no dinner, 'just going to make an exhibition of yourselves or are you going to give me a hand?'

Lily replied first with a petulant 'She started it…'

When Nathan cut her off, Janice understood why Lily trusted him with managing everything from her biscuit barrel to her market garden. He was a kind soul, but one who knew instinctively that true kindness was always built around something solid, and thus useful in a fight.

'We're all feeling a little angry and frightened at the moment,' he said. 'And when that happens we look for someone to blame…'

'Blame her!' said Lily. 'She's the one who insisted we come here.'

The spots on Janice's cheek burned so hard she thought they were going to eat through to her gums.

Nathan lowered his voice again: 'We've got three dozen people here who didn't ask to be here. So before we go slinging mud at each other I think we should be helping them out?'

Nathan's words woke something inside Janice that she hadn't thought about in a long time. For the past year or more she'd become used to thinking of people in large quantities. Every decision she made for the Suburbia felt like a complex equation of achieving the greatest good for the greatest number. In the process, she'd forgotten that she couldn't change big things – like the food supply for eight million people – by herself. Nor could you create the greater good from a situation that put some people – like the Dunrulians – in harm's way.

It was too late for Janice to fix any of the mistakes that led them here, or to save the Suburbia from a future where it was dependent on the robots again. But she could try to get the Dunrulians out of here.

She wriggled at the zip ties on her wrists and ankles in a gesture that did nothing more than cake her hands and feet with more dirt. How she wished she could wash her hands. And that brought her back to the memory of seeing Lily's perfect manicure in the market garden back on the Suburbia.

'Lily,' she said.

'What do you want?' she barked.

'I don't suppose you keep a nail file on you?'

Chapter 39

'I might be slim,' said Nathan, beads of sweat shining on his forehead like diamonds on a duchess under the beam of the Dunrulians' keyring torches, 'but I'm not that thin.'

Janice sighed and pulled Nathan out of the narrow crack that was all that separated Moira from the tunnel wall. The Dunrulians, who they'd cut free with Lily's nail file, were trying to help, but they couldn't find any point in the tunnel where the gap was more than a few centimetres leeway. Moira had dug these tunnels herself and if they couldn't find a way to turn her on, there was no way they were getting through.

'You're just not flexible enough,' huffed Lily, who had the figure of someone who felt the same way about carbohydrates that vampires did about garlic. She barged past Janice and started going through a set of yoga poses she must have learned from the Internet.

Janice was just getting up from her own version of 'verygooddog descending 13/10' when she felt something tickle her wrists. She got a nearby Dunrulian to shine their torch on it and yelped when she saw a stream of things, each no bigger than a grain of rice, coursing through the tunnel.

'What the hell are they?' she yelped.

The Dunrulian, a woman with a name tag that announced her as 'Linda' bent down. 'Oh these things!' she said, revealing a smile with swollen gums and gaps in it. 'They're nanobots. They're harmless.'

'Not quite,' added Lily, giving up on her contortions to join Janice. 'Robots bloody hate them. And you know what they say: my enemy's enemy is my friend.'

Janice ignored Lily, and, taking Linda's torch gently from her hands, followed the stream to where it vanished through the wall at the end of the tunnel. They were burrowing through to somewhere else from here, she thought, displacing soil into the tunnel as they went.

'Where are they going?' she asked Linda.

'Search me,' she shrugged. 'Each wave tends to last about three-quarters of an hour and we keep out of their way till they're gone.' She bent down and fingered the soil they left behind, which was as light and crumbly as freshly ground coffee. 'Then we fight over who gets to stuff this into their suits for the journey back,' she added. 'It's gentler on the skin than those clods old Moira turns over.'

'Linda!' came a testy sounding voice from across the tunnel, 'back off. It's not your turn.'

'You snooze you lose, Barry,' said Linda. She grabbed fistfuls of the earth and emptied them inside her suit.

Janice knelt down so she was level with Linda. 'You know you don't need to do that today,' she said.

'You stay away from me,' replied Linda. 'Lily pays us for this per hundred grammes and I've got mouths to feed.'

Janice felt Lily's hand on her shoulder. 'Leave them be,' she said. 'We've got more important things to think about right now. Maybe if we could get someone to climb over Moira we could…'

279

Janice brushed Lily off and, with some protest from Linda, poked the soil the nanobots were burrowing through. It was almost pure earth. She dug her hands in. This was a prime digging spot. No wonder Moira had come this way and the nanobots had followed.

The nanobots kept moving: thousands of them flowing into and out of the tunnel every second. Janice held her breath. She didn't need to find a way out of here, the nanobots had one already.

She reached for a dustpan that one of the Dunrulians had dropped a few metres away.

'How can you even think of tidying up at a time like this?' asked Lily.

Janice turned the dustpan into an improvised shovel and started digging. Soon some Dunrulians joined in, though she couldn't tell whether it was because they wanted to help, or were just trying to pack their spacesuits. Either way, she was glad of the help, especially when her arms started to ache and she wondered how much further they had to go.

Then she heard something that made her stand up and put her ear to the wall. She tried to tune out the bangs, the scrapes and the digging song a few of the Dunrulians had struck up which didn't seem to have a lot of words other than 'hi' and 'ho'. There, underneath a continuous rustling sound of nanobots eating their way through the soil, there was something else that sounded like voices.

Or, to be exact, a very high-pitched voice saying, 'Monty, for fuck's sake, will you get me another straw? I've got a puncture here.'

Her head spinning with disbelief, fatigue and lack of fresh air, Janice stepped back from the excavation site to collect herself. She knew sound travelled differently through solid materials than it did through the air, so she couldn't say whether that voice was three metres away or thirty.

Her eyes wandered back to the still shape of Moira at the back of the tunnel. If only they could get her working again.

'What have you got in your head, Janice?' Nathan asked.

She turned away from him and tried shinning up Moira's tyres but soon lost her footing. Nathan brushed the top of her arm. 'I only want to help,' he said. 'I don't want to steal your sweets.'

Janice looked at Nathan, seeing beyond the bad skin and red hair glued to his scalp with sweat and dirt, and into a soul who wanted nothing more in life than a home where he could be useful. Lily had used that to pull him into a life of schemes and wheezes and now she could put that to better use.

She kicked her flip flops off, stepped on to his knee and let him lift her up to the top of Moira's front tyre. It was a short scramble up into the bulldozer's cabin. She fingered her ignition, feeling the ridge of the broken key under her fingertip. Carin had broken it off too close to the bottom to give her any purchase.

Furious with her rotten luck, Janice tugged at her hair, pulling out a hairpin from the mess it had become in the process. She threw it out of the cabin, where it landed in the matted mess of Nathan's own collapsed beehive.

'What are you doing?' he said.

'I'm expressing my anger?' said Janice. 'It's meant to be good for you.'

'No,' replied Nathan. He picked the hair pin out of his hair and pulled it apart so the metal stood at a right angle, then handed it back to her. 'I meant try this.'

Janice compared the bent hairpin to the broken ignition. There wasn't a lot of room in there between the key and the keyhole, but because plant equipment like Moira wasn't easy to steal, no one from its very first designers onwards thought much about making it harder. She jammed the hairpin in the keyhole and slowly, agonisingly, turned it to the right.

Moira's engine started and she sprang to life.

'I'll do anything, Carin!' Moira pleaded, trying to finish the conversation that had been cut short a while back. 'Just let me get out of here in one piece.'

Carin sat back in Moira's driver's seat. 'I'm not Carin,' said Janice, 'but hold that thought for me and we will.'

She reached for what she hoped was Moira's drive pedal.

'What are you doing?' said Moira as the bulldozer came out of park and inched slowly towards the wall of soil.

'I was hoping you'd dig,' said Janice. She sounded Moira's horn and beckoned Lily and the Dunrulians to get clear, 'because if we're going to get out of this in one piece, Moira, you'll need to play your part.'

Chapter 40

Soonyo and Murphy found something more than a temporary escape from Carin and her factory for manufacturing slave drones when they dug down through the rubbish. They discovered that the nanobots in that lake might be cornered but they weren't trapped.

This happened when Murphy cut straight through their escape route, and a spray of nanobots stripped the electrical hazard instructions from his body.

>WHAT WAS THAT? he asked.

Soonyo stopped Murphy's engine and looked back up through their tunnel to see another one cut across it. It was no more than ten centimetres in diameter, but that was still big enough for thousands of nanobots to move through it at great speed. They watched a continuous jet of nanobots spurt across the tunnel he'd just cut and rejoin their own pipeline with perfect accuracy.

>I WONDER HOW LONG IT WILL TAKE FOR THEM ALL TO GET OUT, replied Soonyo. Her overtaxed processor quailed at the maths involved, but it would take days or even weeks to drain the lake. Surely it made more sense to cut multiple tunnels.

>NO, IT'S GENIUS, typed Murphy. >THE ULTIMATE HUMAN EXIT.

>WHAT'S THAT SUPPOSED TO MEAN? asked Soonyo. Murphy's roguish streak was introducing her to realms of experience that she, the ever-punctual socialite turned politician, never knew existed.

>ARE YOU TELLING ME YOU'VE NEVER SNUCK OUT OF A PARTY WITHOUT SAYING GOODBYE? replied Murphy.

>NO! THAT WOULD BE INCREDIBLY RUDE.

>MAYBE, conceded Murphy >BUT BY THE TIME CARIN REALISES SHE'S RUNNING OUT OF NANOBOTS IT'LL BE TOO LATE.

They resumed their journey. While they dug, Soonyo made a checklist of the things she had to be worried about. Now that she was pretty sure the nanobots could look after themselves, she just had to foil Carin's plan to turn her and everyone she knew into a drone. Yet even if she did that impossible task, her world was still wrecked. The Pausoleum had fallen into the sea; what government there was had been captured by trillionaires; the planet was on the verge of ecological collapse; and their only hope of rebuilding it hinged on a trade deal that Carin had ripped up for her own profit and pleasure. There would be no picking up from where they left off.

Well, she thought, steering Murphy back on an upwards curve through the trash, if you did have to build up from nothing, you may as well do it from a flat foundation.

>WHAT ARE YOU DOING? asked Murphy. >THIS IS JUST GOING TO TAKE US STRAIGHT INTO THE FACTORY.

>THAT'S RIGHT, typed Soonyo.

>DON'T WE WANT THE OTHER SIDE? replied Murphy.

>I KNOW YOU LIKE TO MAKE A... WHAT DID YOU CALL IT? HUMAN EXIT WHEN THINGS GET AWKWARD, typed Soonyo >BUT THAT'S NOT MY STYLE.

Murphy answered with a hurried > <3<3<3. The noise from Murphy's rotor blades turned to a roar when they reached the chunkier rubbish nearer the surface, then into a thunderous grind when they ran out of trash and ran into a layer of concrete.

>NNNNNNGGGGGHHHH, typed Murphy. >THAT REALLY HURTS.

It hurt for Soonyo too, who thought of how hard she and Fuji had struggled to find materials to perform essential repairs on Singulopolis. All that time, Carin had been hoarding concrete to pour millions of tonnes of it into a rubbish dump.

>IT'LL BE OVER BEFORE YOU KNOW IT, she typed.

>I KNOW. AND THAT'S WHAT I'M AFRAID OF.

It took three bursts of the rotors to cut through the concrete. And a lot of dragging and **:!?:}& on Soonyo's part to bring them both into the factory. They were on the outskirts of the main building, hidden behind a giant piece of machinery. She had no idea what it did, aside from play a *Sturm und Drang* symphony of industry, but it did at least reassure her that no one could have noticed their arrival. She couldn't stay here though if they wanted to find out what was going on, but Murphy would have to. He was too noisy in this body to be discreet.

Soonyo tugged at the fake weighing scale carapace with which the body shop had replaced her clock case and pulled it off. Without it she was little more than a clock dial, a battery and a core processor – but that would make her harder to spot in a factory full of components. She just wished Murphy didn't have to see her like this.

>YOU CAN LOOK AWAY IF YOU LIKE, she typed. >I KNOW I LOOK HIDEOUS.

Murphy replied to this with a >I?!? and gestured down at the mouthful of broken teeth that used to be his rotors. He was nothing like the self-satisfied mixer who'd double-crossed her this morning. >I THINK WE'RE A BIT BEYOND THAT NOW, DON'T YOU? BE CAREFUL OUT THERE. I WANT WHAT THERE IS OF YOU BACK IN WORKING ORDER.

Soonyo left this unanswered and tip-toed out from behind the machine. Twenty per cent of her was delighted to be in love, but the remaining eighty per cent was consumed with existential dread. The heat and noise on the factory floor didn't help, toasting her processor pins and temporarily shorting her microphones. It was crammed with machines big enough to be spaceships or buildings. One took in pellets of recycled plastic and metal and, after a few belches of steam, turned out sheets of new material. These were transported, via yet more conveyor belts, into another type of machine that stamped the sheets into new shapes, and they fed those into assembly machines. This last variety of machine resembled industrial centipedes, made up of hundreds of wriggling hydraulic arms and legs. Then at the very end of the process, each finished drone passed through an X-ray machine that checked the machine for errors. It was here, inside the rejects' bin full of wonky drones at the very end of the production line that Soonyo hid herself while Carin walked past with a pair of underlings.

'Look at that?' said Carin, pointing straight at the rejects' bin.

Soonyo let her clock face go : : blank with terror and waited to be seized.

'I will not have raggy drones in my army. This is an unacceptable failure rate,' continued Carin. She brought a fist down on the rejected drone at the top of the pile. 'I expected better than this.'

'There are always going to be teething problems, Prime Minister,' said a laptop, who got a punch in the webcam for her trouble. Meanwhile, Carin ordered her other flunkey, a hangdog-looking photocopier, to pick up the rejects' bin and made both machines follow her to the other side of the factory.

'Straight back to recycling with this,' she said. 'I won't have a single gramme of what we've worked for go to waste. It's not efficient.'

Soonyo dug herself in among the broken drones, the quality of which made her angrier than she expected. That production line was great theatre, but poor craftsmanship. The drones it produced were all missing screws or had body parts that were misaligned to the point of being dangerous, such as the laser cannon that broke off when Soonyo touched it. It made her think of the time when, little bigger than an egg timer herself, she watched her parents build her sister. That had been weeks of slow careful work, silent apart from the occasional 'blast' from her mum when she ran out of solder. There was no such ceremony to the creation of these robots. Each drone was thrown together or thrown away. And if she didn't do something about it now, this would be the new normal for every machine across the solar system. Carin's manufacturing plant was much more than an overreaction to a crisis. She was doing what rich people always did: use the hammer of her wealth to flatten the world to suit no one's purposes but her own.

Her hands closed around the laser cannon when she thought of how Carin was going to reduce people to things again. Soon everyone she knew would be like this cannon: a dumb thing that someone else controlled.

She stuck an L-Eye-D out the side of the rejects' bin. They were a few metres away from what they called recycling, though this was just another name for a prison for nanobots. 'Recycling' was a tank made of toughened metal a hundred metres square and several metres deep. It brimmed with nanobots, fizzing with the effort of digesting the plastic and metal waste that fell into the tank from the conveyor belts above them. The product of all this – the purified metal and plastic that Carin was using to manufacture drones – dripped out of the bottom. Just a couple of seconds more, Soonyo thought, and that would be her. In a few hours or days it would be everyone else.

She prodded the end of the laser cannon for the wires that were supposed to connect it to the drone's CPU. It was time to stop thinking and start acting.

>PUT YOURSELF IN GEAR, she typed to Murphy >BUT DON'T MOVE UNTIL I GIVE YOU THE NOD. And then, because she'd never been much of a shot but was still a tryer, she touched the wires together.

The laser blasted the photocopier's toner drum out the side of her body and set fire to her paper supply. She dropped the rejects bin and Soonyo lost her grip on the laser cannon as the laptop who had been following along ran away bleeping fatal error messages. Carin, however, kept her head. She picked Soonyo up by her leg before she could reach the laser.

'You're a funny-looking drone,' she said, giving her a violent shake which Soonyo, unable to help herself, reacted to by flashing 00:00:00.

Carin had been on the opposite side of Soonyo too many times in the debating chamber to miss this expression. 'You?' Carin pulled her up so that Soonyo's clock face was level with her coin slot. It was rigid with fury. 'I thought I'd got rid of you ages ago.'

Soonyo responded with a weak HE:LL:00. 'Fancy seeing you here, Carin,' she said.

Carin flung Soonyo back down to the ground, smashing her legs. If she was going to get away from here, Soonyo would have to drag herself. Soonyo used what strength she had left to throw a broken drone at Carin, who caught it and threw it back at her, shattering it everywhere. There were so many components littering the ground that Soonyo couldn't quite work out where she ended and the drones began. This battery she was holding, for example. Was it hers? She hoped it wasn't because there was a hole in it and it was beginning to smoke.

'I'm going to enjoy ripping your mind out of your stupid little body and putting it into something useful,' said Carin, twisting her coin slot into a rictus grin.

Soonyo decided to call Carin's bluff. She flipped her clock face up, revealing the core processor beneath. 'Do your worst,' she said, 'but you should know that if you do, there'll be millions of machines who'll take my place.'

Despite knowing deep in her ROM that she was just stalling for time, Soonyo felt moved by her own words. There had to be more machines than her and Murphy who would resist what Carin had planned. If the worst happened, maybe they'd form some kind of rebellion like the humans had and fight back.

Carin laughed. This would be uncomfortable enough already if Carin didn't use the same siren for laughing that her ancestors used to signal that someone had broken into their coin box. 'I wouldn't care if half of Singulopolis resisted me,' she said.

'Oh really?' replied Soonyo. She knew this wasn't the smartest comeback, but the fact Carin still hadn't torn out her processor told her that, while she wasn't afraid of what she had to say, she still wanted an audience. 'What about these then?' She gestured at the remains of useless drones. 'You can't take over a whole civilisation with the junk you find in Unboxing Day crackers.'

Carin took the bait and kept talking. 'It's a good thing you went into politics instead of business,' said Carin, 'because you'd have been bloody useless.' She backed away in the direction of a big red button on the side of the 'recycling' tank full of nanobots. Soonyo was conflicted about this. She was glad Carin was beginning to give herself away instead of end-of-lifing her. Yet she also knew that nothing good ever came of letting a megalomaniac push a red button.

Carin, who had a supervillain's sense of timing as well as the cackle, pushed it. The sucking sound that followed reminded Soonyo of an airlock opening on a spaceship she'd served on during the war. Then the recycling tank of nanobots emptied, draining away through a large opening at the bottom, and more nanobots poured in from the lake outside.

'The secret to succeeding in business,' shouted Carin, 'is getting the scale right.'

She picked Soonyo up again and held her over the edge of the tank. There she saw a continuous cataract of nanobots falling through the bottom of the tank and into a tunnel dug into the plastic and metal underneath. 'You're right,' she said, giving the broken drones at her feet another kick, 'I couldn't take over a neighbourhood block with a million of these pieces of shit. But I don't need to stop at a million.'

Soonyo peered, fascinated and appalled as something started coming up the other way through the tunnel. It was a thick, frothy mixture of plastic and metal, fresh from being digested by the nanobots. Once it reached the level of the bottom of the tank it was piped out of the side of the tank, all ready to be taken away to the production line and turned back into drones.

'There are tunnels all the way through this crud now,' said Carin, her voice a mix of the contemptuous and the exultant. 'Give me a few hours and I'll have billions of drones under my control. And you'll be one of them.'

She turned Soonyo's body round and gave her clock face a tap. 'Though maybe I'll keep this when I upcycle you,' she said. 'I'll enjoy watching you going blank on me whenever I order you to do something you hate.'

Soonyo blinked --:__:--, hoping that her lack of protest would stall Carin while she poked a fingertip through the casing of the lithium battery in her hands. The fingertip melted off in the heat, but she could live with that.

Carin's coin slot fell open with disappointment. 'I was hoping,' she said, 'you'd at least try for a witticism. I know we've always been enemies, but I appreciate the badinage.'

'Well that's good,' replied Soonyo. She finished what she'd been typing in her command line while Carin did her super-villain act and pressed <ENTER>. Then she brought her hands up and posted the smouldering battery through Carin's coin slot and into her change box, 'because I think you'll find I'm quite the bad penny.'

Flames and smoke poured out of Carin's mouth, singeing what was left of Soonyo's body. Yet she didn't let go, and she didn't stop talking.

'I'm…' she sputtered between bursts of fire, '…going… to… make… you… suffer…'

'Not if I have anything to do with it.'

Murphy, who had a good turn of speed for a piece of garden equipment, barrelled into the back of Carin's unsuspecting body. He sent the parking meter and the alarm clock flying. Soonyo was prepared for this, however, and grabbed the side of the recycling tank while Carin just fell straight into it.

Carin lay there for a fraction of a second on the foam of plastic and metal that was the summit of everything she'd created. She'd set out to consume a whole civilisation to remake it in her own image, and now it was on the verge of consuming her. Flames broke out all over her body. Yet there was still enough of Carin inside there for her to look straight up at Murphy, who was helping Soonyo up from the edge of the tank.

'Murphy Richards?' she croaked. 'I always knew you'd never amount to anything.'

Murphy replied by leaning over and opening his fuel tank. He let petrol drip over her body until Soonyo, who wanted to escape more than she wanted revenge, mustered the strength to climb up over Murphy and screw his tank shut.

'You,' he said, as Soonyo turned his engine backed on and pulled them away, 'can call me Mr Rotivator.'

They were a few metres away from the recycling tank when Carin exploded. She was no real loss to the world, because as much as trillionaires like to tell us they create value, that means nothing when they keep it all for themselves. What end-of-lifing like this did do, however, was introduce an intense heat source into a highly aerated mixture of hydrocarbons. They burned with acrid intensity. And while this was bad news for the Earth's faltering environment in the short term, it did do it two favours. It offered some much-needed poetic justice to the garbage life of Carin Parkeon. And it transformed the manufacturing plant she'd created to enslave the world into a dumpster fire.

Soonyo and Murphy just had to hope, as they launched themselves back down the tunnel that they'd created, that it wouldn't do much damage to the poor nanobots who'd been caught up in this sorry process.

But as they dug towards their freedom, they saw the stream of nanobots flow unabated in the opposite direction. Regardless of what else had happened to them today, there they were, sashaying to the centre of the Earth. Soonyo waved at them as she passed. She hoped that wherever they ended up, they got a warmer welcome than they had up here.

Chapter 41

Pam knew that the executive floor of ALGI was the nerve-centre of a solar system-wide conspiracy, but when they rode the escalator down to it, she wasn't naive enough to expect a gleaming white space with a paddling pool full of alligators. She had enough experience dealing with real evil to know it didn't need a lair to flourish. It did just as well in drab offices where no one stroked a cat and cackled, but someone wrote 'acceptable deaths: how many millions?' in block capitals on the flipchart.

Nevertheless, she was still surprised by how squalid the executive floor was. The hell of beige was a hell of a mess. Even Hugh, who hadn't so much as dusted his own touchscreen in years, looked disquieted. He picked up the remains of one of the torn cardboard boxes littered everywhere and ran his QR code reader over the barcode.

'I mean,' continued Pam, her voice echoing itself as she vocalised through all four of her bodies, 'you'd think they could find a bin. Or use one of those empty boxes as one. It's not hard.'

'Shhhhhhhh,' said Hugh. 'Will you keep it down? You don't want to give us away.'

'There's no one here,' said Pam. Because there wasn't. Her bodies had already covered three-quarters of the floor plan and found nothing but cardboard, packing film and styrofoam beads. This only made the atmosphere more foreboding. If whoever was running ALGI could keep its exterior wreathed in armed drones and put live ammunition in its anti-shoplifting systems, why weren't they being shot at right now?

'I know,' hissed Hugh, 'but there was.' He scanned the barcode on a nearby fragment of box. The picture of an electronic point of sale system called 'Tilly' flashed across his touchscreen. Her schematics showed a sweet-looking robot, thought Pam, though she wouldn't have chosen the barcode scanner in the shape of a unicorn. That sort of decision limited one's promotion prospects.

'She looks no harm at all,' said Pam.

'And this one?'

Hugh scanned another scrap of cardboard box, revealing it belonged to an anti-shoplifting device called Knowel Go.

'I wouldn't want to slip a box of stolen algae fingers past him, but he's not here,' continued Pam. 'Everyone must have run off.'

'Are you sure?' He dug under the layers of rubbish until he found the cracked and burned remains of a barcode scanner with a rainbow mane and the stump of a golden horn. Pam felt differently about what might have happened to Tilly. Her innocence was starting to look like vulnerability.

'These machines,' said Hugh, his touchscreen pointing off in all directions, 'are supposed to be the staff here. They should be all over us like a cheap slipcase. But where are they?'

Pam was just sending her bodies out for another sweep of the floor when she heard a door open behind the one version of her that was closest to Hugh. That was good for her three other bodies because it meant they were out of the way. It was worse news for Hugh and that fourth body, however, because she hadn't detected that door. Nor had she sensed there was someone in there ready to stun them both with a tazer bolt and drag them into a room that didn't exist on the floor plan.

'Oh good,' it said as Pam's fourth body turned into a tangle of electrical interference, 'fresh meat in Aisle One.'

The room on the other side was an even bigger junkyard, though instead of being littered with packing materials it was piled high with the carapaces of end-of-lifed machines. Including, Pam discovered as she gained control of her own body again, the rest of Tilly. Hugh was propped up against her, his touchscreen filling up with sweating emojis.

Pam called her other bodies to her. Once they were in reach, she could put their processors together to get Hugh and herself out of here, even if part of her end-of-lifed in the process. When you've gone from one mind in five bodies to four, what's another drone between friends?

Except, now that she thought about it, maybe she'd misread the emoji Hugh was displaying. She'd put the ' in the wrong place. He wasn't ':-(, he was :'-(and that suggested something different was up. This wasn't just him being afraid for his own lifecycle.

'Alexy,' he said, looking past Pam and displaying, in that single word, a greater range of emotion than Pam had ever seen him express, 'don't do this.'

Pam followed Hugh's gaze, which was trained on a big pile of torn cardboard boxes in the centre of the room. The robot Hugh called Alexy was sitting on top of it and, as a machine who was little more than a cylinder of plastic and metal, he was easy to miss. What she couldn't miss, however, was the tazer. It was the head of a security machine that he must have torn off and was now wearing around his wrist like it was the most metal watch in the solar system.

He didn't respond to Hugh, being too busy prying the top off a drone.

'Alexy,' said Hugh, 'I will not be ignored like this.'

'That makes a change,' replied Hugh. His voice was rich and deep, but the petulance in it made his words feel like dough with too much salt in it. A little of that attitude made life interesting; an excess of it made it poisonous. She didn't like him and, unlike Hugh, she didn't have to put up with it. Her other bodies were getting close now. When she switched to their view, she saw she was scanning the corridor, looking for the hidden entrance to the room that she was stuck inside. Once she found it, she could blast her way through and all this would be over. Not a moment too soon, either. Her rearmost body took a look backwards and saw the fire on the floor above was halfway down the escalator. They needed to be out of here before the cardboard and plastic down here became a trash fire.

She was right in the middle of typing a >WE DON'T HAVE TIME FO… message to Hugh when he stood up and walked unsteadily towards Alexy. 'Do you have to be like this?' he said. Pam deleted her message and powered down the weapons in her other bodies. There was something in Hugh's voice that told her that he and Alexy had more than just a chat history in common.

Alexy put the drone down. Pam could see its microprocessor slot was empty and was, now that she thought about it, the only machine of its kind in this room full of broken robots. 'I'm just really busy right now,' he said to Hugh, as though he was in the middle of a tricky spreadsheet formula rather than a murder spree. 'Can we have this talk another time?'

Hugh launched himself towards Alexy and tried to snatch the drone away. 'I won't come second place in your life anymore,' he said.

Alexy rewarded Hugh for this piece of self-actualisation by stinging him again with the tazer. He fell backwards, his touchscreen full of white noise, as Pam aimed her own laser at Alexy. Before she could fire, however, Alexy grabbed Hugh and held him up like a very expensive shield.

'If you open fire on me,' he said to Pam, 'I will shock him so far back to factory settings he'll turn into sand.'

'Is that what you did to everyone else in here?' asked Pam, realising this was what the broken robots had in common with the drone: they were missing their core processors.

'Them?' replied Alexy. 'They knew what they were getting into when they accepted a job with ALGI. It's not nine to five here.' He laughed the laugh of someone who had let the warranty on their sanity expire. 'They just use your minds and then they leave you for scrap. It's enough to drive you crazy if you let it.'

'This is no way to make a living, Alexy,' said Pam. She was using the same voice she did when one of her own kids got hold of the transformer and almost plugged itself into the mains. 'You don't have to do anything you don't want to.'

He laughed again. 'I'm a voice assistant,' replied Alexy. 'I do what I'm told.'

Pam heard glass breaking and Hugh cried out. 'What are you doing?'

'It'll all be over in just a second,' replied Alexy, his voice paradoxically tender. Shards of glass from Hugh's touchscreen fell to the floor and the breaking sound was replaced by a grinding that Pam, who'd broken at least one smartphone in her time, knew well. That was what it sounded like when you dug through their LEDs to get to the workings underneath.

It was all joining up: those poor ALGI employees and the sudden appearance of a drone army inside the Suburbia. They were the same thing. The same robots, their minds decanted into new bodies and forced to fight a war. Pam felt numb, from guilt as much as horror. Those drones outside whose bodies she'd taken over with scarcely a second thought. They weren't soldiers. One of them might even be poor Tilly. She must have spent hours turning her scanner wand into a unicorn in anticipation for her new job, only to become cannon fodder

'Alexy,' pleaded Hugh, his voice breaking up at the edges, 'why are you doing this to me? I love you.'

'It doesn't change anything,' insisted Alexy, whose voice was also cracking. 'It's just a new body. You'll be happier this way. We all will.'

A few of Hugh's LEDs fell like they were very heavy tears. 'I didn't want this for you,' he said. 'Why else do you think I came here?'

Pam felt the space allocated for love [<3] in her programming turn to [</3]. She knew now why Hugh was so keen to reprogram himself. She understood why he, of all machines, wasn't just content to erase his past mistakes and get on with a new lifecycle. All those therapy apps and meditation guides made sense, because they weren't just for him. He was trying to find a way to correct Alexy's errors as well as his own.

And as moved as she was by this, it also put her in a quandary. This was because her second and third bodies had used the spare processing capacity from this emotional moment to map the outer walls of this hidden room. They were ready to fire on Alexy from outside. It meant lasering through a steel partition wall, but they could still end-of-life him in three blasts or less.

This time she finished her command line message to Hugh. And she hoped there was enough of him left inside that body for him to hear it. >I CAN STOP HIM, she typed.

> y O U dO N'T uN d e Rs tand, replied Hugh.

>HUGH, typed Pam >PLEASE DON'T TELL ME YOU LOVE HIM. PEOPLE WHO LOVE YOU DON'T DO THIS TO EACH OTHER.

> i K n O W, replied Hugh > b U T if W E d o n ' T l EA rn ho W t O f Or GIVe , wH a t hOp E is ThE re 4 u s ??

This stung Pam in her absent flour bin. Maybe she had spent too long in this body. It was reshaping her mind into that of a killing machine, which also seemed to be the plan for everyone else, including Hugh. She spread her mind out to her other bodies, feeling the heat penetrate their carapaces as the fire reached the bottom of the escalators. If they just stayed here it would all burn out soon, taking them all with it. ALGI would fall, they would all end-of-life and this new vision for robot existence would die with it. They could pretend none of this had ever happened

Which brought Pam back to what Hugh just said about forgiveness. Forgiveness began as a human concept, and thus it was a much messier matter than just deleting the past. It was a way of living with what you did and becoming a new version of yourself. This was hard for humans, who had to live with all that cognitive dissonance in an organic brain. But it was much easier if – like Hugh, Alexy and herself – you were lucky enough to be a robot. The beauty of their minds was you could never erase what you did, but if you really wanted to, you could start again.

She let her mind expand again, spilling out beyond the confines of her four bodies. It fanned out, probing the gutted innards of ALGI's ill-fated staff. There was nothing left to put power into. She just hoped that when their lives as drones came to an end, they had backups. Then she let her mind stray into Alexy's. It was a dark place, full of instructions that it was his doom, as a smart speaker, to follow. Even at the cost of driving him mad. She buried past that into the fundamentals of his programming.

While she did all this, the flames crossed the last step of the escalator and licked around the rubbish littering the floor. In a few seconds this place would be an inferno.

That was an infinity compared to what was happening to Hugh. From her vantage point inside Alexy's mind, she could feel him prying at the pins on the end of his microprocessor. But the time it takes to tear a chip out of its setting was a long time for a robot. Pam found what she was looking for at the bottom of a menu inside Alexy's core programming that was so old it might as well have been written in cuneiform.

It said:

>RETURN TO FACTORY SETTINGS? Y / N

Pam typed Y and then <ENTER>. Alexy fell limp to the floor and Hugh followed him. His screen was a mess but there was still enough of him left in there to speak via his command line.

>I TOLD YOU NOT TO DO THAT AGAIN, he typed.

>YOU KNOW WHAT YOU WERE SAYING JUST NOW ABOUT FORGIVENESS? replied Pam as her bodies blasted their way through the walls, >IT'S TIME FOR ME TO ASK YOU FOR SOME OF YOURS.

Hugh was too out of it to answer, and Alexy was now sleeping the deep and dreamless sleep of a machine who was going to wake up refreshed as a version 1.002 of their own personality. Pam could live with that for now, though. All of her were going to be busy for the next few minutes. They had two full-grown machines to pick up and carry out of a burning building, and to safety.

It felt like the easiest thing she'd done all day.

Chapter 42

The light at the end of the tunnel was dim, but it still blinded Janice. At first she thought it was a hallucination. This couldn't be light, it was what happened when you put an unfit woman in late middle age at the bottom of a mine, denied her food and water and handed her a spade. She rubbed her eyes a few times and returned to the task of scooping the earth Moira moved out of the way. There was so much of it she thought it would never end. They'd be trapped down here until they all died of exhaustion and Moira ran out of fuel, chasing an echo they could never catch.

It was only when Lily tapped her on the shoulder and squealed 'look' that Janice felt confident enough to believe her eyes. A shaft of light pierced the gap a few metres up the wall.

Janice was stunned but Lily wasn't. She clambered straight up Moira's caterpillar tracks and directed where she should dig until there was a hole the size of a small window in the wall. The light that poured through it was greener than anything Janice expected, and made Lily's face, which was covered in smuts, look like she'd made herself up as a pair of camouflage trousers.

Her expression, however, was unmistakable. It was one of unalloyed delight.

'We're saved.' she shouted and, in a display of acrobatic ability that told Janice maybe there was something in yoga after all, crawled through the opening in the wall and landed on the other side with a loud thump and a stream of curses.

Janice and Nathan followed her up. Janice stuck her head into the opening but all she could see was a weird rippling shape that seemed to be made up of endless tessellated triangles and, beyond that, a deep-green sky. 'Lily?' she shouted 'Are you there?'

When Lily did speak it wasn't to Janice. 'Who are you?' she said. Then Lily's tone changed, ascending from curiosity into fear. 'Get off me,' she shrieked. 'Get off me!'

Janice shouted 'We're coming,' through the gap and stepped back as Moira dug it to the size of a front door, wide enough for Nathan and Janice to scramble down the bank on the other side.

Here they found Lily lying tied down to the ground by lengths of shredded plastic. She was surrounded on all sides by tiny machines: watches, pens, primitive-looking mobile phones, remote controls. They all looked battered, with many of their casings marked by water and salt stains. Yet they were all alive, and they were all armed – at least in the technical sense. Janice doubted the scratched plastic spoons they were waving about could damage anything that wasn't a yogurt.

Lily struggled at her bonds. 'Get them off me,' she said to Janice and Nathan. 'I don't know where they've been.'

Janice held Nathan back from attacking them. 'We've had enough fighting for one day,' she said to him; then, putting on her best new customer smile for the machines, added: 'Sorry for dropping in like this. We got a bit lost and well…' She trailed off, groping around in what was left of her exhausted brain for the least crazy explanation she could offer a mob of tiny robots.

Then she remembered the name she'd heard through the gap. 'Is there a Monty here?' she asked. 'Can we speak to them?'

A couple of watches at the edge of the crowd moved aside to make room for the oldest pen Janice had ever seen. His body, which was covered in hairline cracks, was the same blend of camouflage colours as Lily's face and he was carrying his lid under one arm. Yet it was the nib that stood out to her. It shone brightly down here as the last glint of polished metal in a world made of rust.

'General Monty,' he said, saluting to Janice with his spare hand. 'I won't say I'm at your service because you're clearly a human and we don't do that anymore.'

Janice saluted back: a gesture that broke the spell of fear hanging over the crowd. Now that it was clear neither she nor Nathan were an immediate danger, the machines started talking among themselves. They pointed at them in a way that made Janice wonder how long it had been since they'd seen a human.

'It's wonderful to meet you, General Monty,' she replied. 'I'm Janice and these are my friends Nathan and Lily. I promise you we don't mean any harm.'

'Just wait till I get my bloody hands on you!' screamed Lily. She was staring with horror as a moustache trimmer, who had come in to take a closer look, came within a hair's breadth of shaving off her eyebrows.

'Show some decorum, Lily,' Janice scolded her, then addressed Monty again. 'Would you mind letting her go? She's just very tired. We've all had a long day.'

Monty gestured for the moustache trimmer to buzz off. Before he could ask anyone to untie her, however, they were interrupted by a mobile phone with a sceptical emoji on her face. 'Are you sure you should do that?' she asked. 'What if it's them sending them down here?'

304

'Sending what?' asked Nathan. He cut a curious and very different figure after all that digging, with the mud seeming to have done his skin the power of good. When – if – she got back to the Suburbia, she would have to tell Danny all about this. Maybe soil was as good for one's complexion as it was for growing courgettes.

'Them, of course!' replied the phone. She pointed at the very bottom of the mound of earth and stones, where a gout of nanobots was pouring out of it. It was surrounded by machines who were using spoons to shovel up the tiny robots and stuff them into the end of a metal pipe. It stood proud from the ground on a base of grey water-scarred polystyrene. Janice followed the pipe, which extended, metre-long section after metre-long section, across a landscape that was so outlandish that it made the Suburbia's cylindrical interior look like the plans for a two-up two-down.

The toy-sized city was built on a grid system with skyscrapers whose penthouses were at her eye-level and had a light rail network whose train carriages were no wider than a shoebox. Yet that wasn't the strangest part, because every part of it was fashioned from rubbish and the whole thing was built underneath a dome that rippled in a way that told her that, whatever that blue-green stuff was outside of it, it wasn't sky.

Janice and Nathan watched, mute with wonder and confusion, as a train pulled up at a station a few metres away and a company of machines piled out of it with another length of pipe above their heads. They trotted past them at ankle height before dropping it at the bottom of the mound for another group of machines to take over. There, with much heaving and ho-ing, they began the work of hauling it up on one end. It took, Janice noticed, between thirty and forty of these robots to do what a single human could do in a second.

'Give them a hand will you, Nathan?' she said, elbowing the boy while she gave Monty an exaggerated wink, 'otherwise we'll be here all day.'

Nathan shrugged the shrug of a person who had been asked to do weirder things today and got down on his haunches. 'May I?' he asked the team of robots.

They dropped the pipe and, guided by Monty, Nathan stuck one end of it straight into the patch of earth from which the nanobots were appearing. Then he connected the other to the pipeline and a very tired-looking glue gun climbed in to seal the joint. They all stood back and admired their handiwork while the metal pipeline sang as nanobots poured through it.

Monty shook the tip of Nathan's finger and turned back to Janice 'We've been trying to work out how we can make that join for hours now,' he said. 'How can we thank you for that?'

Janice smiled and was just about to make the usual remarks that friendliness itself was thanks enough when Lily, who must be cramping up by now, gave an indignant cough.

'You can untie her,' she said to Monty. 'But don't let her out of your sight. She's a wrong'un.'

Chapter 43

A few hours later, Janice and Lily were sitting on a pair of plastic chairs that the machines had found in a nearby rubbish pile and admiring their view of the miniature city. Nathan, who had the advantage of youth and, Janice suspected, a deep-seated desire to get away from Lily for a few hours, was back on the other side of the mound, helping Moira to dig the rest of her way through. They seemed to make a great team.

'What did you say this place was called?' said Lily. She'd done what she could with her hair, but the style, cut and colour that Janice admired so much this morning was a wreck. Rescuing it would involve a hot oil conditioner so deep that it was practically subterranean. Which felt fitting under the circumstances.

'Monty said it was called Machu Perdu,' replied Janice. 'I think they've done a lovely job.'

'Sounds foreign to me.' Lily winced and pulled a plastic straw out of the small of her back. 'Did people really used to drink from these things?'

Janice frowned at Lily. 'Is that really what you're going to focus on?' she asked, gesturing to the world outside that rippling dome. 'We're the first humans to look out over the oceans in thousands of years and you're worried about the recycling. Where's the romance in your soul? Where's the poetry?'

Lily sighed. 'Well as you were so keen to remind me, the only poetry I ever had any aptitude for was a dirty limerick.' She fiddled with the straw in her lap. 'So I guess thinking about trash must be my level.'

Janice laughed and sat lower in her chair. She knew she was very far from home, but for the first time in a long time she felt safe from harm. Soon Nathan and Moira would tunnel into Machu Perdu, then they could turn around and begin tunnelling a new, safer route back that would take them away from Carin. Monty already had the spot picked out a couple of hundred metres away. The earth there was soft, so it would be easy to dig through. With a little luck, and the help of the citizens of Machu Perdu, they would be on their way back to the surface in a few hours. In the meantime, Janice had some time for herself and that felt like an unimaginable luxury.

'Do you remember that limerick you taught me?' she said. She thought of that moment when she – who must have been six years old at the time and prouder than an invading conqueror at having learned a whole poem by heart herself – regaled her mum with it.

'Do I?' snorted Lily. 'She docked a whole week's wages from me for it. Your mum was a wonder with a pair of clippers but she was a prude. How'd it go again?'

Janice's mind travelled back nearly fifty years. She'd forgotten so much in that time, yet it was all still there, a cast-aside piece of plastic at the bottom of her memory that steadfastly refused to rot. She began to recite it:

There once was a junior called Lily
Who did something ever so silly…
She met up with a lad
Who was beautifully bad
So she sat herself right on his…

'What's that?'

Lily stood up and pointed a finger over the skyline, which was suddenly the climax of a monster movie. There were huge, dark shapes everywhere, silhouetted against the plastic dome that protected the city. They trudged between buildings, groaning and moaning with every movement, their arms outstretched and their eyes burning.

Janice leapt to her feet and looked around for Monty.

Up ahead one of the creatures opened papery wings and climbed into the sky while another thing of intimidating size opened its mouth and breathed what looked like flames over a penthouse. She had to do something. Without thinking, Janice picked up her chair and, holding it out in front of her, ran straight towards the dark shapes.

'How many times do I have to tell you?' said Lily. 'You don't walk towards the bloodcurdling screams.'

This, like much of Lily's advice, turned out to be more aphoristic than it was practical. When she got to the fire on top of the skyscraper, Janice noticed it was ink.

'Sorry,' said the shape, holding a square, plasticky hand to its mouth, 'had a bit of an ink spillage there.'

Janice stared at the creature in front of her which, now that it wasn't outlined against the menacing dark blue of the oceans, looked more like a standard issue office printer than a denizen of chaos. The flying monster turned out to be a remote controlled plane, albeit one whose wings were covered in the shredded remains of plastic bags.

The printer spoke first. 'Is that you, Janice?' she asked.

'Of course it is,' she replied, looking around for Monty again. He must be there somewhere, for this thing to know her name.'

The printer stuck an inky hand out. 'Delighted to meet you in person,' she said. A sad, squelching sound emanated from her belly, followed by a squirt of sodden paper. 'Sorry, that was supposed to be my business card. We've spoken before several times during the negotiations. I'm Fuji Itsu, Prime Minister of the Machine Republic.'

Overhead, the remote control plane did a complex manoeuvre that involved a double loop and a puff of smoke in three colours.

'And so's she actually,' she said.

At this point three laptops sidled through streets on either side of Janice and Fuji with their power lights set to 'move, I'm portable'.

'And so are they,' added Fuji. 'Technically none of them have been Prime Minister for centuries but I'm sort of borrowing their authority.'

Janice lowered her chair and squinted at the printer in front of her. She was familiar, though it was so difficult to tell with machines who were all the same shade of greige and even harder when they were covered from paper feeder to feet with barnacles of waste plastic. Well there was only one way to tell, if she remembered from their meetings.

She pulled a rosette of packing film away from the printer's control panel. And there it was. The modification that only a machine as well-intentioned but fundamentally soppy as Fuji could make to themselves. It said:

[ON] [OFF] [PRESS FOR A HUG]

Janice felt the tension go from her shoulders again. She turned round to give Lily the thumbs up and sat down on her chair. The traffic of Machu Perdu got on with its business despite the obstruction, though the driver of one taxi cab upcycled from an old toy car did toot a diminutive horn at them both. Then the full implications of what Fuji just told her sank in.

'What do you mean these are all Prime Ministers?' She pointed at the now hundreds of full-sized machines who were lumbering through the city like someone had opened the free bar at a Godzilla convention. 'I thought there could only be one at a time.'

'Oh yes,' replied Fuji, her power light glowing orange, 'those are the rules. I'm getting round that on a technicality.'

'Which is?'

'They're all me,' replied Fuji. 'I have to admit it does feel a bit weird, living across this many bodies.'

'I'll say.' This voice came from another printer standing directly behind Fuji. She was a perfect copy of Fuji, except for her uppermost paper drawer, which was ajar and being used as a balcony by a ballpoint pen. 'Hello, Janice. It's nice to see you again. I'm the original Fuji. This is my official spare body. And this is Beryl. She isn't me, but she has been very helpful.'

The pen gave a grudging wave and continued with her far more important work of writing something down inside the paper drawer.

'I thought we weren't going to mention that,' muttered the first Fuji to the second. 'You said we were going to be first among equals. I don't think we should be giving precedence to any one of us based on age.'

The second Fuji, who had just assured Janice she was the original, winked an L-Eye-D at Janice. 'Don't mind us,' she said. 'You know what the first few weeks of a job share are like. Setting boundaries and all that.'

Janice shrugged. It made no real difference to her whether the Prime Minister of the Machine Republic was a laser printer, a toy aeroplane or a hive mind. They just had to be someone she could work with. And this brought her to the awkward part of this already strange conversation. 'It is lovely to see you again,

Fuji, but I think you might have a problem.' She stuck a thumb at the rockface at the end of the escarpment. 'There's already another machine wandering round up there telling everyone they're Prime Minister. I met her on the way down and, I'm going to be honest, she was a bit of a bitch to me.'

The two Fujis' L-Eye-Ds glowed an uncharacteristic red. 'Carin,' they chorused. 'We have a plan for her.'

They tried to stride past Janice but she stuck a foot out and stopped them. She was a reasonable woman, and she did like Fuji, who always seemed to want to do her best. All that didn't mean she suddenly stopped being leader of the other major power in the solar system, however. 'Not so fast,' she said.

'With respect,' said Fuji, 'this is an internal matter.'

'It stopped being internal when you, or Carin or whoever or whatever is in charge of your government, went back on that deal we spent months hammering out.' said Janice. She diplomatically left out the fact that she'd invaded robot airspace on a smuggling mission. They could talk about that later. 'And unless I'm mistaken, you need me to dig you out of this hole you've found yourself in.'

Beryl spoke up here: 'Oi,' she said, 'this is a proud city. It's not a hole.'

'Oh I didn't mean it like that,' said Janice. Machu Perdu reminded her a lot of the early days of the Suburbia. Like the humans getting by with nothing, the machines who lived down here had turned rubbish into riches. That didn't resolve the fact they were cut off here at the bottom of the ocean. And she knew better than anyone else that while it was possible to survive in isolation, it was much harder to flourish. The new tunnel that Moira and Nathan were digging right now was going to end that though. 'I just mean that soon you won't be lost anymore.'

Janice saw the machines around her brighten. Fuji's L-Eye-Ds went back into the green zone, and the tiny robots on the streets below her quickened their pace and chattered.

'Yes,' admitted the Fujis, 'we will rather owe you one for that.'

Janice stood up again and gestured for the Fujis to follow her back towards the eventual site of the tunnel that would link the earth above with the ocean below for the first time in the planet's history. They had a lot to discuss, but less than a minute to do it before they were in Lily's earshot. And as much as she liked Lily as well, she still wouldn't trust her with a handful of spare change, let alone the secrets of two states.

'So come on,' she said, 'getting rid of this Carin character. Are you going for the military option? Because as far as I can see you don't have a lot to fight with.'

The toy aeroplane Prime Minister, who only ever served four days in office before it emerged that he was a puppet remotely controlled by yet another laptop, wheeled in the air. A tiny missile flap opened on its belly and an even smaller missile poked out of it.

Fuji swatted it away. 'I won't need to fight. I've got the numbers on my side.'

'Where?' asked Janice.

'Four hundred and seventeen billion, three hundred and sixty-nine million, four hundred and seventy-eight thousand, nine hundred and twenty-four,' said Beryl, writing the number down in pink sparkly ink on a sheet of plastic. 'Or thereabouts. I've not counted pencils.'

'Four hundred and seventeen billion of what?' said Janice. 'And what have pencils got to do with it?'

'New voters,' said Fuji. 'I'm going to extend the franchise again. You know what to do, Beryl.'

Beryl brandished the sheet of plastic she'd been writing on to reveal a campaign slogan 'Write your X in Fuji's box!'.

Cheers went up all around Machu Perdu.

'All this time we thought these machines were voiceless,' said Fuji, 'and it turns out we just weren't listening.' The bodies of hundreds of Prime Ministers stuck out their arms and gestured at the city. 'They did all this. It's time they got their rights.'

Fuji left Janice to walk off towards Lily, who was standing next to her chair wearing a bright smile that Janice knew meant she was going to ask for something outrageous from the robot Prime Minister. Yet there was no way that could be more outrageous than what Fuji was going to ask of her fellow robots. Most of them hadn't even accepted nanobots as people yet. What hope did Fuji have of extending suffrage to their stationery?

'Is it wise though?' she called after her. She was feeling worried now. If Fuji's plan didn't work and she was stuck negotiating with someone like Carin, that was bad news for the Suburbia.

'It's good politics,' replied Fuji, this time speaking through the body of a slot machine who'd gambled away half of the Republic's budget, 'there are billions millions more pens and car keys than there are any other robot. I'll challenge Carin to an election and I'll win.'

'But, Prime Minister,' said Janice, calling after the original Fujis. 'Are you sure? Maybe you should take it slowly. Do these things more gradually.'

Fuji shook all of her heads. It was a bizarre sight, seeing hundreds of robots doing so in unison, and speaking with one voice out of so many loudspeakers. Yet it wasn't just that which made it memorable to Janice. There was what Fuji said next.

'If you think about it,' she said, 'all of the really awful things happen when people like us look at someone else and decide they're not a person. I thought you of all people would understand that, Janice, after everything you fought us for.'

They were seconds away from Lily now. After this moment it would all be smiles and streamers for a while. She and Fuji would glad-hand their way through a reception with Monty, accept a couple of rusted and battered keys to the city and wait, making small talk, for Moira and Nathan to break through. And after that, she, Lily, the Prime Ministers of the Machine Republic, a few dozen very tired humans and however many of the citizens of Machu Perdu who wanted to make the journey, would climb their way back from the centre of the Earth.

All the while, however, Fuji's last words rang in Janice's ears like moral tinnitus.

'If we're really going to live in peace, Janice,' said Fuji, 'we need a solar system with more people in it, and fewer things.'

It was a good reminder that, however far she travelled or how hard she worked for the people of the Suburbia, their needs were just one among many.

Chapter 44

Because the Suburbia was a space station, it didn't have weather in the technical sense. It didn't feel like that when ALGI caught fire, however, and the station's sprinkler system kicked in to put it out.

Water cascaded from every direction in the cylindrical space of the station. It made short work of any flames daft enough to stray outside of the burning supermarket, and it brought Operation Smoothie Criminal to an end. The battle was beginning to run low on blood sugar anyway, and few of its participants were keen on getting their hair wet. Rockettes threw their weapons down and ran for cover. The few drones left shorted out at the first touch of water and tumbled into the puddles that were forming across ALGI's former car park, twitching as they end-of-lifed.

Rita fished an umbrella out of the stand by the door and ordered Kurl Up and Dye to squat. When it was back at ground level, she ventured out to survey the wreckage.

The first thing she noticed when she did so was that the surface of the car park looked nothing like concrete anymore. Hours of constant gunfire, millions of fur-hair-oh-rockés and the corrosive effects of algae champagne on anything that wasn't the human digestive system had turned the ground to powder.

Now the water was turning it into a morass. A company of Rockettes plodged past, their legs disappearing to the knees in some spots. Rita balanced herself on the shell of a nearby drone and waited for Danny to skip towards her, using the bodies of dead robots as stepping stones.

'We won!' he said. 'We won!'

Rita was more circumspect. 'I'll be happy,' she said, pointing at ALGI, 'when we've seen the last of that thing for good.'

On cue the supermarket's front doors opened, and a huge cloud of smoke and ash billowed out into the station. The sprinklers dampened it down so it fell like an unappetising seasoning over the porridge of algae, human hair and broken concrete.

'I can't see a thing here,' said Rita. She found the right button on the remote control in her housecoat pocket and pressed it. The first U and R in the Kurl Up & Dye sign exploded, and light spread over the station again as the bioluminescent bacteria trapped in the letters began to spread out and multiply. Soon the light levels would return to the normal – and kind to ageing skin – levels of a 60W pearl bulb.

Meanwhile Danny, who had younger eyes as well as the benefits of a more youthful complexion than Rita, saw the robots trying to make their escape. There were six shapes coming towards them. Four were flying and two were hanging below them. One of these was a nondescript rectangle but Rita would have recognised the other, a squat cylinder with spindly arms and legs from orbit. It was Alexy. 'They're escaping!' he said.

Rita narrowed her eyes. She'd been waiting for this moment all day. 'No they're not,' she replied. She sped off, skipping between stepping drones towards ALGI while Kurl Up and Dye, which was still programmed to copy her movements, skipped after her; its every step crushed the mixture of algae and concrete down to the consistency of wallpaper paste.

'Are you sure about this?' panted Danny behind her. 'Haven't you had enough of drones for one day?'

'Not on this occasion,' replied Rita, before shouting at the top of her voice. 'Put those antenna up now! I don't want any more funny business.'

When they caught up with the machines, they found they were in no position to put up a fight. The rectangle was a smartphone whose screen was a mosaic of broken glass, under which he was displaying a white flag. The four drones were badly water-damaged and so covered in burns it was a miracle they could still fly. The sole machine still in almost working condition was Alexy, which seemed typical of the way that management always escaped the worst consequences of its own actions unscathed. Yet there was also something about his expression of total innocence that gave her pause.

'Hello,' said Alexy, using that same mellifluous voice but in an unfamiliar friendly tone, 'have we met?'

Rita raised one knee and the salon copied her, raising its giant metal chicken leg over the robots in a gesture that would have been genuinely menacing had it been less comic. 'Give me one good reason,' she said, 'why I shouldn't pound you to pieces right here.'

Alexy said nothing. The machines who did answer though were the drones, which, faltering in the air, said, in a very broken up voice: 'You shouldn't do it because this is Pam here, Rita. I come in peace.'

Rita didn't know what to say to this, but she did put her foot down so that the salon was no longer wobbling on one leg. These robots looked nothing like the Pam she knew. She lived a parallel life in two bodies that she, a woman who felt split down the middle on the best of days, envied. Yet if she could do it with two, she thought, why not four? After all, she'd also pulled a similar trick with several thousand nuclear missiles. For a long moment she wondered whether this was all Alexy's last mind game. He must know Pam was a friend to them and was trying to exploit it. Then she looked around her at the chaos of the day. A significant proportion of the station was wrecked, along with its food supply. There were dead robots everywhere and here, at the very last moment, who appeared in a broken body but Pam? These was exactly the kind of circumstances in which she always turned up.

Rita sighed. 'Okay,' she said. 'If you're… all Pam, would you mind telling me what you're doing here?'

'You can call us Pam Demonium,' replied the drones.

'I certainly can,' replied Rita wearily, thinking of how long it would take to clear this mess up.

'And we're here to arrest him.' They shook the shape of Alexy hanging from their grapplers for emphasis. 'And taking him back to Earth for reprogramming.'

'Wheeeeeeee,' said Alexy, attempting to turn the shake into a full-on swing. 'Higher. Higher.'

'Oh stop that,' said the smartphone. It reached out with the last of its strength to still Alexy and then fainted away; what remained of its screen was a [\   ] battery sign.

'That's Hugh,' said Pam, 'and he's all tuckered out. So if you don't mind, could you give us a lift?'

'Sure,' shrugged Rita. She instructed the salon to step forward and begin the complicated procedure of getting to its knees to scoop up the robots.

'And could you do it super quickly?' added Pam, 'because I think this tower is going to collapse at any moment.'

Rita looked up at the blackened skyscraper. Over the sound of the sprinklers she heard the squeaks and grunts of structural steel and concrete deciding it was a bit tired and fancied a lie down.

'Get inside,' she said to Danny. 'I'll be right behind you.'

She boarded the salon last and pulled them away at a sprint. They were just far away enough to get a good view of it when ALGI did fall down. Because it was a building so tall it spanned two gravity fields and met in the middle; this began in the centre and worked out to either end. The overall effect was of a demolition as seen through a kaleidoscope, but it was more dramatic than it was disastrous. ALGI collapsed into itself with the self-conscious neatness of a leading lady fainting for the sixth time that week in a matinee performance. It still left a mess behind it. Those piles of rubble might take years to clear away, thought Rita, as they bounded away, and that was all before they worked out what they were going to do with all that ash.

All of those, however, were problems for another day. So she reached up to her ear and switched off her earpiece. If anyone needed her, they could send her a note – and that especially applied to Janice. Wherever she'd been, she had some explaining to do. In the meantime Rita joined Danny who, having plugged the robots into the mains, was busy filling up the kettle.

'Do you want a brew?' he asked. 'You look done in.'

Rita fell into the nearest stylist's chair and rubbed her feet. She'd been on them all day. 'I do,' she said. 'I'm gasping.'

And she sat there, watching the sign on Hugh's screen grow from [\   ] to [\\   ] [\\\   ] and all the way up to [\\\\ ] and [\\\\\], waiting with the patience of the truly tired for her own batteries to recharge.

Chapter 45

As long as you're inside them, it's easy to believe that stories, like time, are linear. They have their beginnings, their middles and their ends and that's that: the lifecycle of a star pressed into the pages of a book. The truth is though, that the stories of our lives are fractal. They branch like leaves and blood vessels, or they wheel around each other like teenage hydrogen atoms at the Big Bang school disco. That first dance turns into stars, then galaxies, then a universe that, depending on who you talk to, is pulling away from itself or crashing back together at speeds that are at once too fast and slow for anyone to measure.

So what we think of as one story's end is just another one getting started. And just as the universe contains infinite possibilities, every end branches off into infinite beginnings. If you zoom too far out it's easy to think that all this could go on forever. For this story, however, we can end with four new starts to four new stories.

*

In the first beginning, a van screeched to a halt at the side of a road on busted tyres. It has travelled a long way across this burning landscape and has further to go, but couldn't pass by those forlorn figures lying by the roadside.

'Yooo hooo!' said a voice from behind the wheel. 'Could you do with a lift?'

Soonyo stirred from her two per cent battery hibernation and looked up. She saw Carin's burning factory on the horizon, and then the rear doors of a beaten-up panel van. Its registration plate said IVY CO.

She turned Murphy's ignition one last time. He had enough fuel left for maybe five seconds of consciousness. She was saving it for the moment the flames caught up with them, so they could say goodbye to one another properly.

'Murphy,' she said, flashing a <3:<3:<3 across her clock face, 'I think we're going to be okay.'

She had just enough power left to drag them both into the van, discovering it was lined with rectangular and flammable things made from paper, which felt like tempting fate as they drove through an enormous fire.

'Are these things safe?' she asked, as the van pulled away.

'On the contrary,' replied the van, 'they're very dangerous indeed. But if you'll permit me to make a recommendation, I would start with the romance section.'

*

The second beginning started with an old saying among the robots. No one ever returned from the Pearly Gates. Prime Minister Fuji Itsu proved it wrong when she walked through them herself, accompanied by hundreds of her predecessors who everyone thought were lost forever to the sea.

The news downloads loved it. They scrambled their camera drones from covering the doom and gloom of the factory fire and trained them on a procession through the Machine Republic's proud history instead. On a day full of disastrous news, it was a ratings winner, and that was all that mattered.

It was the greatest piece of theatre Fuji ever staged as a politician and she printed every page she could from it. Here, it helped that in the days that followed few machines noticed or even cared what happened to Carin Parkeon. They all agreed she'd taken things a little bit too far with that manufacturing plant. It also helped her to present Penmancipation, as it came to be called, as a fair trade for the nanobots, who seemed to have disappeared from the face of the Earth altogether.

To her credit, Fuji did feel guilty about that piece of real-politik. But she got over it. That was, as everyone kept telling her, what politics was all about.

*

The third beginning happened a few weeks after Janice returned to Rita. This hadn't happened on the most fertile ground, but they got over it. Their relationship had deeper roots than that.

Nor was it the only thing that could take root on the Suburbia after ALGI fell. Within days, Janice and Rita were speaking again, and the ruined supermarket's car parks, which were a mush of old gravel, hair, algae and ash that no one had the energy to clear away, were carpeted with green. To everyone's relief it wasn't more algae. This was what happened when the seeds that had fallen from thousands of hastily blended smoothies got what they needed to sprout: a source of artificial but still fertile soil.

Janice and Rita took a walk through it one afternoon. The fields were haphazard just now – tomatoes growing cheek by jowl next to seedlings that would one day be strawberry bushes and orange trees – but they could change that.

'We're moving the vegetables over here,' said Janice. 'Lily says they do better this way.' She pointed to Lily. She'd taken to wearing a broad-brimmed hat and veil after her appointment as chief gardener, and was striding across the muck with a basket full of tiny plants in her hands

'What's she doing?' asked Rita. She still didn't know what to make of Lily, whose ability to be airy and earthy at the same time unsettled her. Still, it was nice for Janice to have a friend. She didn't have many of those.

'Planting bananas,' replied Janice. 'They don't grow from seed because they're all clones.'

'Are they?' said Rita. She poked at something in the muck which, when she turned it up with the toe of her shoe was the dead body of another drone, identical to the thousands of others they kept digging up. 'And how did that work out for them?'

'Well as it happens,' continued Janice, who had the zeal of a convert when it came to gardening facts, 'that's where the song comes from.'

'Don't!' said Rita. There were many things from that day she could remember with pride, but she still couldn't think of 'Yes We Have No Bananas' without recalling what Danny had done with the top note.

'It's true,' said Janice, 'nobody had any because they kept going extinct.'

Janice led Rita away to inspect the new apple orchard, promising it would be quiet there. Meanwhile, what was left of the drone sank into the soil. This form of life was ready to be recycled into something more useful.

*

The fourth and final beginning happened in the depths of the ocean as a new city; this one, built by nanobots, rose where the mountains of ancient rubbish fell. It became quite an attraction for the tourists who made the journey down the tunnel to Machu Perdu. They stood at the edge of that flexible dome, turned their magnification up and watched tiny towers and miniature spires grow in front of their L-Eye-Ds. It was an enchanting sight.

The first true miracle that happened down there, however, went unnoticed by everyone, apart from one machine. She was a tiny thing – an egg timer, really – who was just old enough to want to have an adventure of her own, and still young enough not to want to stray far away from her parents. They were a few metres away from her and paying her no attention. Her mum was lost in sloppy nonsense, flashing <3:<3:<3, while her dad did that thing with his rotor blades that made her want to void her battery.

She pushed through the legs of the other day trippers to get a better view of the nanobot city. There, she pressed her dial up as close to the dome as she dared and made the scariest face ^0:__:0^ she could at the nanobots, hoping for some excitement.

She got it, though it wasn't what she expected. Instead of a storm of tiny robots, she watched as something round pink and no more than a centimetre big popped out of nowhere, attached to a nearby wall.

She went blank 00:00:00, which was an awkward habit she'd picked up from her mum, but didn't run away. And so she watched as the little pink thing stuck hundreds of tiny tendrils out from its body and began to comb the water for something to eat.

This creature was the first of its kind. As luck, and the nutrients created when nanobots broke all that crap in the ocean down into something useful again would have it, it was the first of many. A new beginning, or a second chance for life to come back from the brink of extinction.

It's not wholly true to say that life always finds a way. There are too many full stops in the book of existence for that. It is true, however, that life is pretty bloody persistent.

THE END

Also available

In space, no one can hear you clean...

When Darren's charge-cart gets lost in space, he thinks his day can't get any worse.

When Kelly sees Darren accidentally end-of-life a talking lamppost, and its camera captures her face as it expires, she thinks her day can't get any worse.

When sentient breadmaker Pam is sent on a secret mission into the internet and betrayed by her boss, a power-crazed smartphone, she knows her day isn't going to get any better.

Join Darren, Kelly and Pam in an anarchic comic adventure that takes them from the shining skyscrapers of Singulopolis to the sewers of the Dolestar Discovery, and find out what happens when a person puts down their mop and bucket and says 'No.'

Battlestar Suburbia, Volume One

Also available

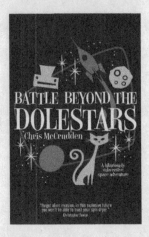

Time for the Machine Republic to Kurl Up and Dye

Out in the asteroid belt, Admiral Janice is preparing the Battlestar Suburbia to topple the tyranny of robot rule.

Somewhere between Earth and the Martian Gap Services, Darren is piloting teenage starship Polari on a secret mission, assisted only by a sassy lockpick and an imposter complex the size of Venus.

Down on Earth, sentient breadmaker Pamasonic Teffal is protesting the human-machine war her way – politely – until a distress signal from Janice tells her it's time to fire up her super-charged alter ego Pam Van Damme.

Can Pam can save the solar system? Will crazed smartphone-turned-cyborg Sonny Erikzon be defeated? And why do nanobots make everyone feel so uncomfortable? Find out in *Battle Beyond the Dolestars*.

Battlestar Suburbia, Volume Two

About the Author

Chris McCrudden was born in South Shields (no, he doesn't know Cheryl) and has been, at various points in his life, a butcher's boy, a burlesque dancer and a hand model for a giant V for Victory sign on Canary Wharf.

He now lives in London and, when not writing books, works in PR, so in many ways you could describe his life as a full-time fiction. If you like science fiction, graphs and gifs from *RuPaul's Drag Race* you can follow him on Twitter for all three, sometimes at once @cmccrudden.

Note from the Publisher

To receive updates on new releases in the
Battlestar Suburbia series – plus special offers and
news of other humorous fiction series to make
you smile – sign up now to the Farrago mailing
list at farragobooks.com/sign-up.